MELTDOWN!

"Listen!" shouted George Twist and silenced the KGB officer with a wave of his hand. "I know what's going on here. Somewhere in this godforsaken Russian wilderness you've had another nuclear disaster and I'm the only person who can help you out of the mess. But you're so screwed up you can't leave it at that! You want power, a lever to use against other people because you're so damned paranoid you can't trust anyone to be straight!"

"George—"

"No!" George stopped. Suddenly he was sorry for Kirov—and for every one else involved in this mess except himself. Then he thought, forget it. This was business pure and simple.

"You need me, Peter," he said. "I've got the whole of bloody Russia by the balls—and I'm not going to let go."

RICHARD HUGO

FAREWELL TO RUSSIA

PINNACLE BOOKS
WINDSOR PUBLISHING CORP.

First published 1987 by
MACMILLAN LONDON LIMITED,
4 Little Essex Street, London WC2R 3LF
and Basingstoke

PINNACLE BOOKS

are published by

Windsor Publishing Corp.
475 Park Avenue South
New York, NY 10016

First Pinnacle Books printing: February, 1989

Printed in the United States of America

Acknowledgments

The Sokolskoye Incident was conceived in the imagination of my friend and colleague Alan Fox, who developed the main storyline and sketched many of the characters. He also did all the research — except for the enjoyable part, the visit to Helsinki, which the author got. Without Alan's support and cooperation, this book would never have been written.

I should like to thank Tarja Koivula for her help and kindness in Helsinki, and also M.S., for reasons M.S. knows best.

Author's Note

The manuscript of this novel was delivered to my publisher in January 1986. Although I believed that a nuclear disaster in the Soviet Union was likely in the not too distant future, I found myself in the uncomfortable position of a prophet when the Soviet reactor at Chernobyl exploded in April 1986. This is the second time I have appeared in the role of a seer into the future, as any reader of *The Hitler Diaries* will be aware. I do not, however, claim to be psychic; but perhaps, occasionally, I see clearly. Specific references to Chernobyl were added after April.

I had originally intended in this foreword to justify my description of the disaster of Sokolskoye. The incident at Chernobyl has made this unnecessary. The nuclear disaster described in what follows is technically feasible, and any inaccuracy in the data contained in the various "reports" contained in the text (for example, the hydrology of the Goskovskoye—Volga system, which is conjectural) does not vitiate the basic premise: a release of plutonium in greater or lesser quantities as described could constitute a hazard of colossal dimensions. I should state, however, that this book is not intended to be an attack on the use of nuclear energy: events in Russia are an imperfect guide to what may happen in the West. Rather, this book is about other things.

West Valley exists, but the names of the companies and people involved there and their activities are fictional and not intended to be understood as corresponding to reality in any "factional" sense.

Prologue

Autumn arrives early at Sokolskoye. The birch trees around the Chiraka lake are quick to show the signs of the coming winter in the turning of their leaves, and the dark firs look darker and bluer as the mists rise from the water and hang in layers on the horizon. At night the lake is never wholly black. On the high wall of the dam sodium lights glow orange and dribble away in reflected beads on the water's surface; occasionally a car drives along the roadway, and its white headlights sweep across the lake, scattering light among the reeds. The silence, too, is rarely complete—though such noises as exist do so almost as aspects of silence: a klaxon sounds to change the shift at the plant, and the blast disturbs the ducks, who echo it and flop around uncomfortably in the sedge, and workers troop in file along the top of the dam, their voices breaking into the stillness like the lonely barking of farmyard dogs in the quiet of the countryside.

The worker—whose name was forgotten in all accounts of what happened—liked to fish. When his shift finished, just before dawn, he would take his tackle out of the locker and trudge through the darkness to a favorite spot on the lakeside where he would sit for an hour or two and catch fish, if he could, as they rose with the sun to feed on the early-morning insects; and he would think for a while, sip from a bottle of vodka and, at the end of his spell of relaxation, trudge back to the dormitory to talk about money and football and turn in for a few hours' sleep.

9

The Chiraka lake was good for fish. It provided cooling water for the plant at Sokolskoye and, in the exchange, gained a degree or two in temperature, which the fish seemed to appreciate. They grew big and fat. And, because the lake was in a security area, there was no competition from other anglers, so that the man could catch the biggest and best, which he regularly did, taking two or three at a time to cook for his breakfast on the small stove in the dormitory and drive the other men crazy with the smell.

The level of the lake was low after the dry summer. He sat by the water on the dried-out shoreline where the bank overhung and the bushes concealed him from view. He baited his line while the light gathered in the east and the mists drifted about, filling with pale color. Somewhere there was singing. A gang of Chuvash laborers. A couple of times during the summer they had sprayed the lake to keep down the weeds, and for a time he had worried about the fish. Now they were mending the banks, clearing the stands of reeds where they threatened to encroach too far into the shallows. They sang in a language that wasn't Russian but sounded like Turkish and wasn't that, either. They kept to themselves, worked hard and sent money home to their wives, wherever the hell their wives lived, and were left alone by the Russians. The man ignored them; he made a cast, heard the plop of the float on the water, and stared down the line to its vanishing point in the darkness.

For five minutes or so the man sat with his thoughts, once or twice taking a pull at his bottle, until, as he reeled in to make another cast, he felt a weight on the line. There was weight but no resistance, the feel he sometimes got when the hook snagged on driftwood; and, come to think of it, there had been a wind during the night, the remnants still sighing through the creaking treetops, and a few branches had probably fallen down. He reeled in and saw a dark shapeless mass floating on the water near the edge of the shoreline. A heave and it was at his side shedding water onto the grass, the sodden carcass of a duck, hooked somewhere under the wing. The man fumbled after the hook under the oily feathers, got some of the water on to his shirt and cut the hook free. He threw the dead bird into the bushes and proceeded to mend his line. And all the while the rising sun filled out the horizon with a broken line of trees and the lights of the dam and the plant faded into daylight.

So he busied himself tying fine knots, pausing once or twice to look up. The lake, washed amber and indigo by the smoky sun, and the dark stands of pine glimmered through the mist. A few birds sang in the trees behind him, but the ducks were silent and the reeds rustled only faintly as the water lapped among them. The man relished the peace, but the lake seemed unusually still, the surface flat calm where insects ought to skate and water rats slink close around the edges. He finished fixing the line, baited the hook again and made ready for his cast; but all the while he had a growing sense that something was odd, and when in the end the line snaked through the air to slot into the water it seemed to him that it cut like a knife into something flaccid, as if the lake had suddenly died on him. He reeled the line in quickly without waiting for a bite.

"Damn!" The man sat for a moment, thought of having another drink, then studied the line as if the problem lay there.

"Damn!" he murmured again. He was not in the habit of putting precise words to complex emotions, and his feeling that something was wrong—either in him or out there—left him to fidget and mutter incoherently until in the end he'd had enough. He stood up, deciding he needed some sleep. He'd forget about the fish for once, pack up and go to bed. He stretched his limbs until his joints went snap, shook himself, then stuffed his tackle back into his bag.

The sun was up now, low in a gray-blue sky, and the lake ran with lean shadows. The man bent down as he tied the last strap on his gear, then straightened and looked casually to the far shore and back across the water. And now for the first time, because of the light, he glimpsed the pale flecks floating on the still surface and paused to make them out, peering with a hand held to his eyes because the sun was sitting on the skyline, until he could fix the nearest one clearly. Then he let out a yell of "Jesus Christ!," dropped his tackle and started running down the path. Running desperately. Shouting breathlessly. His voice screaming itself to soundlessness for want of air: *"Get away from here! Get away from the water!"*—and he tore at his damp shirt until he ripped it off his body so that his torso like something pale and dead was exposed to the cold air.

Behind him in the morning light the lake was still and even, and the air quiet except for the thrum of a wagon driving slowly along the top of the dam. The white flecks he had seen bobbed with the slow rhythm of the water. Fish, everywhere, white belly up and blind-eyed to the sun, and the tense surface of the water freckled with the bodies of a million insects.

Book One

Russia is a country which sets out to mystify the foreigner.

Marquis de Coustine

1

At this date, George Twist had never heard of Sokolskoye. A large, fair-haired, bluff Yorkshireman, in his best days he had probably been regarded as handsome, but now he was somewhere on the spectrum between "imposing" and "jaded," waiting on how events turned out. George himself never gave any thought to the matter. He was not personally vain. His sense of humor was intended kindly even though it was sometimes pointed. It expressed itself in a friendly looking face, somewhat on the fleshy side, with open blue eyes and features with the appearance of general good cheer. Consistent with his generous physical build, George dressed in an easy casual style which, while not sloppy, suggested that not too much thought had gone into it. Everyone agreed that George just looked like someone you'd be happy to know, someone to have a beer with, in fact a man from whom you just might buy that used car—and everyone was not far wrong. George Twist was like everything suggested by his appearance, and also like several things that contradicted it because he was inconsistent; and he possessed, too, other qualities that his appearance didn't hint at at all, simply because he was human. For the moment, however, he had problems.

"Tell me, Lou," he asked his companion. "How do you explain high technology to a beginner?"

"Slowly," said Lou Ruttger, which was his standard reply.

"You should think up some new jokes," George answered, but there were no new solutions to this particular problem: he had asked the question often enough to know that. "Another beer?"

Ruttger shook his head. "I want to think clearly tomorrow." He had an unintentional way of sounding pious about the most ordinary things. It worried George sometimes that the younger man lacked a sense of humor. Oh, Lou could laugh and tell a joke, but George

15

always suspected he was faking it.

"I'll have one anyway," George answered and looked for the waitress.

From the many trips he had made from his base in San José to West Valley, George thought he would have gotten to know all the bars. But there seemed always to be new ones, or maybe there were one or two that he forgot. When George flew over for a couple of days, he and Lou spent the last night in a bar. George reckoned it made Lou relax and tell him more about what was going on. Lou was the project manager at West Valley, even if the whole project was George's baby.

"It's just a subcommittee of the Senate Armed Services Committee," Ruttger was saying. "Alex Burge from DOE let me have sight of their profiles. There isn't one who knows anything about high technology. Think of tomorrow as if you were taking a bunch of old ladies around the place. Or do it as if it were a sales pitch. John Chaseman has hitched himself a ride on this tour. So pretend that you're making a sale to Chaseman Industries. Maybe you are."

"I don't want to be a salesman," George said morosely, then looked around again for the waitress.

"Then why are you going back to England to take over as sales director as soon as we've finished with this business?" Lou asked. "Face it, George, you've got a salesman's instincts. You'll lay them out cold tomorrow. Don't try to analyze it; it's a gift. You should just thank God." And he meant thank God.

The truth was that George wasn't seriously worried about the following day. But sometimes a drink could make him miserable, and there were times when Lou Ruttger, all youth, energy and purpose, could make him miserable, drunk or sober. He wondered why he liked Lou so much. In the car, driving back to the motel, he had a relaxed opinion of the whole episode. A few politicians kidding themselves about their familiarity with the latest in separation technology were not a major problem. As for John Chaseman—he had a vague recollection that Chaseman had been a presidential adviser in a Republican administration, which would explain where he got the clout to join the senatorial party. But Chaseman's interest? At this stage he couldn't guess. And that concerned him.

He left the driving to Lou. Lou was a fan of high performance cars but always stuck to the speed limit, so George wasn't quite sure of the point except that it had something to do with elegant engineering, according to Lou, who would illustrate the argument from the magazines he kept stuffed in a drawer of his desk. Lou was sticking to the speed limit now. George caught a glimpse of him in profile under a passing light as he glanced out of the window to see where they were. He guessed that Lou was probably good-looking—Lillian always said so—but George didn't see it. He had clean features and a good orthodontist, auburn hair and a serious moustache. So maybe George was jealous. He shrugged off the thought and concentrated on the scenery. They were driving past the gray slab walls of the complex at the corner of Third Avenue and Fifth Street.

"I didn't realize we were on this side of town," he commented.

Lou gave an uh-huh and took a look at the plant where they had put in so much time and effort and where tomorrow they would have to face representatives of the Senate Armed Services Committee. In this light it didn't look all that much. You wouldn't think a place like that could pollute a creek with radioactive waste.

Moscow: 0500 hours, September 14

"Kirov? It's me, Victor . . ." The speaker gave another name, but the line was bad or the tape was bad or maybe both. ". . . You know, *Victor*"—meaning you couldn't forget Victor, not forget good old Victor, whoever the hell Victor was. Even Victor was uncertain: "Yeah, well—sorry, Pyotr Andreevitch—I don't know what time you're listening to this—day, night, whichever it is. You said I could always call you—day or night makes no difference. Remember?"

"Who is Victor?" Lara asked sleepily, coming up for air, out of the depths of sleep, out of the depths of the bedclothes, of darkness and drawn curtains and bodies distilling scents into the close air of the apartment.

"I don't know," said Kirov, feeling his way for a cigarette *tap-tap* among keys, clock and ashtrays by the bedside. Lara, not really awake, humming a tune to lull herself to sleep, Tchaikovsky—*Swan Lake*? Kirov lit the cigarette and laid a hand across Lara's naked shoulder, rocking her gently. With his free hand he turned the machine on again. Victor again.

"It's the plant, Petya. Something's happened." No—that was too definite for Victor. "I *think* something's happened. No, that's not right—I know that something's happened; but nobody's admitting

17

anything." The line crackled. Then: "Yesterday morning—bloody chaos for an hour before I arrived, then everything stable. One of my informers told me but didn't know why. I asked the plant director, but all he would say was 'routine alert.' Routine alert! Ha!"

At this point Victor's voice fell away and there was nothing for a minute or so but his breathing. Kirov remembered it from the first playing, and this time he let it run on while he made a cup of coffee.

Yesterday? The call had come at midnight, when he and Lara had been at a party. Theater and film types; some dancers like Lara. Stars of stage, screen, and secret police, the last in the shape of himself, Major Pytor Andreevitch Kirov of the Industrial Security Directorate of the Second Chief Directorate of the Committee for State Security, now making coffee. Midnight—did Victor mean that the incident had happened on the twelfth or the thirteenth?

Victor didn't say. Instead he resumed: "I guess I'd better get on with it. I mean, once I've started there's no way back, is there?" He thought of something. "How long do these tapes run for? Do I get a warning before it cuts me off or do I finish by talking to myself? Hey, maybe I am talking to myself!"

Maybe he was. Kirov sipped the coffee. He reran that last section just to catch the tone, the character.

"I'm wandering," the caller said, more slowly now. "It's midnight, Petya—past midnight; it was midnight when I started—I'm tired." He left a space for Kirov to get the point and there was a clink of glass, which was also the point and partly explained why Victor's emotions were all over the place. He became flat and went on: "There's probably nothing to it. That's half the reason I didn't contact you in the regular way. Out here I can't afford to make mistakes, know what I mean? Someone saying that creep Victor doesn't know what he's doing and starts a scare—it doesn't do me any good, am I right?"

He was right, Kirov agreed. He stubbed his cigarette out and waited for the peroration.

"Do me a favor, huh, Petya? Can you check out a message for me? To Kostandov—you know Kostandov—from his man at the plant. Whatever it is, it's all in there. You'll do this for me, eh? Sure! Call me back, Petya. Oh"—and suddenly Victor was shy—"give my love to Larissa Arkadyevna."

"Who is this Victor?" Lara complained in her sleep.

"Listen to this and get me the file on Victor." Kirov threw the tape on to Bogdanov's desk — Uncle Bog, his subordinate, a thin, lugubrious character with a manner like a dirty story.

"Victor who?"

"I don't know. Play the tape and work it out for yourself." Kirov gave what help he could. "One of the godchildren — he had my home number."

"Wants his bottom wiping, does he?" Bogdanov disliked the godchildren, out-station men who reported to Moscow instead of to the local KGB. They got lonely and had fits of nerves.

"Maybe. Something's worrying him, that's for sure." That was why Victor and all the other godchildren were given a private number to contact. It meant they could voice their concerns off the record, even if it all went on the record and they knew it all went on the record. Something in the psychology worked.

"I'll see what I can do." Bogdanov dropped the tape into the pile of rubbish on his desk.

Kirov had an appointment with Grishin. The Colonel was his superior. Half an hour to discuss progress on an investigation the KGB were running together with the regular police into the pharmaceuticals racket. The KGB were watching the case because of suspicions that the racketeers were paying off the fraud squad. He didn't mention the call from Victor, even though Victor had mentioned Kostandov and any reference to Kostandov was calculated to whet Grishin's appetite. It was a matter of timing. When he had something concrete to offer, he would tell Grishin. Meantime there was only the uncertain feeling of urgency. Which day was Victor referring to?

"This came in last night?" Bogdanov asked when Kirov returned. He sprawled in his chair.

"Around midnight."

"Ah, you were out with Larissa Arkadyevna — a party — all that film crowd. Tea?" Bogdanov pushed an empty glass across. "You should stick with this one. All my wife ever introduced me to was her mother." He picked his long nose lazily.

"Victor," said Kirov. "Who is he?"

"This Kostandov," Bogdanov answered obliquely, "the one Victor talks about. Is this the Kostandov we know and love, namely General

Yuri Trofimovitch Kostandov, head of the Army's Directorate of Nuclear Operations and currently occupying a desk not a million miles away at GHQ in Frunze Street?" He didn't need a reply. He gave one of his melancholy gut-wrenching sighs and said: "I swear to God some of these guys think we're supermen! Does Victor seriously think we can monitor every call into General Headquarters?"

"Probably." Yes, probably. Kirov had his own picture of how Victor saw things. Contempt and respect for Moscow Center would go hand in hand. The sense of Moscow's absence: the fear of its presence. Oh, yes, Victor would have all sorts of ideas about the full extent of Center's abilities. Kirov felt the faintly depressing touch of another's thoughts and brushed it aside. He came back to the point. "Have you identified him?"

"Sure." Bogdanov picked up a scrap of paper. Klyuev — Victor Sergeiitch — Captain. Station officer at the Nuclear Reprocessing Plant at Sokolskoye. Age forty-five. Wife, Galya. Two kids, Sasha and Andrusha. You met him last January when a whole bunch from out in the sticks came to Moscow for a course. A fat guy, all smiles and sweaty hands. I remember him because he had this complaint that on an Army-run site he didn't get any respect. I've heard it all before: it's the story you get from from anyone who has to work alongside the Army on the nuclear program. Why do you think Grishin hates Kostandov?"

"What do you make of the tape?"

"Paranoia." Bogdanov passed the tape back. "Something happens that Klyuev doesn't understand and immediately he thinks it's a plot. You think it's something else?"

"I'm not sure."

"You want me to check on messages between Sokolskoye and GHQ? Just because we're not running taps on GHQ it doesn't mean that nobody in this place is."

"Ask around." Kirov turned to study the fly-specked map tacked to the wall. Sokolskoye. He found the spot, a small place on the bank of the Gorkovskoye Reservoir. You could take it out with a nuclear disaster and no one would notice. "Ask around," he repeated to Bogdanov. "Find out what you can. I'll call Victor this evening."

West Valley: 1100 hours, September 14

"Gentlemen . . ." George Twist let the word draw out, let them hear his English accent. Grab the attention from the start — as Ronnie Pugh, his old mentor, used to tell him — it's all a matter of timing; and in matters of timing, except for the trip to Lagos that got him killed, Ronnie knew what he was talking about. "I want to tell you about a new piece of technology that can be encompassed in one word: *excitement.*"

They were in the plant training room, which had been fitted out for the presentation: George, Lou Ruttger, a technician to work the gadgets, and the senatorial party who carried with them the politician's sense of urgency, the feeling that they were in transit to somewhere more important. Plus one of two others. Alex Burge from the Department of Energy who was doing his young, smart, new act and looking, so George thought, like something you bought in a bubble-pack; and John Chaseman, who was technically an outsider though he had been at one time on the White House staff, and who was sitting composed with a pen and notepad at the ready.

But on with the song-and-dance act.

"This place," George began, "is the site of a nuclear fuel reprocessing facility — or perhaps I should say 'was,' since a stop to that sort of activity was imposed by President Carter.

"Now, the plant out there" — he let his hand indicate the scope — "consisted of the actual reprocessing facility plus fuel storage ponds and treatment systems; and its tanks accumulated material which was both radioactive and toxic. Which, gentlemen, is what gave rise to the problem, because" — he glanced at Lou Ruttger, who was hiding a grin because he knew what came next — "it leaked!"

He was slow with the next line. He knew he had them. They were up in their seats as if they expected the alarms to go off and the place to be cleared for an emergency. He still had the touch.

"You can relax." He let the tension go. He could see the realization in some of their faces: Chaseman gave him a nod. It was working. "The leakage was unspectacular," he told them. "Nobody died. Nobody glowed in the dark. It was just a slow seepage of groundwater into the Cattaraugus Creek, which contaminated the water; and the fallout, such as it was, was in the main political. It contributed to the call for FUSRAP — that's the Formerly Utilized Sites Remedial Action Program. And it led to my being here, for my sins, gentlemen: because my company developed the Sep Tech Process. And the

21

Sep Tech Process cleans up contaminants such as uranium out of water."

So he began his story, relaxed into it, played it and pitched it as the feedback from his audience came to him in raised eyebrows, grins and all the other small gestures that the Americans like to call body language.

There was a time when George could interpret body language better than words. That was back in the seventies when he had spent his time on the international contracting circuit, selling chemical plants to anyone who would have them — which in those days was so many people you had to beat them off with a stick; or so it seemed now, when business was so flat that even the customers who didn't intend to pay weren't buying.

Then it had happened. Lillian, his wife, had fallen ill.

George was in Cairo, locked into a negotiation with a bunch of smiling Egyptians; Ronnie Pugh was out cold at the hotel with terminal diarrhea, and the competition in the next room were waiting for their chance. For some reason the international telephone lines were down, and all he had was a cable that said everything and nothing. Lillian was ill. How dangerously? Was he needed at home? Was he being asked to drop the job and return? "Mr. Twist, give us your best price," said the Egyptians. "Sure, sure." Press on, because if he walked out, the opposition would take the deal. Sit for two days with the cable in front of him on the table among the technical specifications and the spent cigarettes. Stand and tell them the tale, in a close room where the ceiling fan rotated and stirred the muddy air, spicy from the smoke of oriental tobacco.

Never again. He retired from selling. The company wanted him to run their new American acquisition, Sep Tech. No more travelling. He could stay at home and take care of Lillian. He moved to the Santa Clara Valley and ran the research and development program, taking somebody's neat idea and turning it into a full-scale plant here at West Valley, backed by manufacturing and engineering facilities, so that Sep Tech was on the point of taking off. And all the while his wife's health deteriorated in small increments of pain.

Lillian tried. For a while she walked with a stick, leaning on it while she used her left hand to do the housework, and making jokes because she had a sense of humor. It was one of the things he had liked about her. She took to a wheelchair. "I prefer it," she said. "It

22

frees both hands"—and she held them out to take his, and he could feel the tremor in her fingers as he clasped them.

He hired a Mexican woman to help around the house and a nurse to take care of Lillian, and he sent his daughter away to school because she hated the sight of her mother's suffering. And in this fashion he carried on for a couple of years, knowing it couldn't continue. He needed a better-paid job and to live somewhere it would be cheaper to look after his wife. He was forty-three years old.

"Why don't you come back to England? Back home? See the old kith and kin?" said Alasdair Cranbourne, the chairman. "We have a vacancy for a sales director."

Moscow: 1830 hours, September 14

"Victor Sergeiitch!"

Warmth, friendship, authority—all there in the voice, overlaying the tiredness. Did Klyuev really have something for him or was it just an attack of nerves?

"Pyotr Andreevitch, you at home?"

"Yes." Kirov was back at his apartment in the Sivtsev Vrazhek district; a cold, bare place as Lara complained, or home as he told Victor Klyuev. Lara was listening in, striking unconscious poses against the wall as if it were a theatrical backdrop. He raised a beckoning finger to her.

"Hello, Victor," she said at a distance into the mouthpiece of the phone, then pursed her lips as if sucking lemons.

"Larissa?"

"Yes, she's here," said Kirov. And now I'm done with reassurance, he thought. "OK, Victor, give it to me straight. What's your problem?" It was time for authority.

"There's something funny going on here."

Lara lit a couple of cigarettes and passed one to Kirov. The gesture was smooth, elegant. A trace of her lipstick smudged the tip. Since he had first found her in the Bolshoi *corps de ballet*, it had seemed to him that all her actions were as deliberately easy as her dancing.

"What sort of thing?"

Klyuev wasn't listening—or at least, not responding. He was rambling over the same ground as before: worried about how he would appear to the Center; didn't want to start an unnecessary scare; he had enemies—Petya knew all about having enemies, didn't he? Sure he did. Kirov forced himself to remember that Klyuev worked alone except for his informers; and now the KGB was taking on their colors: ingratiating, supplicant. "He drinks," Bogdanov had said—which wasn't on file because someone had protected good old Victor, but you could read it in the silences.

"Don't worry, Victor. Just give me the facts."

So—slowly:

The previous morning, said Klyuev—that was the thirteenth—there had been some sort of emergency at the plant at Sokolskoye. He wasn't certain of the details, but the operators had switched from some of the primary systems to the backups. "Which is OK so far—I mean, sometimes it happens. But then the plant director makes himself scarce and the garrison commander sends a cable to Moscow and—get this—*he uses a code.*"

"A code? What kind?"

"He has a one-time code pad for communicating with his own directorate: but until yesterday it's never been used. It's strictly for emergencies only."

"So you've had an emergency? This is the first time?"

"Yes—no!" Klyuev was getting excited.

"Easy does it." Kirov calmed him down. "Emergencies—you've had them before."

"Sure, sure, we've had them before. That's the point! Emergencies but no codes. *This* code, it's for real emergencies—like—I don't know—like General Order No. 1!"

There was silence on the line and then a tentative "Hello—Petya?"

"I was just thinking."

General Order No. 1.

It had grown out of the nuclear program, out of the imagination of the contingency planners. How did the critical phrase go? *Serious threat to human and economic life.* General Order No. 1 was the prelude to full mobilization of the resources of the Soviet Union to fight a disaster. It was the domestic equivalent of a declaration of war.

Kirov inhaled calmly on the cigarette. He remembered Sokolskoye again. What cities were near? Gorky, further south on the Volga. Too far? Gorky? He looked to the door, as if he could see Victor in the next room. A vague picture. An overweight man sitting in his shirt-sleeves by the telephone in his own room at Sokolskoye, a bottle of

24

vodka and a dirty glass standing next to the instrument. "Are you telling me you've had a disaster but the kind that nobody notices?" He prodded Klyuev out of his silence. "Is the plant stable?"

"I'm no engineer . . ."

"Go on, you can tell me. The plant is stable."

"Yes, the operators are twitchy, but the plant is stable."

"Ah, then, where's the problem?"

"I . . ."

"I understand."

"Sure — look, maybe . . . I don't want to start a panic over nothing. After I got the news I took a stroll around the plant and down to the lake — there's a cooling-water lake, but I guess you know that. Anyway, I get down there and they're starting to fence it off: there are men all over the place and they're all in full radiation protection gear — and they're casting nets on the water."

"What?" Kirov couldn't hide his own surprise. "What are they looking for?" he asked. "What are they finding?"

"Dead fish!" Klyuev blurted out. "The lake is full of dead fish!"

West Valley: 1200 hours, September 14

George Twist scanned his audience. He had them nicely warmed up.

"Uranium or other heavy metals," he resumed. "The Sep Tech Process handles a whole range of contaminants. And across the whole range there is a common problem to which the solution — until we came up with it — has been hard to find. That problem, gentlemen, has been the sheer volume of water to be processed in order to remove small, almost minuscule quantities of these highly toxic substances. Whether in a creek or a pond, or whatever, we are frequently talking about millions of gallons."

There was an interruption from the floor, which suited George since it meant that the Senators were relaxed. He recognized the speaker: Abe Korman, who represented one of the Eastern states, George couldn't remember which, but he had seen him often enough, a fat man with a crazy kind of charm if you liked folksy right-wing slobs. Korman got ponderously to his feet.

"You mean you could treat a whole river with this unit?"

"In principle — sure," George answered and scratched his nose slowly. "Could be, though, that we'd have a hell of a time keeping the river in one place long enough."

There was laughter. They liked that one. Even John Chaseman laughed, and he was no fool. George had been watching Chaseman as a cue to his delivery because Chaseman was smart enough to take bullshit and hard information in the right quantities, and George wanted to make the right impression on him. It was businessmen, not Senators, who had contamination problems and bought plants to clear them up.

He returned to his theme.

"Volume is our major problem, because the real trick of getting every last trace of contaminant out of water is slow and expensive if any form of fine filtration or separation is involved. Imagine trying to push the creek here at West Valley through a coffee filter and you'll get the idea. We approached the problem in two ways.

"We felt first that it was important to devise a quick, energy-efficient process that would reduce the amount of water to be handled to a smaller quantity that could be treated in detail: in other words, a process to concentrate the contaminant. Then we could move to the second stage: the treatment of this smaller volume of water to strip out the toxic material and convert it into a solid form that could be safely transported and disposed of.

"So we come to our first-stage process. Lou, show the gentlemen the membrane."

Lou Ruttger picked up a bundle of floppy white tubes from a table behind the lectern. From a distance they resembled spaghetti.

"They don't look like much, do they?" he said, taking over the floor. The laughter suggested his audience agreed. George nodded appreciatively.

"OK." Lou took a breath for the next bit. "These strands and thousands like them are arranged in our membrane units. The membranes are so constructed that they contain pores which are sized so that small molecules such as water can pass through them, while larger molecules—uranium, plutonium, americium, and neptunium are examples—are held back. We can vary our design to let more or less water pass through, but typically, if we wanted to, we could pass a thousand units of water into our unit such that nine hundred and ninety-nine parts went through the membrane, leaving just one part, containing the larger molecules of the contaminant, ehind. Here's what a unit looks like."

The lights dimmed and a slide was flashed onto the screen. It showed a silver tube about three feet in diameter and twenty feet long. At the exposed end bundles of the white tubes were connected to a plate bored with holes.

"The contaminated water distribution plates. At the other end is the pipe branch for discharging clean water." Ruttger smiled as if he had just told a joke and carried on, trying to mix his dry explanations with George's easy style. He failed, George suspected, because he had no sense of humor, and sometimes his timing was faulty. It was a relative failing. To compensate, he had youth, energy, talent, and ambition. He was even honest and truthful. And despite all that, George liked him.

Lou went on: "The plant at West Valley has five membrane units similar to this one, not very impressive to look at, but easy to install and cheap to operate. The material for the membrane fibers is a special polymer developed by Sep Tech."

Probably he would have said more but George stopped him.

"Accepting that all of this is secret," he said confidingly, "does anyone have any questions?"

From his position apart from the Senators, John Chaseman spoke. "Your unit claims to handle radioactive materials. My company produces a range of polymers and our experience is that they deteriorate when exposed to radiation. Is your material so different?"

Chaseman had an incisive mildness of a kind that could cut through an argument better than shouting. He was one of those clean-cut types with fair hair and blue eyes whose firm features seem to give weighty consideration to everything they hear and say. George put him at about his own age, but Chaseman's Mormon clean living made him look ten years younger.

"Mr. Chaseman is of course correct," he said. "Over time the membranes do deteriorate: but this is a known factor; in West Valley they have a life of about six months. We monitor this and can recognize a failure quickly. Then all we have to do is change the tube bundle. It's a simple operation. Is that OK?" Everyone seemed to think it was. Fine. Then, let's get on with the show. Lou, the lights. Let's pass on to the second stage of the Sep Tech Process."

Moscow: 1930 hours, September 14

27

Kirov waited half an hour before calling Grishin. He sat with his thoughts in the darkness, half-listening to *Don Giovanni* on the record player. Lara plied him with coffee. If he called Grishin with the story he was committed. Whatever happened, Grishin would remember Lara, who was intelligent but played stupid because someone had told her there was more future for a woman that way, recognized his dangerous mood and retired to the bedroom with some magazines. Kirov watched her go, all relaxed, all deliberate action, dancer's training. Like to like? Did she see the same in him, tension in balance? He studied the clock and allotted himself half an hour to decide. At the end of that time he made his call.

Colonel Rodion Mikhailovitch Grishin was Kirov's superior, a small, tidy man of disarmingly bland appearance with apple cheeks and a good-natured look about him that concealed a deep and devious mind and an unrelenting character. He had a line of faintly treasonous jokes which those who did business with him found unsettling. Who dared to laugh at sedition? Who dared not to laugh at the jokes of the KGB? Grishin's special enmity was reserved for General Yuri Trofimovitch Kostandov and the Army's Directorate of Nuclear Operations. It was his goal to assert KGB control over the Army's nuclear reprocessing plants and thereby over the production of weapons-grade plutonium. Colonel Grishin, so Kirov decided, would be very interested in the story told by the KGB officer at Sokolskoye.

"Rodion Mikhailovitch," he began after apologies to Grishin for the lateness of the hour, "I have something to tell you. It affects the Army's management of one of their nuclear installations and, I suspect, may be urgent."

To Grishin's credit, he knew a serious call when he received one. He told Kirov to deliver his story and did not interrupt as the Major repeated what he had been told by Klyuev.

"So they've polluted their lake," he mused as Kirov finished. "Where's the disaster in that? Sokolskoye — it's a plant in the middle of nowhere. Any problem can be contained."

"Perhaps not," Kirov suggested.

"Why not?"

"The lake is artificial: what goes in has to come out." He paused there, conscious of reaching a point at which he had to speculate. "There's a stream. It was dammed to form the cooling-water lake

28

before that it used to flow into the Gorkovskoye Reservoir. According to Klyuev, after the spring thaw and whenever there is heavy rain, the flow into the lake exceeds the capacity of the dam and they open sluices to get rid of the excess into the Reservoir. Ultimately it discharges into the Volga. So, sooner or later, whatever is in the lake will finish up in the Volga and be carried downstream, maybe as far as Gorky. I'm sure you understand the implications."

"You think they've identified a threat to Gorky and are suppressing it."

"Yes."

There was silence on the line. Kirov imagined the other man going over the same pattern of reasoning. A few dead fish — it seemed a flimsy base on which to construct the threat of a disaster. But Kirov had considered not the fish but the human reaction.

"How do we get from fish to Gorky?" Grishin came back as if reading Kirov's mind.

"From the way people behaved. The panic among the workers, the plant director hiding himself, the coded message from the garrison commander to Kostandov — it's all out of scale for a minor operational problem. They're frightened of something far worse."

"How much worse?"

"I believe," Kirov ventured slowly, "that the message to Kostandov was a request to invoke General Order No. 1."

"Stop this conversation now," Grishin said curtly. "Meet me in my office in half an hour."

West Valley: 1300 hours, September 14

The screen showed a large steel tank. George was describing the second stage of the Sep Tech Process.

"We talked about the concentration step," he told them. "In the next stage the concentrate passes into vessels like the one on the screen. They contain a large number of tubes packed with another of our special materials, an ion-exchanging resin — in this case a naturally occurring inorganic substance mined up in Wisconsin, known as a *zeolite*.

"The zeolite has unique properties. It has a structure like a maze which allows large molecules into the structure but then traps them there. We can enhance this effect by putting opposite electrical

29

charges into the body of the vessel and the core of ion-exchanging resin so that the contaminating substance — uranium and the transuranics we talked about — is attracted into the zeolite. *But* it's a slow business, which is why we go through that first stage to reduce the volume of liquid that the second stage has to handle. However, at the end — and this is where we want to get to — we have achieved pure water at one outlet and a concentration of contaminant at the other, all ready for long-term disposal."

He signaled to the assistant. "We'd like to show you a sample of the zeolite." It was passed to the first row of the audience. Kids playing with dough, thought George: they were picking at it with their fingers as if it were a miracle. While they were fooling around with that, a tray of glasses was brought in. George took one.

"On this plant," he said as the zeolite passed to the next row, "we have three vessels sized at 25,000 gallons each, and they contain roughly twelve tons of this material. Please, gentlemen," he added as the first of the Senators raised his glass to his lips, "refresh yourselves. This is pure water, straight from the West Valley decontamination plant. Guaranteed free from plutonium."

The collected hands holding the drinks froze. George examined his own doubtfully.

"Would I lie to you?"

Senator Abe Korman broke the spell. He dipped his long, fleshy nose toward his glass. He looked at the others through dark, cautious eyes, then at the clock, the walls, the screen. "No olive," he murmured and took a sip. He paused. His lips writhed. He coughed.

"Well?" George asked.

"It tastes like a dry martini."

George opened his eyes wide and then put his mouth to the clear liquid. He stared at Lou Ruttger.

"Damnit, Lou, we got the process wrong!"

He turned back to the Senators with the same expression of alarm on his face, then let it break down slowly as the men in front of him got the point and each took a sip of his cocktail.

I'm overweight and I'm forty-three years old, but I can still do it, George thought.

The audience was applauding.

Moscow: 2045 hours, September 14

Kirov drove to Dzerzhinsky Square. Slack evening traffic. Crowds queuing to get in at the restaurants. A few militiamen bouncing the early drunks. He parked his car and went straight to Grishin's office.

"Well, Pyotr Andreevitch, is this the occasion when we finally catch up with Kostandov?"

The outer room was normally occupied by a secretary. Now it was in darkness. The door to Grishin's inner sanctum was open and an Anglepoise lamp burned over the desk. The man himself was there in his shirt-sleeves. Having spoken, he looked up from his papers and greeted his visitor with a pale smile.

"Difficult to say," Kirov answered. "The situation is obscure, but . . ."

"You feel it in your bones, eh? Me, too. Definitely. Something is happening out there, I know it. The only question is: what do we do?" He returned to bending over his papers, exposing his thinning hair and a freckled scalp that reflected the light. "Sokolskoye . . ."

"Yes?"

"It was commissioned in the middle seventies. Remember then? All the problems we had?"

"I was in Washington with the Residency." Washington — the halcyon days before the Ouspensky Case. He didn't care to think of Washington. Himself and his fat sidekick, Yatsin, living like kings because that was the style of the time and the place. Before Oleg Ouspensky.

"I was forgetting." This was Grishin at his most benign and considerate. He glanced upwards. Small eyes like bright beads in the sharp reflection of the lamp. "Talk to Bogdanov," he grunted. Bogdanov had also been deputy to Kirov's predecessor. "He'll remember the details. It was all part of the rush to build up our nuclear capability. Plants springing up overnight, and the usual waste and confusion and corruption. Operation Fall-Out — it was all hushed up. Talk to Bogdanov," he repeated. "Maybe it affected Sokolskoye — maybe not. Or maybe we couldn't prove anything or were stopped. The Army was riding high in the saddle back then, and in this area there were limits on how far we could touch them. There still are." Grishin didn't mask his resentment. He concentrated on the papers, the tip of his tongue moving over his lower lip. In this light it looked unusually pink. Pink tongue, pink skin: Grishin was fair-skinned and smoother

31

than his years. "What to do, what to do?"

"Invite Kostandov to apply General Order No. 1."

"How? Throw the whole system into an emergency, evacuate the town and put the whole region under a security blanket — all on the strength of a few fish?"

"The first stage of General Order No. 1 is only to convene an investigating committee to confirm the emergency. Until the committee confirms the finding, everything stays as it is, with minimum embarrassment and disruption. How can Kostandov risk a refusal?"

Kirov left Grishin to consider the point and moved into the shadows of the room. The Colonel's voice followed him, quizzing the wording of the General Order. Kirov gave his informed answers and picked over the trophies from the other man's own spell of foreign service. An empty Ricard carafe. An ashtray with a Gitane gypsy dancing across it. Junk from a posting in Paris. Kirov stretched a hand to open the slats in the blind and look down into the square at the people passing across the front of Detsky Mir, the children's shop, thinking of his own junk variously bought or stolen in Washington — it was always the stolen junk that captured the indefinable. Did Westerners here in Moscow find the same? He wondered why Russians craved the West's rubbish as if their own country were empty of something.

He heard Grishin say: "I'll do it. Did you hear me, Pyotr Andreevitch?" Kirov let the blind snap back into shape. "This way, using the committee, there will be no obvious appearance of KGB intervention. What do you say?"

"Yes," Kirov answered.

"Good. Then the disaster at Sokolskoye is official." Grishin smiled cheerfully, a cherub in an open shirt and baggy corduroy trousers.

"Let's drink to it," he proposed.

West Valley: 1500 hours, September 14

They broke up into an informal session. George Twist and Lou Ruttger mixed with their guests and answered questions. They were mostly idiot questions or scripted by the senatorial staff, in which case the questions made sense but the answer was unintelligible to the person asking it. George fielded a few while keeping an eye on Chaseman. The latter had ditched his cocktail and provided himself with a

32

glass of orange juice. He was engaged with Lou in a conversation the Englishman couldn't overhear. Then Abe Korman cut a swathe through the other Senators, who parted as though they might catch something, and brought his bulk alongside.

"So what are the British doing on a project like this?" Korman asked. He had a pugnacious voice and a habit of grabbing microphones and making pronouncements about defending the rights of the little guys, so that the listener got the impression the international forces of darkness were about to knock over the neighborhood drugstore. As a style it was gross and pushy and had instant appeal.

"Like most things," George answered, "Just chance. I work for a British company, Chemconstruct — you ever heard of them?"

"No."

"I guess not. Well, they're process-plant contractors, which in simple terms means they design and build gas processing and chemical installations. Most of their market has been in Eastern Europe and the Third World, but a few years ago they decided to expand into North America. They bought a local engineering outfit to give them a foot in the door. And along with the deal came a small research and development subsidiary of the American company. That was Sep Tech."

"Who built the plant that you've just been explaining to all us ignorant schmucks."

"You got it. Sep Tech had a good idea what they were playing around with; but they didn't know how to handle it commercially and bring it to a full-scale plant. I was sent over here to help them do that; and that's just what I've done. After this I go back to England and Lou Ruttger takes over from me."

Korman cast his eyes over Lou Ruttger. "Looks like a good guy." Then back at George, who wondered: What is he seeing? One tall Englishman with too much tired flesh around the eyes and thirty pounds of excess weight he was planning to get rid of when he could find the time and energy. Not exactly star quality. "A good guy," Korman repeated, staring at George. He put down his glass and conjured up another.

"You know, George," he said, just-between-us, the way he spoke in his television slots, "no offense, but I don't like to see this sort of technology in the hands of a non-American. I don't claim to understand all this high-frontier-of-science stuff, but I can recognize some-

33

thing good when I see it. And I pride myself on thinking" — he slipped a hand onto George's shoulder — "strategically. The idea of foreign control of anything with an application in the nuclear field — well, it gives me the jitters."

"I wouldn't worry: the government has us tied up in knots as to what we can and can't do with this technology."

"The government couldn't tie its shoelaces," Korman answered testily. He scrambled the broken bits of his face into an appearance of good humor and went on: "If you really want to exploit this thing, you should look for an American partner."

"Make me an offer," said George.

He was in the control room when John Chaseman found him later. George had a glass and a cigarette and was watching the instrument readouts — making his farewells, he guessed. The Senators had gone, Lou was taking a walk around the place like he had just inherited a property, which in a sense he had, and only Chaseman was left. He stood at the back of the room watching George until the last of the technicians had left, and then he broke the silence.

"So what's the trick, George? What makes the Sep Tech Process so special?"

George turned the swivel chair and eyed the other man. "I thought you'd gone," he said easily. "No offense."

"None taken. I hung around in case there was a better story than the official tour."

"I don't know that there is. You heard the spiel: everything about Sep Tech is special. It's cheap, it's quick to install, it works. I thought Lou had answered your questions — didn't I see you two getting your heads together?"

"Talking to Lou is like listening to a sermon."

"He can get a little earnest. What do you want to know?"

"Tell me about that second-stage process again. There was something in there that I missed."

George examined Chaseman cautiously, but the examination revealed nothing: a friendly face with a sincere smile as impenetrable as the truth or a well-thought lie. It occurred to George that they were both in business and somehow worlds apart. Maybe it was because Chaseman knew he was successful while George wasn't so sure. Forget it. He took a sheet of scrap paper and began to sketch lazily. Watching him Chaseman remarked: "I hear that Chemconstruct is in trouble."

George continued to work at the drawing.

"That's just a story our friends spread about."

"That so?" said Chaseman. "I've seen the last couple of company reports," he added. "They don't look too good. Chemconstruct is overborrowed. They don't need an expensive development program like the Sep Tech Process. They need ready cash from sales. Is that why you're going back as sales director?"

"No, it's just pin money for my retirement." George put his pencil down. "Are you interested in this thing?"

"Show me." Chaseman leaned forward and looked at the outlines on the paper.

"OK." George breathed out. "So let's say we've gone through the membrane phase: the volume of contaminated liquid has been reduced to one-thousandth of the original. Here"—he indicated the drawing—"the active concentrate enters the vessels in the second phase. In effect we have two electrodes, the shell of the vessel and the zeolite core. By putting a charge through the solution we attract the contaminant to the core, where it engages in the structure of the zeolite. So far so good?"

"Sure. But what then? You junk the zeolite?"

George laughed. "Like we explained, it's a neat trick. With the contaminant enmeshed in the core, the liquid in the vessel is clean: we can draw it off and reduce the volume. Then we adjust the liquid that's left to a slightly alkaline condition. And then—*zap!*—we reverse the polarity of the current: and this time round the zeolite sheds the contaminant and precipitates it as a hydroxide sludge into the small liquid residue. The zeolite is as good as new, we take the sludge out of the bottom of the vessel with a sludge screw, and everything is clean and ready to repeat the process. The sludge you can do what you like with: encapsulate it in glass or concrete, or bury it—whatever suits you. The point being that you start with a contaminated creek and you end with a clean creek and a few barrels of crud. That's the trick."

Chaseman picked up the sketch. He had fingers with square tips, clean nails, and a college ring: no tobacco stains. George watched the other man's eyes running over the lines. He had a feeling that was how a man with vision was supposed to look. Chaseman put the sketch down with an audible snap.

"What are the industrial applications — just nuclear, like at West Valley?" he asked.

"No. We could use the technique on any heavy-metal contaminant. Mining, metal processing, plating, paint manufacture: there are plenty of industries with that sort of problem. In principle there's a hell of a market out there just waiting for us."

"I can see that," Chaseman said thoughtfully. Then, with his penetrating way of asking ordinary-sounding questions, he said: "But just how good are you, George?"

It was a question for which the answer still had to be tested. But George found an answer for now.

"Give me a big enough plant and enough time, and I could clean up the Pacific."

2

Kirov underscored the words in his notebook, lounging back in his seat, waiting for the meeting to get started. Smoke and edginess; and cups of coffee, more or less drained, ranked on the large conference table among the papers and the ashtrays. Rows of faces in blank expectancy. The first meeting of the Committee of Investigation into the Sokolskoye Incident. Pokrebsky was on his feet, an *apparatchik* to his toes, in his cheap suit with the hero-of-something-or-other medal ribbon pinned to the broad lapel.

"Nuclear Reprocessing Plant No. 7" — Pokrebsky's voice was a cracked tenor — "is situated thirty kilometers from the town of Sokolskoye in the province of Ivanov on the west bank of the Gorkovskoye Reservoir. It was commissioned in 1975 and has been in continuous operation ever since. The location of the site is among dense forest of spruce and pine on shallow soil overlying a granite base on a promontory formed by a stream or small river, the Chiraka, as it enters the Reservoir. With the object of providing cooling water for the storage tanks and for other purposes, a man-made lake has been created by damming the Chiraka with a concrete structure approximately six hundred meters in length, which, at full capacity, holds back some 1.4 million cubic meters of water in a shallow lake of more or less a kilometer in length. The lake is not self-contained. During periods of heavy rainfall and during the spring melt, the capacity of the dam is exceeded and water is discharged into the Gorkovskoye Reservoir."

Yuri Maximovitch Pokrebsky was Director of the All-Union Nuclear Inspectorate. Nominally independent and responsible for supervising the safe design, construction, and operation of nuclear installations; in fact Kostandov's civilian deputy, an Army nominee, the linchpin of Kostandov's control over the nuclear program. "But not Kostandov's choice," as Grishin commented pointedly. "Inherited with the job — implying, perhaps," he suggested to Kirov, "a lack of commitment to Pokrebsky. I've always thought — *wondered* — whether, if the occasion arose, one couldn't exploit that possibility."

Pokrebsky, having halted to sip a glass of water, resumed:

"On 13 September, observations carried out at the lake indicated the presence of large numbers of dead fish with no signs of the cause of death. Subsequent investigation conforms that there are no live fish in the lake and suggests that this mortality has also affected amphibians, insects, and other indigenous animal life. Concurrently, there is evidence of illness among a small section of the work force, but at this date there are no fatalities. It is agreed that the phenomena can only be explained by toxic contamination of the lake water, but the nature and quantity of the poison in the water has not been determined. This uncertainty arises from a lack of reliable data as to the behavior of the lake in dispersing any contaminant, with the result that we cannot be sure that our samples are representative of the lake as a whole. Preliminary analysis suggests the presence of paraquat herbicide and a higher than expected radioactivity."

He glanced at Kostandov — OK so far? Kirov acknowledged the gesture and continued to make up his notes. Grishin sat next to him, a smile on his face as deceptive as his public manner. His body was pointed reassuringly at the General.

General Yuri Trofimovitch Kostandov, Head of the Army's Directorate of Nuclear Operations. A career soldier, hard-featured, bushy-eyebrowed, his identity hidden beneath his uniform. A basilisk compared with Colonel Grishin of the KGB, whose face was always fluid with emotion, even if the emotion was bogus, a trap. The Directorate of Nuclear Operations was itself a misnomer, since it concerned itself with the coordination of civilian and military uses of nuclear installations and not with offensive military operations. Kostandov concentrated on Pokrebsky's words, even though it was to be assumed that they had been rehearsed.

"Operating data from the plant," said Pokrebsky, "show that during the months preceding September the radiation monitors installed on all potential alpha-discharge lines sounded no alerts. These monitors have been checked and found to be functioning. It therefore appears to the All-Union Nuclear Inspectorate that the absence of such alert excludes any possibility of leakage from the main plant. This leaves

38

only two further possibilities." And he paused before elaborating.

Academicians, Corresponding Members of the USSR Academy of Sciences, directors of several institutes, deputies of the foregoing — various. Kirov did a quick count, twenty people in all, a nice round figure, all nominated to the Committee of Investigation into the Sokolskoye Incident by Kostandov in collusion with Pokrebsky as was permitted by General Order No. 1 at this stage in the development of the crisis. Not that there was a crisis, if one believed Pokrebsky.

"The first possibility," he was saying, "is suggested by the presence of paraquat herbicide in the lake-water analysis. As you will be aware, this summer has been exceptionally dry throughout the northern areas of the Soviet Union, and it will not surprise you that the water in the Chiraka lake has been maintained at a low level. Under these conditions, the plant reports unusual growth of water weed, which has from time to time blocked the filters at the inlet end of the systems utilizing water from the lake. This weed has been suppressed using paraquat herbicide. Our first hypothesis must therefore be that the unregulated use of this chemical has been responsible for the death of animal life in the lake. If this is so, then the problem falls outside the remit of this Committee of Investigation and will be treated as an operational problem by the Inspectorate and probably solved by draining the Chiraka lake into the Gorkovskoye Reservoir, where dilution should reduce the contamination to safe levels.

"The second possibility is that the lake has been contaminated from a radioactive source outside the limits of the main plant. Such a source exists in the land waste-disposal site, where low-grade radioactive waste is dealt with by burial, and it is conceivable that the seepage of groundwater from this site has introduced radioactive material to the lake. If this is the case, the contamination, though unfortunate, is not fundamentally serious and is unlikely to lead to human fatalities. If, comrades, the Committee reaches this conclusion, then the Inspectorate would propose that the problem be resolved by reorganizing the land waste-disposal site and by draining the Chiraka lake into the Gorkovskoye Reservoir, where dilution should reduce the level of radioactivity to safe levels."

While Pokrebsky delivered his introduction from notes, his voice rising and falling like the meaningless chant of a village priest, Kirov completed his brief sketch of those present, looking at this point for the indefinable. Not for action, that was certain — nothing in the

39

meeting was geared to action. Kostandov had seen to that. Perhaps for opportunity, human opportunity. All subjects, as the KGB recognized, even technical ones, were reducible to human behavior. Study human behavior.

Pokrebsky was closing with a short peroration.

"Although we are optimistic about the outcome of the investigation, the possibility of serious radioactive contamination remains, and for this reason the Army's Directorate of Nuclear Operations has taken the step of invoking General Order No. 1. The first stage of that procedure requires the calling of this Committee of Investigation to confirm the nature of the disaster, if any, as a prelude to taking emergency measures."

He looked around briefly, perhaps for thanks from Kostandov, then sat down with an expression of evident satisfaction on his face, having generated the calculated level of tedium. Kirov glanced at Grishin. The Colonel wore a smile of ancient wisdom. He had been at his most patient since the list of Committee members had been thrust into his hand like a blackmail demand by a supercilious staff officer in the lobby of the GHQ building. Kostandov was saying dully: "The shortage of definitive data precludes any useful discussion of the problem at this stage. It is frankly too early to say whether we have a disaster on our hands or not." This provoked a grunt of assent from the only person to have provided a name card. It was folded on the table in front of him: Director P. Y. Yermolin of the State Committee for Hydrometeorology and the Control of the Environment. Kirov suspected a combination of fussiness and vanity and made a note against the name. How would a subordinate react to Yermolin? A scan of the back row where the aides and stenographers sat in a line against the wall didn't establish which of them might be Yermolin's creature.

Kostandov continued: "I propose that at this first session we should confine ourselves to allocating areas of activity to members of this Committee with a view to compiling a report confirming the disaster—or not, as seems more probable."

Pokrebsky added: "If you wish to delegate this responsibility within your respective organizations, that will, of course, be acceptable."

A nice touch, Kirov thought. He tried to resist the drift of his eyes from the sly weariness of Pokrebsky's face. The implication that the task was both tedious and, at bottom, not terribly important was

40

made without overstatement. He found himself staring out of the window over the gardens behind the Lenin Library. Yes, effective. He pulled his gaze back into the room, passing briefly over the woman sitting in the line behind Yermolin — one of the stenographers, he supposed. Kostandov was talking of the secrecy undertaking which members would find with their papers and should sign and return. "Security considerations," he amplified, "also demand that strict control be exercised over access to the site at Sokolskoye, which will be arranged through the Directorate of Nuclear Operations."

This caused Grishin to intervene with a question. "Couldn't the KGB assist?" he offered with a suggestion of doing a favor. "Sabotage, as an explanation, remains at least a theoretical possibility."

"There are many theoretical possibilities," Kostandov answered drily. "I don't think we can address all of them or any of them until there is at least some evidence pointing in that direction. And security generally in this area is a matter for the Army."

"Naturally," Grishin conceded, having tested the initial resistance to his idea. He grinned in turn at Pokrebsky, then at Kostandov, and finally at Kirov. His words were merely a reminder to the spectating Academicians that there were other powers than the Army. "It was an invitation to dissent," he remarked to Kirov afterward. This was a reference to a theory stemming from the more fashionable intellects of the KGB, according to which the KGB was as much a vehicle *for* as *against* malcontents. Dissent, said the theoreticians, was after all personal rather than ideological, negative rather than positive, and capable of being alleviated by the destruction of the dissenter's enemies. There was therefore a choice: denounce or defect. In that sense the KGB was a force for liberation, an essential part of the democracy of denunciation. Kirov wondered if it were operating here. He looked at the list of names again, without any particular one in view. He found that of the woman, not a stenographer but an assistant to Yermolin; a man's name crossed out because he was unable to attend, and hers penciled in: I. N. Terekhova — evidently not a first choice.

In full flight Pokrebsky was saying: "The provision of data from the site will be done by the Inspectorate. This will include a definitive analysis of the lake water, a review of all designs, engineering data, and operating experience relevant to the plant, and the conduct of any dissections, autopsies, and analysis of animal life affected by the contamination. Requests for such data should be made to myself.

41

There is no representation on the Committee by any body with experience in hydrology, but it is desirable that a report be obtained on how quickly any contaminant will be diluted and distributed if released from the Chiraka lake. Such a study will be commissioned by the Directorate of Nuclear Operations through the Frunze Military Academy under the guise of a defense-planning study. In conjunction with this, Directors Yermolin and Velikhov will be asked to report on the effect of the contaminant on the population and environment of the area Sokolskoye—Gorky with emphasis on toxicity and persistence of contamination."

And so on. They were checking their watches. Kirov glanced at his own. He scanned the faces again looking for—resentment? Not necessarily. The emotion might be resentment or anger or even integrity: he would recognize it when he saw it, the flicker of an attitude that was out of tune with what was happening. Its source was immaterial; it could be cultivated in the desired direction. *Where are you?* he wondered. He turned to the list again and worked through the names again as if searching for that of an old friend. Which one would be his collaborator?

"Should . . . " A clear voice broke Pokrebsky's speech like a stone dropped on ice. Kirov looked up sharply. Pokrebsky had halted and directed a withering stare at Yermolin. The latter was whispering to his female assistant. She answered his questions but her eyes returned a cool gaze to Pokrebsky. Close to Kirov someone asked, "Who is that bloody woman?" but without any serious interest.

"Director Yermolin?"

"My apologies."

"Yes?"

"Comrade Terekhova merely enquires whether the studies of my own institute should be confined to the area Sokolskoye—Gorky. If the degree of contamination is not known, should investigations not be directed at effects along the whole length of the Volga?"

"I . . . " the woman began, but was arrested sharply by Yermolin's raising his hand.

"We are talking," Pokrebsky said with undisguised sarcasm, "of a disaster, not a holocaust"—which was the nearest he came to mentioning the catastrophe at Chernobyl. "Now . . . " he continued and went on to discuss the need for information on the climate of Sokolskoye and the province of Ivanov while Kirov half-listened, but was distracted by the woman who in that suppressed atmosphere had shown the one spark of life and interest. Meanwhile Kostandov was wrapping up the meeting, asking whether anyone present had encountered such a problem. One of the Academicians, an ancient character buried in an old suit and cardigan, spoke up.

"Not here — not in our country." He had a sharp, combative tone, daring anyone to disagree, and an old man's carelessness. "We never used to mess around with this environmental stuff. Too expensive. Too much interference with production. We leave that sort of thing to the Americans."

"Does that mean you have information or not?" Kostandov asked patiently.

"Could be — or perhaps not. There's a place in the United States — West Valley — old plant — polluted stream. The Americans have done something about cleaning it up. I dare say it isn't the same problem as ours, but it may be worth a look."

Kostandov looked to Pokrebsky for a cue. Kirov wondered how far they were really allies, remembering Grishin's theory that the alliance was one of necessity: that Kostandov on coming to office had inherited the Directorate's relationship with Pokrebsky like a family curse. Grishin hadn't given particulars, merely referring darkly to Operation Fall-Out. Kirov had tried a records search against that name, but the computer failed to recognize it. Pokrebsky — Kostandov — Grishin — Fall-Out. Kirov had a whiff of old plots and stale malice between KGB and Army. Fall-Out, a plot with no record — dangerous.

Kostandov was saying to the old man: "Can you investigate this American technology?"

"No information — embargoed." A monkey grin on a crabbed face. "Maybe the *spies* can come up with something."

"We'll investigate," Grishin volunteered, and Kirov took a note. Then Kostandov launched on his conclusions: despite the potential gravity of the situation, there was a window in the course of events: the problem was apparently confined to the Chiraka lake and would probably be locked there by the onset of winter until the spring thaw. Assuming the Committee reached its conclusions and gave recommendations by the end of October, there would be five months in which to take the necessary actions. He gave the Committee thirty days in which to complete its investigations.

And with that the formal part of the meeting was finished though the ending occurred in the same ragged way as the rest. Kostandov's voice trailed off into a murmur and there was a gradual sense that nothing more was happening and then a sudden realization that that was so. No peroration, no dramatic plea. No *direction* — yes, thought Kirov, that was it, the source of the subtle dissonance between the subject and its treatment.

"Pokrebsky has them where he wants them," said Grishin, his round face smiling and his eyes glittering with anger. "No one knows whether we have a problem on our hands or not. This is supposed to be a crisis meeting, but it's starting to sound like a plot by Kafka or some experimental play — by the way, isn't your woman in the theater?" he added inconsequentially.

"A dancer." Kirov was looking beyond Grishin to the General. "Kostandov believes in this disaster, or at least has his suspicions. And he isn't alone." Beyond the General the woman, Terekhova, was scooping up her notes with a look of quiet concern. In repose she had a handsome face, perhaps at one time even beautiful, with dark hair and strong features. She looked up, and Kirov saw a pair of expressive eyes regarding him with frank curiosity. Her clothes, on the other hand, were indifferent, tidy but without style, the sort that most Moscow women would make for themselves. But then, he was conditioned by Washington and the *svelte* beauties who had fallen for his Russian charm in the days before the Ouspensky Case.

"We have to find some way of opening this investigation up," Grishin was saying. "We need to get at the truth without seeming to involve ourselves out of our area." He was looking at the various underlings holding briefcases and opening doors for their bosses. They smelt of servility and ambition. "There should be somebody here who is open to an approach."

"Leave it to me."

"Yes. You'll find a way to turn this investigation inside out and destroy Pokrebsky, won't you?"

"Yes, if that's what you want," Kirov assented without any indication of his personal desires. People were leaving. The Terekhova woman was leaving with her boss, Yermolin.

"You have some ideas?"

"Perhaps." Kirov regarded her clinically, noting her height and the way she walked. Competent, he thought. Vulnerable to what? He glanced at some of the others. One or two harassed younger men. Also vulnerable. It was a matter of choice.

He stood beside Terekhova in the lift. She ignored him. Yermolin, a fussy man, kept glancing at his watch and following the floor indicator. Avoiding something? She was speaking.

"How do they expect to get to the truth of this matter when all the key data are controlled by Director Pokrebsky? The Inspectorate is too involved in the design and operation of the plant. Its personnel may have been involved in whatever went wrong."

"*If* anything went wrong," Yermolin reminded her. He turned from watching the lights and treated her to a superior smile. "Don't concern yourself, Irina Nikolaevna," he murmured. Then: "This is where we get off."

The doors opened and as they stepped out Yermolin remarked: "You have always been a promising candidate for other things. Let's hope you continue to be — promising."

3

London: September 16

For a homecoming businessman on a transatlantic flight, it is always raining at Heathrow. This is true whatever the weather.

George Twist collected his bag from the carousel in Terminal 3. It was one of those bags guaranteed to hold a suit without creasing and to fit under the passenger seat as hand-luggage. It did neither. It was another piece for the collection, like the travelling iron, the multi-current adaptor, the stuffed mongoose and snake picked up at Bangkok airport, and all the other junk that gets bought in air terminals because it seems like a good idea at the time and because browsing through the flashy boutiques makes a change from hanging around the bars. He was tired. He hadn't shaved and his face had relaxed like a pudding that wouldn't set. For the trip he was wearing a diamond-patterned sweater, jeans, and flat-earth shoes, and he was stopped at Customs because something in his manner and appearance fitted with one of their prejudices. He stood with the patience of exhaustion. When he was finally released he was scheduled to go to a board meeting at eleven that morning; he was to be the white knight who would pull in the sales and put Chemconstruct on its feet.

"You'll be the company hero," Alasdair Cranbourne, the managing director, had said on the occasion of his appointment.

The offices were in Borough High Street, set back from the rainspattered pavement in a blackened Victorian pile encrusted with gargoyles and vagrant pigeons. The receptionist was a woman in spectacles who was also the union convener. Like the other sedentary staff, she resented anyone who went on foreign trips and showed it by demanding a bicycle shed for the workers whenever she got the chance. But for now, maybe because the departure of Graham Talbot had sated her taste for red meat, she smiled a knowing smile and said, "Congratulations, Mr. Twist. They're waiting for you."

He shaved in the executive washroom and doused his head in cold water. Evans, the company lawyer, was there, preening in the mirror. He was a cheerful type who wore bow ties and tried to impress people by being eccentric. Between straightening his tie and flattening his hair he said: "Let's have a bit of sparkling wit, eh, George? Since I'm taking the minutes."

"Where's the towel?"

Evans passed a paper tissue. "By the way, congratulations on your new appointment."

"Thanks."

"We need new blood to run the sales department."

"Sure." George liked the image. In the sales department there was always blood on the walls. When things were tough, the company could always be relied on to sacrifice a sales director to appease the gods. But not this time—he told himself—not if he could help it.

The board was already in session, gossiping about an item not on the agenda, namely the managing director's new car. George caught the words "overhead camshaft" as he came in. He guessed that Cranbourne didn't know what one was, but from listening to the words, you could never tell. In any case, Alasdair could always rely on Harold Barnes if he got out of his technical depth. A hesitation and Harold was in there with the detail. The two of them had a double act going.

"Hello, George, how was the flight?" Cranbourne asked. "Manage any sleep? Get in this morning on the red-eye special? I find that on these night flights the economy class is half-empty and you can usually manage a couple of hours' shuteye. Always provided, of course, that you don't mind bunking with the proles. Which airline was it?"

"I don't remember. It was OK. I got some sleep, and it was OK."

"Fine, fine." Cranbourne had a light tenor voice and an airy way of speaking, his voice floating over the words as if he didn't mean any of them. He was a slim, donnish-looking man with an active manner like a starling looking for worms. "Well," he added, "feel free to doze off if all this gets too dull for you—only joking—it's good of you to come in."

"You know how it is after a long trip. I had to watch my back."

"Oh? Ah, yes." Cranbourne gave a small laugh, and the rest of them followed at intervals like glass breaking. George thought: Christ, five minutes back in the office and I've scored an own goal. I must be losing my touch.

But the meeting was passing him by. It had reached "Matters Arising from Previous Minutes," which had to be good for an hour; and since George hadn't been there last time he decided that his mind could drop out and wait for the rest of him to catch up like misdirected luggage. Instead he could ask himself: What made me take this job? More to the point: What made them give it to me? They don't even like me. Alasdair Cranbourne meanwhile smoothed the meeting over with his neat line of patter. The story was that he was a sometime accountant who had got into contract negotiating and made his reputation weaving fine words around the East Europeans back in the days when they were too unsophisticated to recognize bullshit when they smelled it. He was diplomatic with everybody. "I keep open house where ideas are concerned" was one of his catch phrases. Another was: "I like competing thoughts on a subject. I call it Creative Tension." Others called it Divide and Rule, and maybe it explained why George was on the board.

There were three other directors. Stan Chambers, the finance director, was a bookkeeper by instinct, cautious in his own area but otherwise prepared to consider most things. Sandy Murchieson was responsible for operations. He had long field experience with the pluses and minuses that went with it: the last including a nervousness of technical innovation, which history told him never worked the first time. And that left Harold Barnes, another engineer, who was technically sharp but almost paranoid about guarding his turf. Between them they had got Chemconstruct to where it was. Wherever that was.

George was drawn back to the meeting by the sound of Barnes cracking pencils, which he did from a pent-up frustration that he carried to everything so that after any meeting he attended his place could be located by crushed polystyrene cups.

"Now the state of the order book," announced Stan Chambers.

48

"Bloody terrible!" murmured Barnes.

"Downturn in the economic cycle," suggested Cranbourne with his fine ear for jargon. And then he smiled and allowed Chambers to explain that Sep Tech was swallowing cash to fund Lou Ruttger's research and development program and that Chemconstruct wasn't generating enough new business to produce the income. It took Chambers time to say it, since he had an insecure man's urge to cling to what he knew best and so talked about cash-flow and forward projections, but the message was clear enough. Chemconstruct was quietly going bust.

"And with that I think we should have coffee," Cranbourne said.

Coffee was brought by an elderly woman who was treated by Cranbourne as a family retainer so that he made a point of remembering her birthday and asking after her grandchildren.

"Have you noticed," Evans whispered, "that Alasdair can't bear rows? I thought Harold would fall off his chair when Alasdair suggested coffee." They stood together by the mahogany sideboard that served as a bar and studied their reflections in a tarnished silver wine-cooler which was engraved with the date 1923 as if it were somehow a better time. Cranbourne found them there.

"How's your wife, George? Lillian, isn't it? Brought her over yet?"

"I'm waiting for the house to be ready. Everything is in storage. And I have to make arrangements about the nurse and about Sarah's school." George didn't mention that he also needed the time to rest from the physical exhaustion of caring for his wife these last few months as her illness went into another decline.

"And how is Lillian's trouble?" Cranbourne asked, expressing his ignorance of the details diplomatically.

"I live in hope, you know how it is."

"That's what I like, George—an optimist!"

They resumed.

"The problem lies in the States," said Barnes sharply. "We should cut Lou's budget, tell him to stop messing around with the Sep Tech Process and sell what he's got. The West Valley Project has given him a reference plant and he should be looking for repeat orders instead of frigging around trying to make new resins and better membranes. And on this side we should be going for volume: the profit on our standard plants is too thin to support the

49

company, and the only way to correct the position is to sell more of them." He glanced in George's direction. "Whichever way you look at it, it's essentially a sales problem."

"What do you have to say to that, George?" asked Alasdair Cranbourne evenly. "Do we have a sales problem?"

"What do I have to sell?"

"You heard Harold: our standard plants."

Barnes amplified with the information that everyone already knew. "We've sold nearly two hundred of them over the last fifteen or twenty years—and as far as I know, the market hasn't gone away."

George said, "You've seen the figures: every year for the last five years we've taken a smaller share of the cake. What does that mean to you?"

"That Sales have fallen down on their job. That's why Graham was given the push, isn't it? I mean, tell me if I've got it wrong, but when the sales director gets the sack, it does mean that all is not well in the State of Denmark, doesn't it?"

George nodded. Graham Talbot was the last sales director. George hadn't been present when his predecessor was fired, but he could imagine the scene: Talbot being dragged out of the board-room to the cellars of the Lubyanka to be shot. George had been thinking a lot about Russia lately.

Cranbourne said, "I'm glad to see you agree, George. We're looking to you for great things."

"I wasn't agreeing." George felt too tired to add anything more. He was following Stan Chamber's eyes drifting around the framed photographs on the wall: pictures of plants the company had built in the sixties, water stains on the paper and flyspecks on the glass— was that really all they had to show?

Barnes leaned across the table. For a quick-tempered man he had a surprisingly mild face—round, even jolly. "And what is our problem, George?"

George found that the others were all looking at him, even that cynical bastard Evans, as though he had come down from the mountain bearing the tablets of the Law. It lasted a second and then they began to fidget, but while it lasted it was real. He said, "The product."

"I don't follow."

"No." George stretched himself. "OK, I'll tell you. When we started on the standard plants twenty years ago, we had one competitor and an arrangement that cut up the market leaving the contractors happy and the clients screwed."

"I'm not sure it was exactly like that, George," intervened Alasdair Cranbourne. To the others he said, "There was an orderly marketing arrangement"—an expression which in his mind made it all right.

George went on: "Five years ago we had six competitors and the sales position collapsed into a free-for-all. This year there are maybe twenty companies that can do what we can do and prices for everyone have been slashed to the bone. And that's how it is. We don't have a product; the last major job was taken by a Korean and the four before that by the Japanese. And there is no way that this company is going to match the Far East on prices and stay solvent." He let it drop there. They either believed him or they never would.

"So what is your solution?" Alasdair Cranbourne asked.

"Innovate."

George paused and waited for a reaction, but there was silence. Had he used a word they didn't know?

"OK, let me go on. For years we've been kidding ourselves that we are up among the Fluors, the Davy-McKees, the Bechtels of this world, when the truth is that we were standing still while even Costain passed us by. There are only two areas where maybe we are ahead of the game. The first is Sep Tech, which has made progress only because it's located in the States and hasn't been too closely controlled from here—let me finish," he said to avoid the obvious protest. "And the second is in liquefied natural gas treatment, where we have a good process but haven't had the guts to sell it." He paused. Then: "Sep Tech has got to sell plants, sure—but it still has to invest in development. If we cut the budget like Harold suggests, the company will be dead in two years because the technology is moving too fast and what we have will be out of date. That means that the States is still going to need cash. And that brings me to the LNG plants, because that's where the cash is going to come from."

George halted there, because for the moment, the others looked as though they had had all they could take in. What the hell, he thought, he might as well tell the truth and go out in a blaze of glory. But when it came the response was subdued.

"Where are you going to sell these LNG plants, George?" Alasdair Cranbourne asked.

George breathed in and let it out.

"Russia."

One day in a pub, Jim Evans had told George the story about Russia. In fact George had heard it before, but the lawyer had a way with words. "Somewhere in the history of every contracting company," he said, "there lies a disaster, the big project where everything goes wrong — by the way, stop me, George, if I'm telling you what you know already."

"Go on, Jim, I'm listening."

"OK, let's get the drinks in while I talk. Every contracting company, as I say, has its big disaster."

"Two pints of bitter," said George to the barmaid.

Evans said: 'Sometimes it doesn't have a name, sometimes it's referred to as 'the Fall' as if it marks the day when the company lost its innocence. But, whatever it's called, it becomes the company's taboo, like incest, a thing that can be talked and thought about only obliquely — perhaps under a smokescreen of jokes — because the subject is too serious.

"The truth about the Fall is never known, not by the company itself, not even by those responsible. I mean, George, that those who are caught in the open when the firing starts get scattered and their recollections lost. And the survivors — well, the survivors tell so many stories that they themselves get lost in the legends and mythology of the thing.

"The chairman — God bless him — the chairman has a report on the incident. It sits in its binding in his bookcase and probably represents less of the truth than anything else because the people who contribute material are mostly concerned to blame the client and, in any case" — Evans paused to take a sip of his beer and mumble into his glass — "the report is written by the company's lawyers." He smiled and went on, "This is partly the point, George, the point about the Fall and about large contracting projects."

"Oh," said George. "What's that?"

"That there's never one story or one problem. That's the point. And the result is something that exists as a series of conflicting myths and moral precepts."

"And what's the other point? You said 'partly'—that was 'partly' the point."

"Did I? Yes, I remember."

"Well?"

"Oh, the other point is only that the company always learns the lessons of the Fall."

"Since when?"

"Since it says so in the Annual Report," said Evans. "So it must be true."

In the case of Chemconstruct, the Fall occurred in Russia. There was a second incident in Lagos when Ronnie Pugh was robbed and murdered on his way from the airport, which meant that the company stopped doing business in Nigeria—but in general this was regarded as simple bad luck. The incident in the Soviet Union was different.

Its popular name was "the Omsk Job," and—whatever it was—it happened in the early seventies. The process didn't work, the plant blew up, the client never performed his side of the deal, no one ever got paid—these were all true to a degree or, at any rate, part of the legend. As Evans said, the details weren't important: it was the legacy that counted.

It was after the Omsk Job that Alasdair Cranbourne became chairman and Stan Chambers, Sandy Murchieson, Harold Barnes, and Rod Willis became directors. Rod Willis was the last sales director but three.

Sandy Murchieson said in his low Scottish burr, "We don't do business in Russia—not since the Omsk Job."

"That's right," Harold Barnes agreed. "The profits are too small and the conditions are too tough. We don't have enough local knowledge, and I wouldn't trust the Estimating Department to price a job there."

Alasdair Cranbourne asked, "Do we even have representation there, George? I mean, after all this time?"

"His name is Jack Melchior."

"He didn't get us the Omsk Job, did he?"

"No, we've never done any actual business through him. He has brought in a few enquiries, but we've never bid on any of them."

"Still, better than nothing, I suppose. Sorry, go on, George, why Russia?"

"Because it's the world's biggest potential market for LNG plants. It's no secret that the Soviet Union has the largest reserves of oil and natural gas. But the Eastern Bloc still has problems in balancing its energy budget. On the one hand, they're expanding their nuclear plant capacity and, on the other, they're trying to extend and make optimum use of their fossil fuels."

"So?"

"So one of their options is to process their natural gas. Instead of just burning it for fuel, they can strip out gasoline and chemical feedstocks and still have an acceptable fuel gas left. Common sense and the latest information say that that's exactly what they are trying to do."

The others were silent for a moment. George felt like a starlet doing a turn before a show's backers.

Cranbourne asked, "Have there been any actual enquiries for LNG plants from the Russians? I don't recall that Graham mentioned anything."

"Graham had more sense. He'd have thrown anything like that straight into the bin." Barnes had stopped looking at George.

Chambers suggested, "Graham might just have forgotten to raise the point. He was fairly sick toward the end."

"Which was why we had to let him go," Cranbourne agreed, which was one way of putting it. "Well, George?"

"The Russians have put out two enquiries and are supposed to have two more ready for issue. The story is that they're looking for thirty to fifty plants over the next five to ten years. We didn't receive either of the two enquiries out already, so it's clear that Chemconstruct aren't on their bidders list. The first problem is to attract their attention and get there."

"How do you propose to do that?"

"There's a British Chamber of Commerce trade mission fixed to visit Moscow next month. One of the targets is the Ministry of Gas, which is the ministry supporting these plant purchases. If we're agreed that this is a strategy that's worth pursuing, then I intend to be on that mission." And with that George stopped. He had thrown down the gauntlet. No one picked it up. If Barnes had been going to, the chairman stopped him.

"That seems a thoroughly sound suggestion. After all, a trip to Moscow doesn't represent a commitment. Whether thereafter we change our policy—well, that's a different matter, but we have to keep an open mind, eh?" To the others he said, "George has to be given some leeway to put his own stamp on the Sales Department. This new policy is all very provisional, very preliminary, what we might call early days. I don't think we can honestly object to George's sticking a toe over the threshold of the Soviet Union. After all, there may be nothing in this story about gas plants. Or there may be everything."

George asked, "And the R and D budget for Sep Tech? That was the other side of the coin: the building up of a new long-term business."

There was another silence of seconds, during which the chairman glanced at Harold Barnes. Then he said genially, "Oh, no question that we have to continue investing. Sep Tech is a valuable business. It would give altogether the wrong impression if we didn't support it with money. There, George, you can't complain at that. You've got all your own way—only joking—we needed the new contribution, very stimulating."

"Thanks."

"Don't mention it." Cranbourne stared around now at each of the others, so that George had a sudden feeling that all along he had been at a different meeting and wasn't really here. "And now you must be tired," Cranbourne said. "I don't see that you need to hang around for the rest of the routine stuff."

Tiredness, that was it—jet lag catching up.

"Would you like a driver to run you home? You kept your house on, didn't you? Wasn't it Hampstead?"

George looked up. He remembered that Cranbourne himself lived there. The chairman still professed to be attached to art and socialism. There was a story that he had forgone the company Rolls for a Volvo estate. Socialism was hell.

"West Hampstead," said George.

"Thought so. Thought I'd seen you walking the dog. Which part?"

"Uxbridge."

*   *   *

Jim Evans followed him out. The lawyer collared him near the stairs among the fire buckets and surplus filing cabinets and last year's spare diaries. Evans fingered his bow tie and tried to look game. He said, "Don't trust Alasdair too far, will you, George?"

"When are they going to redecorate, clean this place up so that it's fit for clients?"

"Cash, George, everything's a question of cash—you heard them. Anyway, we have the VIP suite for the clients."

"Furnished with the taste of a high-class burger joint." George stared down into the depths of the well and summoned the elevator. "This working?"

"Probably. It does most days."

They waited. George said, "I wasn't planning on trusting Alasdair."

"Good show. That was Graham Talbot's greatest failing. The sales strategy that Graham put his name to was really all Alasdair's doing; Graham was no more than the chairman's errand boy. Left to himself, I think he would have taken a similar line to yours."

The elevator came. Evans said, "Mustn't stop. I told them I was only popping out to water the flowers."

George blocked the automatic door with his foot. He asked: "Why did they bring me back from the States? Don't tell me I have a fan club over here."

"I don't know." Evans looked away, at the walls, at the ceiling, where an inspection hatch had been removed and not replaced. He focused on George. "I do know one thing, though. Alasdair is intending to visit the States in the near future. I'm talking about our Alasdair who was hardly ventured out of Hampstead these ten years except to stick a knife into his friends. Make of it what you like." He gave a conspiratorial smile. "Must go," he added. He pushed through the swinging doors and turned right, toward the boardroom.

George watched him go. He took his foot out of the door and went into the elevator, where he stood for a second facing the control panel in a moment of blankness, as if the instructions were written in Russian, before pressing the ground-floor button.

Russia. Surely it couldn't be worse?

4

"Irina Nikolaevna Terekhova, age thirty-eight, born in Simferopol, educated at the University of Kiev, degree in applied physics, doctoral thesis on the something-something effect of nuclear radiation on the something-or-other, a couple of minor qualifications in nuclear engineering. Seems to have had problems in pursuing an engineering career — who knows? It's a man's world. Switched to studying radiation effects on the environment, maybe something to do with her doctoral thesis. Now works about three rungs down the ladder from the chairman of the State Committee for Hydrometeorology and the Control of the Environment, Doctor P.Y.Yermolin. Also lectures at the University of Moscow —" Bogdanov broke off. "Do you want me to go on with this, boss? All that talent, already I hate her."

"Just give me the facts," said Kirov.

"Whatever you want." Bogdanov shook his shoulders loosely inside his oversize captain's jacket. He had myopic eyes and a long beak of a nose with a reddened indentation from his spectacles. He was thin as drawn wire, a collection of mismatched bones and flesh, like the scraps in a butcher shop.

"What's to know?" he went on. "She's whiter than white. Father a hero of the Great Patriotic War, mother a daughter of the soil and a Party member. Good communist education, a member of Komsomol and probably pretty as a picture waving her flag, and in favor of virginity. I've seen the type before, all strength and virtue."

"Anything negative?"

"Her confidential work record shows that she pestered the Inspectorate with a couple of papers on radiation hazards to the environment—no one complained, but you can tell they didn't like it—maybe that's not so bad. And then there's her marriage."

In the corridor outside the cubicle that Bogdanov used as an office, there was laughter and the thud of a body against the flimsy partition.

"That's Kuzmin chasing the typists, dirty bastard."

"Terekhova's marriage?" Kirov reminded him. Bogdanov forgot about Kuzmin and picked up his notes.

"She used to be the wife of a Yid poet, Osip Abramovitch Davidov. He was OK at one time, held a card in the Writers' Union and turned out verses for the usual journals. Then a few years ago he went off the rails and started publishing political poems in *samizdat*. They locked him up in a special hospital. Maybe he's still there, or maybe he's dead—no one's sure since the file was removed and not returned. In any case Terekhova divorced him in 1976 before the trouble started. She must have fallen for that Yid charm—who can blame her? Nowadays she's married to Colonel Konstantin Aleksandrovitch Terekhov. It seems he's a hero. He's out in Afghanistan, fighting the *dushmani*. They have one kid, a boy."

Kirov picked up the papers from the mess of spent ballpoint, cigarette stubs, and coffee cups on Bogdanov's desk. A record of interviews, reports by colleagues, and her own self-criticism written in a well-formed hand. That and the usual anonymous denunciations scrawled in large letters on recyled paper.

To: Dr P.Y. Yermolin,   18 September 198-
    State Committee for Hydrometeorology and
    the Control of the Environment

REPORT ON THE CLIMATE OF SOKOLSKOYE AND
GORKOVSKOYE RESERVOIR REGION

For climatic purposes the subject region is treated as part of the East Russian Plain, an area in which the onset and transit of autumn and spring are alike more rapid than in more western areas of European Russia. September is a colder month than May and October is colder than April. The temperature usually falls some 15°C during the months of September and October, and in the latter month frosts with temperatures of –15°C occur fairly frequently. The ground is usually covered with snow by mid-October. Precipitation in both autumn and spring is similar, about 3 cm, even close to the Urals. Between the date of writing and the onset of seasonal ice cover, one may therefore expect only negligible rainfall or other precipitation.

In winter the average temperature will be in the range –15°C to –10°C and the January isotherm of –10°C runs almost directly from Moscow through Gorky. The absolute minimum temperature has been recorded at –45°C.

Spring occurs two weeks later than in western areas — for example, Belorussia — but comes suddenly and is a much shorter season. Temperatures for March will still average below freezing and it will not be until the middle of April that a substantial thaw begins. However, by mid-May temperatures in the river-basin area will generally exceed those found elsewhere in western Russia.

For more detail, please refer to the attached Table 1 (temperature averages by day: 25-year study), Table 2 (precipitation by type: weekly over 30 years), Table 3 (temperature and precipitation by season: a 100-year study from records, in bar-chart form).

In response to the specific questions raised in your request, it is impossible to give a categorical answer, but all data indicate that it is highly improbable that temperatures in the subject region will not exceed 0°C during the period 15 October to 1 April for any significant period. Precipitation over the same period should not exceed 18.5 cm and will be mainly in the form of snow.

> (Signed) P. E. Schcherbitsky
> Senior Researcher,
> Climate Research Laboratory,
> Computing Center, Moscow

"In my opinion, " said Bodganov, "we forget about Terekhova and go for the throat. Interrogate the plant director at Sokolskoye. He's an Armenian, name of Fuckyoursisterian — well, maybe not exactly that — and he must be pretty isolated working up there instead of sunning himself in Armenia. Trust me, I know this character. We could crack him easy and get all the dirt on Pokrebsky and the Inspectorate."

"Too direct. The Army would put everything down to KGB pressure. In any case, we can't get at him: Kostandov has him locked up at Sokolskoye, and at the moment this is a technical not a political or criminal investigation. We would have to make a case to Kostandov, and for that we don't have the material."

"No problem." Bogdanov's hand rested on Kirov's shoulder. They had reached the anteroom to Grishin's office and were waiting for him to be available. Bogdanov was suffering from one of his macabre enthusiasms. "There are ways," he said. "Our guys in Erevan could go through their records. Fuckyoursisterian didn't get to be plant director without making enemies back home. There must be a lot of people who would like to cause him trouble. We can dress up a criminal case against him, base it on something totally unconnected — black-market speculation — and get the fraud squad from Petrovka to pull him out of Sokolskoye." Petrovka was headquarters of the Moscow CID, who were not a part of the KGB.

"OK," Kirov agreed. "But I want direct access. If he starts confessing to the regular police, then the lid will blow on this whole business. And I still want Terekhova. Using the plant director is crude tactics: we can keep him in reserve for supporting evidence." The secretary announced that Grishin was free to see them.

The Colonel was at his desk with the climatology report in front of him. As the two men sat down, he pushed the report toward them.

"This confirms that we don't have a serious problem until the snow melts in spring." He pushed his chair back. "If then," he emphasized. "For the moment, we don't know that we have a problem at all. Are you making any progress?"

"I have a target on the Committee of Investigation," said Kirov. He produced Bogdanov's abbreviated report and handed it over. Grishin took it, glanced at the name.

"Irina Nikolaevna Terekhova. Why the woman? Wouldn't a man carry more weight?"

"There's always a risk that whoever we pick would run to his chief for protection. Terekhova seems to have differences with her own chief, Yermolin. And she distrusts the Inspectorate from past experience." Kirov paused. "There is also her first husband to consider. Marriage to a counterrevolutionary may give us a lever over her if she doesn't cooperate willingly."

"Perhaps." Grishin read through the rest of the report. "Terekhov," he said when he had finished. "I've heard of the present husband. *Komsomolskaya Pravda* did a piece on 'our brave boys fighting the bandits in Afghanistan.' You should read the papers: the Army is building him up as a popular hero. That gives him a lot of protection—and his wife, too. I don't think you'll be able to pressure her over some Jewish poet who went crazy." He put the paper down. "On the other hand, I agree that she may want to cooperate."

"Do I have authority to use her?" Kirov asked.

"What harm can it do?" said Grishin.

To: Major P.A. Kirov,   19 September 198—
     Industrial Security Directorate,
     Second Chief Directorate,
     Committee of State Security

Copy to: Director K.I. Skryabin,
          Nuclear Physics Institute

REPORT ON THE DECONTAMINATION OF WATER BY ELECTRICALLY
ENHANCED OSMOSIS AS PRACTICED IN THE
UNITED STATES OF AMERICA

In response to your request of September 15 I attach a report compiled from information held by this Directorate relative to the above technology. Most of this has been gleaned from patents and articles published in western scientific journals and indicates the existence of a working technology for the removal of heavy metals and transuranic elements from contaminated water as demonstrated at a full-scale plant situated at West Valley, New York State. The available data would not allow Soviet industry to replicate the technology or manufacture the associated equipment other than conventional items.

Although this technology has a nuclear, and therefore military, application, because it is not directly used in production its acquisition has a low priority. The most recent report from an agent of

First Chief Directorate, Source David, who visited the West Valley installation, confirms that it is in an operating condition. This agent has no technical experience and his further use would probably not be productive. His status requires that any request for his services must be directed to the First Department and also sanctioned by I. A. Yatsin, Washington Resident.

This technology is owned by an American corporation, Sep Tech Inc. of San José, California, which is a subsidiary company of Chemconstruct PLC of London, England. The exportation of drawings, data, or equipment relative to this technology from the United States of America to the Soviet Union or to any member of the Council for Mutual Economic Cooperation is strictly prohibited by Federal law.

(Signed) V.I. LESSIOVSKY
Scientific and Technical Directorate,
First Chief Directorate,
Committee of State Security

He knocked at the door of her apartment, listened to the movement. She lived quietly: no television noise, no music; most people did not, but were ignorant of the background accompaniment to their lives. When she opened the door she appeared to him to be older, but still with the same fine eyes. Beautiful, he thought, once upon a time, but not now.

"Comrade Terekhova, may I come in? I should like to speak to you." He saw the lack of recognition. "Kirov — Pyotr Andreevitch."

"Major Kirov — yes — I remember." She examined him with unmixed curiosity where he had expected caution. "Please, come in."

He followed her down the short hallway into an undistinguished room with Finnish furniture and some East German stereo equipment. It was clean and well ordered except for a pile of books on the floor. The walls were bare of decoration other than some framed certificates. *Arkady Konstantinovitch Terekhov has successfully passed his 25-meter swimming test.*

"Where is your son?"

"In the bedroom. Arkasha . . ." She didn't need to raise her voice. The boy's head came around the doorway. Dark hair and an intense, almost insolent stare. Perhaps eight years old. He had a book in one hand and seemed annoyed. "This is Major Kirov." The child said hello, then disappeared back to his reading. The mother said, "He's fond of books."

"A precocious child."

"He likes to read." The way she said this sounded like dissent.

They exchanged more polite observations and she offered Kirov a drink. While she poured from the bottle, he regarded the room more closely. On the table a large map of the Volga river system was spread out, and there were open books with animal and plant diagrams on the exposed pages and others with demographic data.

"You've started working on our problem at Sokolskoye."

She passed him a glass, not having one herself, and took a seat facing him from an upright, composed postion. "This is very preliminary," she answered. "Until I know the exact nature of the contaminant, its concentration and distribution, I can't predict what its effects will be on animal and plant life."

She had not asked him why he had called.

"Have your received the water analysis?"

It occurred to him that he resembled a priest with his unspoken right of access to every house. Except, of course, that he didn't bring absolution.

She said in response to his question, "I've received three. They show above-normal radiation and pesticide contamination, but there are wide fluctuations. The Inspectorate states that there are still problems in obtaining representative samples, since they have no model to explain how any chemical deposited in the lake would distribute itself."

"Is the radiation serious?"

"No. The pesticide would be enough to kill the fish, but it could be disposed of safely by dilution into the Gorkovskoye Reservoir."

He thought she seemed tired. Of course, she had the child to take care of as well as her work. With exceptions such as Lara, the women of Moscow all seemed tired. Unlike Washington, as he remembered it. Noticing the silence he commented, "When it's quiet like this, they say a policeman is born." He smiled and drew a smile out of her.

"Why are you here?" she said at last.

"You are concerned at the behavior of the Inspectorate?" he countered. He saw her hesitation and suspected a first flash of fear behind it. "Please," he said soothingly. "I'm not here to represent the Inspectorate. I'm simply concerned that the investigation get to the truth of the matter. Perhaps I can help you. If there is information you need, I may be able to get it. If you wanted to visit Sokolskoye, perhaps to take plant samples or see the patients at the hospital, I may be able to arrange that, too. I know that at the moment there are difficulties, but things can be done."

"The Inspectorate is concerned with production at the expense of everything else," she answered laconically. It was a reply he admired. From the record he could only speculate about her feelings toward the Inspectorate. They might easily have been a mere petty resentment that her reports on environmental hazards were ignored. Instead, there was a transparency and objectivity in her observation. She was telling the truth.

In the next apartment someone was singing. Kirov stooped to the bag he had brought with him, opened it, took out some papers, and placed them on the table. Her eyes followed. Taking the bait, he thought—and for once the thought made him sad.

"I was wondering," he enquired quietly, "if you could also help me." He gave her another measured smile. "It's purely a technical query—nothing sinister." He laid the pages apart and then ignored them. In an apparent aside he asked, "Do you remember that Pokrebsky reported the condition of the plant as stable?"

She turned her eyes from the papers and frankly at his. "Yes. I was curious how he knew."

"The plant director phoned him after the incident."

"But how did the plant director know? No one has admitted knowing what is in the lake. All that the plant director could have told Director Pokrebsky was that the lake was full of dead fish and what actions he had taken on the plant. How would he know what actions to take to stabilize the plant?"

"Yes," Kirov agreed. "How would he know?"

As she spoke, her manner was beginning to become more animated and her face was alive with intelligence.

She said, "I think that Pokrebsky suspected the cause, and something in the way the plant director handled the emergency confirmed his opinion."

"I think so, too." Kirov told her. He thought that he had quickened her curiosity—and perhaps her anger. It was time. "I have managed to obtain some documents," he said, "from the plant. The emergency actions taken by the plant director were recorded in the plant log. Would you like to take a look at it?"

Her lips registered surprise. A step backward. A wondering how the conversation had reached this point. But then, the question was harmless.

"I . . . yes, if you like, Major. I don't know if I can help. Without knowing the layout of the plant, I may not be able to interpret the log."

"There's a sketch of the layout with the papers." He moved the sheets toward her. He judged it was probably superfluous, but added quietly; "This could be important, Comrade Terekhova. I only want to know the truth."

He left her to study the records and stretched his legs in the small room. At the window he stared out into the street where Bogdanov was parked in a black Volga saloon. It was dark. On the otherwise empty pavement, a party of soldiers and their girls were trying to force too many of them into a taxi. The singer in the neighboring apartment had changed the song.

Irina Terekhova rustled the papers as she turned them over, and her bracelet clinked as it caught his empty glass. After a while she said, "I've finished what I can do."

He extinguished the cigarette he had unconsciously lit.

"Have you found anything?"

She turned. The last breath of smoke hung between them.

"I'm not certain," she said. "I'm sorry, it's difficult to explain." He appeared to sympathize, and she responded with a slight relaxation of her guard. "Come here and I'll show you." He moved to her side, where he could see alike the open plant log and the brown hairs on the nape of her neck.

"Here," she began, and he allowed his attention to be directed to a line on the page, "the plant director notes receiving the information that there are dead fish in the lake; and although there has not been any alarm sounded, he decides to take no risk: it is possible that the water may have been contaminated by the plant. Yes?"

"Go on."

"The next few lines are routine emergency instructions to clear people away from the danger area and so on. Only then does he start to address the problem as he sees it."

"I follow. What does he do next?"

"That's what I don't understand."

"Ah."

She must have sensed his disappointment, because she corrected herself. "I'm not making myself clear. I know what he did; but I don't understand why he did it. Let me explain to you." She waited for his approval—no, not approval. For a second he thought that she was indulging him. Then she was giving her explanation.

"The plant consists in part of storage tanks holding plutonium nitrate; I don't know at this stage how many, but there must be several. They are carefully designed so that their shape does not allow the plutonium to form a critical mass—otherwise there would be an explosion." She bit her lip and smiled wanly. Kirov joined her, knowing what "explosion" meant in this context. She went on, "The plutonium gives off heat and the tanks have to be cooled, so they are connected to the lake by cooling-water systems—two for certain, perhaps more. In theory plutonium could leak from a tank through its cooling system into the lake; but in practice this is inconceivable: the care that's put into design and construction of the plant, the backup equipment in case of a fault, the safety systems—also, if there were a leak, a radiation monitor would have sounded an alarm. We know this didn't happen: the plant log confirms it."

"So?"

"So why did the plant director take emergency measures on the plutonium storage tanks?"

From the bedroom the child complained. Irina Terekhova broke off abruptly and left Kirov in order to take care of the child. A minute later she came out of the bedroom. He thought her face looked softened, but the impression was fleeting because without pause she returned to the subject. "He didn't take steps on all the tanks, but only on one."

"He? The plant director?"

"It's clear from the log that he switched from the primary to the secondary cooling system on a tank he calls T1/2105. Then he proceeded to empty its contents into one of the other tanks. And after that he noted that the plant was stable. It doesn't make sense!"

Her voice had risen, and noticing it, she let it fall away, then said calmly, "The Inspectorate are trying to reserve this part of the investigation to themselves. Perhaps you can see now why I am concerned."

"How do you explain what was done?"

"I can't," she admitted frankly. "First, I should have to see a fuller layout drawing of the plant. Perhaps I've misunderstood something."

"That can be arranged."

"Thank you."

"Don't thank me. You are also helping me."

"Yes, I suppose I am."

They were silent again. Kirov was used to silences: normally they were out of fear, but this time he detected a difference, an embarrassment as though they had been talking of other matters, of something more intimate. He stored this impression, too, not allowing it to intrude.

'What do you think?"

"About . . .? Ah . . ." She paused. "It's clear that the plant director has suspicions—bad feelings—about the primary cooling system of T1/2105. Or . . . "

"Or?"

"He knew something."

"You took your time, boss," said Bogdanov as Kirov got into the car. The captain grunted as he shifted the gear stick. "Did she agree to cooperate or were you giving her one?"

"She agreed to cooperate," Kirov said dully. "She agreed without even realizing."

"Did she, now? You're getting cynical in your old age."

They drove into the city, left the car, and went for a drink in a bar on the corner of Pushkinskaya Street and Stoleshinikov Lane. Bogdanov struggled through the crush with two Zhigulyovkoye beers and complained, "I don't know why we drink here, boss. The service is terrible, the beer stinks, and in that suit everyone thinks you're a Georgian black-marketeer—honest to God, the approaches I get and the stuff I could sell in here! We should drink among our own kind. Here nobody knows who we are."

"Nobody knows who we are," Kirov agreed. He stared out of the window into the night lit grayly by the streetlights and the shops.

Now, in September, with the light failing and the last rags of summer hanging in the trees like soiled underwear, he looked forward to the first snow. He would wake one morning and it would be there, white and untouched as a palimpsest.

"Have you read the report on the American technology?" Bogdanov was saying. "Yatsin—the Washington Resident—wasn't he your legman when you were over there? How come he got the plum job and you finished back here? What went wrong?"

"Nothing."

"Nothing. Oh, yeah, sure," Bogdanov said regretfully and sank his nose into his drink. When he surfaced he asked, "Who do you suppose Source David is, the guy who got to see the American plant?"

"I don't know." Kirov finished his drink. Bogdanov had finished his and was looking for another. "It doesn't sound as though he could be of any use to us."

"No. Another beer? No?" Bogdanov looked around the bar; Kirov knew he had an informer who hung around the place—not that in his current job the other man had need for his own sources, but informers got to be habit-forming: they spelled power over another human being, more concrete than the power that could be exercised from an office. Finding no one, Bogdanov resumed his theme. "This Yank technology could have interest. Maybe it's what we need to clean up our present business?"

"Maybe." Kirov checked his watch. The crowd in the bar was hot and stale. "I've got to go."

"OK. And this American report?" Bogdanov persisted. "Do you want any action taken?"

Kirov stopped long enough to consider the point. Maybe it was something. It was impossible to tell. He said, "Find out what you can about the English parent company, Chemconstruct. Get me any details we have and the name of the sales director."

He returned to his apartment. Lara was waiting for him. She was wearing a new dress and her face was carefully made up to please him. He spoke to her kindly, hearing his words like a record playing. Something was wrong, but he couldn't put words to it, except that Lara was in some way an example. He had known in advance about the surprise dress; her behavior that morning had been ostentatiously secretive; she had checked her purse carefully and had searched for a large bag that would hold something without creasing it. He knew exactly what she intended and he hated the knowledge.

They made love. She had a strong, lithe body, golden in any light, precious as a child's present. He made love to her gently but avidly, and afterward lay back still unconsoled. During the night he woke up and read for a while. There was a book of poems by his bed, poems by Walt Whitman which he read in English. Oleg Ouspensky, the traitor, had given him the book one time during their long conversations walking the streets of Washington talking about American women, how unbelievable they were, you couldn't get enough of them; and Yatsin trailed behind, watching their backs, overweight and complaining of his feet.

"This," said Ouspensky, tapping the book, "is why I shall always stay in America."

But he wouldn't stay. Kirov knew that he, Kirov, would bring Ouspensky back home to Russia.

5

There were moments when the plant at Sokolskoye seemed to exist as a rumor. Kirov was conscious that he had not yet seen it, not yet talked to the people involved. And the disaster itself was little more than a rumor, still unconfirmed, represented only by the slow accumulation of reports produced by the Committee of Investigation and mostly addressing side issues. Still the main one remained unanswered: had anything significant *really* happened?

As Irina Terekhova requested, he obtained drawings of the plant and had them delivered to her.

"Asking for them really shook Pokrebsky," said Bogdanov, who enjoyed the idea. "He's reinforced his team at the site. His deputy, Nechvolodov, is there and a picked crew to watch over all the operations—tight as a gnat's arse; our guy won't get much out of them."

Klyuev made one call from Sokolskoye to report that the condition of the men in quarantine was deteriorating. "There have been two deaths," he told Kirov. "That's for sure—and there may have been others. It's like being under siege here. Every time I step out of my office, one of Nechvolodov's men follows me around—for safety, he says. None of my sources will come near me while this is going on: they don't want to be identified as informers; and, in any case, Nechvolodov has told them that the KGB wants to take over the plant, and that isn't an idea that appeals to anyone." Kirov gave him a few words of encouragement. Klyuev gave a final warning:

"Don't trust the autopsy reports when you get them. Pokrebsky will try anything, believe me."

Wanting information to eke out his scraps of knowledge, he telephoned Irina Terekhova. She recognized his voice. In the background her son was making some childish complaint. Kirov glanced at his watch: it was ten o'clock at night. She sounded tired, and he tried to imagine her life, her work, the taking care of the child. What did she do in that last quiet hour of the day when the boy was in bed? Read the dry, censored prose that he imagined so carefully penned by the dutiful husband, Colonel Konstantin Aleksandrovitch Terekhov, as he wrote his weekly letter from Kabul?

She asked, "Why are you calling so late?"

Yes, why? To hear another voice in uncertain times.

"I wanted to know how your researches are going; to offer my help."

There was a silence. She wasn't used to help. He had a sudden picture of loneliness. A woman who had had two husbands, and indeed still had one. Loneliness, but not to be confused with longing.

"That's very kind of you," she said, and the pause explained itself as a yawn. "I'm sorry . . . I'm tired. It is kind of you. Give me a moment while I collect my thoughts. There was something."

"It's all right. Take your time."

He made a note to have her mail intercepted. She was rustling among the papers stacked on the remembered table by the window. The boy was still making petulant noises. She told him to make himself a drink; she warned him not to fill that glass; that it would cause him to wet the bed. He was highly strung, the Colonel's child.

She was back on the line, asking clearly, "Could you confirm when the construction of Sokolskoye was completed?"

"Nineteen seventy-five," he told her.

"I thought so." She was fumbling with the papers again. He felt the tension. She had found something. "The flowsheets that you obtained from the Inspectorate are dated 1973," she said.

"How significant is that?"

"It means that Pokrebsky has shown us only the intended design of the plant. But we don't know what was actually built."

71

·SUBJECT: TOXIC EFFECTS OF PLUTONIUM

Please find attached to this note the report on the above subject prepared by Senior Research Scientist A.Y. Marchenko of this Institute. You will understand the difficulty caused by the present emergency, in that we have been asked to consider not the explosive or radiation hazards of plutonium, but the effects of its direct consumption by the drinking of contaminated water or similar action. Because experiment on human beings to test the toxicity of plutonium taken in this form would undoubtedly prove fatal, such experimental data as exist are confined to animal studies, but they establish that, quite apart from its other well-known dangers, plutonium is one of the most toxic substances known to man. Since, however, it is a man-made substance and exists only under the most strictly controlled conditions, the free release of plutonium into the environment has not hitherto been considered as a serious risk, and the absence of data on its effects on human populations is thus explained. In summary of our opinion, however, you may wish to consider the following facts.

The maximum permissible body-burden of Pu 239 is $0.0005\mu g$ — or five ten-thousandth parts of one-millionth of one gram. If, in the absence of certainty, we make the conservative assumption that this is only a thousandth part of the level that would be needed to cause cancer and a ten-thousandth of that which would kill, we can see that a single kilogram of Pu 239 would contain 2×10^9 dosages sufficient to cause tumors, or 2×10^8 dosages sufficient to cause death. In easily conceived terms, we may say that one kilogram of Pu 239, evenly distributed among the human population, would kill two hundred million people. Slightly more would wipe out the Soviet Union.

Reducing this to practical terms is more complex. It is certain that distribution of any quantity of plutonium in the manner theorized above is quite impossible. Even distribution through the air is not universal but modified by winds and pressures. On the other hand, plutonium is far more toxic in one sense than is indicated by a simple dosage analysis. This is because of its extreme persistence. Plutonium will exist in the environment for a half-life of 24,000 years. It is not degraded or rendered harmless by passing through the body of its victim. It will remain poisonous for any creature feeding on or decomposing the body and for any creature feeding on that creature. It is therefore erroneous to imagine plutonium as a series of doses each with a single effect. Once introduced into the food chain, its toxic effect is long-term, perhaps permanent.

I do not intend by this note to cause alarm. There are several factors that suggest that, in the case of Sokolskoye, we are dealing with a containable, even minor, problem.

(1) The currently available water analysis indicates no more than traces of plutonium in the Chiraka lake water, consistent with groundwater seepage from the land waste-disposal site;

(2) The distribution route for any contamination will be by the Gorkovskoye — Volga water systems and limited by them;

(3) Even in the event of serious plutonium release, the enormous volume of water held in those systems is capable in theory of reducing the concentration to humanly safe levels by simple dilution. I would observe, however, that the *practical* capacity of the Gorkovskoye Reservoir and the Volga to handle this problem would require further study.

I would recommend action in two fields. First, a hydrological study of the capacity of the Gorkovskoye-Volga system to distribute and dilute contaminants should be commissioned. Second, it is necessary to obtain a definitive analysis of the Chiraka lake water. I should have thought that this would have been possible by comparing the existing analyses with the inventory of the Sokolskoye plant. Any serious leakage of plutonium should appear as an inventory loss. On this point the All-Union Nuclear Inspectorate is being needlessly evasive. Could you apply pressure to Director Pokrebsky?

(Signed) G. S. VELIKHOV
Director,
Institute of Biochemistry and Radiobiology

During the night of September 23 an autopsy took place at Sokolskoye on the bodies of a Russian plant operator and a Chuvash maintenance foreman who had died during the evening. In the presence of Major Akhmatov, the garrison commander, and Deputy Director L.V. Nechvolodov of the All-Union Nuclear Inspectorate, an army surgeon removed selected organs and tissues from the two corpses and placed them in shielded canopic containers for shipment to various research institutes. In the course of this operation, but unknown to those in attendance, there was a disturbance in the isolation ward, where three of the patients who could still walk barricaded themselves in a sluice room to avoid contamination from the others. This futile demonstration was soon overcome by the military orderlies and calm was restored inside half an hour. For reasons of morale, news of the disturbance was kept from other persons at the plant.

When daylight came, the two surgically mutilated cadavers, the detritus from the postmortem, were taken from the hospital under conditions of technical and military security and carried to the pilot encapsulation plant, which was a prototype unit for the handling and long-term storage of high-level radioactive waste. The body of each man was folded into a fetal position, tied with a cord, and placed inside a stainless-steel drum; and because the drums had not been designed to take a human body and were too small, the neck, in the case of the first man, and the legs, in the case of the second, were broken to make them fit. The air-space inside the drums was then displaced by filling them with a special cement formulated for its long-term stable properties, and the sealed drums were moved to an engineered storage area where they were ranked with others in columns according to serial numbers stenciled on the exterior of the containers.

Since permanent disposal of the bodies would follow that of the other waste in the store at the encapsulation plant, no record was kept of these particular drums.

Bogdanov took the call from Irina Terekhova.

"She wants to see you," he told Kirov. From the chaos in his room he extracted a file. "By the way, this is what you asked for. This is all we have on that English company, Chemconstruct, and the sales director. His name is George Twist. He's been to the Soviet Union before, but he kept his nose clean and we have nothing on him. There's also a note from Skryabin. He read the report on the American technology and he says we may need it. He wants more data."

"It's embargoed."

"I told him that."

"And what did he say?"

Bogdanov kicked his chair back and reached for a toothpick kept among all the junk.

"Steal it."

MEMORANDUM

To: General Y.T. Kostandov,   24 September 198—
    GHQ Moscow

As requested I have obtained a report from the Hydrology Research Institute on the subject of the Gorkovskoye reservoir and the Volga river. May I record my surprise at both the nature and the urgency of your request. If this is a prelude to a demand for further time and resources from this department in relation to this topic, then I wish at this time to register a protest. Even a cursory examination of the logistics of waging war by chemical attack against the major river systems of the USSR reveals that such a strategy would be impractical and futile to a potential enemy. This department would not wish to be involved in such wasted effort.

(Signed) GENERAL G.T. GALICH
Director of Studies,
Department of Defense Studies,
Frunze Military Academy

WAR-PLAN STUDY ON THE EFFECT OF CHEMICAL ATTACK ON SOVIET RIVER SYSTEMS. REPORT ON THE HYDROLOGY OF THE GORKOVSKOYE RESERVOIR AND VOLGA RIVER FOR THE AREA SOKOLSKOYE — GORKY
Summary

The attached report has not been prepared at the request of the Department of Defense Studies of the Frunze Military Academy. For reasons which will become apparent, all conclusions are tentative and further long-term study is recommended if this subject continues to be of interest.

We have encountered three main areas of difficulty in giving an exact response to the questions posed. The first is that for obvious reasons it has been possible to conduct experiments by introducing poisonous chemicals into the subject water system and it has therefore been necessary to proceed by theory. Second, in calculating the behavior of both the reservoir and the river in diluting and distributing contaminants, we have relied upon a computer model and at this stage we are not convinced that our model is reliable. Third, the specification of the toxic chemicals as presented to us was vague in the following respects:

(i) quantity
(ii) lethal dosage
(iii) tendency to degrade into harmless forms
(iv) miscibility in water and tendency to precipitate
(v) volatility and response to temperature and pressure.

For purposes of the study we considered the nerve gases Tabun and Sarin, a range of defoliants, and, as an extreme case, contamination by a radioactive agent, namely plutonium.

Our detailed response is contained in the full report, but the following are general considerations. Because of its enormous extent, the Gorkovskoye reservoir is subject to wide variations in temperature and currents, which have the effect of separating the water into horizontal and vertical layers and prevent the dilution of any contaminant by the full volume of the reservoir. In imagining this effect, you should think of the contaminated water not as evenly distributed but as a packet suspended in the reservoir that becomes relatively larger and more dilute over time. The westerly streams are relatively slow and contain occasional warm pockets caused by the discharge of industrial water into the system, e.g., from the Chiraka lake some 30 km from Sokolskoye. Any chemicals entrained in these warm pockets would be sandwiched between colder layers and disperse relatively slowly. Generally one could expect some contamination along the whole western shore of the reservoir, but in the case of all the chemicals studied, except plutonium, the effect would be negligible: these chemicals being volatile and non-persistent or reduced to a harmless condition after allowing for dilution. Plutonium is the natural exception, being stable and exceptionally toxic.

On passing the Corodetz dam into the main stream of the river, the flow is more dynamic and one would expect further dilution of the contaminated stream. Taking a warm pocket as the worst case, we would still expect dilution by a factor of 100 at the point where Gorky draws its water from the warm stream. In practical terms the result would therefore depend upon whether the chemical at the point of introduction was in a concentration of 100 × lethal dose or not and the initial volume of water meeting that condition. If a significant body of water were initially contaminated at 100 × lethal or greater, then the affected water on passing Gorky would still be fatal. In this example dilution in fact worsens the problem, in that the water, on passing Gorky, is still lethally contaminated and its volume has been increased a hundredfold.

We do not, however, regard this as of great concern. To constitute a serious threat to life, the initial volume of water contaminated must be large and the contaminating material must be exceptionally toxic. Only plutonium meets these conditions.

(Signed) P.Y. GORDIEV
Deputy-Director
Hydrology Research Institute

He called at her apartment bearing gifts: a ham from the special section at GUM such as you couldn't buy even at Yeliseyevs, a bottle of export vodka, and for the sulky boy, a bar of chocolate. He stood in front of her door as if coming to woo her. No, that was an illusion. He dismissed it. He was something else. An executioner offering the friendship of a final cigarette. Also not true. He was aware of the ambiguity of gifts.

"I would have suggested that we meet at the University," he said, "but I didn't want to cause any confusion between your other work and this business. An association with the KGB," he added tolerantly, "can sometimes be misunderstood."

She took his offerings and placed them to one side. She had already prepared *zakuski,* and there were glasses on the table but only fruit juice and Narzan water. He smelt—washing? Yes, he was smelling the effort she had made to receive him. Behind closed doors to the other rooms he imagined laundered clothes hastily hung to dry. An effort—but with what design? He couldn't suppose that the intent was neutral. Her dress appeared to be new, but something she had made herself, simple in recognition of her own limitations and from a restrained sense of style. The deep blue gave a dark luster to her hair. She wore no makeup. Faint sags marked the corners of her mouth and would become more pronounced as she aged. He wondered how she had appeared fifteen years ago.

They chatted briefly with tense casualness. Kirov mentioned the rumored deaths at the plant.

"So it's started," was her comment. Almost indifferently she asked, "And Pokrebsky? Does he still maintain that we are not concerned with a leak of material from the main plant?"

"He doesn't commit himself. How are your researches going?"

She didn't answer. Kirov considered his timing: he was still not sensitive enough to her responses, but it would come. There was no point now in pressing the question. In any case there was distraction: noise from the boy; and she was saying, "Excuse me," and going away to do something for the child. Kirov poured himself a drink and passed the time examining the room. "May I borrow this?" he asked, holding a slim paperback of Davidov's poetry: it was entitled *Poems* with a simplicity that was almost arrogant.

"If you like," she said blankly.

He read the dedication: "To Irina—for now." It suggested that Davidov, even then, in his respectable period, had felt their marriage to be impermanent. Kirov made a mental note to order a search for the mislaid files on the poet.

He heard Irina Terekhova saying, ". . . by looking at the drawings."

He slipped the book into his pocket. She had brought herself round to the subject. "I'm sorry—did you find something in the drawings?" he inquired.

"Yes."

She unfolded the papers on the table. Her manner now was detached, authoritative. "I think we should start with an outline of the whole process."

"Yes, if you like." He eased to a position by her side.

"Sokolskoye," she began, "is an installation for taking spent fuel from nuclear power plants and reprocessing it to extract waste and return uranium as a fuel to the power plants. It produces plutonium as a by-product.

"Here"—she indicated the block diagram—"short-cycle fuel from the reactors is brought into the plant in flasks, the fuel rods are extracted and their contents dissolved in concentrated nitric acid. This solution is then treated through a solvent extraction process which takes out plutonium and uranium nitrate and removes high-level waste to storage tanks."

If you say so. Kirov caught himself before the words came out. They would sound sarcastic, and that was not his intention.

"The next phase," she said—she had paused slightly, noticing his hesitation, and her dark eyebrows held a question, but she went on—"the next phase is for uranium extraction and separation." Her fingers moved easily over the symbols to another part of the diagram. "There is a further cycle of solvent extraction which removes medium-level waste to storage, leaving the plutonium and uranium to be separated. The uranium is denitrated and converted to fuel grade, and the plutonium is conditioned and stored in tanks as plutonium nitrate. The point of all this"—she directed her eyes away from the chart and to Kirov's—"being that the high-level waste storage, the medium-level waste storage and the plutonium nitrate storage-tanks are all cooled by water drawn from the Chiraka lake. A leak from any of them would cause the effects seen at Sokolskoye."

At this point Irina Terekhova stopped. Kirov felt the pause as a challenge, and then not: there was nothing combative in her demonstration of her expertise. He said, "Did the plant director have any basis for selecting between the three possibilities?"

"No—at least, none that we know of."

"But he did . . . choose."

"Yes. It's clear from the plant log that he immediately turned to the plutonium nitrate storage tanks." Her finger pressed firmly on the paper. "And this tells us why."

"Why?"

"I think they had problems with their equipment. I don't mean simply now, but from the beginning, from the moment the plant was built."

"Tell me about the scandal."

"Which scandal?" Bogdanov asked. "How many scandals do you want?"

"The one which affected the nuclear industry in the early seventies. Operation Fall-Out—wasn't that the name?"

"Where did you hear that name?" Bogdanov snapped. "You didn't turn that one up in the files. Operation Fall-Out—the computer would spit in your eye if you tried to call that one up."

"Grishin told me. He said I should ask you about it; it affected equipment used in the nuclear program. He said you were involved." Kirov found the older man looking at him with suspicion. Grishin hadn't warned him about that.

"Operation Fall-Out!" When Bogdanov sighed there was a weary amusement. "Jesus! Fall-Out—that wasn't the real name, you know."

"No?"

"It was a joke. Fall-Out: all the crooks who were going to fall out when we shook their tree. Get it?"

"Yes," Kirov said sympathetically.

Bogdanov wasn't listening.

"Only it didn't work out like that," he said, substituting a look of intense misery for the hint of amusement. "There were too many of the old Brezhnev crowd involved. You never knew where the thing would lead. The bosses put a lid on it just when it was getting interesting. We had to make do with a few dumb bastards who were caught at the bottom of the pile."

"But it was important," Kirov pressed.

"Important? Sure it was important. And big—who knows how big? The names would make your hair curl. What the hell," he murmured. "You understand what I'm telling you?"

Kirov understood. Success didn't always succeed—wasn't even meant to succeed. It had happened to him in Washington. It had happened to Bogdanov.

"I want the files," he said.

"There are no files." The shutters came down over Bogdanov's eyes. "That's why Grishin told you to speak to me. The records were broken up—oh, they probably exist in bits and pieces all over the place; but there's no total picture. Forget everything—that was the deal they made. Army and KGB, both at each other's throat. Brezhnev himself stepped in to make the peace. If Grishin wants to reopen Fall-Out, then he's going for the big one: he wants to kick the Army out of the nuclear plant business altogether."

Kirov did not answer. Bogdanov, oppressed by the silence, asked: "Has Grishin formally asked you to reopen Fall-Out? Is this a request in writing?"

"No."

Bogdanov looked away. His fingers stalked a coffee cup.

"There's a limit to what I can give you. I only had a little piece. The rest is under lock and key; even Grishin doesn't have it. Andropov, when he was head of the KGB, used to keep it in his jockey shorts."

"Tell me what you know. Just your piece."

"Yeah, why not? But don't expect proof." Bogdanov looked for a sign that everything left unsaid was understood, then he began.

"Atommash—ever heard of them?—an outfit based in Volgo-donsk; they make vessels, tanks, heat exchangers, stuff for the nuclear industry—don't ask me, because I'm no expert." He stretched his untidy bones and stared at the ceiling. Talking to himself, except that he wasn't. Sometimes it helped to do it that way.

"This was all before your time. Trapeznikov was running our show—I'm talking before Grishin got his knife into him. That's the background, OK? So here we are: it's the middle of a big expansion program for nuclear plants. The plant has set targets way over everybody's head. Everybody is working his balls off. You know how it goes. Yeah." He stretched again, murmuring "Yeah" and remembering that he, too, knew how it went. His bones crackled like pistol shots which gave him an animal satisfaction so that he finished with a grunt and helped himself to a cigarette.

"So—ah—the complaints start to come in. Everything is running late; the suppliers are delivering short; the quality is lousy. You can't put your finger on anyone in particular—the whole world's in trouble—but Atommash are in the thick of it. You get the picture?" Kirov got the picture as if it were a conspiracy between them. He held out his lighter. Bogdanov stooped to put his cigarette to the flame, inhaled slowly and eased the pressure on the dents on his nose caused by his spectacles, rubbing the spots between finger and thumb. He carried on.

"Trapeznikov gets it into his head that Atommash are dealing on the side, quietly selling some of their production, which is why there are shortages and late deliveries. Don't ask me where he gets the idea from: after all, Atommash are making specialized equipment for the nuclear industry—not exactly stuff you can sell from the back of a lorry on the Ring Road; but that's the theory we're working on.

"So we decide to put on a big show—you understand, this is going on all over the country—lots of light and noise and a cast of thousands straight out of Mosfilm. A big team from Moscow flies down to Volgodonsk. We do a dawn raid on the plant and the homes of the managers. The chief of Atommash is called Nefkin, a shifty little character with two dachas and a swimming pool and a house stocked like a Beriozka store—and who can blame him? It would be bloody peculiar if it were any different. We drag him bollock-naked straight out of bed and parade him in front of Trapeznikov, who really gives him the business. Trapeznikov—ever meet him?—no?—he's an old-style *chekist*, full of sweat and righteousness, hairy fingers and garlic breath—Trapeznikov huffs and puffs and storms at Nefkin, and Nefkin is ready to confess to all sorts of terrible things that you wouldn't believe. But the one thing he won't admit—it's funny how people can stick on a point of principle—is that he has been selling Atommash equipment on the side."

"No," said Kirov, who understood Nefkin. Criminals had an acute sense of justice. They expected to be condemned, but only for the crimes they had committed. "He didn't confess because that wasn't the cause, was it?"

Bogdanov didn't answer directly. It was obvious why Trapeznikov wanted this particular admission: because any explanation other than Nefkin's crimes was an implied attack on the system. "It was the usual trouble," he said at last, "plain bloody incompetence. Oh, sure, there was bribery going on, but that was just a symptom. The truth was that Atommash had more business than they could cope with and were screwing up the job and delivering short, trying to keep everyone happy—you know this country, half a loaf is better than none. And where he thought there'd be trouble, Nefkin would pay somebody off to keep quiet. We never got to the bottom of it. The paperwork was a mess and we could never figure out exactly who got what. We had a lot of specific complaints, but there were other cases where Atommash had failed to deliver or made a dog's breakfast of it but Nefkin had settled the right people to forget all about it; and these we never heard of. And then"—Bogdanov slipped into the brevity of caution—"Fall-Out was stopped."

"And Nefkin?"

Bogdanov stubbed out his cigarette and stared at his fingers.

"We charged him with fucking about with State property." He looked up at Kirov. "He died of it."

She waited for him to ask for an explanation. Kirov thought of Bogdanov's story. Nefkin, the crooked director of the enterprise, was a character who took form in his imagination. He understood Nefkin and his contemptible little rackets. But Irina Terekhova? Watching her now he had the sense and fear of missing something; that she was escaping his comprehension.

"We know about the equipment crisis," he said. "There was an investigation—Operation Fall-Out." He let her know that he was sharing a confidence with her. It invited a confidence in return. He wanted to deepen the collaboration so that it became unreflecting—personal. Cooperation was not enough unless it was on his terms. The alternative was too dangerous, a step on to the ice that might fail at any moment. Of all bases for collaboration, morality was the most treacherous. "Please go on," he said.

She was in no hurry. That look was also one of evaluation. She flicked a strand of hair from her eyes.

"You have a problem?" Kirov asked.

She shook her head regretfully. "You ask questions," she said, "as if you already know the answers. Is that part of KGB training? Or does the KGB really know the answer to everything, like God?"

"Not like God. Now, show me, please."

She returned calmly to her papers.

"There are twenty-five plutonium nitrate storage tanks at Sokolskoye," she resumed. "Each tank has a primary and, in case of fault, a secondary cooling system. This"—she indicated a drawing—"is a typical example. The principle of the system is simple enough, not unlike a car radiator. The heat from the contents of the plutonium nitrate tank is transferred to a jacket of cooling water around the tank and then through a heat exchanger.

"Now, from this first heat exchanger there is another cooling-water loop. It picks up the heat from the first loop, runs with it to a second heat exchanger, and loses it there before returning to the first heat exchanger. The tank and these first two cooling loops are all closed systems, which means that the contents of any one of them never come into contact with the contents of any of the others. The only thing that moves through the system is heat."

"I follow," Kirov encouraged her. But she needed no encouragement.

"There is a third cooling-water loop," she said, "but this one is different. It isn't closed. It takes water directly from the lake and returns it there. So" — she took a piece of paper and began to draw on it boldly: a box — "here the storage-tank, here the first heat exchanger, here the second heat exchanger, and here — Ah!" — the pencil snapped; she took another — "the Chiraka lake." Four boxes labeled in her firm hand. "And now," drawing a circle connecting each box in a chain without the circles touching each other, "the cooling-water loops forming the links, each link separated from the next one. Heat passes through the chain but nothing else. It's foolproof."

"Then how does plutonium get into the lake?"

"It doesn't."

The child called. Kirov felt its fretful nature. Her face clouded with weariness. She didn't go immediately, but sat in stillness in case the sound was a mere cry in the child's sleep. They sat together in stillness listening, as if it were a burglar in the night. Tensely she continued her explanation.

"It doesn't," she repeated, "except by impossible accident."

"Like what?" Kirov found himself listening and wondered: Was it always like this for her, night after night, tied by Terekhov's child?

"Let's say," she began in answer, "that there's a leak within the storage tank. Plutonium and nitrate will escape into the first cooling-water loop, but it will stay there because the loop is closed. And at this point the alpha emissions from the cooling water will trip an alarm causing the operators to take action. Let's say, further, that there is a leak in the first heat exchanger. In this case contaminated water from the first loop will get into the second loop . . ."

"But get no further," said Kirov, "because that loop is also closed. Yes?"

"Yes."

"And I suppose more alarms would go off?"

"Yes," she said good-humoredly, implying: You see how silly this all seems. But he knew that she was serious. She went on: "It's only if there is another leak, this time in the second heat exchanger, that the plutonium can get in to the final section of the cooling system, the part that returns its water directly to the lake."

"And that's what the plant director assumed? That the system had sprung three leaks and that the radiation monitors in every section had failed?" He wondered: Was she playing games with him? The coincidences were too much to believe. But it was obvious that her clear intent was to convince him.

"I don't understand everything," she said. "I don't have all the pieces. But there is something—something that the plant director knows. What"—she paused to order her thoughts—"what I just described is the way the plant was originally designed. It's what was shown on the original layout provided by the Inspectorate."

"The one that you said was out of date—it didn't represent the plant as it was built?"

"Yes. Now, think what the plant director did during the emergency. He didn't check all the tanks: he went to a specific one, T1/2105. Here, on the drawing, this is it."

Kirov scanned the drawing, recognizing under the symbols in which Irina Terekhova was fluent the elements of plutonium nitrate storage tank T1/2105 and its associated systems: the tank, the first cooling-water loop, the first heat exchanger, the second cooling-water loop, the second heat exchanger—except that there was no second heat exchanger! The cooling system was truncated; the second loop, instead of being closed, was connected directly to the lake.

"That's the change," Irina Terekhova said quietly, almost matter-of-factly, folding the drawing and returning it to the file. "It's what Pokrebsky was hiding by sending us an earlier design for the plant. I don't know why it was done." She anticipated his question. "There isn't any technical justification. The change simply saves on equipment. And it doesn't fully explain how the accident happened: we

85

still don't know why the radiation monitors failed. But"—she hesitated and he saw chinks in her detachment, a glimmer of her anger—"at one stroke they sacrificed half of their protection against a disaster."

"Like at Chernobyl?"

"Chernobyl?" She appeared surprised, and Kirov sensed again traces of that collective suppression of memory that Chernobyl evoked. Which explained perhaps why it remained possible for him to consider the risk of disaster at Sokolskoye so calmly; why it was possible for Grishin and the Committee to regard the incident as a mere political event and not a catastrophe waiting to happen. Because in their hearts they had never allowed Chernobyl to become fully real.

But she was thinking of other things.

"Not like Chernobyl," she said.

"No?"

"This could be worse."

6

October 1

Sokolskoye. The plane flying into the dawn light. Moscow somewhere in the darkened west. Trees in dark smoking masses and the
Volga brown under a rolling mist. There were lights along the airfield
strip, and in the shadows stood ranks of Antonov transports with
their massive noses in line like pigs at a trough with litters of suckling
service vehicles. Klyuev—the KGB resident—was on the tarmac
waiting, a big, tight man, strapped into his suit till his eyes popped
and wearing a herringbone overcoat and a fox-fur hat. By his side
was a black Volga with a uniformed driver in a cap with the blue band
of the service.

"Flight OK?" Klyuev asked eagerly. "Coffee?" The driver had a
flask and cups. He placed them on the bonnet, poured the coffee and
shots of brandy, and they stood there in the open, stamping their feet
against the autumn chill, their white breath irradiated with the glare
of the airfield lights.

"Let's be going." Kirov slung his empty cup to the driver. He decided to give Klyuev a sense of security by playing the Moscow pro,
curt and efficient, and Klyuev was responsive, bobbing about to
accommodate the visitor and meticulously correct toward Irina
Terekhova, who had begun to identify a certain KGB politeness;
perhaps they were compensating for something in their work.

Klyuev talked. He was lonely, isolated from the center where every
day it seemed he could feel the patter of damp soil being shoveled
onto his face. He wanted to talk stale gossip about people he knew
"back there," but the woman's presence inhibited him and he had to
speak of other things instead as they sat squeezed into the overheated

car. Kirov listened and wondered who the other man's friend was. He was sure that Klyuev had a friend — someone you could tell things to because they wouldn't go any further. Honest.

Klyuev said, "Am I glad to see you! I hope you've got clear instructions for me. Here it's . . . well, you'll see for yourself. I've fixed you a place to stay. There's no hotel, only a bug-house you wouldn't want to . . . I've arranged something in the barracks, separate rooms, a bit Spartan, but clean. And the food's OK, everyone's on good rations — but there's no drink; it's a safety matter. You have to go boozing in town if you want that sort of thing."

The interior of the car was unlit. The road was a dark channel between the trees. The driver blasted his horn to pass a convoy of trucks in drab green livery stenciled with the name of their enterprise.

"Akhmatov — that's the military commander — he's all right," said Klyuev. "A straightforward soldier boy. He doesn't want to get involved in any odd business — everything by the book and orders in writing. Scared, if you ask me."

He was a heavy man who sweated freely and mopped his forehead with a cotton handkerchief that smelt of lemons.

"The one to watch is the new guy, Pokrebsky's legman, Nechvolodov." An expression of distaste caught in the lights of an oncoming car. "Tricky sod. But you can't catch him out — at least, I can't. Everything is 'technical' or 'an emergency.' What am I to do? I'm not an engineer. He crawls over everything, taking out bits of this and that, and I can't stop him because he says it'll be dangerous if he doesn't do whatever it is he's doing. And in the end he'll have buggered around so much that no one will ever be able to figure out how things stood when, you know, when whatever it was that happened happened." A glance at the visitors, then, "Here we are!" They were at the outermost perimeter of the plant, an electrified fence backed by a mined security strip. Everything blazing with lights. Off the road, two tanks and a troop carrier roped down under tarpaulins and a couple of soldiers smoking.

Kirov asked, "What part of the plant is he concentrating on?"

"Nechvolodov?" Klyuev rubbed his nose to think. "The herbicide store. Nechvolodov ordered a detailed inspection and an inventory."

"These . . . herbicides . . ."

"This year was the first year we had them. They were used to keep down water weed and stuff in the lake. Something to do with the summer. Too hot, too dry, whatever. But I think it's only a blind."

"Why?"

"I pulled Nechvolodov's record. He's an engineer, not a chemist. He talks a lot about sloppy procedures in handling the weedkiller, but his real interest is in the plant hardware. He crawls over it every chance he gets. Then twice a day he's on the blower to his boss."

"What does he have to say to Pokrebsky?"

"You can hear for yourself; I've got recordings. Some of it I understand, some of it I don't. I think they're working a code but I can't put my finger on it. They talk a lot about *Kerensky* — I think that's you, "K" for "Kirov," get it? Or it could be Grishin, but that doesn't fit so well — but I'm only guessing. Anyway, this Kerensky scares the shit out of them."

"It could be Klyuev."

"Now, there's an idea!" But Klyuev knew the limits of his own powers.

They were already at a barracks building, a low concrete structure streaked with water stains. A squad of soldiers in fatigues were working around it, painting something white. "Not very homey," Klyuev admitted, "but it's better than it looks." He suggested that Irina Terekhova unpack, and carried her bag himself with the same careful politeness. "Have you had breakfast? There's something in the canteen; it's not too bad. If you like, I could have it brought here." While she unpacked and freshened up, he returned to the car and brought Kirov's bags.

"There's something I wanted to mention," Klyuev said, "but not in front of the woman."

They stood by the door in a fall of leaves. A damp early breeze swept across the sparse grass.

"What is it?"

"The plant director, we've got him on ice. What do we do with him?"

"What do you want to do?"

"Not my decision."

"I suppose not." Kirov guessed that the other man was glad for that. KGB officers on a long-term posting could get sentimental about people they got to know closely. They developed blind spots. Old So-and-So couldn't be an enemy of the people: I know him too well. That was why after a security lapse a few heads in the KGB rolled along with those of the traitors, and from nothing more than friendship. It was ridiculous. So was Bor'yan the friend that the resident at Sokolskoye had?

Klyuev was saying, "For me, I'd put him through it — make him tell us what's gone wrong at his fucking plant — but my instructions are just to question him. And the bastard stays quiet. OK, so they don't want any bruises and his brain has to stay in one piece; I can accept that: there's a reason, something political, maybe. But there are other ways — no damage to him or drugs or anything."

"Oh?"

Klyuev bit his lip and tried a knowing smile but was out of practice. Intelligence work at Sokolskoye was largely a question of collecting gossip and counting the pencils; the main political vetting was done before anyone was posted to the plant. "I don't know a lot about interrogation technique," Klyuev said. "But I don't get rusty. I mean, I read about it, think about it, get me?"

"Yes."

"I mean" — Klyuev stepped as close as the bags he was carrying would allow — "I heard about a case in Washington a few years ago. You know, the Ouspensky Case. That was the one where one of our guys took this traitor and charmed him right out of a public restaurant and into the embassy. No violence, just words — 'Come home to Mother Russia and all is forgiven,' something like that — just words like casting spells until this Ouspensky falls for it and walks to the Soviet embassy with him like they were in love, and the CIA following them in a prowl car watching the show with not a damned thing they could do."

"I heard about it."

"The case officer that time was also called Kirov." Klyuev heaved one of the bags and pushed open a door while Kirov followed empty-handed. The big man was out of condition, panting and staring through his bulging eyes. He opened the door to a small cell with a bunk, a clothes rack and a washbasin. "Christ! It's not what I ordered. Don't worry, I'll get you shifted to the VIP block. I'd forgotten this shithole existed." He put down the bags to regain his breath, turned and saw the other man still studying him.

Kirov asked, "So how exactly are you going to get at Bor'yan? What are you proposing I do?"

"Oh, that. Well, Bor'yan is a big family man. Three kids. Photographs on his desk. The kids' first shoes hanging on the wall at home. You get the picture?"

"You've seen the shoes hanging on the wall? So you've been to his home?"

"A few drinks together, that's all," Klyuev answered quickly. "It's how you find things out, right?"

"Right," Kirov agreed and smiled and kept on smiling until he forced one out of the big man and Klyuev warmed to his conclusion. "So he's a family man. What do you suggest we do?"

"Bring in a heavy squad — from Moscow if you like — and knock his old lady about a bit," said Klyuev. "You know — just like that! A cold surprise, right in front of him. Magic!"

The sun was up. Kirov and Irina Terekhova went on an inspection tour of the installation. Akhmatov, the garrison commander, escorted them in silence, checking them through the security points, asking no questions and answering briefly any that were put to him. Klyuev wasn't there. He was moving their bags to new accommodations. Nechvolodov had sent his compliments and locked himself in the main control block like a magician in his cave. He was trying to call Pokrebsky in Moscow and finding the lines blocked on Kirov's instructions.

"Are these the normal operators?" Irina asked. The place seemed hopping with people.

Akhmatov consulted one of the plant foremen who was acting as guide. "No. Most of them were drafted in by the Inspectorate." There was nothing more. No opinion, no inflection of voice betraying what he thought.

"Where are the uranium and plutonium nitrate storage tanks?"

The foreman led them to the secure compound where the bank of tanks stood masked behind radiation shielding, their cooling systems connecting them in rows to the lake. The presence of water and the cold air drenched the place in mist.

She turned to the foreman directly. "Have any changes been made?" He glanced at Akhmatov, who nodded. The man's mouth worked in nervous silence as if he were counting his children; then he spoke.

"They've blanked off three of the tanks."

"Which ones? T1/2105?"

"Yes, and the other two like it."

"What about the cooling systems?"

"They've been dismantled and scrapped on the land waste-disposal site."

Kirov watched Irina take the information. She was calm but pale, accepting and evaluating each fact as it came. But he could sense a tension in the workings of her mind.

She asked, "What about the tanks themselves?"

"They were only standby tanks. We only used them when we were working at full capacity. T1/2105 was emptied during the emergency. The other two were already empty."

"And have they been tampered with?"

There was no reply. Kirov knew why. The man was terrified with the unformed terror of the innocent. Akhmatov said, "Speak up, comrade!"

The man responded to power and found his voice.

"They said that their investigation showed nothing wrong with the tanks or the cooling systems. But all their messing around, the cutting and carving, had made things unsafe. That's why they scrapped all the pipework and the heat exchangers."

"And the tanks?"

"They broke into them through an access port and filled them with concrete."

Kirov heard Irina Terekhova catch her breath. She said something, but in a voice so low as to be almost inaudible. He thought she had whispered, "Dear God!"

"Do you want to speak to Nechvolodov?"

They were walking back to the VIP block.

Irina shook her head. "No, he'll only lie. Everything will be explained. He'll tell you I'm not an engineer, just a theorist — and a woman. He'll say that I don't understand the practical side of the problem — and to some extent he'll be right." She stopped so that Akhmatov walked on a few paces. Kirov halted with her. Her eyes were turned away, watching a bird overhead. He was looking for what? Self-pity, he supposed. But she was reporting nothing more than the truth. She said, "Pokrebsky must be desperate to destroy the evidence." The bird was gone and she looked now at Kirov. "Scrapping the contaminated materials and filling the tanks — it's almost inconceivably dangerous."

The real name of the plant director at Sokolskoye was Bor'yan. He was a stocky middle-aged Armenian from Erevan who had decided long ago in his youth that the future of the Soviet Union lay with the largest national group, the Great Russians, and he was going to do his damnedest to join them. And if his looks were against him — he had black hair, an olive skin and a great beak of a nose with flaring nostrils — he compensated by shouting with the loudest and volunteering with the shrewdest. He was sharp, evasive, dishonest and successful. "I think I'm in love with him," Bogdanov had said when he fished out the papers. "This guy is a good communist."

Kirov had the papers with him; he carried them in the Gucci bag he had bought in Washington. It was the same bag he had carried on the day he met Ouspensky for their last lunch together. But on that day there had been no papers in the bag, just a silk scarf he had bought for a girlfriend back home because he had a premonition that after he'd finished his business with Ouspensky he would be returned to Moscow. "What do you think of it, Oleg?" he asked the traitor. "Will it do?" A silk scarf, that was the only prop he used before starting on their conversation which subsequently became so famous that it was in the textbooks. There were no papers because he knew all about the other man by heart, and even that didn't comprehend the subtlety and complexity that made up Ouspensky. And there was no script. "It was like an improvisation in music to an unknown song," said Kirov's debriefing officer admiringly after the encounter. "It was played out with passion. To the limit." That was the point that everyone was made to understand. Ouspensky represented the limit, the man who was won over by someone who pushed himself where his own thoughts, emotions, loyalties became in doubt in the tangle of sympathies. Everyone agreed that only someone who *ultimately* fell back on his professionalism could have got Ouspensky.

Instead and for now, there was Bor'yan, a man without personal enigma; the only mysteries being — as the anonymous denunciations pinned to the file stated — where did his car come from? How did he acquire his West German suits? How could he buy so many bottles of Scotch? And these were hardly mysteries at all.

"These people are here to see you. This is Comrade Major Kirov, and this Comrade Doctor Terekhova." Klyuev made the introductions.

Kirov examined the prisoner. In his internal passport there was a photograph of Bor'yan in the days of his prosperity, respectability and honesty: a black-and-white affair of the stocky Armenian pinned against a white background like a specimen moth, leering at the camera, his features caught with a flash of guilt. Now, penned up in a barracks cell at Sokolskoye, his criminal complicity on the point of exposure, here was a man terrified into the appearance of innocence. Bor'yan bobbed up from his bunk at the sound of the bolts being drawn.

"What about my wife? How is my wife?" The plant director spoke good Russian. He had a pleasant voice, a sympathetic voice that didn't go with the rest of him.

"She's OK, as I keep telling you," answered Klyuev. He glanced at Kirov and added, "What kind of people you do take us for?"

"I don't know," said Bor'yan. "I thought I did, but now I don't."

This caused Klyuev to lose his temper. He shouted, "What the hell do you mean by that?" and then, remembering the others, he collected himself, pulled out a couple of chairs from the scrubbed deal table and offered them to the visitors. To Bor'yan he said; "Now you listen! These comrades want to say things for your own good. They *know* everything — understand?"

Did that one come from the textbook or from the heart? Kirov wondered. He asked Klyuev to leave so that he could consider his subject alone without the KGB man's emotions getting in the way. He knew he had been right. Bor'yan had been the other man's friend. It was a pity, really.

They sat until the air seemed to crackle with silence. Kirov smoked two cigarettes, lighting each one with elaborate care. He watched the plant director twitch his nostrils and rub together his first and middle fingers. Bor'yan was a smoker. It was finally he who spoke.

"I want to see Pokrebsky. He can explain everything. There's been a mistake." Even Bor'yan couldn't put any conviction into his words.

He flapped his arms loosely inside an oversized suit so that the folds of material swayed as they caught up with his movements.

"Would you like a cigarette?" Kirov pushed the pack across the table and extended a light. Bor'yan hesitated, not realizing that he was being rewarded for that first surrender — his willingness to speak — then he accepted and rushed to gulp down that first lungful of smoke. Kirov watched. Predictable. A confirmation of that first impression of a man without enigma. He said, "Comrade, I want to be your friend."

Kirov paused. Bor'yan had unbelieving eyes but — if he was right — a need to believe. Each of them knew that the statement was a lie, but there was something in the chemistry of this lie that elicited the truth. That was another lesson from the conversion of the traitor and defector Oleg Ouspensky as now enshrined in the training manuals.

"Have you been mistreated here? You can tell me, I have authority here: even Major Klyuev takes my orders."

Bor'yan snorted. "Klyuev was my friend. We worked together on plant security. We sometimes went hunting together." Kirov was pleased with the answer. The other man would not have allowed himself anger if he had not relaxed.

"That's all in the past. Now he's your enemy. So is Pokrebsky. They have to be, in order to save themselves. I am the only friend you have. Believe me or not, what choices do you have? What greater risks do you run in trusting me?"

Bor'yan chose not to answer that question. Kirov permitted the Armenian to talk about his wife and children. He answered a few questions about their well-being. At the moment they were well. For now there was nothing to fear. For the present the plant director's salary was still being paid to his dependents. This was explained softly so that the words and what was said each seemed transitory.

"I can save you." Kirov took up the thread of conversation. "Do you understand? There are others involved; you are not important; in a complicated story, the parts played by insignificant people can get forgotten. We can work this thing out together. Please, let me ask you again: have you been mistreated?"

Bor'yan shook his head.

"Now, you see?" said Kirov. "Things are changing. There are laws. They can protect you. But we have to fight for them, some of us, against the past. We need help."

Dull, dull. Bor'yan was a man without interest, a man who responded like a machine to the pulling of levers. To a display of power — a reaction. To an uncovering of his guilt — a reaction. To the barest glimpse of a deal — a reaction. Kirov was tired and oppressed by the ordinariness and emptiness of his opponent, whose motivations and responses could be lifted out of him like filleting a fish. And then, at last: "What do you want to know?" Bor'yan asked. He was relieved, even eager.

"The pollution in the lake," Kirov asked, "it's nuclear material?" Bor'yan nodded. Did he know how much? The other man shook his head. The tank T1/2105, was it the source of the leak? Yes, tank T1/2105 was the source of the leak. Had the design of the plant been changed? Yes, the design of the plant had been changed: there was a shortened cooling system to three of the storage tanks because the heat exchangers were not available. Was this done under an arrangement with Atommash, with — what was his name? — Nefkin?

"I don't know this Nefkin," said Bor'yan.

Kirov paused. Bor'yan was ready to cooperate but not to confess. But the need was there: Kirov had known it too many times not to recognize it now.

"Nefkin? Remember? Alexei Tromfimovitch Nefkin, a director of Atommash in 1974? Let me help you, let me suggest how things happened — yes?"

"Go on," said Bor'yan, this time quietly.

Slowly, Kirov told himself. *Remember Ouspensky, even if this is not him but some little nobody as transparent as glass.*

"Nineteen seventy-four — I am talking of that year. The plant at Sokolskoye is still being built and you are responsible for seeing that construction is completed and the plant brought into operation according to the Plan — yes?"

"Yes."

"But things are hard for you. The quality of labor is poor. The Inspectorate has no clear policy on the plant. The delivery of materials is late. All of this is very difficult for an honest man, eh? And then there is this Nefkin."

"I don't remember Nefkin."

"But he existed."

"If you say so. I forget."

"You forget?" Kirov queried, but his voice was indulgent. *Everything can be worked out. Some little things you will even be allowed to forget.* "Let me remind you. He calls you, Nefkin calls you. How does it go? You have been complaining to Atommash for months about the late deliveries of the storage tanks and the heat exchangers — I think so; that's what a diligent man would do." Bor'yan nodded. "I think so," Kirov repeated. "And then? What? Nothing happens? For months nothing happens until, one day, Nefkin calls. So you fix a meeting, possibly here, but perhaps in Gorky, maybe in a hotel where Nefkin is staying. This is all very proper: after all, there is a plant to be built; you cannot be criticized. So now do you remember the meeting?"

"It was the name," Bor'yan said. He glanced at Irina Terekhova, but she seemed not to register with him. "It confused me," Kirov followed that glance. What was she thinking? What did she make of the two "friends?" He needed her there to prevent Bor'yan from blinding him with technical argument, but her presence made him hold back.

"OK," he resumed. "We are in our meeting at Gorky — on reflection I think it was Gorky."

"Yes."

"And Nefkin has a message for you. He tells you that Atommash has too much work, that certain deliveries will be very late, years late, perhaps. And in this case nobody will look good. You, of course are innocent of any delays, but Nefkin has an answer. He says, 'Who cares about innocence? Does the KGB care about innocence?' Yes, let's be frank: Nefkin says something about the KGB in order to frighten you. I think so." Bor'yan made no answer. "And then he offers you a deal."

"A solution."

"Of course, not a deal, a solution. That's more exact, isn't it?" Kirov said. "Because there was nothing corrupt in your motives."

"I was trying to be practical."

"Exactly," Kirov agreed. "Now, let's talk about that solution."

Bor'yan turned his eyes away and stared about the room as if he was looking for lies in the dark corners; but the room seemed as stripped of them as of furniture. He helped himself to another of the cigarettes laid out on the table.

"This what's-his-name—Nefkin—asked me to take fewer heat exchangers. He said the plant was over-designed."

"Over-designed?"

"The capacity was bigger than he would ever use—at least three of the plutonium storage tanks were surplus to requirements, just there for standby. Each tank had two cooling systems with two heat exchangers on each line. So—says Nefkin—why not take out one heat exchanger from each line and run the last loop direct to the lake? That would save six heat exchangers. And there was still a safety margin because there was no direct connection between the tanks and the lake."

"So you agreed."

"No!" Bor'yan was emphatic. "It wasn't for me to say. I couldn't authorize a design change. It had to go to Moscow, to the Inspectorate."

"To Pokrebsky."

Bor'yan nodded.

"But you added your recommendations."

"Yes."

"May I ask a question?"

It was Irina Terekhova. Kirov caught the surprise on Bor'yan's face. *Only a woman—she can't know anything and she doesn't count.* Kirov wasn't certain whether or not Bor'yan was right. Her presence was a complication as well as a help. He would have preferred to use the KGB's own scientific personnel if his chief, Grishin, hadn't insisted on using the Inspectorate's own investigation to destroy it. "Go ahead," he said.

"The design change made the chances of an accident greater," she said to Bor'yan, "but it wasn't the cause. It doesn't explain how plutonium nitrate leaked from the storage tank into the closed cooling-water cycle or from the closed cycle into the direct cycle leading to the lake. There had to be a materials failure. Where? In the tank and the heat exchanger?"

The statement and the question hit Bor'yan like a blow. He froze for what seemed a minute with the ash of his cigarette crumbling down the front of his suit, then he muttered, "This is a very technical issue. There are explanations one would have to go into."

"What's your problem?" Kirov said impatiently. "This goes against your deal with Nefkin?"

98

"I've told you, there was no deal with Nefkin!"

"No? What about your car?"

"My car?"

"Your car," Kirov repeated slowly, reminding himself to keep his temper, that for all his pointless evasions Bor'yan would eventually come round. He went on, "In 1974 you bought a car—a nice car, a Western car."

"So? It was secondhand. I bought it in Gorky. A Westerner working on one of the car plants had sold it, but I bought it legitimately for rubles from a Soviet citizen. You can see the records."

"I have them," said Kirov and he placed a thin folder of papers in front of Bor'yan and laid open a page as if it were a gravestone. His expression remained equable, reasonable. The other man's cigarette had burned down to the tip, and a curl of acrid smoke lay between them to be picked up by the ventilator and whirred away.

"The previous owner," said Kirov, "the man from Gorky—he owned the car for only a week. Isn't that strange? A good Western car and he owns it for only a week?"

"That was his business," said Bor'yan. Kirov turned another page.

"This man"—he licked his finger, pressed down a fold, then laid down an open palm as if looking for an offer: *help me to help you*—"He bought the car originally in Volgodonsk. You follow? Volgodonsk, where Atommash and our friend Nefkin have a factory. You see the implications?" He turned another page to suggest that there was more incriminating material; then, as if no more were needed, closed the file and laid it where Bor'yan was forced to see it. "How was it?" he asked. "Nefkin asked you a favor—that's what people will say. And you agreed. Then—suddenly—you bought a car which came from the home town of this Nefkin, a good car, a valuable car, at a very modest price. I know," Kirov added, "that this could be merely a coincidence, but there are people who could build this up into a case against you, if they cared to draw the wrong inferences. Yet," he said, "it doesn't have to be that way. People can forget about these things. *I* can forget about these things." He looked Bor'yan straight in the eyes. "Help me. I want to be your friend."

7

George Twist couldn't remember how long it was since he had last been in Moscow. Ten — or maybe it was twelve — years. He wondered whether it had changed. Then he decided that the question didn't make sense since he had never really known Moscow in the first place — just hotels, airports and offices, the way that he knew every city. And change, when he noticed it, tended to be in the plumbing or in the price of the taxis.

The British Chamber of Commerce trade mission to the Soviet Union started in a bar in Terminal 1 at Heathrow with a couple of stiffeners because it seemed like a good idea and because someone said that being drunk was as good a way as any of spending two or three hours at Sheremetyevo waiting for baggage and immigration formalities. So they all had drinks except for the teetotaler from Sheffield, who drank orange juice, which was all right because there was always a teetotaler from Sheffield who drank orange juice; and someone told the story about the trip to Karachi when a couple of fellas had pissed in the teetotaler's bed but they couldn't remember who, and someone else said they knew the story except that it was Cairo, and they hadn't pissed in his bed, they had paid one of the porters to provide him with a boy for the night. George wondered what he was doing drinking with this crowd of clowns, but laughed with them, which made him wonder whether he wasn't a clown, too; and in any case it was too early in the morning to be a hero and tell them to stuff it.

They had their photograph taken for the first time. This was on the steps of the Boeing 737 in London when they still looked full of hope. It would turn up later in one of the glossies issued by the BOTB or the Department of Trade or in some company's house magazine, and wherever it showed up it would be thrown into the bin unlooked at. On the plane the girls handed out newspapers. Mostly they chose the *Sunday Times* because you couldn't get English papers in Moscow, not even the *Morning Star,* except once in a blue moon, and the *Sunday Times* would last you the week. But this was the day when the review section ran a story entitled "Fat Cats of the Kremlin," so when they landed in Moscow there were a lot of newspapers left on the plane because they knew that in Russia, though not in the rest of Eastern Europe, visitors are generally searched for literature.

This was how George got to Moscow.

Sheremetyevo is a modern airport, but that doesn't alter the problems. The British hung around the baggage carousels trying to guess whose luggage was going around in circles because the indicator board was showing the wrong flight. Either that or a group of Vietnamese soldiers in flimsy green cotton fatigues had been on the London plane and no one had noticed. They looked like boys of twelve, and their luggage consisted of fiber suitcases painted emerald and scarlet in a camouflage pattern. The British caught up with them later by the white trays containing the currency declaration forms in four or five languages. The boys, who probably didn't have any money anyway, were squatting in a circle around the pole holding the tray marked "Deutsch," and George saw them struggle to fill out the forms in German. They scratched their heads and gabbed to each other and borrowed pencils while the Russians and the other passengers, except for George, ignored them. He watched the crazy scene come and go and he remembered from last time that in Moscow people didn't stop and stare or point or laugh and there was a whole area of life that was going on out of the corner of his eye. They were already out of sight when this occurred to him, and he was going through a special channel that had been cleared through Customs and was halfway to the Intourist bus.

The hotel was the Mezhdunarodnaya. It stands by the bank of the Moscow river opposite the Ukraina. The Hotel Ukraina is a Stalinist pile, a mausoleum that looks as if it was finished by a *pâtissier* it has a wearisome charm and sense of Soviet atmosphere that appeals to people who want to get a feel for the country and it annoys the hell out of businessmen. The Mezhdunarodnaya, on the other hand, was built for the 1980 Olympics. George felt that he had stayed there before: only last time it was called the Hyatt and was in a different country altogether. It offered American bars and showers that worked, and George sampled both before unpacking his case to hang four days' worth of clothes in the wardrobe. Then he paced about the room because he felt twitchy in the way that traveling always made him twitchy, and tried to read a little but couldn't. He heard the traffic outside and the air-conditioning and a few English voices going past suggesting they go for a drink because there was damn all else to do, and for a while he hung around the window looking out on the city as the night fell. He looked and he tried to pick out the places he knew, but didn't recognize any or maybe recognized them all because he had been everywhere and they suggested nowhere.

Then there welled up inside him that jaded feeling of tiredness and anticipated failure that he knew came from traveling and selling his heart out. It could be fixed with a few drinks in the American bar of any hotel you cared to name.

Leningrad lived up to its reputation. It was raining. A thin drizzle crept coldly and slowly off the Baltic under an umbrella of stained cloud. Irina Terekhova arrived unaccompanied on a scheduled Aeroflot flight that was running on time, which meant thirty-five minutes late. There was no explanation; even the fact of the delay wasn't acknowledged, as was normal. Irina didn't notice. She was looking for the KGB man.

His name was Ivanov. He was waiting in the arrivals hall, a tall character with small mobile features like nomads on an expanse of face, a massive domed skull and red wavy hair. He wore a brown, hairy overcoat, a gray suit and black moccasins and had nothing to say except to check her identity and his orders from Kirov and offer her transport.

They drove into the city in a blue Chaika, past the workers' apartment houses and along the quays of the old city where the stone classical buildings of St. Petersburg stand in the rain and sulk after the past like counterrevolutionaries.

The Central Research Insitute for Atomic Science was in a new building off the highway to Pavlovsk, if you knew where to look. There was a side road sharp off behind a red billboard with a Party slogan, a screening line of pines with a security fence behind, and then a spread of open ground posted with cameras and a few man-made hummocks under the turf which could signify anything. They arrived with rain still tumbling down and the guards dodging about in streaming raincoats.

Mukhin, the head of the Institute, was waiting for them, a fat man with long cheeks and slit eyes, as if he were staring into the sun. He sported a home knitted cardigan in green with ill-matched bands of color, and was as friendly as the circumstances allowed—which meant that he was cautious because the orders he had received from KGB Leningrad were ambiguous. *He's frightened of me!* Irina thought. She was surprised at first because she wasn't used to the idea, then amused and then vaguely sad, though there was nothing about Mukhin personally to be sad about. Mukhin was asking after her journey and the state of things in Moscow and offering tea. And all the while, to keep the conversation light, he fired off random shots of laughter.

"But what can I do for you?" he asked at last. He had his orders and a note in front of him from his own KGB resident, who on Kirov's instructions had impounded all the Institute's files on Sokolskoye. "This"—waving one of the papers—"doesn't make it clear. Something about radiation monitors at Sokolskoye, yes? Did we design them? Is that the question?"

I know you supplied them," Irina said. She was remembering Bor'yan blabbering excuses at this point. *Why was the design fo the plant changed? Why did the equipment in the cooling line fail? Why didn't the radiation monitors sound an alarm?* "I've talked to the plant director," she explained. "He says he received a batch of them two years ago with an instruction to fit them and report on performance. They were prototypes?"

"I've answered this question before—"

Little girl—no, he hadn't said "little girl," but Irina heard it in his tone. Arrogant, fearful, patronizing, ingratiating—Mukhin had an *apparatchik*'s voice like a palette of colors muddied into grayness.

"—from Comrade Pokrebsky at the Inspectorate and from Professor Yermolin, who is, I believe, your superior."

"Please," Irina said quietly, "answer my question."

"And I tell you the same thing," Mukhin went on, now smiling and pretending to ignore her. "It would be inaccurate to call the monitors 'prototypes.' Rather, they were a pre-production batch."

"Meaning?"

103

"That their design and testing were complete. We were waiting for a manufacturing slot in order to produce a larger quantity, but . . ." He gave one of those you-know-how-things-are shrugs of complicity. Irina knew it well enough, the invitation to join in the conspiracy of inertia against the system. "Anyway," Mukhin said, "there were customers — Sokolskoye, for instance — who needed monitors; so we ran up a pre-production batch. And that's it."

"That's not Bor'yan's story. He says that the monitors were forced on him."

"This Bor'yan, he's in trouble?" Mukhin asked; but he knew the answer. "So what else can he say?" He leaned on his desk and stared across at Irina Terekhova, and again she caught the real meaning of the gesture. Neither was being frank with the other, but each knew that in a perverse way there was a flow of truth between them. Yes, she thought, that was how it was: a currency of lies passing from hand to hand like useless ruble notes and, beneath it, a profound flow of truth, so that the Party educated the people better than it ever knew. Information, on the other hand, was as scarce as gold; and for now that was what she needed.

Mukhin enquired cautiously, "What did Sokolskoye do with these monitors?"

"They installed them in all their potential alpha-discharge lines. When there was a leak from one of their plutonium nitrate storage-tanks into the cooling water, an alarm should have sounded but didn't. Bor'yan says that the monitors you designed were faulty and failed. He says he complained about them."

"Not to me."

"No?"

"No." A pause. Then: "This whatchamacallim . . ."

"Bor'yan."

"Bor'yan — an Armenian, eh? — so he had problems. Everyone has problems. But failures — no." Mukhin was emphatic. "There were no failures." He turned his eyes on Ivanov and asked the KGB man, "Please, let's settle this. I need the files. The story is there." Ivanov picked up the telephone and made an internal call. When he had finished he gave Mukhin a dog-dirt look. Irina noted that the red-haired man didn't carry power in the same easy ways as Kirov. She asked, "What were these problems?"

Mukhin picked up the question. "This and that, mostly calibration. You understand, these new-pattern monitors were highly sensitive. Sokolskoye had problems calibrating them to filter out background radiation. And without proper adjustment they picked up the radiation ordinarily present in the environment of this type of plant and sounded an alarm. But failure?" He shook his head. "That wasn't the problem."

When the files on Sokolskoye arrived, Mukhin took Irina Terekhova through them to demonstrate his point with the correspondence from Bor'yan and his engineers. She picked out key items and had Ivanov copy them. Two hours later she pronounced herself satisfied, which only seemed to worry Mukhin.

"I'm sorry I can't help you more, comrade," he said.

She nodded and understood: he wanted to help and not help, being uncertain which was best. And that, too, was part of the way things were.

"It's all right," she answered. "I know what happened." And now the man looked genuinely surprised, so that she thought: *He really doesn't know!*

The travel agents had laid on a British pub in a room off the foyer of the Mezhdunarodnaya. George Twist turned up there after dinner to find the evening under way, a game of dominoes in progress, and those who hadn't bothered to turn up for the meal tucking into a dish of pie and peas. Two other contractors were sitting in one of the corners, but George didn't join them: he wanted to work up a strategy for ditching the competition by having a quiet word with the Russians away from the crowd; but for the moment he had no ideas. He got himself a glass of beer and sat on his own in the shadows. He was still there when Wormold, a bluff Midlander who had come to the Soviet Union to sell soft-drink franchises, breezed in from the foyer and found him.

"Hello, George, just the man!" Wormold had bright eyes that went peekaboo over the rim of a glass of gin and tonic. He claimed expertise in tonic water, could tell any brand from the taste. "There's a fellow outside looking for you. He says he's your agent. I wasn't sure it really was you he wanted since he kept going on about spare parts for cars — that isn't your game, is it?"

"No, but I think it's me he's looking for. Thanks." George eased himself out of the chair and took a stroll into the foyer looking for Jack

Melchior, the company's local agent.

What George knew about Melchior was negligible. He had been the company's agent for five or six years — somebody thought — but only a couple of people claimed to have met him. "After all, George, there wasn't much point. Everyone knew we didn't bid into Russia — not since the Omsk Job. In fact it was news to me that we had a man there at all."

Jim Evans knew him slightly from the Great Agents' Jamboree — "Remember that, George? We had them over in England for a week, the whole lot of them, even the little Chinaman. Pep-talk and jolly rolled into one. Pissed all the time, every man-jack of them."

What was he like?

"Jack Melchior? A funny little cove, George. Must be getting on a bit now, I should think. Likes his grog and comes over as a pukka sahib, but there's more than a whiff of "other ranks" about him. He rattles on a bit about the time he was in the Palestine Police, though I'm buggered if that has anything to do with anything. His party trick in front of the Russkies," said Evans, "is to do trimphone impressions — honest to God, he did them for us to prove it. It's the only international joke that Jack knows," he added, "apart from baring his arse."

There was a clock in the foyer of the hotel, a thirty-foot affair in the style of the famous Fabergé Easter eggs, with a cockerel on top which crowed the hour. As George reached it, he was approached from out of the crowd by a small man in a navy-blue blazer and gray trousers, who came straight for him like a coast guard cutter and said, "*George Twist,* am I right?" in a snappy voice with a slightly distinguished tone. "Thought so!" the stranger went on before the reply could reach him. Then he looked stern and said, "Five years — my God, but it's taken you chaps some time to get out here!" — so that George was reminded of his mother asking: *What do you think you're doing? Staying out until midnight!*

"Jack Melchior?"

"Himself. Am I right in supposing you've been here before?" Melchior gripped George by the arm and led him towards another bar. "Wet the whistle while we talk, eh?"

"I was here a few years ago," George said.

"Good egg, then you'll know the rules; don't change money on the black market, don't roger the waiters — oh, and one or two others that one soon gets the hang of. Got the spares for the car, by the way?"

"An air filter and some plugs? They're in my room."

"Spot on! It can be devilish difficult getting Volvo spares out here." Melchior turned to the barman: "Two splashes of vodka *spasibo*, Boris, and chop-chop." He planted George on one of the stools and took one for himself. Then he sat and waited, staring at his visitor with an eager, fragile smile until the drinks arrived.

"You asked for some cigarettes, too," George said. The other man had taken his drink and was distracted by it. A thin mouth lined by a white moustache dipped into the glass. Beneath the blazer Jack Melchior was wearing a drip-dry shirt set off with a regimental tie, which, in turn, was held in place by a mother-of-pearl tie clip. As he replaced his glass on the bar he showed a stretch of shirt cuff and an enameled cuff link with a dart board motif. He wore suede shoes, meticulously brushed.

"I'd almost forgotten the cigarettes," he said.

"Park Drive?" George asked. "That was the brand? Tricky to get; they don't stock them in airports as a general rule."

"No, that's why I made a point of it. They're not for me but for a friend, you understand. Something to remind him of back home. Have you eaten, by the way?"

"Yes"

"Good show. Got to get the right balance between nourishment and alcohol over here and no mistake. One slip and you'll find yourself in bed with a girl from the Gas Board and *pop-pop* from the old cameras before you know where you are."

"The Gas Board?"

"You-know-who, the Kremlin Gas Board—KGB—your favorite police force and mine," Melchior answered casually. "Not that they are anything to worry about if you keep your nose clean. I expect they spend most of their time helping old ladies across roads and rescuing cats from trees, much like anywhere else. But it's as well to be on the *qui vive,* if you take my meaning."

George took his meaning.

They finished their drinks and had a couple more. The visitor tried to move the conversation toward business but couldn't interest the other man.

"Get your feet under the table first, George, and save business for tomorrow. There's plenty of time. Have another, eh?"

So they had another, and George felt the momentary lift. Jack Melchior gave him a jovial smile with a set of glossy white teeth that sat too loosely in his mouth, and told a few stories about the local scene in a confidential voice while George's eyes drifted aimlessly about the bar and he wondered, in the dissociated way of travel and booze, why it was that he was there.

"Who's that?" he asked without particular interest. His glance had alighted on a middle-aged man in what appeared to be a duffel coat, who was sitting on his own, drawing pictures in the beer-spills. "Don't tell me he isn't English. I haven't seen a coat like that since God-knows-when."

"Who?" Melchior screwed up his eyes and peered across the room. He shrugged his shoulders and caught the barman's attention. "Same again Boris, *spasibo,* and *molto pronto por favor.* The name is Lucas," he answered to George. "Neville Lucas—ring any bells?" He nodded at the stranger, who acknowledged with a tilt of his glass.

"Should it?"

"It all depends." He nibbled at a piece of lemon and spat the pits out into his hand. "Old Neville caused quite a stir back in 1965."

"How?"

"Oh, you know, he climbed over the wire, chucked in his lot with this crowd—what's the word I'm looking for?" Melchior slipped the lemon pits into an ashtray and wiped his fingers on his handkerchief. "Defected."

George glanced at the man again, but the nondescript figure suggested nothing dramatic. Jack was saying, "I'm surprised you don't remember—though, come to think of it, there have been rather a lot of British traitors over the years. The *Daily Express,* in its own original way, called him 'the fourth man'—I think it was the fourth but it could have been the fifth—you get the general idea, I'm sure."

"Sure."

"Not to worry. Aside from a few unsavory acquaintances in the Gas Board, Neville is a good scout and always willing to do a good turn for a fellow Briton. So far as he's allowed to, of course. I'll introduce you to him some day. Come on, drink up and we'll have another."

"I think I've had enough," said George. Waves of tiredness were starting to break over him. Jack Melchior seemed disappointed but ordered himself a drink, called for the bill and left it dangling on the bar in front of George.

"Well, I'll be off," he said. "Thanks for the drink. I'll see you tomorrow." Melchior started from his seat and was stopped by the other's hand on his own. George had decided on one last push towards business.

"I was wondering, Jack, whether you could set up a meeting with the Minister of Gas — a chance to make my pitch away from the others."

The older man smiled sympathetically. "What are you looking for from this trip, George?"

"Just a chance, that's all." That was the way it came out, and to George it sounded like a last chance for everything.

Jack Melchior shrugged off the hand. He shook his head. "You're five years too late, old son." He paused for a second's thought and then went on: "Look, I'm close to retirement — not long now and I'll be growing chrysanthemums — so I'll do what agents can't normally afford to do. I'll tell you the truth."

"Do that," George said and, like most people suddenly promised the truth, realized he didn't want to know.

"Frankly," said Melchior, "here in Russia, you don't have a bloody hope."

Irina Terekhova returned to Moscow by another scheduled flight, back to her apartment and her son and the letters from her husband in Afghanistan, and to cooking and cleaning and writing up her notes when the boy was in bed and she could be alone in the half-darkened room with her papers spread out in the light of a desk lamp and the cold flicker of pictures from the silent television set.

Kirov gave her three hours to take care of her chores and have something of the evening to herself before he telephoned. And she supposed that, in its way, this showed a sort of consideration.

She gave a brief account of her journey to Leningrad, of Mukhin's story and the contents of his files. She stood by the window as she spoke into the mouthpiece. In the dark street there was a new car parked across the way, which might, as far as she could ever know, be just a new car parked across the way. Someone was singing, a radio was playing; a dog was barking and scratching against a closed door as if someone had stolen its soul.

"So the Institute supplied Sokolskoye with an untried design of radiation monitor," Kirov repeated back to her over a faint line that made him seem far away in the night. Irina caught herself nodding, which was pointless, since he couldn't see her.

"I've been reading some of Nechvolodov's calls to Pokrebsky," said Kirov, which made Irina remember that the KGB had tapped the line between Pokrebsky and his man at the plant. "He confirms that he tested the monitors on the cooling-water loops and they were all in working order. Even Pokrebsky can't understand why an alarm wasn't sounded if there was contamination of the water." There was more but it was lost in the crackling of the line. Then: "Pokrebsky has an analysis of the lake water. It shows some insignificant low-level radiation consistent with minor malpractice. But the main toxin is chemical—the herbicide used to keep weeds down on the lake during the summer. The analysis has been given to Yermolin—you should get it tomorrow—but the conclusion is obvious. There is no problem with the lake: if we flush it out into the Volga, the chemical poisons will dilute to a safe level. That's what Pokrebsky will recommend, and Yermolin will be bound to support him."

More static and interference on the line. She thought: even the KGB couldn't provide a decent telephone service. The thought distracted her from her anger. Lies! The world was rotten with lies! The line cleared. She said as calmly as she could manage; "The water analysis is a fraud. I've seen the men in the hospital at Sokolskoye. They are suffering from radiation poisoning, not the effects of some weed killer." She went on, but there was a gale of white noise on the line so that she was not sure he could hear her, *"Please,* there has to be another analysis. You must get it. You must!" And suddenly his voice was there, so loud, so close that it was as if he were next to her, and she recoiled with the sensation of an intimacy that she didn't want. He was saying, "The radiation monitors—they worked, and yet there was no alarm sounded. There can't have been a leak from the storage tanks."

"But I know what happened to the monitors," she answered. "I know!"

There was no reply.

Irina said, "I know what happened, but I don't know how to prove I'm right unless the plant director confesses to it."

"Don't worry about Bor'yan," Kirov said. "Just tell me."

He spoke with a certainty that chilled her so that she couldn't speak. She felt herself frozen with the phone in her hand. Somewhere the dog was howling pitifully and people were shouting. She found her voice and said, "Mukhin unintentionally gave me the answer. Bor'yan's complaint was that he couldn't screen out ordinary background radiation; the monitors supplied by the Institute were too sensitive. If he had tried to run the plant with them in place, he would have been shutting his operations down continually to trace nonexistent leaks."

"So?" Kirov asked.

She thought: *How can I know?* But she knew.

"He turned the radiation monitors off," she said. "It's a simple as that."

Kirov's call to Sokolskoye pulled the local man out of bed and to attention like the Last Judgment.

"I want a written confession from Bor'yan," he said.

Klyuev, the KGB resident, licked his lips, found a pencil and wrote down the words.

"He has to admit to turning off the radiation monitors in the cooling-water systems."

Klyuev grunted, read what he had written, then said, "Difficult — that's worth thirty years to anybody. You're asking him to sign his death warrant."

The reply was quick and clear: "Arrest his wife and children. Bring them to the plant. Confront him. Understand?"

Klyuev understood. He put down the phone and got dressed. He went to speak to Bor'yan, the Armenian plant director at Sokolskoye. And he remembered to forget that it was his friend with whom he used to go hunting.

At midnight in Kalinin Prospekt the military guard at the building of the All-Union Nuclear Inspectorate changed duty. The reliefs arrived in two trucks and a staff car carrying the officer of the watch. The vehicles formed a line by the main entrance, engines running and their headlights reflecting dully off concrete.

The captain of the relief guard was first to the entrance of the building. The sentries snapped to attention but barred his way while the sergeant manning the duty desk scanned the scene via the three cameras pivoted at first-floor level, issued the appropriate challenge on the voice intercom and called his own officer on the internal phone to report the punctual arrivals.

It took two minutes for the officer of the watch to appear. The lifts had failed, and he had to use the stairs. His footsteps could be heard rattling through the hollow chambers of the building, and he arrived tugging at the skirts of his jacket, out of breath but relaxed. He gave the order to admit the newcomers and, while his men, tired but laughing among themselves, and the newcomers, fresh, stiff and uncommunicative, jostled in the foyer, he adjourned to the protocol office with the relief commander, gave a rundown of the night's events and signed off the log. With the watch handed over, the two officers exchanged cigarettes and made small talk. The outgoing guard loaded themselves into the trucks, and one of the wits rattled the tailgate until his officer got the message and came out of the building stubbing his cigarette on the pavement of Kalinin Prospekt.

At 2 a.m. three black Volgas drove into Kalinin Prospekt from the direction of the Sadovoye Ring Road, parked outside the building and turned off their lights. Twelve men in civilian dress got out. Four of them left the group and stationed themselves in pairs at the nearest junctions. A fifth, in black woollen overcoat and brown felt hat, walked straight inside the building without being challenged and was met inside by the duty officer who was waiting in the protocol office. After a few words the rest of the civilian team was summoned inside.

They took the stairs to the fourth floor, a paneled corridor with the usual portraits of the leadership and a strip of carpet to show that the occupiers were important. Two of them carried Samsonite cases. One of them opened the door to the office.

The office had an impersonal executive luxury. A hardwood desk with a figured-leather top. An armchair and a couple of swivel chairs in oatmeal gray and brown, textured like muesli. On the desk there was a millefiori paperweight of Italian glass, a set of pens in an onyx holder and an ashtray with the Exxon logo stamped on it. In the corner of the room stood a safe.

One of the men opened his case and fingered the tools inside. He looked at the safe. It was of West German manufacture, squat and gunmetal gray. In addition to whatever hardware the Germans had included for its protection, it was sealed with six wafers of lead alloy embossed with the security code of whoever was responsible for accounting for its contents on a daily basis. It took two minutes to open.

The man in the brown felt hat inspected the contents. Files held in racks, a couple of box files, a gray cash box with a fancy transfer print of the maker's name on the lid. He picked through the files with delicate hands sheathed in leather gloves and selected one by the title on the spine. This he handed to one of his technicians.

They ran an extension lead from a power outlet to the desk, set up a lamp and took a rostrum camera from the second case. Each page of the file was photographed three times for safety and then the whole was reconstructed in its original order and replaced in the safe. While this went on, five of the men lounged in the shadows of the room and fidgeted because they couldn't smoke. Like many other jobs, this one was overmanned.

The whole business took half an hour, most of it in restoring the seals, and this partly because a fragment of one of the old seals was mislaid and had to be found. It was a tidy affair, mostly done in silence except at the end, when they took the vacuum cleaner from the storeroom and cleaned the place up.

And when they had finished it was as if they had never been there.

Kirov was woken by a phone call to his apartment at 4 a.m.

"It's me, boss, calling just as you asked," said Bogdanov. "They've got it."

"Where are you?"

"The office."

"I'll see you in twenty minutes."

"I'll put the coffee on."

He slipped out of bed. Larissa was still asleep. As he moved, her arm draped itself over the hollow in the sheets. A beautiful arm, smooth and shapely, with skin that reflected light like pearl. Kirov kissed it and got dressed by the light of a table lamp.

There was no traffic. It took him only fifteen minutes to reach Dzerzhinsky Square and park his car. There were few people about, and those mostly clerks manning the foreign desks where the overseas stations were generating messages from different time zones that had to be transcribed and decoded for the morning analysis session in time. There was nobody in his section except for a group called the Fire Brigade who were there for emergencies and spent their time sleeping or playing cards.

"How long?" he asked Bogdanov.

"Five minutes, as soon as I get the hang of this thing." He was wrestling with a projector, feeding slides into a rotating magazine and trying to locate the latter on its spindle. He was tired and bad-tempered, and a little drunk.

"I waited up for this lot," he said. "Two o'clock they promised me — latest — guaranteed." As an explanation he added, "I had a few drinks at the club. I heard this joke?" — he grunted — "got you, you bastard" — the magazine was engaged in place — "I'll tell you the story later. Will you turn the light off?" Kirov turned the light off, and they both sat in the darkness illuminated only by the cone of light from the machine and the nacreous reflections of the screen.

Click. The screen threw up a cover page with a series of eyes-only security tabs and a circulation list. Bogdanov fiddled with the focus, then sat back, stringing out his sparse bones in the chair.

Click. The second frame gave a title: REPORT ON THE ANALYSIS OF LAKE WATER AT SOKOLSKOYE.

"Same title as the one we got. You don't suppose that Pokrebsky's been playing straight with us do you? Your little Terekhova could be wrong boss; maybe it's weed killer all along."

"Shut up and recall the last shot," Kirov answered.

"Suit yourself." Bogdanov flicked back to the preceding frame and showed the circulation list again.

"Yermolin isn't copied in. Neither is Grishin. This is the Inspectorate's private report."

"Naughty, naughty; they've been keeping secrets. Next page?"

Kirov nodded.

The next page and the few that followed contained a description of the analytical method and a table of results expressed in units that neither man understood.

"Next?"

"Run through the rest until you find the conclusions."

"Just say the word." Bogdanov pressed the button and the slides clicked on in sequence. They found the conclusions. And there they paused.

They sat for a moment. The conclusions were set out on two pages. Kirov had the frames played and replayed. Bogdanov worked the machine while reading the text, mouthing the words and sharpening the focus of the image as if that somehow brought out the meaning. Then he snorted and reached into his pocket for something.

"I don't think I want to believe this, boss," he said and struck a match to light a cigarette. He stood up and walked around the office, jogging his shoulders to loosen up, and then stared at the screen again. Kirov turned the machine off and switched on the main light.

"Well, we've got them — Pokrebsky and the whole Inspectorate," he said evenly and gave a thin, dry laugh that had no satisfaction in it. *Got them.* Grishin would be pleased. He could present the report to Grishin in the morning and invite him to look on the Inspectorate like a naked woman. And that was what he would see. To Grishin the plutonium content in the water at Sokolskoye was of secondary consideration. But to Kirov it was different because Irina Terekhova had told him about the effects of even small amounts of plutonium contamination.

"How do we explain it this time?" he said quietly. He glanced at Bogdanov. "Put this stuff away and go get some sleep." The words were as adequate as any others.

8

Klyuev was woken at dawn. There was a hammering at the door. A voice was wailing, *"For Christ's sake, open up! Oh, Jesus, are you there? Wake up, damn it!"*

He grabbed his trousers and slipped them on. A panel on the door was starting to split. A voice he knew—Denisov, the little runt who had taken over as plant director. He got to the door holding his gun in one hand and the waistband of his trousers with the other. He opened the door with his gun hand and Denisov fell in.

"What's going on?" Klyuev grabbed him by the coat collar: he wore the overcoat over rumpled pajamas and a pair of boots, and his face was unshaven, ashen gray with slack lips like dead poppies. He was still jabbering. Klyuev pushed him up against the wall and slapped him around until he made sense.

"Spit it out, man! Spit it out!"

Denisov hung slackly from the KGB man's fist. Klyuev threw him a look of disgust, then dumped him against the wall and poured them both a drink. By the time he returned with the glass, Denisov had come out of his panic and stuck himself against the door.

"Nechvolodov is in the control room!"

"So what?" Klyuev was shaking the air into his brains, holding the glass and scratching his backside.

"He's waving some bloody order from Moscow! He says he's going to open the sluices on the dam and dump the whole goddam lake into the reservoir."

"Order? What order?" Klyuev felt his thoughts stringing apart like a thing only partly glued. He said lazily, "There aren't any orders— can't be. We control the telephones and telex. Nechvolodov is boxed in."

Denisov didn't care. He was chanting plaintively, "I've got a wife

116

and kid in Gorky. I've seen the poor bastards dying here. I don't want anyone flushing poisonous crap into the reservoir until I know exactly what it is."

Klyuev began to hear sense. He shut the other man up.

"Stuff your wife and kid!" He saw Denisov wince and said quickly, "OK — wife, kids, — yeah, OK. But what's this about an order?"

"Couriered by plan from Pokrebsky himself."

"Shit!" Klyuev grabbed his overcoat and with Denisov at his heels ran out of the barrack building.

It had snowed during the night. Thick drifts of the stuff lay white across the floodlit expanses of the plant and tumbled down toward the shoreline between the bare granite outcrops. In that direction lay the lake, still ice-free because of the heat load on the water caused by the plant, covered by a milky web and a layer of mist within a black rim of spruces. The sky winked with fading stars.

"What now?" Denisov prompted.

"Fuck off," snapped Klyuev. What now? Good question. "Nechvolodov, you bastard! Come on out!" His voice echoed off concrete and steelwork. There was no answer, just the scuttle of operators in the shadows. He looked towards the control room. It was on the upper floor of a small block. Lights in the window. A flight of railed steps led directly from outside. There was a soldier at the bottom.

"You can't go up."

Klyuev looked the man up and down. Sometimes it worked. "Get out of my way."

"You can't go up."

He stepped back and glanced at the lit windows again. He yelled again, "Come on out, you bastard!" He turned on the soldier. A conscript. Red-faced, smooth-cheeked — scared stiff. Klyuev murmured, "I'll have you shoveling shit in Siberia." He stuck his gun under the boy's chin and muttered, "Move!"

He clattered up the metal treads. The frozen handrails cut like knives. At the top he remembered Denisov. The plant director had stuck with him. A kid afraid of the dark. Too bloody right — how could he judge what Nechvolodov was doing? It was all black magic, nightmare stuff. "You," he said to Denisov, "clear out. Find a switch and cut the power to the sluices if you can." He watched the other man hesitate and then retreat down the steps. Klyuev turned to the door, took a deep breath and kicked it in.

Nechvolodov was sitting in front of a console with an operating manual in front of him and a glass of tea. He glanced at the KGB man and swung round idly in his chair. He had nerve — Klyuev had to admit it — that was probably why Pokrebsky had sent him.

"What do you want?" Nechvolodov asked. He had the confidence of a man with the Inspectorate and the Army General Staff behind him. Snow drifted through the break in the door. He pulled his coat around him. A fur coat — expensive. "Well?" It was a bitter, lisping voice issuing through tight lips stuck fast to his teeth. Calm, but not so calm. His red hair was uncombed and fell over his forehead. He had blond, invisible eyelashes. "Why the commotion?"

Why the commotion? Klyuev felt his guts stir. He recognized his own fear — not physical — that he could smash the other man into pieces. But what if he was wrong? Black-magic stuff. Leave it to the witch doctors. What if he was *wrong?* "I don't know what this is about — but you and your boss must be desperate to pull a stunt like this."

Nechvolodov's eyes flicked open and shut. Then he stirred in his chair and answered contemptuously, "You don't know what you're talking about. This is a technical matter."

"Bullshit!"

Nechvolodov flinched. Klyuev registered the thought: *physical coward.* Use it! Use it! The other man had recovered and went on in the same scornful manner, "You really wouldn't know, would you?" His voice changed to an aloof monotone, emphasizing that he was giving a lecture to a know-nothing. "Scientific tests indicate that unless the lake is emptied quickly, the drop-out of contaminant will foul the lake bed. Then we'll have a long-term problem." He eyed Klyuev, searching for advantage. An ignoramus — yes — not frightened of violence, but of abstract power. He pressed on: "If we empty the lake, everything will be flushed out and diluted by the reservoir and the Volga. That's a lot of water. It can handle it."

"Tell me another one," said Klyuev. But there was doubt there.

Nechvolodov returned to examining the manual. He said slowly, "I don't care whether you believe me. This is a technical and operational question. I don't have to listen to you." He looked round again bleakly; and for the first time Klyuev knew that there were other powers than the KGB.

"You're forgetting who I am," he ventured.

"I remember," said Nechvolodov. "But this is an Army-run site. Your job is to stick to politics; and this isn't politics." He deliberately stressed his contempt, willing the other man to understand it. "Go write out a complaint. Denounce me. You'll never make it stick in Moscow."

There was silence. Klyuev looked down at his gun and sensed its uselessness. He heard noises now, outside: ammunition boots rattling on metal. Akhmatov, he guessed, with reinforcements. Klyuev searched for the vestiges of initiative and courage that the system had leeched out of him.

"I'll offer you a deal," Nechvolodov proposed. His eyes watched the door, waiting for Akhmatov. "Fix Denisov. Go back to bed, and no one will ever know. That way you never get called on to make a decision. This" — he leaned forward — "is *serious* business. What do you think has happened here? How do you think it was all done without important people becoming involved? Do you follow?"

"I follow."

Akhmatov was in the doorway, holding a pistol of his own. Klyuev dragged his eyes from Nechvolodov and tested the Major. He sensed a professional neutrality.

Nechvolodov exhaled slowly, and his fingers slid over the pages of the manual. His eyes gave a lizard stare, and Klyuev felt his bowels twisting. "So?" Nechvolodov asked, and Klyuev knew he had to answer.

"So, if you touch any of those controls, I'll blow your head off." It was crazy, but he had a sudden feeling of satisfaction. He had always wanted to say something like that.

Moscow: 0800 hours

"Pokrebsky is already at GHQ," said Bogdanov, putting down the car phone and turning his red-rimmed eyes on Kirov, who guessed the other man hadn't slept. Not after finally obtaining the water analysis — finally understanding what Sokolskoye meant. Bogdanov mimicked Pokrebsky: "He's making his pitch to Kostandov. 'Let me drain the lake and everything will be all right.' The bastard was at his office early — waiting for Nechvolodov to call him and say that it was all over. He doesn't know how much we've found out, but he must be shitting himself. Why else would he do this?" There was an underly-

119

ing satisfaction in Bogdanov's voice. This was Operation Fall-Out —
the old, dead case had gone live again and come up with a prize:
maybe not the biggest, but still a prize.

.They arrived in two cars, lights blazing, clearing the dim streets of
traffic. Two KGB legmen, the sort who wore.raincoats in summer,
were in the rear car. The four men piled out of their vehicles and took
the steps three at a time to Irina Terekhova's apartment.

She received them at the door, pale and tired but composed. She
was wearing a workaday dress and flat shoes that made her appear
more diminutive as she stood in the doorway. She asked, "What's
wrong, Major?"

"Not now — get your coat and come with me." Kirov was curt with
her, then regretted it.

"My son . . ." The boy was standing in the bedroom doorway,
staring with his dark, expressionless eyes; and for a second there was a
silence, as if the other people in the apartment block were holding
their breath and had their ears pressed to the walls.

"Don't worry." Kirov spoke more softly, recognizing his own tension
and tiredness. After receiving the report he had spent the balance of
the night working at home; sitting at a table in a pool of light, trying to
collate the facts, admit their enormity even to himself; hearing the
rustle of bedclothes and the catching of breath as Lara slept restlessly;
senses acute to the changes of the night, the rattle of wind against a
window, the clink of a spoon against a cup — yes, he told himself, *he
knew!* To Irina Terekhova he said, "My colleague will take care of
Arkasha." He laid a hand on her forearm.

"They call me Uncle Bog," said Bogdanov with an engaging smile
strung across his worn face. He swung his bones through the gap in
the door, followed by her eyes. He pinched the boy on the cheek and
said: "OK, kid, today we have some fun, huh?" Kirov was already
hustling the mother into her coat. Irina didn't resist; there was no
denying him. He took her hand, at first simply to force the pace down
the steps past the guard stationed on the landing and the other at the
entrance to the block. Then, as the driver opened the passenger door,
he found himself facing her, holding her fingers like a gift. He
dropped them and they got into the car, which set off with the second
car hanging on its tail and a cassette going on the player, filling the car
with bland Muzak until Kirov switched it off.

She repeated her question: "What's wrong, Major?"

"I have the Inspectorate's own analysis of the lake," he told her. He passed a copy of the papers to her. "They've finally done a reconciliation of the water analysis with the plutonium inventory and matched the two. There's no guesswork: Pokrebsky *knows* what's in the lake" — he paused until her divided attention was his — "and he wants to drain it."

The call had come through from Klyuev. The KGB man was still in the control room at Sokolskoye, training a gun on Nechvolodov and on the garrison commander, who was also armed. They faced each other, waiting for instructions and frightened of the slip that would turn the place into a butcher shop. *Tock* — there was a digital clock on the control-room wall that dropped numbers like bricks so that the phone picked them up even as Klyuev asked, "For Christ's sake, what's going on? Where are the bloody instructions?"

Kirov told Irina Terekhova, "It makes sense. Pokrebsky has already scrapped the equipment, so if he can drain the lake the critical evidence will be destroyed." She was looking out of the car. She had made no comment on the report, but her face had weariness etched on it. It came to him that she was thinking about the boy; that Sokolskoye was not important to her; but he knew that couldn't be true. A Gastronom shop flashed past with something in the window that probably wasn't available inside. A Melodia record store. Traffic lights, which they ignored.

"Pokrebsky can't do that," she said at last. She spoke calmly, but Kirov had learned to suspect her calmness.

"He can if Kostandov authorizes it. Technical necessity — that's how it will be put. Flush everything into the Volga and the problem goes away."

"But it doesn't!" she came back sharply. "It just changes the nature of the problem."

Her naivete surprised him — but perhaps it was just honesty. "The problem becomes somebody else's responsibility," he answered, "and that's the same as solving it." The car stopped at a junction. A black Kremlin limousine with the curtains closed and an escort of motorcycle outriders tore by at right angles. Kirov glanced at his passenger, wishing he could penetrate her thoughts. There were people who could lay open her thoughts to him, display them as in a case, to be picked up and handled. Bogdanov, if he had cause, would order it as a matter of course. Uncle Bog — his subordinate. The traffic moved off again.

"Is this the woman?" said Grishin. "Good morning, Comrade. Does she have the full story to tell Kostandov?"

"Comrade Terekhova can explain everything."

Grishin was uncomfortable in his KGB uniform but wore it as a badge to warn the General. He ran a finger around the inside of his collar and cast an eye over the staff officers who were toing and froing across the lobby, crowding in and out of the Frunze Street entrance to GHQ. At the desk an army clerk was trying to reach Kostandov on the telephone.

"I may not be believed," Irina Terekhova said. Grishin reacted as if the voice had come from an unknown source. He looked first to Kirov, then at the woman. She added, "I'm not a practicing engineer. Pokrebsky may point that out—and it's true."

Grishin looked her up and down thoughtfully. The comment remained unanswered. To Kirov he said, "She'll have to do." He took the other man into a corner.

"We must be careful," he cautioned.

"Why?"

"Kostandov is so far not directly implicated in Fall-Out, merely tainted."

"Meaning?"

"That at this date he is not a party to the fraud—but at some date he may be. Whatever suits us."

Kirov nodded in understanding. He could still see Irina Terekhova. She had found a chair and was sitting quietly. From the reception desk keen eyes watched them. Kirov looked around idly for the monitoring camera and found one tucked under a cornice on its rotating arm. It was pointing at them. Did it have a directional microphone attached? Was Grishin speaking for its benefit?

"Forget the woman," said Grishin. "Bear in mind that Kostandov may have lost faith in Pokrebsky. He may—should—be frightened of what he is being drawn into. He may be willing to sacrifice Pokrebsky."

"If he does that, then he will preserve the Army's reputation—and control. Is that what you want?" Kirov felt distracted. He turned from

Irina to Grishin, detecting a subtle change of emphasis. Grishin was warm, almost fatherly.

"We can't win everything—not in a single turn."

"Can't we? How far does Fall-Out go? Kostandov may not have been involved in 1974, but someone in the Army supported Pokrebsky in his deals with Atommash over the equipment and the design changes. Expose that and the whole foundation of army control over the nuclear program will be shown to be rotten." Kirov stopped. He had gone too far. Fall-Out was not to be talked of: it was something more than Sokolskoye—magic words that brought curses.

"Fall-Out is not in question," Grishin said circumspectly. "This investigation isn't a reopening of Fall-Out. Forget I ever mentioned it. Yes, it does go further than Pokrebsky. It goes too far—you understand, *too far.* Yes," he added uncomfortably and then, reverting to friendliness, he put a hand on Kirov's shoulder and confided: "If we press too hard, then the Army will rally behind Pokrebsky to save itself. It's enough that we separate the Army from him. Any new appointment to the Inspectorate would, in the circumstances, only be made with our—advice. And after that—who knows, eh?"

"Who knows," Kirov agreed, thinking that not once had Grishin mentioned the substance of the disaster at Sokolskoye: as if it were no part of the subject.

The Colonel meanwhile said briskly, "Let's be off to see our friends. Oh, and you'd better bring your damned woman along."

0900 hours

Kostandov and Pokrebsky were waiting in the General's room. Kostandov was stonily calm, greeting Grishin with punctilious correctness. The Director showed a nervous mobility, now friendly, now aggressive.

He knows, thought Kirov with a bitter satisfaction.

"Well, Colonel, it appears that we have a problem at the plant," Kostandov stated flatly.

"Some confusion," Pokrebsky intervened. "That's all. Nothing that can't be solved between us," he offered tentatively. He eyed Irina Terekhova with suspicion and surprise. Kirov had directed her to a chair and sat next to her. "What do you say?"

"No confusion."

"Excuse me?"

"There is no confusion," Grishin repeated. He drove his first wedge, at the same time giving Kostandov a way out. "You have been lied to, General. May I have a cigarette? Yes, lied to. I hate to say it." He reached for a cigarette from the tortoiseshell box on the other man's desk, taking one and passing a second to Kirov. The gesture established his command of the situation.

"Nonsense!" Pokrebsky retorted. "This is just a cover for a blunder by the KGB! What do you have?"

"Yes, what do you have?" Kostandov enquired.

"Some fool report from a person not qualified to form an opinion," Pokrebsky continued in a shrewd guess aimed at the weakest of his opponents. "Dr. Terekhina, isn't it?"

"Terekhova."

"Not a name familiar to me," he remarked to Kostandov, implying that further comment was unnecessary.

Not the way, thought Kirov. Irina was opening her file of papers impassively. Pokrebsky had not recognized his misjudgment. An attack against such an insignificant target only lent it significance. Kostandov, having initially ignored her, now examined her carefully.

"Dr. Terekhova volunteered her help," Grishin explained. "Out of her concern," he added, without bothering to hide his insincerity.

"What are your qualifications?" Kostandov asked her.

She told him, keeping her voice clear and precise.

"Irrelevant," snorted Pokrebsky.

"Not entirely," said Kostandov more guardedly.

"We could put Dr. Terekhova's findings to the full Committee," Grishin offered. "They could be checked. Do you want them to be checked? We are only lending assistance to the Army."

"And I'm supposed to thank you for that?" Kostandov responded with a hint of testiness.

"If you like. I don't insist. Shall I ask Dr. Terekhova to begin?"

"I object!" Pokrebsky blurted out.

"Shut up!" Kostandov snapped back. Pokrebsky recoiled as if bitten. For a second there was silence. A policeman being born, Kirov remembered again, this time thinking how the simplicity of the words sounded like a tale for children. He wondered how Bogdanov was getting on with the boy. Irina Terekhova was probably thinking of the same thing: balancing the two matters, Sokolskoye and her child, as

124

he supposed women, in various fashions always had to do. Kostandov was saying to her in a mild tone, "Please explain, comrade."

She put her file down. Doing it without notes — without a safety net — all of them without safety nets. Including Klyuev — Kirov reminded himself that while they were talking, the standoff in the control room could have broken down into a bloodbath. The lake could have been emptied into the reservoir. Echoes of *Chernobyl* — the word that must never be used.

"I should like to take notes," said Kostandov, and he rang for his secretary to bring a pad. Still giving Pokrebsky time to come up with an answer. He passed the moment with a few friendly remarks to Grishin, and the Colonel responded in kind. The secretary came in with a pad, handed it to the General, then left with a studied glance at the other woman. "Please," he said next. "Would you like to begin?"

Sokolskoye: 0955 hours

"A cigarette?" Nechvolodov asked. "Why not? — or do you think I have some secret weapon in my cigarette case?"

"Shut your mouth!" Klyuev answered. *Relax,* he told himself, feeling the sweat globules tickling his hairline: too fat — bad for the heart — lose weight and don't drink so much. "OK, smoke if you want to."

The case was on the console. It was made of crocodile skin and had a gold monogram. Nechvolodov smiled and picked it up. He took out a cigarette and lit it, then extended the case to Akhmatov. The Major helped himself stiffly and accepted a light.

"And you?"

"Sure," said Klyuev; he held out a hand, and Nechvolodov dropped a cigarette into it. The KGB man fumbled after his own lighter, then remembered that it was by his bedside. The cigarette hung limply from his lip.

"You want a light?" the other man asked and proffered his lighter.

"Just get back! The cigarette will keep." But Klyuev kept it in his mouth like a baby's pacifier and felt the end go damp and by degrees fall apart. The gun was still pointed at Akhmatov, who remained stone-faced. Klyuev looked at the gun. He couldn't remember having used one in anger. He supposed he must have.

Waves of lassitude swept over him. Maybe the others felt the same

125

way, but they didn't show it. He rested his gun hand on his lap, but it didn't seem to help; the fingers were still so tensed that they felt rigid. They had become an object to him. He didn't trust them to work if it came to — No, it wouldn't come to that; those things didn't happen to fat, middle-aged men.

It was more than two and a half hours since he had called Kirov. What were they doing in Moscow? Did they understand what was happening? Did they care? In the stillness his detachment became more pronounced. The stiffness of his hand was spreading up his arm like an infection. *Pitter-patter*, the dust of his body crumbling on the floor. Sweat on his forehead. *Pitter-patter*, the damp earth on his face. It was a pity he didn't have Bor'yan to talk to. The former plant director was a good guy. You could always talk over your troubles. He even seemed to understand why Klyuev had abandoned him. Well, he had to, didn't he? People went too far and had to be given up. It was necessary. Even Moscow — him, Klyuev — if it were necessary. It was a bloody shame, though, about Bor'yan.

Outside it was daylight, and on the level ground outside the control block the soldiers and the plant operators had formed a mute crowd in the snow, waiting for a sign like peasants petitioning the Tsar.

Moscow: 1000 hours

"It was all part of a gigantic fraud," Grishin said in a voice so subdued as to be almost philosophical. After Irina Terekhova had finished her explanations there was a pause for questions, but instead there came only silence. Irina had delivered her account with such completeness and lucidity that questions seemed superfluous. More — in her description, from the finding of the dead fish through the design changes to the plant, the failures in the equipment and the switching-off of the radiation monitors, she had established a mood. Her frankness and clarity made evasiveness and ambiguity appear naked. But at the same time they became intensely necessary because the truth exposed was too much to face. So Grishin added consolingly to Kostandov, "Of course, it was before your time — nothing you could do about it — not your responsibility." Kostandov nodded appreciatively.

"Fraud —" Pokrebsky caught himself and interjected, "Why does everything have to be fraud?" To Kostandov he pleaded, "There were equipment shortages and sound technical reasons why designs were changed to economize on equipment."

"We are still continuing our criminal investigations," Grishin went on, still feeding the General a lifeline. "But to what end? Water under the bridge. The criminals may have moved on." He let his eyes drift over Pokrebsky, but not too pointedly. "Isn't there something more *constructive* we can do?"

"Like what?"

Grishin suggested, as if this were an idea newly come to him, that they might talk about a reorganization of the Inspectorate — a joint Army–KGB steering committee: "a collaborative effort," he called it, to disguise any implication of victory. And to preempt any need for Kostandov's agreement, he began to discuss details so that the General was diverted even before he had considered the principle. It was all understood, Grishin implied. Not once did he refer to Sokolskoye.

Kirov let his attention fade, feeling that the problem had been somehow flattened into two dimensions. Where was the urgency, the sense of scale of the disaster? He saw Irina Terekhova bite her lip, but he could not interpret the action. Anger? Determination? He was nagged by the sensation that she was beyond him, evading his attempts to understand — more mysterious than what had really happened at Sokolskoye, which at bottom was mere human folly and corruption. He wondered whether she had followed the subtle drift of Grishin's offer to Kostandov: that even Pokrebsky could be saved from the debacle if the terms were right. On behalf of the KGB he could offer absolution of a kind.

Sokolskoye: 1030 hours

The tip of the cigarette crumbled and fell to the floor, leaving a shred of paper clinging to his lip. Klyuev licked at it circumspectly. He spat the shreds of tobacco out. The wall clock dropped another digit — *click*.

Kirov had told him that there was a solution to the contamination in the lake. Petya had confided in him — a real pal. What was it? There had been talk about raising the height of the dam and about diverting the Chiraka and all the streams that fed the lake — it would at least give them time if what was in there was really terrible. But Klyuev didn't believe in those solutions, even though some surveyors and civil engineers had visited the site and looked the place over. It wasn't possible—not in a matter of a few months, not during the dead of winter. No, said Petya, that wasn't the answer. Then what was? Some fancy American technology. No details. But there was a man, an Englishman, and he was here in Moscow. Just hang on, Petya told him. Just hang on.

"I'll have that smoke," he said. Nechvolodov shrugged, opened his cigarette case, took out a cigarette, and threw it across the room. Klyuev tried to catch it one-handedly. He missed, and it fell to the floor. He stooped to pick it up, moving his eyes fractionally from Akhmatov. It was a mistake.

Akhmatov leaped out of his chair. Klyuev was leaning forward, hand groping on the floor. Akhmatov's foot lashed out. Klyuev felt the blow on his chin, his head reeled backward, his finger tightened on the trigger. There was an explosion, and a bullet passed through the ceiling. He rolled over to avoid another kick, but Akhmatov wasn't out for blood. The Major put a foot on Klyuev's gun hand and pointed his own weapon at the KGB man's head.

"Let go," he commanded coolly.

Klyuev let go of the gun. What the hell, he had tried his best. Akhmatov scooped the pistol from the floor and then set the fallen chair upright.

"Sit!" he ordered, and Klyuev sat. I'm too old for this, he thought. They couldn't complain back in Moscow. He felt a curious sense of relief. Let them drain the lake! It was on their heads! Fuck them!

From his own seat Nechvolodov collected himself, and a smile curled about his features. He stared at Akhmatov then at the console.

"I'll get on with the business," he said, and his right hand flicked over a page of the operating manual.

"Stay where you are!"

"What?" Nechvolodov swung round abruptly and saw in the Major's face not the expression of an ally but dislike, contempt.

"Don't touch a thing," Akhmatov hissed.

"But . . ."

"Nothing's changed except that the Army is back in control. I'll kill you just as easily as he would. We still wait for the telephone call." Akhmatov held the two guns, one pointed at each of the other men. "You may as well have that smoke," he said to Klyuev.

Outside there was a rising noise from the crowd waiting in the snow and a couple of shots in the air as soldiers maintained order. There was a jingling sound but it wasn't the harnesses of the Tsar's cossacks, just someone rattling the door and a voice asking whether everything was all right in there.

Moscow: 1045 hours

"You seem to be assuming that we have a disaster at Sokolskoye," said Pokrebsky. Eyes turned slowly toward him. Kostandov and Grishin, who had been conversing with growing intimacy over coffee, now regarded Pokrebsky as an interloper. "So there may have been errors," Pokrebsky conceded. "But disaster? What evidence do you have? So there's some plutonium in the lake — so what? Two hundred and fifty grams maybe — you've seen the water analysis. The Gorkovskoye reservoir will dilute that without any difficulty." To Kostandov he said, "The plutonium in only a problem so long as it is concentrated in the Chiraka lake. The level of toxicity there is undoubtedly causing problems. But in the reservoir it won't signify. That's why it's so important that we drain the lake." With that, his own voice drained away and he slumped back in his chair with a self-regarding look as though one part of him were dissociating itself and saying to the other, "It's not my fault."

The resistance by now was purely reflexive. Kirov had seen it close enough to be certain. It was ingrained by the system. Deny everything. There is nothing so unforgivable as to ask for forgiveness. Deny — and luck and good connections may save you. There but for the grace . . . This is what Irina Terekhova doesn't understand. What does she make of the silences as the truth unfolds? He glanced at her.

"There is another water analysis." She dropped the words slowly and singly. A chair creaked, and attention followed the intrusion as if it were important, and only by degrees was the subject picked up. Someone said, "Good — good," in an unattributable voice as though the walls participated.

"Another water analysis?" Kostandov questioned her; and shuffling his papers he inquired after the dates of the earlier analyses. "Do we have that one?" he said quietly, and to the others, "Do we have that one?"

"It wasn't circulated," Grishin answered cryptically.

"Not circulated?" Kostandov threw up his hands, but unemphatically, meaning that he could not be expected to have an opinion. Pokrebsky sat in silence.

Irina asked, "Do you remember the report on the toxicity of plutonium and the hydrology report?" Yes, they remembered those. "They tell us the scale of the potential disaster."

"Do they?"

"Once we know how much plutonium is in the water."

"Two hundred and fifty grams," Pokrebsky repeated wanly. "More or less. Analyses are unreliable in this area."

Kostandov asked, "Why wasn't this one copied around?"

"Discrepancies—high margins of error—unreliable sampling techniques." The words dribbled out, then Pokrebsky recovered and said, "The matter is significant only if the body of contaminated water is large and the level of toxicity exceeds one hundred times lethal dosage."

"There are five kilograms of plutonium nitrate in the lake," Irina Terekhova said. There was no reaction. "On the Inspectorate's own analysis"—now she seemed embarrassed—"in theory it's enough to kill the population of the Soviet Union three times over."

"In theory," Pokrebsky objected without taking the point further. And for a fraction Kirov saw Irina hesitate. *Destroy him! Destroy him!* Kirov wondered why she held back. It wasn't failure of confidence. Something else. *Don't feel sorry for him!*

"The lake," she resumed carefully, "contains 1.4 million cubic meters of water. The concentration of plutonium in each liter of water is 1,440 times the lethal dosage. Dilution and dispersal in the Gorkovskoye–Volga system will not handle that volume at that concentration—at least, not as far as Gorky. There are 279 million people in our country. A quarter of them live in the Volga Basin. It contains a third of Soviet industry and grows a fifth of our agricultural produce. Sokolskoye . . ."

Sokolskoye what? Kirov waited, but she allowed her words to fall there, implying that the truth had to be received as well as given.

Kostandov sat palely back, and when she had finished leaned forward and wrote in brief words his understanding of the Sokolskoye Incident.

Sixty million people.

Book Two

The first law about doing business with the Russians is to remember that you are not selling to them. They are buying from you. But once you have learned that, they can be the most reliable customers in the world.

Executive World, August 1985, p.7

9

There was a girl.

George Twist had always known there would be. He had no particular image of her; still less was he looking for her: but the state of his home life, the state of his business, his blood-alcohol level, his whole life all made it as certain as if he had picked her number out of one of those famous little black books which he didn't possess and asked her to meet him in the bar next to the Japanese restaurant off the foyer of the Mezhdunarodnaya, say, around eight o'clock.

In other words, it was an accident.

George had had accidents before, things that happened in his life like falling under a bus—except that some accidents fall into the special class of those we conspire with. That last drink might have been one of them. "Come on, George," said Jack Melchior, "another day, another dollar, chin up—the Russkies may be in a better mood for business tomorrow. Meanwhile hit your tonsils with this little concoction, old lad, a little gin-and-something that used to work wonders for morale." So George took it and drank it, which made him feel better, and he left Jack Melchior drinking with Wormold and took a stroll to get away from the Boy Scout outing that was going on in the British pub.

He stood outside the hotel in his jacket and open-collared shirt where the Russians had to brush past him in their overcoats except for one or two who were maybe keeping an eye on him but you never could tell. The night was there but not so dark, the river flecked with dribbles of light, the sky glowing orange through a veil of falling sleet that ran away as black water in the gutters. On the farther bank the Ukraina was piled up in dark stacks in the form-less shades.

Moscow Nights.

It was the name of the only tune that ever seemed to get played in the hard-currency bars — that, and sometimes "Kalinka." There was a jazz-clarinetist who had made a hit of "Moscow Nights" back in the early sixties — he seemed to remember — back in a time when innocence and the novelty of bowling seemed to go together. How did the tune go? Dum-dum-da-dee-da — mumbling the melody on his lips until he was cold and his hair was damp with sleet and it was time to have his accident with the girl.

If George had been a real hero, things would still have been all right. For one thing, he would have remembered that no one could be trusted who felt as cheerful as he did after that last drink. But then, George had only a temporary commission — Acting Company Hero — valid for the duration, which made him not too far removed from Jack Melchior, who sometimes claimed the rank of major — "A field-commission, earned under fire. Not confirmed, though. Envious rivals back at HQ. Pity, really." So things were not all right. George shuddered from the cold and went back in to the lobby and into the bar next to the Japanese restaurant.

The girl was not very pretty — by Western standards few Russian girls were — but her makeup was good and her face had a natural friendliness and charm, with a snub nose, high bright cheeks and two neat rows of teeth that bit her tongue just so when she wasn't speaking but listening sympathetically with her head cocked slightly to one side. Her name was Natasha and she said she worked at a clerical job with the Moscow city authorities; and she sat alone at one of the tables with a sequined purse in front of her, a pack of H&B cigarettes and a glass of Coca-Cola — the last because she didn't really like alcohol, it turned Russian men into pigs — and she came to the bar on account of the good company because her daytime job was so boring.

George asked if he might sit at her table. She said that was OK, using the English expression, and smiled. George brought his drink and took the seat next to hers while a tune struck up which turned out to be "Moscow Nights."

"You are an American?" she asked with one eyebrow raised.

"No, sorry—English. Is that OK by you?"

"English?" She laughed, showing her neat white teeth. "Yes, is OK, in fact wonderfulest, more wonderfulest than American, who talk too much."

"I'm glad you think so."

"I do! I do! English is my preferredest nation," she said, and smiled again in a way that seemed to George to be particularly frank. And it was the openness of this smile that caught him rather than her sexuality—though he was aware of the smoothness of her skin and the scent of her perfume, which was also called "Moscow Nights"—because George, without knowing it, was at an age when sentimentality is almost as powerful a drive as sex. She put her hand confidingly on his.

"Please," she said, "tell me: what is your name?"

George thought for a moment, knowing the significance of the question. Her age made him think of the time when all his girlfriends were eighteen or so, in an era when it was death to be called "George" and he had wanted to be known as "Elvis" but had settled on "Rick" as more plausible.

"What is your name?" she repeated, thinking that he hadn't heard.

He looked at her, seeing all the girls of eighteen he had ever known, and then answered, "Gordon," and took a sip of his drink.

How do you remember a woman's body? George had long since lost interest in abstract perfection of form. When he saw photographs of nudes, wonderfully shaped, with mouths that pouted with dreams, he found it difficult to see them as women at all. Women—real women—in his recollection, existed as details of flesh, their bodies scarcely remembered as whole, only their personalities existing in entirety. So it was with Natasha, too.

First, her scent—but he thought the word should be "smell," because it was the delicate but real smell of her body that he remembered beneath the wearing fragrance of "Moscow Nights" (how did the tune go?), a faint, salty, animal smell, made mild by a clean and plain soap and, here and there, a dusting of talcum powder that was caught in pale lines where the skin folded softly. There was a vaccination scar just visible. It was on the flesh of

135

her upper right arm, a small medallion, lighter in color and surrounded by faint freckles. He had touched it with his fingertips as she took her clothes off and laid them with great care over a chair in his room.

He noted the small imperfections of her body. She lay for a while on the bed, the swelling part of her belly glazed by the diffuse lights of the city filtering through the window. Her breasts lay full and flat, the large aureoles deeply colored, and, beneath the left one, a small mole brown as a nut.

He remembered her skin not as waxed bald into some imitation of plastic, but as fine with invisible down so that as they lay afterward in the darkness side by side where the air would cool them, the hairs on his arm grazed against hers and he felt her electric presence.

It's passed, he thought in that moment of sadness after love, not certain what it was that had passed. He listened to her faking her own release, her timing wrong, perhaps through inexperience but perhaps not, which didn't matter since he knew that it was done out of consideration for him and he liked her for it. And, too, when she smiled and said, "That was perfectest," which both of them knew to be a lie; but she said it as if it were a shared joke, affectionate, not to be taken too seriously—perfectest, perhaps in a wholly different way.

He paid her well, so she was in no rush to go. They lay in bed with the sheets tucked up to their chins and dozed and talked about this and that, since there was no way of screwing for eight hours on end. They smiled a little and laughed a little, had a drink, smoked a cigarette. At one point she cried a little, her face turned away into the pillow, which wasn't supposed to happen but George knew that it sometimes did, an accident just like the whole business was an accident. When she stopped, she said, "You are nicest," and rested her head against his so that he could smell her hair, a cheap shampoo, not unpleasant, with a scent of roses. He slept then for a few hours with his arm around her until it was daylight and someone was hammering on the door.

George slipped into some trousers and a shirt while the banging went on. The girl stayed in the bed with a scared look on her face, clutching her sequined purse. He looked at her and thought, "So this is where it starts. This is how it happens." But he didn't care; he asked who was at the door, and a very English voice replied, "A friend of Jack Melchior. Come on, man, let me in." George slipped the latch and opened the door.

"George Twist?" A big man, somewhere in his fifties, with light brown hair and a friendly enough face that was slowly being taken over by a pair of spiky eyebrows. He was polite, maybe even a little shy, and he waited for George to step back before entering; then he came in, stooping slightly though the door was big enough for him. He wore a duffel coat. "George Twist?" he repeated and stuck out a hand to be shaken. "Yes, I suppose you must be—a bit obvious really." He seemed out of practice in meeting Englishmen. "My name is—"

"Neville Lucas."

"Ah—you know. Well, that saves a bit of time."

"Jack pointed you out to me. The other night. In the bar."

"Yes. Well, good. And gave you the whole unsavory story of my career as a traitor, I imagine. Neville Lucas, alias 'Working Class Shit of the Year, 1964' or 'The Man Most Likely to Fail.' "

"I'd never heard of you."

"Not surprising. It merely goes to prove that even spying against your own country is only a nine-day wonder. Hope I'm not interrupting anything," Lucas added, eyeing the girl. When George didn't reply, he spoke a few words to her in Russian which seemed to soothe her, and she got out of bed and began to get dressed. He waited until she had gone, passing his time picking up small objects about the hotel room and putting them down again like a shopper hunting for bargains.

"Not a good idea, picking up girls in a place like this." He had taken off his coat and made himself at home in a chair. He was wearing a brown corduroy jacket and a fawn-colored cardigan with buttons that looked like footballs.

"Because they're in the KGB?" George was trying to identify the other man's accent; he thought it was from the northeast, Northumberland or Durham, because of the lilt.

"Not exactly, but that's the general idea. They report to the KGB, anyway. It's the paperwork, not the shagging that gets the poor bitches down."

137

"And then the KGB put the bite on, is that it? A bit of blackmail? Because, if it is, it won't work with me." He looked at Lucas, but the other man didn't react. *Stuff him!* George ignored him and put on his socks. "Nobody cares. Least of all me."

"No?" Lucas sounded indifferent. "No, I suppose not. Hadn't really thought about it. Don't imagine that the KGB did, either."

"But they provided her?"

"Oh, sure. You don't think you'd have been able to slip her past the *dezhurnaya* otherwise, do you?"

"The *dezhurnaya?*"

"The floor lady who keeps an eye on the guests. They must have told her to let you pass with the girl. It's a standard KGB tactic, one of their reflex actions. They're a bit short on imagination and not absolutely up-to-date on the current state of Western morality. People tell me that everybody back home is fucking like rabbits and nobody gives a damn. I wouldn't know." Lucas spoke easily; he had a voice with a little humor, a little wistfulness.

"But you're here," said George, "and you're in the KGB, aren't you? What rank—a colonel?"

"Something like that," said Lucas unconcernedly, then added; "Back—you know where—*home,* I only made corporal when I was in the Army. Over here, on the other hand, I'm a colonel. The Soviet Union is a land of opportunity for the working classes. Mind if I smoke?" He took out a packet of Park Drive cigarettes and rambled on while he lit one. "I don't rely on the rank much, though it comes in handy if you want to get theater tickets. Do you like the theater?" he asked, as if there were some urgency in the question. Then he sighed and said, "You know, it's good to be able to talk to an Englishman."

George continued dressing. He went into the bathroom to shave. Lucas was evidently unembarrassed. The conversation was kept up between rooms.

"Those cigarettes," George asked, "are they the ones I brought? Jack wanted them for you?"

"That's right. I can't get them in Moscow and I like a taste of Olde England. I get fed up with Marlboros. Any chance you could manage a couple of bottles of beer next time you come out here? Mackeson? Yes," Lucas said thoughtfully, "I could fancy a Mackeson—or a Guinness at a pinch, I'm not too fussy."

George returned to the bedroom, wiping his face on a towel. "I don't know that I'll be coming back."

"Ah—business not too good, eh?"

George didn't answer.

Lucas went on: "These things take time. Here in particular. It's the system; you get used to it."

Time is something I don't have, thought George; but all he said was "Sure, sure," and dumped the towel on the bed. Lucas, meanwhile, was rummaging through his suitcase.

"What the hell are you doing?"

"Sorry." Lucas dropped a pair of ties and gave a friendly, apologetic smile. "Nothing sinister intended. Should have asked. Simple curiosity—you know how it is—wondering how people are really living in England." He stood aside for George to close the case.

"Nothing much has changed."

"No? I'm surprised you say that. From where I stand—not having been to the old place in twenty-odd years, not since I legged it over the frontier—everything seems to have changed. You could have knocked me sideways when Marks and Spencer started selling food."

"I'd forgotten that they didn't use to—just clothes before, wasn't it?"

Lucas nodded. "You tend to remember that sort of thing, living in exile. In that respect treachery has the effect of making you terribly loyal." He sat down again and lit another cigarette.

"What do you want from me?" George asked. Lucas seemed surprised.

"I hoped I'd be able to do you a favor, George. I can call you 'George,' can't I?"

"Whatever you like," George answered impatiently. "What favors are you going to do for me? Or am I supposed to be doing favors for the USSR?"

"Oh, favors can be mutual, George. Just because something helps the Soviet Union, it isn't necessarily bad. I mean, provided that everything is open and that everyone can see the joint benefits."

"So you *do* want me to help the Soviet Union."

Lucas chuckled pleasantly. "Be reasonable. In my position I can hardly offer you a deal that doesn't have something in it for the Russians. What do you care? Tell me what you want; I don't know your business. Jack Melchior says that you are trying to see the Minister of Gas. What for? Tell me these things and perhaps I can help you."

"I want—" George hesitated. The question suddenly sounded like a wildest-dreams invitation: three wishes and a crock of gold. "I want the contracts for the fifty LNG plants that the Soviets are going to build over the next ten years. Or, at any rate," he added, "a few of them."

"Is that a lot to want?" Lucas asked calmly. "I wouldn't know— not my line."

"Yes, it's a lot."

"I see." Lucas got up and approached the suitcase again. "You don't mind if I have a root around, do you, George? Helps me to think." He lifted the lid and fumbled over a couple of paperback novels. "Any chance of letting me have these? I mean, after you've finished with them."

"Help yourself."

"Very grateful." Lucas pocketed one and flipped through the other, speaking all the while. "One of the big problems the Soviets have—stop me, George, if I'm teaching you to suck eggs—one of their big problems, as I was saying, is the American embargo on high-technology exports. How do you feel about that?"

"We don't sell computers. It doesn't affect our company."

"No? But it isn't just computers. There are other things on the blacklist."

"I suppose so."

"I don't know them offhand, but they exist. The point being that in many cases the Russians are willing to buy these things but they can't find anyone prepared to sell. They resent that, George, resent it quite a lot. They regard high technology, the achievements of the human intellect, as the common property of mankind." Lucas glanced in George's direction and went on casually, "Of course, I can see that there may be a different point of view. But I'm sure you'll admit that this sort of thing only adds to East-West tension."

"I can see that."

"Good."

George waited, but Lucas was apparently satisfied with whatever he was trying to achieve. He was ready to leave, hunting for his coat and smiling his embarrassed smile as he thrust his arms into the sleeves. He held out a hand, and George took it.

"Well, it's been good to see you, George. I"—he was searching for a word—"appreciate the chance to talk to another Englishman. Oh, and don't worry, I'll see what I can do for you, talk to people and so on. No promises, mind you."

"OK, fine." George couldn't think of anything else to say. *I need to freshen up. I need a drink.* He said, "Call me if anything turns up," and showed Lucas the door. He closed it behind the visitor and stayed for a moment staring at the fire regulations and thinking that you would need a guide and compass to find the emergency stairs shown in the floor plan. And then he remembered that Lucas had just invited him to sell American-embargoed technology to the Russians.

And he remembered, too, that he hadn't said no.

10

"His first name is George," said Kirov. "Remember that because you'll be meeting him." She raised a cautious eyebrow at this. "His father's name was Ronald, but the fact is immaterial since the English don't use their father's name: but I imagine you know this already because you speak English."

"Yes, Major."

He had telephoned her with a sense of urgency in his voice. She knew that there had been a Politburo meeting to discuss the report and conclusions on the Sokolskoye Incident, and divined that in some way his pressing request to see her stemmed from that. And she agreed, though common sense told her that she should distance herself; that her part was done. She was surprised at her own reaction.

"I wasn't sure you would know," he was saying. "You've never been to England, and that makes a difference—a matter of customs, of fine distinctions."

"I suppose so," she answered. "I should like to go there; as a visitor, of course."

"Have you ever been to the West?"

She shook her head. "But next summer I expect to be visiting Geneva. There is a conference on nuclear hazards to the environment. I have been invited to attend as a delegate."

"I promise you'll enjoy yourself," he said, and smiled.

She found his urbanity superficial. From the beginning he had struck her as naturally tense, though he was now more at ease in her apartment. When he picked up a book to study it, he felt no need to put it down when she came back into the room; and when she moved the photographs into new positions, he noticed and asked why she had done so, as if the old arrangement had been part of a familiar home.

"Remember the name — George," he repeated.

"George."

"He'll expect you to use it, not immediately, but after only a little while. Try not to appear embarrassed speaking it; that would only make him feel uncomfortable and suspect an ulterior motive. Say it again."

"George."

"How does it feel?"

"I'll get used to it." It felt distasteful. It was an act of intimacy with a stranger.

"Please," he said, revealing one of his rare flashes of sympathy. "This is important; George is important. In fact, for the moment, though he doesn't know it, he's the most important person in the Soviet Union."

She agreed: George was important.

"He's forty-three years old," Kirov said. He produced a photograph from his wallet, as if he wanted to show her his children. It was recent, she thought, taken here in Moscow: that was just a feeling; there was nothing from which you could tell. Forty-three; she would have guessed a little older. Not that it was an unattractive face, but it seemed tired and the eyes had the lackluster gaze of a subject who doesn't know he is being photographed.

"Married," said Kirov. "He has one child, a girl. He's a qualified chemical engineer and, as of last month, sales director of Chemconstruct PLC. His salary is forty-five thousand pounds a year, which," he added, anticipating her question, "would be a considerable fortune in this country; but in England George is not a rich man, though his style of life is high. He would say that he lived 'comfortably' — that is his word: it's a very bourgeois conception."

"Is it?" she asked. What did he want by bringing this Englishman to her like a cat bringing a dead bird into the kitchen? "Has he been to Moscow before?"

"In 1976."

"Why?"

"He was a salesman trying to sell a fertilizer plant. Unsuccessfully, as it turned out."

"Ah." She tried to picture the Englishman younger, inexperienced. "Not a very good salesman, it seems." She imagined his failure, and it made him more accessible.

"He was considered quite shrewd," Kirov partly contradicted her. "This was Techmashimport's assessment—and they had to deal with him. On the other hand, he was unsuccessful; so perhaps that assessment was mistaken." The contradiction apparently troubled him. She assumed that there was an attitude he wanted to adopt and he was looking for material to support it. He wanted to despise the Englishman?

"Three years ago he was sent to America to manage a small subsidiary company, Sep Tech. This, of course, is where our interest lies. George Twist built Sep Tech up. We must assume that he wants it to succeed."

Irina saw now what he was doing: constructing a picture of the other man as a creature of needs which could be fed and manipulated; a man of weaknesses who could be disregarded so that his fate became immaterial. Poor George, who was hardly human at all.

She asked, "What is his wife like?"

"She's an invalid. She has suffered for ten years from a wasting illness, and now she is bedridden. That's why there is only one child."

"Is that all you know?"

"Isn't it enough?"

She couldn't tell whether he was being serious.

"Is she a person? Is she important to him?"

"She's his burden," Kirov said after a moment's thought.

"Nothing more?"

"His job takes him away from home for long periods. He employs a full-time nurse to take care of her. The child is sent away to school because her mother can't look after her. Isn't that a burden—a financial burden, at least?"

"But he could leave her."

"Or kill her—people do. The fact that he hasn't murdered her doesn't mean that she isn't a burden to him."

Arkady was whimpering in his sleep. Irina excused herself and went into the bedroom. Her son had woken and was sitting up in bed in the darkness.

"It's too dark," he complained.

She went to the window and drew back the curtains. The night haze of the city lifted the darkness a little so that objects in the room stood out as black shapes. In the street was parked one of the unfamiliar cars that followed Kirov around like an evil rumor. The driver stayed in the vehicle, smoking. She sat for a while on the bed with her arm around the child, comforting him until she felt him lean against her breast, asleep. She kissed him and laid him down and then returned to the other room to find Kirov fingering through a stack of records.

"Do you have any Mozart?" he asked.

"I don't know. It belongs to Konstantin—my husband. He likes only folk tunes and military bands."

"And you don't have any tastes in music?"

"Yes, I enjoy music."

"Ah!" He smiled, not unpleasantly, and left the subject alone, but she felt his question as a nerve that had been touched. It had of course always been possible to buy records that pleased her. Konstantin would not have objected to her playing them on his record player. Somehow it had not occurred to her.

Kirov replaced the records, passing his hand as he did so over one of Terekhov's letters; the military censor's chop was impressed on the envelope. She saw, next to it, a bottle of wine and length of *chorizo* sausage such as couldn't be obtained in Moscow, even at Yeliseyev's.

"I hope you don't mind," he said.

"No—thank you." She remembered Terekhov wooing her in his decent fashion with practical presents that he affected not to notice. "Just a little thing that I came by. I thought you might need it." Terekhov was a man of imposing appearance and fearsome reputation, but at times surprisingly gentle.

"George is unfaithful to his wife," Kirov said, perhaps to shock her.

"Does she know?"

"Who can tell?"

"She's an invalid," Irina hazarded an answer. "He's a business-man who travels and stays in hotels where there are women. That's how it is, isn't it, even here in our hotels in Moscow? She understands this. Perhaps she knows and forgives him."

Without any sign of intentional cruelty, Kirov said, "She is dependent—physically, financially—she has no choices."

"Perhaps." Irina felt herself reacting to his dismissiveness. Kirov evidently wanted her help to understand the Englishman, but he needed a model of the other man that was simple, mechanical, a series of levers to be pulled. She said, "Your picture of George has no depth to it. All you have are uninteresting facts. Where did you get them from?"

"We have records."

"Ah. You investigated him when he came to Moscow in 1976. What for? To see whether he was spying for the British? To recruit him for our side?" She provided her own answer. "No, it's more simple than that, isn't it? He was investigated just because he was there, without any thought or plan, because there is machinery for investigating people and it has to be used on something."

"Please, let's eat," he suggested.

She made a light supper of the food he had brought and laid it on the table among her papers. Kirov picked at his portion without interest. Between moments of attention to her own plate, she caught his brown eyes studying her and wondering if he saw her, too, as a specimen pinned out for dissection.

"Does George have a mistress?"

"No."

"What does he do?"

Kirov halted with his fork poised. "He picks up prostitutes in the hotels where he stays. Sometimes, not always. It depends whether he has been drinking. He feels lonely, disoriented; that is how it happens." He placed a piece of *chorizo* in his mouth; it was full of meat and crunched when he bit it. "This is good. Do you like it?"

"Yes." She responded by taking a piece. It leaked red spice like blood where her fork went in. "So George's adultery is not deliberate—not planned."

"What do you think?"

"That he has never made a decision to be unfaithful to his wife."

"You are right: he is not a courageous man."

Kirov got up from the table and went over to the chair where he had placed his papers. He returned with a dossier tagged and classified and marked with warnings that its contents were danger-

146

ous to the uninitiated. He opened it and produced several pages of flimsy paper.

"This is a report of George's activities on his present visit. Two nights ago he slept with a prostitute who works the bars at the Mezhdunarodnaya. She has been interviewed." He began to read from the page in what seemed a contrived flatness of expression. To distance himself from his material?

"Question: What name did the man call himself?

"Answer: Gordon.

"Question: Are you sure that it wasn't George?

"Answer: It was Gordon. Who is George?"

Kirov looked up with an expression of disinterested pity.

"See what sort of man he is? What did he hope to achieve by such a feeble lie? He couldn't suppose that we didn't know who he was. It wouldn't protect his wife, who in any case had no way of knowing what he was doing. It was just a small act of cowardice. George is not a hero." Kirov delivered himself of this as if it were a mathematical demonstration.

"Question: Did the man talk about his business?

"Answer: No. I asked him, but he wouldn't tell me even what he did for a living.

"Question: So he was deliberately secretive?

"Answer: No—I don't think so. He seemed worried, maybe it was about his business. He just didn't want to talk about it."

"Please—stop," Irina interrupted, but he gave no sign of wanting to hear. She found the flatness of his voice almost insupportable: it turned the human exchange of words into a desolation.

"Question: What *did* you talk about?

"Answer: Nothing—well, I don't mean *nothing*, I mean we just talked about small things. He told me a little about how it was in England. This was only when I asked about it. I liked that; it made a change. Lots of times men want to tell you all about themselves and their wives, a sort of confession; it's boring. Or they ask me questions: Why do I do what I do? Do I come from an unhappy home? He wasn't like that. Not that he wasn't interested in what I had to say; but he left it to me. It was different. It was nice. He asked me about my perfume. I said it was called 'Moscow Nights' and that made him laugh; I don't know why. He had a nice laugh— gentle, not poking fun."

Kirov paused. He asked, "Why should George laugh at the name of a perfume?"

"I don't know." Irina wasn't sure she wanted to know. There was a level of knowledge that was like shining a light on to a subject, a light so bright that in the end there was just light and whiteness and everything that had made for the subject's reality was gone.

"It's probably unimportant," said Kirov.

Suddenly she had an intuition.

"All of this was recorded, wasn't it?" she asked. "There were microphones in the hotel room."

"There aren't always recordings."

"No, but this time there were, weren't there? George Twist was special from the moment you identified him. Everything he has done has been observed, hasn't it? There are photographs, too — what are they? George in the bathroom? George wandering around his hotel room naked? George making love — yes, I can imagine that; you would be very particular to get those. And there was George thinking that he had some privacy, probably not even thinking about it, just assuming it; when all the while he was on public show." Irina stopped. She thought: he doesn't understand; but he knows I do. He would like to dismantle me like an ignorant child taking apart a watch. She was suddenly frightened of Kirov in a wholly new way because there was no malice in him: just a dangerous power and curiosity and a terrible acceptance of the way things were.

With an implication that everything was small talk and not too serious, he asked; "Would you like some wine? I'm sorry, I should have suggested it before."

"Thank you."

He poured a little into a glass, held it lightly to his nose, examined the color and whether the wine was corked, then took a careful sip before pouring a second glass. His manners were suave and civilized, and he seemed to her to be at ease with them as if they came to him naturally. Fear had heightened all her senses: the light seemed brighter, sounds crisp and sharp like breaking glass, her sexual awareness suddenly alive and acute. Fear contracted her perception of space: the distance between them no matter where he was in the room was too small so that her skin prickled with the sensation of him. She realized — again suddenly, and with a feeling of shock, almost revulsion—how intensely attractive he was, his hard, physical self-possession complete.

"There is something you want to ask me?" he said.

She remembered her intuition.

"Something happened," she said. "Something that couldn't be explained by the tapes."

"Recordings aren't always perfect," he countered.

"No, that's not the explanation. What is it? You had a recording, but you wanted the girl to confirm it?" She saw his eyes flicker. "You wanted the girl to confirm *everything*, and you weren't certain that she would. She was in KGB pay, but, once she had met George, you lost confidence in her." She felt now Kirov's own surprise. "Did George make such an impression?"

Kirov put down his glass and dabbed his lips with a cloth.

"He made her cry," he said simply.

"He hurt her?" Irina didn't believe that. Not George.

"No."

"Then, what?"

"They were talking—this isn't in the girl's interview—and all at once she started to cry. When she stopped, she thanked him—thanked him; though not for anything in particular."

"What were they talking about?"

He offered to refill her glass; she refused and he replenished his own. "Football," he said. "Would you believe football?" Now he picked up the bottle and studied the label. Irina realized for the first time how metaphorical his actions often were. Studying the label so that he should understand the Englishman, or perhaps herself. Analyzing the wine while he analyzed them both. He said, "George was leaving the girl to lead the conversation. She has a regular boyfriend—they often do—and he plays football for the factory where he works: she watches him regularly, stands on the sidelines and cheers like a faithful wife. She tells George this. It worries her: standing on the sidelines, swapping stories with the other wives and girlfriends; stories about other people, the way most interesting stories are; wondering whether these same women are telling stories about her. George isn't interested in football but he lets her talk and talk and then, suddenly, she is crying. So, why?" Kirov paused. He put the bottle down and let his gaze drift to hers so that Irina was caught by those brown eyes, eyes that were too close to escape. "Her motives," he went on, "her motives are quite transparent. We can see the tension of her relationship, her fear of losing her boyfriend, which makes her sensitive to rumors. She has a difficult life. But George—why did George allow the conversation to go that way? He wasn't there to listen to her troubles. If he had given any indication to her that she should stop, she would have done so—after all, she was being paid."

With that, Kirov was finished. He left his glass on the table and turned to Terekhov's collection of records again. The action implied a question about Irina Terekhova and her husband, but it was left unasked. His fingers glided over Terekhov's letters lying in their envelopes by the record player. Every small gesture that he made seemed an unwanted intimacy to her, but her body responded as if her skin were magnetized to his presence.

"So," he said, the vowel drawing out to a long close.

"I think you should leave," Irina said. "I must work tomorrow, and I have some preparations to make."

"Yes, of course," he agreed quietly. Then: "Do you have any thoughts on George?"

"Your gloves." She found his gloves on a chair and passed them to him. He took them and put them on slowly, slotting each finger carefully into the leather.

"Well?"

"George likes women," she answered at last. She saw curiosity in his eyes, a need to know. "I meant he *really* likes them—as people. That's why he isn't a hero."

11

October 15

The telephone call for George Twist came at eleven o'clock in the morning. It was Harold Barnes, but from the background clamor George could tell that he was on a speakerphone with the full team in the room. George pulled himself out of the lethargy that had affected him since his arrival in Moscow. OK, it was time to do another turn.

"Hi, Harold," he said brightly. "How's tricks back on the farm?"

"Bad news," said Barnes pleasantly.

"Really? And what can get worse?"

There was a burst of laughter at the other end of the line. Good old George, always good for a joke. Barnes came back with his hard note of self-satisfaction.

"Bulgaria—the Italians got the job."

The background murmuring rose. The Bulgarian job, dammit, which George had inherited. He had been told it was all stitched up and ready for signature. Alasdair Cranbourne chimed in like a close friend of the deceased, "Awfully bad luck, George. I know how much store you set by getting that contract. Don't take it to heart."

"I'll try not to." George tried not to.

"I don't know what else we could have done, do you, George? Hello, George, are you still there?"

"I'm here."

"I mean," said Cranbourne consolingly, "technically the Italians came second, a very poor second, that's right, isn't it, Harold?"

"Absolutely. You wouldn't let them mend your roof."

"And the price was keen — very keen — we're all satisfied about that." A languid pause during which George wished he would come to the point. "So what could it be, George, any ideas? Italian jiggery pokery? Sniffing round the client's back door, were they? Our agent didn't pick up anything of that — you'd think he would if there were anything of that sort about, wouldn't you?"

"Maybe."

"Maybe. That's very true; one can never be sure, things are so uncertain. Do you think," Cranbourne asked delicately, "that it might have gone differently if you'd been there personally, glad-handing the client, so to speak?"

"I was told that the contract was already ours. It was in Graham Talbot's papers."

"Well, there you are, do you see? Perhaps all it needed was the personal touch. Some people are impressed by that, the sight of a bigwig on the job. It shows our seriousness, adds to our credibility, a bit of extra push and maybe . . . eh?"

What does he want? To fire me already? Why the hell bring me back from the States in the first place? George snapped back: "Maybe it was Graham who had his wires crossed." That was it — fight back. Alasdair likes to watch conflict but he doesn't like to get into the ring himself.

"Yes, that's a thought; you could be right. Graham wasn't thinking right, not at the end. Perhaps I shouldn't say that — it makes your predecessor sound like a dissident we've locked up in an asylum — but you know what I mean. I'm sure it won't happen to *you*, George. Well" — Cranbourne sighed and bounced back with his usual optimism — "there we are, we get over these things. I'm sure you considered all the factors before deciding your priorities. Bulgaria or this Russian business, one of the other; you can't be in two places at the same time." He paused, and George could hear him searching for some final words of bereavement, some pale assurance of the afterlife. In the end he came up with: "It doesn't do to judge these matters with hindsight, does it, George?"

George agreed, it didn't do to judge with hindsight. The distant voices of the others echoed the same sentiment. They sounded like disembodied spirits at a seance.

* * *

"I've fixed for you to see Licensintorg," said Jack Melchior with a sense of achievement. "No guarantees, mind you, just generalities at this stage, expressions of goodwill, OK?"

"OK."

Licensintorg was a foreign-trade organization. Its offices were out of the city center along Minskaia Street. Moscow this morning was mellow in autumn sunshine and haze, full of rich color like the land flowing with milk and honey. It was the time of the year for apples.

"Moscow has more seasons than I-don't-know-what," Jack Melchior explained in one of his more philosophical if not most eloquent moods. "Last May, for example, it was gents-underwear-season, more jockey shorts and woolly whatnots than you could shake a stick at, all the shops full of them. But it came and went. A bit like asparagus, really. At the moment it's apples."

George looked out of the car. When they went past a food shop, the window was stuffed with apples. He asked, "Did you fit the new air filter?" He wanted to make small talk. He needed the mental jogging to escape the sense of lassitude. He needed the diversion to stop thinking about real life. After the incident with Lucas that morning, he had called home. Lillian was taking a turn for the worse despite the care he paid for, though Bloody Brenda, the nurse—who was a decent enough woman, God knew, despite her support stockings and everlasting Harry Belafonte records—wouldn't come out and say it; and he didn't dare to think—didn't dare to think.

That and the fucking Italians.

"I certainly did," said Jack with satisfaction. "Fitted it myself. I learned how, and a lot more besides, when I was in Palestine. Well, you had to, didn't you?"

"I suppose so." There was a girl standing at a bus stop, a pretty girl in a drab coat, eating an apple. She stood in a pool of warm, feathery sunlight away from the shade of a building.

"They've had a bumper crop this year. Dry summer. Record grain harvest. Feeling proper pleased with themselves, and good luck to 'em, I say. No doubt they've got some disaster lined up around the corner. They always have. That's Russia. Don't suppose the world will hear of it, though—we never do."

"Your friend, Neville Lucas, paid me a visit," George said. But he was thinking of the girl. Lillian—poor, frail Lillian—had once been so pretty, pretty enough to break your heart; though, come to think of it, it was the way she laughed that had first attracted him, that laugh because at the age of twenty he had said something stupid and she caught him out at it and laughed where another woman might not have. He wanted to be home with her instead of on his way to a pointless meeting with a bunch of *apparatchiks* who would mouth platitudes and do nothing. He needed the dose of reality that came from loving and caring for her.

"He's not my friend," Jack was saying, "more of an acquaintance—but visit you, did he? My, my. Of course, I dropped in a good word. Good old Neville, I wonder what he's up to? Well, seize the opportunity, George, but—a nod's as good as a wink to a blind thingummy—watch your step, there's a good chap, eh?"

"I'll try to," George answered. He checked the side mirror as he had done regularly since they started. "And I'll begin now. Whose is the car behind us?"

Jack Melchior gave a small shudder and caused the car to veer to the left with a braying of horns from a heavy truck in the outside lane. He pulled back and carried on as before. "What car would that be?"

"I can't tell the make. The white job with the aerials that's been following us ever since we left the hotel."

Jack glanced in the mirror, watching the car with its bronzed windshield.

"Probably nothing, but could be the Gas Board, I suppose," he suggested cautiously. "I say, George—first Neville, now this. You *are* attracting a lot of attention. A positive Playmate of the Month."

"Hello, George."

On his return Neville Lucas was waiting in the lobby of the Mezhdunarodnaya, smiling his uncertain smile. He kept his distance, diffident about coming forward; his hands fumbled with a copy of *Pravda* that he had been reading for want of anything to do. George was struck by the apparent innocence of the man, an air of puzzlement about him as he looked around.

"I've got someone I'd like you to meet, George. Please, there's

154

no compulsion. How about it?"

"Who is he?"

"His name is Peter. He's a . . . fixer, I suppose you'd call it. He knows people, does deals, that sort of thing. He'd like to chat to you, see whether he could help. What do you say?"

George looked about the lobby. He noticed Wormold. The fizzy-drinks man was standing around with some of the other English, who were too polite to ask each other for a drink. One of them looked through George as if he wasn't there.

"KGB?" he asked, turning back to Lucas.

"Peter? Does it matter? Sorry, George, it probably does to you. Over here you forget about it. Some of my best friends—"

"It's OK. But I'm supposed to be going to a function. A party given by our Soviet hosts. They hand out medals to favored British companies—I'm not joking."

"So I've heard." Lucas smiled gently. "Any medals for you, George?"

"No."

"Maybe next year."

George nodded. But next year would be too late. Next year he would be forty-four and without a job, and there would be Lillian to care for, and his daughter to send to school and Bloody Brenda to be paid. He asked, "Where is he?"

"In my room."

"You have a room here?"

"Next to yours, George." They were at the lifts. Lucas punched the button. He was still looking about him like a man who was lost. "Sorry about that. It wasn't my idea."

"Forget it." George stepped into the lift.

"Peter. George Twist. George, this is Peter Kirov."

"Hello, George."

"Hello, Peter."

"Come on in, George," said Lucas. "Don't be shy. Close the door." Lucas was ushering him froward into a room with drawn curtains and a figure sitting on a bedside chair.

"Why don't you take a seat?" The stranger spoke English with a sincere American accent and, now that George could see him, he had, too, that clean American look in his sporty slacks, pale blue sweater and open-collared shirt, so that for a moment George had an uncanny feeling of attending some revivalist meeting at which he was being asked to step forward and be saved.

"What has Neville said?" Kirov asked. "That there are opportunities for you in the Soviet Union, I hope."

"Something like that . . ."

"Peter," stressed the Russian.

". . . Peter."

"And that I can help you, yes?"

"Perhaps."

"That's it, right on the nail." Lucas intervened. He was standing by the window, fidgeting with the curtains as he seemed to fidget with everything. To Kirov he said, "I told George that there was no compulsion. That's right, isn't it, Peter? I mean, George, that you're as free as a bird. You can go tell us to go jump in the lake if you want to. I wouldn't"—under some internal strain Lucas's voice heightened its pitch and a trace of his Tyneside accent was audible—"be a party to anything—you know what I mean."

"Sure."

George sat down on a corner of the bed. The clothes smelled fresh, unslept in. The sliding door of the wardrobe was open and nothing hung inside. Otherwise the room was identical to his own, and in the absence of his own possessions, he had the feeling of having been emptied out of it, as if his personality had been flushed down the drain and they had retained the vacant form. *George. Yes, George. What do you say, George?* Both men kept repeating his name in almost every sentence.

"Peter here," said Lucas, "has put together a meeting. Very important people. What do you say, George? Give us a sign and we can see them tonight."

"I have a car outside," Kirov commented.

"Peter has a car."

They're rushing me, not giving me any opportunity to think. George noticed the ashtray by the bedside. It was full of cigarette butts with plain white filters—not Lucas's brand. Someone else had been using the room, sitting there for hours. Doing what? Listening? *Ah, Neville, you pathetic liar: you were never in this room before in your life!*

156

"We need an answer, George," Kirov was saying in his business-school manner. "We've had our eye on you, but you know business: there is always competition."

"I'll bet you've had your eye on me." For how long? Watching his every move since his arrival? Watching him as he stood outside the hotel staring through the sleet across the river to the Ukraina? Watching and listening as he made love to the girl, and afterward as they talked, tender in their own company, about unimportant things that became important because in a moment of affection they had decided to talk about them? He felt sorry for the girl. She knew, or guessed, or feared. She was denied even the illusion of privacy.

"OK, for Christ's sake let's go," he said quietly.

In the lobby George checked the time against the great gold clock. Only ten minutes gone. The Englishmen seemed to have dropped the idea of a drink and were chatting amiably. Travel also took people sometimes that way. After two or three days you caught a dose of morality and started to nurture your stomach on salads and soda-water and go to bed early. Jack Melchior was intoning *"Breep-breep"* to Wormold; he paused only to glance blankly in George's direction and then turn his back to go on with his joke, the one international joke other than baring his arse.

They continued across the lobby, George walking between the other two, their shoulders bumping against his. He remembered the Vietnamese soldiers at the airport that nobody noticed. He felt like them, invisible, a part of some other Moscow. Someone opened the door for the three men and George was bundled into a waiting car. Lucas and the Russian sat on either side of him. Kirov gave instructions to the driver.

"Relax, George," said Lucas, "it really isn't as bad as all that. Say the word and we'll stop and you can get out." He sounded as though he wanted to believe, wanted to be sincere. His eyes floated around vaguely, sometimes looking at George, sometimes out of the window. They drove along the Krasnopresenskaya Embankment.

"Is it far, where we're going?"

"Not far. You want some music?" Lucas tapped on the driver's shoulder and he turned on the radio, which played an innocuous romantic song. Lucas smiled and hummed along with it. "When I was a kid," he went on, "we used to play 'pub cricket' whenever we were traveling on a long journey. You ever play 'pub cricket,' George?"

"No."

"We had to count runs for the heads and limbs in the pub names. The 'Lion' would get you a six—I forgot to tell you, you score for the tail, too—and the 'Bull's Head' got you a single, follow? You lost a wicket for a pub with no animals in the name."

"I never played."

"No, well, I don't any more. It isn't suited to Moscow. I often think about it, though—the way you do."

"I played it once," Kirov remarked casually. "Someone taught me—in London."

"Very English of you." George supposed that Kirov was telling him something. Probably that they were all civilized men, just in case George had his suspicions.

Daylight was fading rapidly. Dull lights shone from the shops. People were piling into and out of a subway station—Kutuzovskaya, if he got the name right. The streets seemed full of soldiers in walking-out dress. Moscow nights. He tried to think of the girl's perfume. Road signs flashed past before he could decipher the letters.

They passed the city limits, the Moscow Ring Road, heavy with convoys of wagons. Everywhere dusted with faint lights. Over a black mass of trees, the clear dome of the sky and a sprinkling of stars. More romantic music to tell them that they were all on the brink of a love affair. Lucas had something to say.

"Not far. I never thought to ask, George, but have you eaten?"

"I snatched a bite at lunch."

This seemed to comfort Lucas, but he reached into his pocket and produced some hard candy which he handed round. They sat in the darkness, sucking them. From time to time, as Lucas kept up his small talk, George could hear the sweet rattle against the other man's teeth.

Another road sign, *Zhukovka*. The driver turned off the main highway into a side road bordered by birch and spruce. He flashed the headlights and slowed as they approached a barrier. More soldiers than George could count. Lights all over the place. Lights so bright that they seemed to wash them out of the car. Voices snapping requests for passes.

"Sorry about that, George," said Neville Lucas as the car rolled on slowly down the road. "They're sticklers for red tape. Didn't give you a scare, did it?"

"No."

A bend in the road. To one side an expanse of lawn and a large frame-house with a veranda and a shingled roof. More trees. A gas station with a couple of BMWs parked on the forecourt and a soldier filling the tanks. More houses, rich but rustic. Outside one a pile of logs under a shelter and a man sweating away with an ax, seeming to enjoy the exercise. Another one surrounded by a wire fence, with a leering Doberman prowling the compound. An American-style supermarket, brightly lit through the darkness as if happiness were on special offer this week. There were cars outside and women in fur coats who issued orders to soldiers to load up the groceries.

The car cruised on slowly through the village past the reticent houses peeping through the trees, past the floodlit tennis courts where soldiers in fatigues swept up the autumn leaves, past the small white clapboard building that looked like a Southern Baptist chapel but had troop carriers parked outside it, past all the houses where, in the evening, behind the lit windows, the good life went on and Soviet mom served Soviet apple pie.

"We're here," said Neville Lucas mildly. The car wheels crackled over the gravel drive towards a large house built of tarred wood, with a turret in one corner, a litter of lean-tos, and big friendly windows that lit up the grass. A servant in peasant blouse and soft-top boots appeared from nowhere to open the doors.

"Where's here?" George thanked the servant, who seemed nonplused.

"The Minister's dacha; that's to say, the Minister of Gas's house. Couldn't mention it before. Not strictly allowed to say where the ministers live. Something to do with protocol."

"Sure—the fans, the groupies—they make a minister's life hell."

"Sorry, George, didn't catch that?"

They mounted the steps to the open doorway; George, Lucas and Kirov, taking off their topcoats and handing them to the

Minister's batman. They were shown into a large, brightly lit salon set for dinner. Three people were already waiting.

"This is the Minister," Lucas whispered, giving one of his vague smiles for the benefit of everyone. "He doesn't speak English, so no jokes, George; they don't go down in translation."

"I can do trimphone impressions. They work in any language."

"Pardon?"

"Forget it, Neville. No jokes, I'll remember."

Kirov was already making the introductions.

The Minister was a small man with small feet in tight gray shoes. He relaxed in a cardigan and open-necked lumberjack shirt, and his small, mobile features rattled about his face like abacus beads as he shook George's hand while speaking effusively to Kirov.

"The Minister is delighted to see you, George. He asks after your health. He hopes that you are enjoying your stay in the Soviet Union. He looks forward to mutually beneficial economic relations based on the recognition of the common benefit of amicable exchanges between sovereign peoples."

"Hello," said George.

"This," said Kirov, "is Madame Lubachova. She is personal assistant to the Minister."

"Good evening, Mr. Twist." Madame Lubachova spoke English in a glitter of smiles as bright as sequins. George guessed her age as thirty or so, though she was making a monument out of her tight-skinned beauty. She laid a long-fingered hand lightly on his. Behind her, modestly in her shadow, was another woman who registered at first only as a plain brown frock behind Madame Lubachova's blue silk creation.

"Hello, Mr. Twist."

George didn't catch the name. She had come forward now, a small dark figure with auburn hair, perhaps at one time an attractive woman, but to George's eyes a little dumpy though still pleasant-featured, with a mouth that looked as though it might have something to say—unlike Madame Lubachova, who was for some reason talking about Paris. George said hello and then was turned away by Kirov and offered a drink. The Russian fixed himself a small dry martini and pointed George in the direction of the Minister.

"The Minister would like you to explain the capabilities of your company. This is important, George, a real opportunity; he is extremely interested. Please keep your vocabulary simple, though, since I have difficulty with the technical words."

George wanted to ask: Why? Why are we doing it like this? This isn't business. But instead he launched into his standard sales patter, his song and dance act. *I'll be baring my arse next.*

"Speak directly to the Minister, not to me," Kirov suggested as a friendly hint. The Minister's eyes were twinkling with some secret enjoyment.

"Yes, of course." George tried to comply, but found the words hanging on his lips like spittle. He took a sip of his vodka. It came from a bottle with an unintelligible label and a sprig of something green and foul floating in the liquor. As he mumbled something Madame Lubachova, dying of ennui, proposed that they eat dinner. She took the Minister's hand in her own delicate one and led him to the table.

The meal was excellent, and excellently served on porcelain and crystal. The Minister, sitting in his checkered shirt behind the gilt and glitter at the head of the table, spoke at length in Russian, so that for George there were long periods of silence broken only when Kirov delivered the translation, flatly like a series of Bible readings, in his oddly American accent.

"The Minister says that we are in a period of unprecedentedly impressive expansion of social productive forces."

"Oh, doing well, are you?"

"The Minister can forsee a synergy—that's the word, isn't it. 'synergy?'—between the capital—plant requirements of the social-ist economies and the high technologies of the developed market economies."

"You want to buy something?"

Kirov paused in his interpreting and said quietly, "Yes, George: that's what it's all about, isn't it—buying and selling?"

"Sure, but what do you want to buy . . ."

". . . Peter."

"Peter. What?"

"In good time, George, in good time. The Minister hopes to establish fraternal relations with progressive Western companies based upon mutuality and respect."

161

"I think he's said that once already."

The food was cleared aside and only the bottles were left on the table. George stared at them, thinking: It's time I cleaned up my act. He didn't feel drunk, but his senses were jaded with trying to catch the undertones of what was happening. It was Moscow, he decided—the place wouldn't stay still, wouldn't define itself. Everything advertised itself as something different and moved when you weren't looking. It was a wasteland of snow, where all you ever saw were the footprints of things that vanished.

"We have a need for gas-separation plants," Kirov was saying. "That's what you sell, isn't it? Your specialty?"

George shook himself together to agree.

"But we require other things."

"Like what?"

Kirov was staring at him, coming to a decision.

Am I so important?

"We have a small water pollution, George—a lake which has been affected by heavy-metal contaminants. It's a matter of ecology, of defending the environment—yes, the Soviet Union is also concerned about these things; we are a civilized nation."

Maybe George hesitated a fraction too long, because Lucas interrupted.

"Don't be too cynical, old man. Even if they are technically behind the West here, they share the same concerns: the good life, healthy kids, a place where you would like them to grow up."

"Your company has access to this technology," said Kirov.

"In the States," George answered.

"Precisely—in the United States."

"It's subject to the COCOM embargo. They would never let the USSR have it."

Kirov smiled and sighed. "You know that there are ways around the embargo. It's just a matter of goodwill."

"Sure."

That was the end. Shortly the party broke up. The Minister made a farewell speech. Madame Lubachova suggested that she could provide "her friend George" with tickets for the Bolshoi. The Minister's batman brought the coats.

"I'm sorry that we were unable to talk together, Mr. Twist," said Madame Lubachova's small, dark companion. She was the only person who did not call him George, and he liked her for that. He was tired of hearing his name ground into fine powder.

"Perhaps another time, Mrs. . . . ?"

"Terekhova."

"Mrs. Terekhova," he repeated.

In the car on the way back to the city, Kirov announced that he would be in London the following week.

"Shall I see you there, George? To talk details?"

George turned to him, but there was no light in the car and the other man's face was invisible.

"I'd like to be there myself," said Neville Lucas, "but you know how things are." He spoke casually, as if it was simply other business that kept him away.

Do they let me out of the car if I say no? There's no compulsion, George; that's the story.

"I'm looking forward to it . . ."

". . . Peter," said Kirov out of the darkness.

"Peter."

"Christ, George, you were the last man I expected to see again."

"Bug off, Jack, I need to think."

"But this is serious, George, bloody serious!" Jack was hopping from one foot to the other while George Twist sat peaceably at his table in the British pub mulling over his beer.

"Trust the place to be empty when a man needs a drink and company even if not to talk to. More beer, Boris! Have one yourself, Jack." George looked around for a waiter. There was one busying himself in the shadows where the lights had been turned off and the stools up-ended, but he paid no attention.

Jack Melchior was saying, ". . . currency, I should think. Bloody black market. God knows, I tell them about it, warn them off: 'Don't touch it with a bargepole.' But there's always some smart-ass who thinks he known better . . ."

"Isn't there always?" George smacked his glass on the table. *The last thing I need is a drink.* "Come on, Boris, chop-chop!" Hell, he was starting to imitate Jack!

The bar was closing around them; only their table was still lit. Now that the English were leaving, they were dismantling the fittings. The pub was turning back into another piece of Moscow—it was happening over there in the dark corners where George couldn't see clearly.

"We were quite friendly," said Jack Melchior as if he wanted to cry. "I gave him a few tips, you know, just friendly, nothing in it for me. Told him about currency: stay away! What more do you do?"

"Nothing," George answered without listening. He wondered whether Neville Lucas and the Russians were watching. Why not?

"George?"

"Sorry, sorry." George pushed away his glass and smiled. "Things on my mind." He stretched his limbs, tired—tired. "I've just seen the Promised Land, my son. I've been taken to the high place and offered the kingdoms of this earth. They can do that to you in this dream machine."

"I don't follow you. Are you pissed?" Jack sounded concerned.

George shook his head and laughed. "Nope. I've just had a contractor's wet dream, that's all. But soon it'll be back to reality. I want to get out of this place."

"You're the lucky one!" Melchior suddenly blurted out, so that George was shaken into listening.

"Why? What is it? What's been going on, Jack?"

Jack Melchior paused to calm down and then, as quietly as he could manage, he said, "They've only arrested poor bloody Wormold!"

12

In London it was raining. There was a Tube strike, and the streets were jammed with traffic in long, glistening queues.

"The end to a perfect summer," Alasdair Cranbourne remarked ironically as they watched raindrops trickle down the windowpane. "I gather that the Russians got our summer this year, Moscow positively blooming and the Politburo no doubt out on the lawn in their cricket flannels. No need to take note of this small talk, by the way," he said waggishly to Jim Evans, who was sporting a new bow tie. . . . "And, while I think of it, have you seen this morning's paper, George?"

"I left home too early."

"Well, there's a piece that may interest you." Cranbourne passed across a copy of the *Daily Telegraph*. There was a story under a byline on the front page: "British Businessman Arrested by KGB" and then "Foreign Office sources denied today that Mr. Brian Wormold . . ."

"Know him, did you?"

"I met him in Moscow." George put the newspaper down.

"Thought so. Any truth in this story about the fellow being a spy?"

"I shouldn't think so. More likely he was just dabbling in black-market currency."

"Ah—make money at that, can one?"

"Who wants to be a ruble millionaire?"

"Good point, good point. Still, it goes to show you, eh? Tricky place, Russia."

George agreed: Russia was a tricky place.

The board meeting resumed slowly. It was the first since George's return from Moscow and a lackluster affair like a breakfast conversation between unfaithful spouses. Evans without much interest inquired where they were in the agenda.

"I wouldn't know about that," said Cranbourne. "I think we should have a freewheeling, no-holds-barred discussion: we haven't had one of those for ages. I'm sure Jim can sort things out into agenda order for the minutes later." As if inspired, he suggested, "Let's talk about the figures, shall we?"

This was agreed, and Stan Chambers, the finance director, fumbled through his papers, taking them out of order. He had not been expecting to be called for another hour. The story was the same as before: the company was bleeding to death.

"The problem lies with Sep Tech," said Harold Barnes testily. He looked around for dissenters, then went on. "Lou Ruttger is out of control. His development budget looks as though we're funding the first landing on the moon. Doesn't he know that money has to be earned?"

"He's still within budget," George answered. From his own papers he took a sheet. "This is the budget I got, the one I was working to before I came home."

"Which revision is that?" Stan Chambers asked.

"Revision? This is the one you brought out to the States when you did the books."

"There was a March and a June revision," interposed Cranbourne. "Anybody got a copy of the June revision?" That's the latest, isn't it?"

"March and June are provisional only." Chambers had found his copies. "We didn't actually approve them. Technically I think George may be right."

"Is that what the minutes say? Oh, well, we'd better approve the revision, then—yes?"

"March *and* June, or just June?"

"Just June, I suppose. March is pretty much a dead letter." The chairman initialed his copy and passed it to Evans for inclusion in the minutes. Benignly he said, "Well, that's the paperwork. George, have a word with Lou and tell him to mind the pennies, will you? What now? Shall we have an inquest on the Bulgarian business or ask George about his trip to Russia? George?"

"Let's talk about both." Why not? It was just words. Everything was words and nothing ever got done except in an accidental fashion as if between breaths. George began to wonder if it had always been like that but he had been too young and inexperienced to notice. *In the beginning was the Word.* In the beginning, the middle and the bloody end.

So he began to tell them about Russia, about the British mission, about Jack Melchior, about his meeting with the Minister—at which point the room seemed to come alive. He left out the bit about the Soviet request for embargoed technology, because what they didn't know about wouldn't hurt them. And, before he knew where he was, George found himself lying to the others, telling them how good and certain the prospects in Russia were. Because after the Bulgarian fiasco it was what they needed to hear; and he needed to tell them because he had to keep his job in order to care for Lillian and pay for his daughter's schooling and employ Bloody Brenda with her bloody Harry Belafonte records, and do all those other things which he supposed the Russians knew about. He found himself wondering if Peter Kirov was really going to visit London as promised. He needed the business—damn it, he needed the business!

"So how many of these Russian gas plant contracts are we going to get in the next twelve months?" was Harold Barnes's question, dropped like a stone in a pool as George tried to mesmerize the others. He broke off to fix his eyes on George.

"Five—a minimum of five."

"Five," Barnes repeated. Then, "Is that a promise, George?"

"It's a promise."

"Wonderful," said Alasdair Cranbourne. He's satisfied by words, thought George. The chairman smiled and said lightly, "Well, that fairly hitches our wagon to the Russians, doesn't it? We'll all become proper little communists—only joking, fellows, only joking."

George called Lou Ruttger as soon as the American office was open for business, told him about the budget position and promised to send him a copy. Ruttger took the news of budget stringency too easily; it made George wonder if he was looking for another job. He hoped not; he needed Lou if everything was going to work. Sep Tech was the linchpin of the whole deal. He surprised himself at how he had fallen into thinking of Kirov's proposal as a real piece of business. Would the Russian come to London?

"So, how's tricks on the funny farm?" Lou Ruttger was saying.

"Much as usual; like the last act of *Hamlet* — bodies all over the stage. What's the question?"

"I just wanted to know what was with Cranbourne's trip to the States?"

"Trip?" Then George remembered that Evans had mentioned it at that first meeting after his own return to England. Since then nothing: there was no report.

"He called on you?"

"The hell he did. One of our guys was in New York. He saw Alasdair passing through Kennedy on his way to somewhere else. He had his pet reptile with him."

"Harold Barnes?"

"Got it first time. They came and went like Batman and Robin. No calls, no messages, no nothing — we wouldn't have known about it at all if Al hadn't spotted them at Kennedy. What's it about?"

"I don't know, Lou, that's the truth."

"OK, I believe you. Now, try this one for size. We've had visitors."

"Who?"

"Remember Abe Korman? The senator? He came on the tour of West Valley — an asshole."

"I remember."

"He sent one of his aides to look us over and walk out with every piece of literature we could let him have. He gave us a line about defense procurement, some senate committee selecting preferred contractors. Total bullshit; that isn't the way it's done. It was a snooping exercise for something he doesn't want to talk about. Your guess is as good as mine."

George had no guesses.

" 'Visitors,' you said 'visitors.' There was someone else?"

"John Chaseman, the man himself!" Lou sounded satisfied. "He made no secret that Chaseman Industries regards us as a very sexy business he would like to get into. He talked about the West Valley project, admired the way we'd done it, wanted to know all about the technology. He asked us about working together, some type of collaboration or joint venture. He knows we need the work. By the way, George, when are you going to throw a deal in my direction?"

"What did you do?" George pressed him. Now he was worried. Strange trips by Alasdair Cranbourne, added to Korman and then Chaseman, made for a dangerous mix for what George had in mind.

"I told him that, provided he signed a secrecy agreement, he could have a look at our portfolio to evaluate it. Hey, George, you still there?"

"I was thinking." George was thinking that to sell embargoed technology was hard enough, but to do it through a company that was under scrutiny was like wire-walking without a safety net. He asked, "What do you think, Lou? Does Chaseman want to work with Sep Tech or buy the company out?"

Ruttger laughed. "That's the question, George. You tell Alasdair that he's going to have to treat us nice if he wants to hang on to this technology."

The message that George had been waiting for came two days later.

"George!" said the voice warmly over the telephone.

"Peter? Where are you calling from?"

"I'm in London, just as I promised. We have a place in Highgate," Kirov added casually, as if it were an apartment where he kept a mistress. "Can we meet sometime—lunch today, perhaps—to talk things over? I may have good news for you. You made a great impression on the Minister, George. This could be the start of something big." They agreed on a pub in Hampstead.

Kirov was already there when George arrived. He sat at a small table facing the door, drinking a half-pint of lager out of a dimple mug, his fawn Burberry draped negligently over the back of a bentwood chair.

"I'm pleased to see you, George. Do you want a drink?" he

asked and added, quaintly, so that George wondered whether the man had been taking lessons from Jack Melchior, "What's your poison?"

George accepted a half-pint of bitter and the two men sat opposite each other, almost shyly. Kirov spoke first.

"I've booked a restaurant for lunch. I forgot to mention it on the phone."

That sounded innocuous enough. George asked, "You know London well?"

"Oh, I've been here before. Business; you know how it is."

"Sure." It occurred to George that the telephone line might have been bugged and that was why Kirov had failed to name the restaurant. You couldn't tell from the Russian's easy manner.

They left the pub and strolled down to Finchley Road in the fine air. It was a sunny day after a damp night and the city looked as fresh as a watercolor. George felt clean and fresh with it.

"Where are we going?" he inquired.

"Cosmos. Do you know it? I'll treat you—unless you think that would be a bribe. Otherwise we go, you say, Dutch? For me, you understand, the expenses can be a problem. Unless," Kirov suggested with a smile, "they take rubles. What do you think?"

"Cosmos? Maybe they do." The place had a middle-European atmosphere. Elderly émigrés. Women in tired fur coats. Cream cakes and *heimatweh*.

They sat in the restaurant over plates of *sauerbraten* and a bottle of Moselle. At the other tables people read newspapers and talked. There was a conversation going on in German, which the waiter had joined in, talking familiarly with his customers. Kirov read the German wine label, commented on it, sniffed the cork, went through the usual rigmarole. He was bright and at ease. He made small talk as they plowed through most of the meal.

"So, George," he announced at last, "you've decided that there may be something in talking business with us."

"Maybe," George answered cautiously. "But first things first. I need something from you." On reflection "need" was a word he shouldn't have used. It was giving a hostage.

"What can I do to help? Anything. After all, we are developing"—Kirov was searching his vocabulary like a rational filing system—"relationship. That makes it a two-way street."

It sounded reasonable enough at face value—a sharing—but George was skeptical. All this "George" stuff made him uncomfortable.

He looked around. An old woman with mottled hands. An aging man with a Slavonic face and a faded suit. What were they talking about? Estonian independence? The homes, property and positions they had left in the Ukraine? Many of the diners ate lightly, there only for the company and the reminiscences; picking delicately at their food and chewing over their memories. The restaurant was another dreamland, another piece of Moscow leaking through into the world of the real.

"You were saying, George?"

"I was saying . . ." He took a mouthful of his wine and replaced the glass. "If I'm going to persuade my company that there is something in this Russian business, I need a sign, something visible. You follow me, Peter? The company won't commit resources just on my word without anything to show for it."

"What sign do you need?"

"To start with, a formal inquiry document from one of your foreign trade organizations—say, Techmashimport. I'm talking now about the gas plants. The other business is different: the COCOM embargo makes it different."

"I see. How many enquiries—one?—two?"

"I've promised five."

"Five?" Kirov inquired mildly.

"Five out of fifty that the Soviet Union has planned. That's not many."

"Oh, no, I'm sure I can arrange that. It may take time, that's all." He let the last sentence come out slowly.

George thought: he wants a reaction; he wants to know how hungry I am.

"That's OK."

They changed the subject, each perhaps feeling the strain in a different way.

George asked, "There was another Englishman with me in Moscow. His name was Brian Wormold. He sold fizzy drinks."

"The man who was arrested?" Kirov responded without interest. Then, seeing that George was interested, he asked, "He concerns you?"

"No—well, maybe yes. I knew him." The past tense made Wormold sound dead. George added, "I suppose it's nothing more than curiosity," but the truth was a feeling that it could have been himself—*he* could have been arrested. In Moscow, who needed reasons?

A plain dish of vanilla ice cream arrived for each of them.

"Over dessert we should talk about something more lighthearted," Kirov said.

"I was told that he had been arrested on currency charges. Then it was reported that he was accused of spying. You don't like your ice cream?"

Kirov had stopped eating. The gray metal spoon rested in a foam of melting ice cream.

"In most respects the West is in advance of the Soviet Union . . ."

"But not in ice cream—I know, I've eaten one in GUM." He had been standing on one of the bridges that spanned the ornate arcade in the department store. Below him a dark stream of Russians in heavy topcoats walked by grimly eating ice cream. George remembered them now, here in Cosmos Restaurant, with the traffic cruising by in the Finchley Road, the restaurant door opening as a red London bus went past, and a florid woman in pancake makeup coming in and beginning to address a friend in a voluble language that George took to be Hungarian.

Kirov, oblivious of this, said, "OK, George, I'll tell you. Your friend—acquaintance?—has been arrested on spying charges. I know few details because it is not my business, but this is the story: that he was a courier for your SIS. It's serious, but not so serious. They will naturally find him guilty and he will spend a little time in the *gulag*, and in twelve months or so he will be exchanged for a Soviet spy. This is normal. So"—Kirov leaned forward, and his face became heavy like a father giving good advice—"what is it, George? You are asking if your friend is innocent? No, he is not innocent. I don't know the facts, but I know that he is not innocent."

"Why not? Why couldn't it have been me that got arrested?"

"Because you are a legitimate businessman, George. Be serious. You've been reading too many stories, seeing too many films. It isn't like that. We are a civilized people. And besides, where is the

172

advantage? Your government would not do an exchange for an innocent man because it would be giving in to blackmail; and businessmen—like you, George—become nervous and that hurts us, too. So?"

"OK."

"Believe me," said Kirov earnestly.

"Sure."

They dropped the subject and couldn't find another. A silence fell between them and they watched the waiter clearing plates and a customer paying her bill from a purse with an animal motif cut into the leather and a fringe of red beads, the product of that *ethnic* culture that is as universal as Coca-Cola. The tension of silence began to get George down. Maybe Kirov with his "George, George" had captured it: this was conspiracy, not business—and conspiracy was personal.

"Peter . . ." he began, with nothing in view but to get the conversation going.

"We need to talk about the *other* matter," Kirov answered. "To us it is important that we sort it out."

"I know: it's a two-way street."

"That was the right expression I used?"

"Exactly right: I want the gas plant contracts; you want the Sep Tech technology."

"And in principle it is agreed?"

George was about to say yes, but instead nodded and then scratched his neck so that his agreement took on the appearance of an accidental gesture.

"OK," said Kirov, breathing out as he said it, "let's have a drink on that. What do you say to a brandy, George?"

They had a brandy. As they drank it George asked his questions.

"You mentioned a lake to me. How big is it, what volume of water does our process have to handle? What is your contaminant? You mentioned heavy metals, but didn't say which. What is your time scale for delivery and installation of the equipment? So far I've agreed to go along with you, but I don't know for sure that what you want is feasible: I mean, I don't know that we have the manufacturing capability or can meet your program."

"Details, George, details. I'm not an engineer, but we have

engineers who are working on a technical specification. It takes time—a week—ten days. Can you come to Moscow the week after next? All this can be discussed then and I shall have the inquiries for you on the gas plants. Also we can decide how we avoid the COCOM embargo. Have you had any thoughts on that?"

"I thought that was a Soviet specialty—beating the U.S. embargo."

"We have methods, people who help us and so on. It is a battle of wits with the American investigators."

"So?"

"We cannot afford to play games. A system that was set up from your end would be less likely to attract attention and scrutiny. Well, you don't like the idea of taking risks?"

"George didn't answer. He knew enough about the COCOM embargo to realize that its existence made the whole deal illegal— highly illegal. Kirov was waiting for a response. This was the point at which George was supposed to say, "It's a risky business," the way the big boys said it. He guessed the Russian had it in his script.

"I've had some thoughts," he said finally. Behind Kirov's chair he noticed one of the other diners who appeared to be getting agitated. A big man with a heavy, lolling head like an anvil, hair cut *en brosse* and a skin erupted with veins, who sat alone, draped in a shabby blue raincoat. "We can set up a dummy project in Finland and place the order through there. Provided the window-dressing looks good, the Americans will grant an export license and we can ship the equipment to Helsinki. There's no embargo between Finland and the Soviet Union, so all we need do then is truck the stuff across the border." His voice wound down and he found himself looking beyond Kirov at the big man until the Russian called him back. "Sorry, Peter, where was I? Sure—well, there's the outline. I need to work on the detail." He added, "I'll need money."

"For yourself, George?"

"What was that?"

"For you, George, *personally*." Kirov waited, then saw that he had made a mistake. "I apologize," he said. "What is it you want, working capital?"

"Just enough to get the show on the road."

"Fine," Kirov agreed.

"Good."

"Yes, good."

"What is this, a lovers' quarrel?" George said at last.

They changed the subject again. Kirov talked about the weather. George wondered where he had picked up the habit. Maybe they talked like that in Moscow, too. Then Kirov remarked, "I liked your answer to my question. I prefer to deal with an honest man."

An honest man. George hadn't thought about it.

"That's right. I'm as honest as you'll get. I only commit crimes for the company."

Kirov laughed. "Yes. I'm an honest man, too." And George guessed that maybe he was. Maybe there were places where you could kill people and pay your bills on time and that made you an honest man. He was going to say something about it, but there was a noise at the next table.

They looked round. The big man had stood up and was coming towards them. His large frame hid his age—it could have been seventy. He began to shout at Kirov, abusing him in Russian, his body shaking with hatred. Movement in the restaurant seemed to stop. The stranger's voice suppressed all other noise. Spittle formed on his lips as they mangled the words.

"I'm sorry," Kirov said in English. "I don't understand you." His face was expressionless, but his hands were tensed on the table. A waiter came over and took the old man by the shoulders. He allowed himself to be gently led away.

"I think we should go," Kirov said. He glanced at the bill, tore off the receipt and left some money on the table.

George looked at the old man being ushered politely to the door. The hatred was gone and he seemed collapsed on himself. George turned to Kirov. "He must have recognized something in your accent. What was all that about?"

"Nothing. Just a crazy man, a crazy refugee, not even a true Russian. He needs a psychiatrist. Please, let's go; this is not a good place after all. People come here to be obsessed by their sufferings. They have fantasies; it is not healthy." He took up his coat, and George followed him into the sunlight and the busy London street. By then Kirov had recovered and seemed as cool as ever. He took George's hand and shook it. "I look forward to seeing you again in Moscow. And—please—forget about that business with the old lunatic. It is something out of the past. Things are not like that any more. Believe me."

"Sure," said George, and he turned away to look for a taxi and return to the office. It was time to approach Jim Evans with something of the truth.

There was a story that Evans had formerly practiced as a barrister.

"Which is why he's full of shit," said Harold Barnes.

This was in a confidential moment when Barnes needed George's help for one of his periodic paranoid campaigns against his rivals.

Philosophically he added, "I've never known what Alasdair sees in him—the bow tie and all that arty crap—except that bullshitters swallow it as well as dish it out."

Not everyone would have put it the same way, but it was generally agreed that there was something faintly unreliable about the company's head lawyer, from his dark, slightly thinning hair via bow tie and business suit to his polished shoes.

"Well, George, you old devil," Evans murmured as the story came out. George hadn't been sure of the response he would get. It turned out to be quizzical, slightly amused. "Who else have you told this to?"

"Nobody. The board have had only what you heard at the meeting. They know a little about the gas plants, but nothing about the other business."

Evans nodded. He had a number of little habits: biting and filing his nails was one, and he filed them now. He asked, "Why are you telling me now? Haven't you seen the sign on the door? 'Legal Adviser.' That means I'm the company virgin. I'm not supposed to know about sex."

"And I'm the company hero," George answered. "No film has perfect casting. I need a reliable legman, someone to handle the commercial and legal side."

"Why haven't you told Alasdair?"

"Because he's up to something."

Evans didn't answer. George changed the subject to one that was still puzzling him.

"Why was I brought back, Jim? I haven't sold a thing in years and yet they make me sales director. What's the point?"

"Did you know that Alasdair and Harold slipped off to the States on the quiet while you were away?"

"It has something to do with my question?"

"Search me, George, but it's an interesting coincidence, isn't it? Of course," Evans went on, "there may be nothing nefarious in it. You know Alasdair's style: he tackles every problem sideways on; he's one of nature's born conspirators. But maybe he wants to do something with the Sep Tech operation, and getting you out gives him a free hand over there."

"He could have simply fired me."

Evans shook his head. "Not Alasdair. He likes watching the arena, not fighting with the gladiators. He wouldn't have the nerve to face you, not when your record in getting Sep Tech from kitchen-sink technology to a full-scale plant at West Valley was so successful. It would go against his socialist conscience."

"So he made me sales director to set me up in a position from which he could fire me—is that what you're saying?"

"Just a thought, George. It's not as if sales directors have got what you might call a long shelf-life. There used to be a joke that Graham Talbot, after he got the job, wanted a revolving door put on the office. Did you hear that one?"

"No." George hadn't heard the joke, but he understood the meaning well enough. He wasn't meant to succeed as sales director. If he did, well, that was a bonus. But the whole object had been to get him back from America so that the company could carry out its plans over there, whatever they were.

Evans meanwhile had passed on to the other topic.

"So, what do you really want?"

What did he really want? Put like that, George Twist wasn't sure. He wondered sometimes if he hadn't been too long in the States and fallen into the trap of confusing jacuzzis with happiness.

"I want you to come up with a scheme, something that will get around the COCOM embargo. I'd thought of Finland; we could get an export license to ship the equipment technology there."

Evans's eyes, which had been focusing on George, now drifted off around the furnishings of his office. Among the third-rate junk which was all the company could afford, the books and the sober calendar sent every year by the insurance brokers, the lawyer kept his own exotica, a skull placed on his desk and used as a pencil holder, and a framed certificate attesting to his proficiency in ballroom dancing. He seemed to be considering these as he replied.

"What do you think the COCOM embargo is, George?"

George had heard that sort of question before.

"Go on, Jim, tell me something new."

Evans wasn't to be put off.

"The COCOM embargo — no apologies for laboring the point — is the mechanism whereby the U.S. State Department, with the help of its friends and allies, carries out American foreign policy towards the Soviet Union by means of an agreement among the main Western countries to deny advanced technology to the Russians and the rest of the satellites; in pursuance of which there is a committee which monitors said exports. With me so far?"

"Go on."

"Right. Now, George, have you heard of the United States Atomic Energy Act of 1954, or Title 10 of the U.S. Code of Federal Regulations or the Export Administration Regulations or the Department of Commerce?"

"Can't say I have."

"Thought not. Well, they add teeth to COCOM; in fact, not to put too fine a point on it, they allow the American courts to lock people up for long periods of time for breaching the embargo." Evans sighed. "All of which means that you don't want a legman, George, you want a crook." Almost as an afterthought he added, "Anyway, Lou Ruttger heads Sep Tech nowadays, and he'll never go along with any scheme. Lou is Boy Scout."

"Lou won't know," George answered. "All he has to do is fulfill the order. For him it'll look like a kosher contract from a client in Finland. That will keep the American end clean."

"And me?" Evans asked. "What about my position?"

"You're an English lawyer working for an English company.

American laws aren't binding on you here in London." George picked up a pencil from between the teeth of the skull on Evans's desk and passed it between his fingers. He glanced at the skull, then at the lawyer. "Well, maybe you won't be able to retire to Miami."

Evans gave a sardonic smile. "You should have been a Jesuit." He bit his lip. But he didn't disagree.

For a while they talked about something else, leaving it understood between them that this was the way it was going to be done, because business was business and there was no way you could get around that. Evans asked about Lillian: how had George's wife stood up to the strain of moving back to England? George said she was OK; she had Bloody Brenda to look after her and that was all right. Evans sympathized, suggesting in subtle ways that a less decent man than George would have cleared out years ago; but, since he didn't say it outright, George couldn't explain how it wasn't like that, how love made it different.

Finally, to show he had a conscience, Evans asked, "Why are we doing this, George? I mean, what does this deal offer?"

"I don't know. How about a hundred million dollars' worth of gas-plant business coming out of Russia?" Now that he had said it, it didn't seem enough—only money. "How about 'salvation'?"

"I suppose so." Evans seemed to share the same reluctance. He posed another question. "If this is salvation, what's the other thing?"

"The other thing? That's a tough one." George examined the lawyer. How old was Evans—thirty-five? Thirty-seven? "Maybe it's being forty-four years old and without a job."

"Oh." Evans was still curious. "And what's so special about being forty-four?"

"Your balls drop off."

On this same day an incident happened to Irina Terekhova that was of no intrinsic significance. Walking with her son, Arkady, in Sokolniki Park, she was approached by a stranger. The approach was a shock. The man's manner was open enough, but there was something about his appearance in his shabby overcoat and boots that came to her from the past: but she was unable to identify it

179

because the stranger was pressing her with questions. Which was the best exit from the park to reach the Rizhskaya metro station? Was that the nearest one or should he be aiming for Sokolniki or the Park of Economic Achievement? Which way was north? She answered his questions patiently and then watched as he limped away from her. And then she remembered Davidov as she had last seen him. The soles were splitting from his boots, and he had a vodka bottle in his pocket. He stared at his feet and said in a fervid voice that his poetry was going well — everything was going well with him — everything. The resemblance to the stranger was passing and superficial.

13

Moscow: November 1-2

Moscow in November. The first snow had fallen to be greeted with relief and then annoyance because it wouldn't last; it would come and go for a few more weeks. Muscovites at this time of year experienced a longing for the real thing. So Moscow changed like a flickering image from an old film; now white and indistinct, seen under its gray sky as if through eyes clouded by cataracts; now black and streaming with meltwater.

George Twist was back in the city, booked again into the Mezhdunarodnaya. Kirov had him watched. Bogdanov was running a specialist team, twenty operatives working shifts and a host of casuals with a fleet of cars and technical support pulled from here and there out of the KGB machine on the strength of a Politburo directive. Kirov had their reports.

The Englishman was behaving quietly, seeing no one except his company's agent. Jack Melchior had visited him in his room, itching for a drink and reminding George that, whatever deal he was hoping to conclude, he should include two percent as Melchior's commission.

"Fair's fair, George. It was my introduction that brought you the business. By the way, have you brought the new set of points I asked for and the two hundred cigarettes for Neville? He asked after you. I think he's taken a shine to you."

After that meeting George had drifted downstairs, looking for the British pub, but finding that it had disappeared, went outside for a few minutes to stare across the river at the Ukraina under its cap of snow and then retired to his room. He had a bottle of duty-free Scotch in his case, but he didn't open it.

"Classic case of depression" was Bogdanov's diagnosis. "Mark me, as soon as he relaxes, he'll go on a bender. I've seen it before."

From among the reports from the borrowed Sluzhba team who were keeping the Englishman under surveillance Bogdanov produced a thin folder and laid it out on his desk where the two men were breakfasting on rolls and coffee. Kirov had an appointment in half an hour to collect George from his hotel.

"This came in overnight." Bogdanov handed the papers over. The file had a First Chief Directorate classification, indicating the material was from a foreign source, and a technical digest from Directorate T attached to the main report.

"Source David?" Kirov remembered the Soviet deep-cover agent whose name had come up when he first investigated Sep Tech.

"He's turned in another piece on Sep Tech. Another visit: First are mad with him; they've told his controller to steer him away from Sep Tech and back to his own field—whatever that is."

"Why?"

"Because they know that we're trying to get at Sep Tech and, if our operation goes sour, they don't want their man tainted by association. In any case, they say that Source David's material on Sep Tech is useless, just gossip. Directorate T agrees: they say that the technical content is zero."

"So why are we interested?"

"It's up to you, boss. Source David says that there's something going on with the Sep Tech operation: the managers are nervous; the English owners are coming in and out all the time. He suspects that the owners may be dressing the company up for a sale. That might make sense: the parent company needs cash, and a sale of the American subsidiary would raise it."

Bogdanov didn't need to say any more. Kirov knew the consequence. If Sep Tech was sold off, George Twist would have no power to deliver the technology that Sokolskoye needed.

"George."

"Morning, Peter. Well, anything good laid on?" After a long night's rest, George was feeling refreshed. It was wonderful what sleep could do. He was eager to start. He was ready to seize the situation as an opportunity, not as a threat. The two men crossed the hotel lobby for the exit and Kirov's car.

"As I promised," said Kirov, "I've fixed a meeting with Techmashimport. They are letting the gas-plant contracts that interest your company so much. So this is your chance. Are you ready for it?"

"Lead on."

They drove in light traffic. The snow was melting. Moscow was bright under the clear sky in a way that George had started to notice: physically its colors were warmer and more responsive than the drab gray that passed for its description in the West. Many of the older buildings were brightly stuccoed, and among the newer glass and concrete the red Party hoardings sometimes had an air of almost festive gaiety. Just maybe — George thought — you could get to like the place.

Techmashimport was based in an office in Trubnikovskii Pereulok. George stayed in the lobby while Kirov hunted out the Soviet negotiating team, which took a quarter of an hour and George knew was par for the course. Jack Melchior had given him a refresher course one night in a bar at the Cosmos.

"I've got one word for you," Jack said solemnly.

"OK, I'm ready. Hit me with it."

Jack breathed in and said loudly: *"Biscuits."*

"Thanks for that, Jack, I'll remember it."

He remembered it now.

Kirov returned with a party of Russians, and George found himself ushered with the crowd into a conference room with partition walls and a view over the street and the sound of Kirov's American accent making the introductions.

"George, this is Director Milyutin." An aggressive terrier of a man in a shiny new suit like a dance band leader and a pair of scuffed shoes. "May I introduce Engineer Kuznetsov?" This time a shy man with a long face and thick black hair brushed to the left and flying off like a wing. "Mr. Twist has done business in the Soviet Union before, though this was some years ago. George, please meet Mrs. Turayeva; she is an economist and will also act as translator as necessary." She was a gangling young woman with small breasts crushed flat and lumpy as beanbags under a powder-blue sweater.

They carried on coming, but George lost track of the names. He gathered that the first three were the Techmashimport home team, but there were another half-dozen, generally stooping and smiling and distributing nods and handshakes, who, it gradually emerged, had come from Neftagas and were the technical experts on gas production and technology.

"Remember, George. *Biscuits*."

George remembered as they all settled into the seats and it gradually became clear who had speaking parts on the Soviet side — Milyutin and a cock-sparrow character with a goatee beard on the Neftagas squad — and Kirov asked the woman, Turayeva, to go outside and see what was happening to the tea. One of the men followed her, and this was the start of a periodic entrance and exodus that went on the whole time he was there so that he only ever had an approximate idea of the numbers.

"As well as the biscuits," Jack had said, "look out for the numbers game."

"I remember." He remembered. He had been there before — was it ten or twelve years ago? He still couldn't be sure — and recalled the floating numbers on the Soviet side.

"They're quite capable of working the poor visitor over in shifts. They pop off for lunch and tea breaks and bring on substitutes to keep the pressure on. It's always been a mystery to me where they get the manpower from."

It was a mystery to George, too, but he didn't have much time to think about it because Kirov was already pressing him and he saw the attentive faces waiting for him to speak, and Kirov was saying: "This is your chance, George. Give them your presentation."

So George did.

He began slowly, describing first his company, Chemconstruct, its history, its organization and capabilities. As he worked his way into the subject he found his easy, jovial fluency returning. He warmed up, and his audience seemed to warm with him.

The tea arrived in tall glasses with dull lumps of sugar and no lemon. The biscuits came with it.

George turned to the company's past projects, talking through the reference list of blue-chip clients and the major jobs executed in every corner of the world, speaking with excitement and some humor of those in which he had been personally involved, so that Chemconstruct began to take shape in the imagination as something exciting, something creative that took dreams and made them come true.

The biscuits stayed on the plate. George watched them out of the corner of his eye. They started to lose the character of biscuits; they lacked the shiny sugariness of the real thing; they looked inert, permanent and not consumable.

"It's all a question of pecking order," said Jack.

George switched his speech to the technology of gas plants.

Kirov took a biscuit and nonchalantly bit into it. After an interval Milyutin followed, then a nondescript type on the Neftagas team, but not the one with the goatee who did all the talking but evidently got nowhere.

George spoke of the techniques of processing natural gas to recover the various hydrocarbons, of the advantages of the Chemconstruct technology, its low capital costs, its energy efficiency. He opened up a little to questions and fielded those that were thrown at him easily and quickly. He was on his home ground, speaking with knowledge and assurance.

Kirov took a second biscuit.

"Peter?" said Neville Lucas. "He's a . . . *fixer*, I suppose you'd call it."

Some fixer.

George didn't care. He was going to show Peter that, on his own ground, he was the best.

"So what do you think?" Kirov asked.

The presentation was over. The questions were over. He was in Milyutin's office with the director and the chief engineer sent by Neftagas. The place smelt like an ashtray because Milyutin was a chain smoker with square, heavily stained fingers which he used now to stroke his chin and answer testily, "What does our opinion matter?"

In this case, nothing. But Kirov didn't want to say it. Listening to the Englishman, reciting his case for his company, explaining the technology with a lucidity that even a non-engineer like Kirov could follow, he realized: George was *good*. And he wanted George to succeed on his own merits.

"OK," Milyutin was saying grudgingly, "I admit that this guy seems to know what he's talking about, and the process has its attractions. But Chemconstruct . . ." His right hand rocked doubtfully. "They did a job in Omsk, ten, maybe fifteen years ago. Total fuck-up." He looked at Kirov as he spoke, and Kirov understood the message. Milyutin was preparing the ground to say that he was forced into a deal by the KGB in case anything went wrong.

Kirov said, "And none of it was our fault, I suppose."

"It's not allowed to be our fault," answered Milyutin. He added, "But this Twist—OK, he's good."

"Then, we go ahead," said Kirov and he went back to the other room where the Englishman was waiting. He closed the door and fitted his face for a smile. "George, you were excellent!"

"Sure I was," said George flatly. They sat down on opposite sides of the table.

"But *really*—I was proud of you."

"Like my father."

Kirov caught the remark. His answer had a note of appeal in it.

"You have to understand. It's all part of the system. On the one hand, it's bureaucracy. On the other hand, it's personal. You follow? If everything goes wrong, it's my head that will roll. So when it goes right, I am naturally pleased. This applies to Neville Lucas, too—for him it is also important. You like Neville?"

"He's all right," George answered neutrally. Why mention Neville?

"So," Kirov went on, "if this business is going to work, we have to be friends." He leaned across the table to punch George lightly on the shoulder, laughing as he did it. "We've had a success! What do you say to a drink?" He reached into his bag for a bottle of vodka. "How many inquiries did you say you needed?"

"Five." George noted the glasses in the bag. "You came prepared."

"I was hopeful, George, hopeful. And I have a surprise for you. There are ten! Aren't you pleased?"

"I'm pleased." George put the glass to his lips, sniffed it, put it down. "Sorry, Peter, I get too much of this stuff."

"That's all right." Kirov put his own glass down. "Is there something wrong? You sound sad."

George heard the concern and wondered whether that was in the script, too. He shook his head and murmured, "Forget it. It's the selling—the song-and-dance act—it takes it out of me. I should sound delighted. Sorry."

And for the moment that was that.

Kirov said, "The package of inquiries is too large to give to you now. It will be delivered this afternoon to your agent's office for air-freighting to England. Also, George—and this you did not ask for—there is a study which our client wishes to have done. He has analyzed several gas streams and wishes to have your opinion on how they can best be processed to recover chemical feedstocks. He is prepared to pay for this work—cash in advance—twenty thousand dollars. You can expect the order within two weeks. This is very unusual for us, but it is a measure of our good faith. See, George? It is the Soviet side which takes the first step toward friendly cooperation."

"That's peaceful co-existence for you."

"Please," Kirov said solemnly, "don't be cynical."

George accepted the rebuke. "You're right. If I'm not prepared to trust you, I shouldn't be in the game. What next?"

Kirov was reaching into his bag again. He took out some papers.

"OK, now we come to the other business." He placed the papers on the table. "I have here some basic technical data on our pollution problem, just as you asked. The geography, the climate and the physical circumstances of the lake are described. The contaminant is cadmium—a very toxic metal, I'm told. Here you will see the amount of water to be processed and cleaned. And there is a program. Listen, George, because this very important: we have to have your equipment installed and the lake decontaminated by next April at the latest. After that date we face the problem of the spring melt when we cannot guarantee the capacity of our dam to hold back the floodwater. Is this understood?"

"Understood."

"Good." George could feel Kirov's eyes scrutinizing him. "This is feasible?"

"Maybe." George picked up the document and looked it over. "Sep Tech has nothing on its books that it couldn't clear so as to give this job attention. We could produce the membranes and the ionizing resin pretty quickly. The vessels and the heavy equipment you must make yourselves, but installation is fairly easy. And to process the water—I don't know, maybe a month." He paused and ran his fingertips over the paper, picked up a sheet, smelled it and held it to the light. He looked at Kirov. "You'll have to get this stuff run off again. It's supposed to be an inquiry from a Finnish company. They'd have a classy presentation, not this crap. You want a professional job, don't you?"

"Yes, we want a professional job." This time there was a note of respect in the Russian's voice, which to George sounded genuine. "OK, I'll get it done and delivered to your hotel today. You have decided on Finland, have you? In some ways Austria would be easier for us."

"Let's stick to Finland. There are a million lakes there, so it makes our story hang together better: any one of them could be full of shit. Now"—George paused, remembering the last time they had discussed the subject—"if we're going to move, I need to talk about money."

Kirov gave one of his cold smiles. He shared George's recollection. "Fine," he said. "Tell me what you need."

It was George's turn to riffle through his papers. He had talked this aspect over with Jim Evans and pulled together some ideas. He explained them now.

"COCOM—the American embargo—has been beaten before and can be beaten again. People do it all the time: stuffing microprocessors into their bags and walking on to a plane with them; and sometimes dispatching the odd packing case. But for us it isn't so easy. We are not talking about a few chips you can slip into your pocket: we are looking at equipment by the wagonload leaving a traceable trail of paperwork as we shunt it across the Atlantic. On this sort of scale, COCOM have been quite successful at intercepting and stopping shipments. That's our problem.

"As I see it," George went on, "the weak link in all these schemes is the identity of the buyer, the middleman who stands between the exporter and the real customer. A lot of the time the buyer is a trading house that has no obvious use for the goods, or a hundred-dollar shell company with no assets other than a nameplate on the door. It's an arrangement that doesn't stand up to inspection. A quick check will tell any investigator that the buyer has no substance, that he can't be keeping the stuff for himself and that it follows he must be selling it on to a third party—maybe the Soviet Union."

"I agree with you. So, George?"

"So we have to beef the buyer up, make him look good, make him credible."

"In what ways?"

"First, credit checks. It's the obvious starting point; the moment this enquiry comes through Sep Tech's door, I can tell you Lou Ruttger's going to run a credit check on the client. There needs to be money in the bank. He may ask for a Dun & Bradstreet report—in which case they'll be looking for references, people who've done business with the buyer: so there have to be customers. And just maybe—if anyone is really suspicious—they'll want a physical inspection. And for that eventuality there have to be assets you can walk around." George broke off. He wondered whether he was teaching Kirov something he already knew, but the Russian was listening intently. *He wants to be sure I know what I'm doing.*

"Well?"

It was no time to hesitate.

"Above all this, Peter, our Finnish company has got to have a history, a story that explains why it needs what we propose to sell." And that was it. George folded his sheet of notes. He said, "It's a tricky exercise, but it can be done if we spend the money."

Kirov asked: "How much do you need?"

"I can't tell you exactly. It depends on the size and cost of the plant, and until I get these specifications"—he tapped the material that Kirov had given him—"over to the States I can't get Lou Ruttger to price the job. But, whatever the price, the company has got to look as though it can afford it."

"I understand. What is your guess?"

"Ten million for starters—that's U.S. dollars. The money won't be lost. If you deduct five percent for expenses, we'll hold the rest as cash, stock and buildings. When this business is over, you'll be able to break the company up and sell off the assets—and, if we buy the right stuff, you may even end up with a profit. Well?"

"All right, George."

They stopped there. Kirov went to the telephone and made a

call. Afterwards he was evidently waiting for something. They passed the time in small talk.

"So," Kirov announced cheerfully, "we are in business. We should celebrate more, something better than a simple drink of vodka. What are you doing this evening? Perhaps we can have dinner together?"

"I've already got an appointment."

"Oh, where?"

"Snacks, cocktails, with the British commercial counselor."

"Ah—with Mr. Archibald Lansdowne?"

"I think that's the name."

"Then, surely you can make your apologies. I know these cocktail parties for visiting businessmen; I'm sure you won't be missed."

"You're probably right," George admitted, "but having accepted, I don't want to refuse now." He looked for a reason, when the truth was that he had had enough of Kirov's attempts to manipulate him. He wanted to be somewhere where the other man wasn't. He came up with, "This isn't the time to start attracting our embassy's attention by doing anything out of the ordinary." It seemed to be enough.

A secretary came into the room. George guessed it was in response to the telephone call. She gave Kirov some more papers and he laid them on the table before George so that he could see they were printed sheets with the Crédit Suisse logo on the top.

"What are they?" The text was in German.

Kirov passed a pen across. 'For you to sign. These are mandates and other bank formalities to operate an account in Berne."

"You guessed what I wanted."

"More or less, George. The funds have still to be deposited, but I shall arrange that. This bank account will entitle you to raise drafts to cover all your costs for the Finnish operation. I shall give you the name and address of a man in Helsinki who will act as a counter-signatory with you. You understand, this second signature is just a procedure, a precaution that our bureaucracy insists on." He took the top off the pen and held it out with the tip pointing at the papers. "We—I—trust you, George. I know you won't run off with the money."

"Sure," George took the pen and signed, placing each signature in the incomprehensible German text as if it were a series of blank checks. He replaced the cap and handed the pen back, and as he did so he caught the note of relief in Kirov's eyes. It reminded him that there was also a reason why the Soviets needed him, if he could ever get round to figuring out what it was. What he said was, "Sure you trust me. After all, who needs auditors when you can always have me killed?"

He meant it as a joke; or maybe not. Whichever, it made Kirov recoil.

"Please, George, don't joke. You know it isn't like that any more."

George knew.

"So you keep telling me."

He only hoped that it was true.

14

George Twist returned to his hotel. He needed to rethink his arrangements now that he had a more exact specification of the Soviet requirements and a timetable to work to. The time frame was short, and, if he was going to get things moving, he would have to visit the States. He had his airline ticket rewritten, then went to his room to wait for the retyped package of specifications to arrive. In the meantime he called the office and told them about the inquiries for the gas plants. When he was finished he rang the operator and asked for a second number.

The package came before the call. George collected it in reception from a flashy type in a leather jacket with military pockets and took it back upstairs, where he sat on the bed and had a first shot at studying the material.

It was the same that Peter had shown him earlier, but this time run off on a good-quality paper which might plausibly have originated in Finland. To make double-sure, he held each sheet to the light and checked it for any giveaway Soviet watermarks. Then he started to read.

He was still reading when the phone rang and the switchboard confirmed that his call was through, and next he could hear his own voice resonating on the echoing line.

One word: *Lillian.*

She was there and not there. Her voice, abstracted by distance, was muzzy with drugs—George couldn't remember which ones: her medications seemed to have run the whole gamut and finished up in the haunted wing of the pharmacopoeia. So now she seemed to be fleeing from him.

George was not an eloquent man. His salesman's patter was just that—patter. He needed reactions, a face to look at, features to play back his words. Without that response he found every syllable on the telephone painful.

He repeated, "Lillian."

"Hello George," she drawled.

"How are you?"

"Oh, a bit flat. I've had uppers and I've had downers; but the latest ones seem to iron me out. Little pink things. Look like cake decorations. How are you?"

"Oh, I'm fine."

"Business good?"

"Yes, excellent."

"Oh, good. That's nice for you."

"Yes, nice."

He told her about America, that he would have to go there directly from Moscow. She accepted the information placidly, and George realized that she thought it was something she had already known but had forgotten. Her memory lapses were becoming more noticeable, and she now anticipated them and withdrew from life so as to have less to forget.

There was a bang and then another voice, this one brisk and strong.

"Sorry, Mr. Twist, but Mrs. Twist just dropped the phone—didn't you, darling?"

"Thanks, Brenda. Put her back on, will you?"

This, too, had happened before as Lillian lost muscle tone and her limb functions diminished. But this time she could hold the receiver.

"Hello again," she said, trying to sound cheerful.

He didn't reply. She sensed his need for silence and they waited, hearing nothing but the whisper of each other's breath. He coughed, meaning to speak, but the words wouldn't come. He wanted to say, "I love you," but knew that there should be other words that palely but more adequately filled out what he felt. Was his own memory fading like hers, or was it only now after twenty years of marriage, in these last days as she wasted away beyond his reach, that he had discovered his inexpressible love for her? He prayed that it wasn't: that he had shown his love while there was time.

As he waited George thought of Peter Kirov, who would undoubtedly listen to this conversation. He found himself wanting to deny Peter this piece of knowledge.

Lillian broke the silence. She said tenderly, "I'm getting tired, darling. I'll pass the phone to Brenda. She can tell you all the news."

George answered, "Yes, do," and held on while the nurse took the receiver and in her no-nonsense Irish voice began to tell him about the state of the washing machine, and he nodded and grunted and made faithful promises to fix it on Thursday.

And this—he thought—was where it came to: Lillian retreating by degrees from life and Brenda taking over all the banality of marriage so that he and the nurse would begin to assume towards each other the attitudes of an elderly couple. And, in the end, he knew, his wife would be reduced to a husk, and he and Brenda would carry on in this mundane way; and Lillian and her needs would become a daily marriage rite, like putting out the cat at night.

But not today. Lillian came back on the line to say her faint goodbye. Behind her voice George could hear his future. Bloody Brenda was humming the tune to "My Way."

Bogdanov was waiting for Kirov back at the office. He handed over a packet with the Sluzhba official chop on it and sat back in his chair waiting for a response. Kirov opened the envelope. It contained half a dozen photographs and a badly typed report in stilted police talk. The report was signed *Mivernadze* in a big childish hand with unlinked letters that teetered against each other like a row of drunks. One of the photographs showed Irina Terekhova.

"So what's this about?" Kirov asked. He fingered the first photograph. It showed Irina Terekhova apparently talking to a stranger. He didn't recognize the location—snow and buildings—a shot taken in gray daylight. Because of the poor light, the man appeared in silhouette. The focus looked to be guesswork. Half the man's body was masked by a passing figure. It all indicated that there was no time to compose the shot. "Who ordered this rubbish without telling me? You?"

"Would I do that to you, boss?" said Bogdanov, and maybe he wouldn't; but Kirov knew that the other man had access to enough Sluzhba legmen to follow half of Moscow and was enjoying his spell of power.

"OK—who's this Mivernadze?"

"A nobody, just meat. He was working Sokolniki Park on the hoof with a camera and a few kopeks for his bus fare, taking snaps of our loyal Soviet citizenry just in case something turned up. A dope's job. I ran a check on Mivernadze and he was doing penance for getting pissed and insulting his chief. A real winner!"

Kirov flicked through the other photographs. Mivernadze had chosen to follow the man, snapping away until he ran out of film. More rush-shots, mostly of the man's back. A three-quarter profile with the outline broken up by the foliage of a bush. Useless.

Bogdanov was saying, "They ran a check on the woman and came up with Terekhova. Our interest was noted on the file so they sent the stuff across here. There was talk of the Sluzhba bringing her in for questioning, but I put a stop to it. What do you think?

"What's to think? Terekhova talks to a man in a public place. It doesn't become a crime simply because a policeman with nothing better to do takes a photograph. Where's the suspicion? What made him take the shot in the first place?"

Bogdanov shrugged his shoulders. "Who can say? That sort of street work, it's all instinct, emotion. Maybe she seemed excited, evasive. There's no point in asking Mivernadze because he can hardly string two words together. Maybe it's just prejudice. Here, look at this one." Bogdanov took up the picture of the stranger in profile.

"What am I looking for?"

"The nose—or maybe it's a leaf from the tree in the background—Mivernadze says the nose."

"So?"

"Mivernadze figures the man for a Jew-boy. I say *that's* why he took the shots. I have a feeling about Mivernadze: this guy is a real anti-Semite. He sees Terekhova—there's something about that woman—and she stirs him; he doesn't like the idea of a Yid talking to a white woman, see?"

"Perhaps." Kirov looked through the pictures again to find that of Irina Terekhova. He asked, "How far did Mivernadze follow the man?"

"He lost him near Shcherbakovskaya Metro station. He says the guy was deliberately trying to lose him."

"He'd have to say that to explain why he was shaken off. If the man was so suspicious, why didn't Mivernadze arrest him?"

Bogdanov smiled thinly. "I should have told you: Mivernadze is a famous coward. He has medals for it."

"He could have called for help."

"There's never a policeman when you want one."

"That's what he said?"

Bogdanov didn't answer. Kirov turned to the photograph of Irina Terekhova. Her face was expressive of something—pain? surprise? She had revealed a little of herself to the stranger, something Kirov felt she denied to him. He put the print down. He said, "I'm not concerned with Mivernadze's prejudices—and that's all this business amounts to."

"It's up to you, Boss," answered Bogdanov. He took the photographs back and put them into their envelope. Kirov watched him slowly tying the lot together with an elastic band.

"What's eating at you?" he asked. Bogdanov let slip the band and looked up.

"What if Mivernadze is right? Even a star like him is right once in a while. What if this guy is a Jew? Does it tell us anything about Terekhova? Remember she was married to that Jew poet, Davidov." He hesitated. "I'm talking about loyalty."

"Irina Terekhova's loyalty is my problem!" Kirov snapped. He thought of her cooperation with the KGB. It was complete and yet incomplete, as if he and she were trains running along the same track but towards ultimately different destinations.

"Sure," Bogdanov replied, and Kirov caught the other man regarding him curiously. "Whatever you say, boss," he added cautiously. "It's your funeral."

That night George Twist went to the cocktail party at the British commercial counselor's apartment over the office near the Ukraina. He took a taxi there, through snow-covered streets where the traffic was beginning to slacken and the dimly lit buildings seemed to withdraw to the edge of vision. The taxi driver had a radio or cassette playing. For a change the tune was "Moscow Nights."

Receptions for visiting businessmen were a regular feature of embassy life. There was a feeling in the embassy that, if they could do nothing else for businessmen, they could at least keep them supplied with sherry and small talk; and this somehow justified the embassy's existence. "Now that actual diplomacy is done on television," as Archie Lansdowne put it. He received each guest in turn with the same remark and a tinkle of limpid laughter which excused it, and he made sure that the visitor was provided with a glass of liquor and a plate of canapés, after which, balancing the two, the stranger was pushed gently into the throng. And there they milled around, twenty or so men in an assortment of jackets and ready-to-wear suits, skirting carefully past each other and making uncertain overtures to other strangers, as if it were a gentleman's excuse-me at a dance they had by chance been invited to. Lansdowne's wife, a desperately thin Scotswoman, orchestrated the proceedings by asking each newcomer in turn, "And what do *you* do?" and appeared to be surprised and delighted by the answers.

George found himself a quiet corner where he was regularly supplied with drink and vol-au-vents by a square-built Russian waiter who looked as though he carried a gun but probably didn't. He had come along simply to avoid drinking alone at the Mezhdunarodnaya or—worse—in company with Jack Melchior, who, with familiarity, had started telling stories about the time he spent in the Palestine Police in 1946 with nudges and winks as if they were shared reminiscences. "The good old days, eh, George?"

"We'll never see them again," George answered, remembering that he hadn't seen them the first time around.

Then, too, George had told Peter Kirov that he would be taking drinks with the commercial counselor. The alternative had been dinner with the Russian, which was something else that George couldn't face. Peter had taken the rebuff in good part. In fact he had telephoned George at his hotel later that day and inquired good-humoredly whether George had received the package of technical specifications and how he was getting on with them.

"I'm getting on fine," George answered, which was more or less true. He had quickly read through the specifications and they seemed to make sense except in one instance: the Soviet engineers stipulated that the Sep Tech membranes had to be made of steel and not of polymeric material. And that was a mystery. They had to know that Sep Tech membranes were polymeric—and it troubled them.

"And what brings *you* to Moscow?" Archie Lansdowne was saying. He was a tall man, handsome enough, with black hair slicked to one side and a pronounced cleft to his chin.

"I'm trying to sell gas-processing plants." George found himself looking up; the commercial counselor was of a height which allowed him to look down on people, and this seemed to suit his temper.

"Really? *Fascinating!* Which FTO? Licensintorg?"

"Techmashimport."

"Ah, well, never mind—they're all the same when it boils down to it. Know anybody here, do you?"

George wasn't sure how much territory "here" embraced. He assumed that Moscow was meant.

"I've come across a character called Lucas."

"Really, what do you know? Good old Neville!" Lansdowne glanced about him as if good taste had required him to invite the traitor along. Having satisfied himself that Lucas wasn't among his guests, he inquired, "I suppose he's enlisted you into his catering corps? He seems to treat all the ex-pats as a branch of Fortnum & Mason. Have you brought him anything?"

"A few cigarettes."

"Cigarettes? You surprise me; I understand that bottled beer was on his current shopping list, the brand that used to be advertised by the actor, the chappie who was involved with the Mermaid Theater, name on the tip of my tongue. Do you go to the theater much?"

"No."

"Me neither. Used to, though. We get the reviews out here—in the papers, you know. But can't get to the shows. A pity, that. We have to make do with videos at the embassy club—Clint Eastwood films—one gets a taste for them after a while."

George sympathized reflexively and stuck his nose into his drink. He was thinking: Why not polymeric membranes? From a mere point of curiosity the oddity had begun to annoy him.

Archie Lansdowne meanwhile was saying, "Another of Neville's tricks is to get people to place bets for him. Has he asked you to?"

"No." George felt the conversation drifting away from him. Polymeric membranes. He asked, "What does he bet on?"

"Oh, mostly on the big events — Epsom and the FA Cup. I imagine he'd like to bet on more, but of course he can't keep in touch."

"No?"

"No English sporting papers, see? Mind you, what he does bet on he's quite good at."

"Is he?"

"Absolutely. And he paints the town red if he has a big win. In fact, not long ago he picked the winner in the National and was drunk for two days on the strength of it — or so I'm told, though this is hearsay, you understand: the embassy discourages any direct contact."

"I suppose it would," George agreed. But he was thinking of any possible interaction of cadmium in the lake water and the polymeric material of the membranes Sep Tech would supply. Chemically it didn't stack up. So why should the Russians specify metal? Without considering the point he remarked, "I also met Brian Wormold."

"Wormold? You've got me there. Businessman?"

"You're joking." George was about to laugh, but as he scrutinized Lansdowne's face he saw only incomprehension, and for a second he thought: I'm mistaken; Wormold hasn't been arrested — but he knew that he had been. Then Lansdowne suddenly came to life.

"Oh, God, of course! Forgot the name. Wormold! The businessman chap who was caught doing black-market deals."

"I heard that he was spying," George said, but the other man wasn't listening.

"Fiona, darling! Do you remember that fellow Wormwood, the one who was arrested?" Lansdowne shouted across the room. "Did he come along to the party we gave for the mission?"

"I don't think so," his wife replied in her acid Lowland Scots burr.

"Well, there you have it," Lansdowne said, returning to George.

"I couldn't put a name to the face. Sorry, you were saying something?"

"No."

"Ah well, there we are." The commercial counselor tapped his empty glass and stared at his shoes. Then, with a sigh: "Must mix. Been nice talking to you and all that. By the way," he added as an afterthought, "I don't suppose you could let me have a note, a telex or something, summarizing where you are with the Russians? It's just that the Minister is coming here next month and we could brief him." He went on doubtfully: "I dare say it would help your case."

"Things are too early to say."

"Yes? Sorry to hear that." Lansdowne's face was momentarily solemn so that George had an uneasy feeling of just having announced the loss of *Titanic*, but then the other man said brightly: "Well, must move on, circulate. It's nice to have met you, Graham—it is Graham, isn't it?"

"Sure."

"Good." Lansdowne looked around blankly. "There's someone here who sells photocopying machines; you might like to talk to him. Machinery is your line, isn't it?"

"Something like that."

"Thought so." Lansdowne offered a hand to shake, but withdrew it when he realized that George was occupied by a glass and a plate. He smiled instead, pleasantly, and withdrew to mingle with the other guests, leaving George to stare at his back, seeing not the British commercial counselor, but Brian Wormold, whose face he could no longer remember. And, in the way that these things happen, the distraction suddenly provided George with the answer to the other matter that was troubling him. He knew all at once why the Russians had specified steel for the membranes. Polymeric membranes wouldn't be a problem—unless the contaminant in the lake were radioactive.

"Oh, Jesus," he whispered. "They've had a nuclear accident."

15

Some night they will come for me, the tellers of the deliberate lie.
To tell their lie, is it necessary that they know the truth?
And, if they knew it, would they let me know?
Perhaps, as we walk to their car,
And pause with the street lights shining on the shiny shoulders of their raincoats.
Secretly, between humans, as we light a final cigarette.

One of Osip Abramovitch Davidov's crimes was to publish a book of poems in an illegal *samizdat* edition. It was called *Iskra* — "The Spark" — which was a joke against Lenin, who, when still a revolutionary, had published a newspaper of the same name. Now Pyotr Andreevitch Kirov, major in the KGB, was able to read the Jewish poet's words reproduced in flimsy typescript bound loosely in thin card, blue and water-spotted from when the book had lain hidden behind a water cistern at Davidov's last address, a run-down apartment in Parkovaya Street. He had lived there briefly and desperately after his divorce from Irina Terekhova. It was there that the KGB had arrested him. They had carried the poet — weeping and raving drunk, his pants full of shit — bodily down to their car. Despite Davidov's feeble poem, Kirov considered it unlikely that the men arresting him had either told or known the truth.

He visited Irina Terekhova at the University. She was giving a lecture, so he waited for her in her room, which like her visible life, was sparsely furnished with textbooks, files and a photograph of her son.

He had begun to read her mail, which he obtained from the Postal Inspection Department in Komsomolskaya Square. She wrote to her husband — the present one — regularly, at least once a week; and the Colonel regularly replied, writing with restrained, decent passion.

"Dearest Heart. As I sit at night in the silence of the curfew, I think always of you and of our dear Arkasha . . ." The soldier struggled with words and images from cheap fiction, expressing his modest feelings with poignant banality. Kirov had called for Terekhov's file. The Colonel was a soldier's soldier, a risk-taker, a notorious hell-raiser. Dearest Heart. . . .

Irina Terekhova's letters were different: affectionate, full of lively incident, often gently humorous, compassionate, caring. He had taken a bundle of photocopies of them home to his apartment and read them slowly and intently while Lara tried to engage his interest in the incidents of the day at her rehearsals. She raised her voice, just enough to catch his attention; but it was as if he had suddenly been caught in an act of adultery. Yet it wasn't adultery. Nothing so tangible. He played with the thought and discarded it with the other detritus of people that he might have been. And Lara kissed him with one of her precise kisses like a ballet movement.

"Good morning, Major," she said. "I wasn't expecting you." She had come into her room to find him there already.

"Good morning, Dr. Terekhova."

Today she looked pale and tired. There was a grayness, a slackness about her face, which he noticed as she placed her books on the table and turned to give him a guarded look. She suggested tea and set about arranging it. She appeared harassed and impatient to be rid of him.

She asked, "What brings you here, Major Kirov?"

For an answer he said, "George has been in Moscow again."

"Really?" She seemed pleased by the news.

"He came to collect the specifications for the project at Sokolskoye so that his company can work on it. And, of course, to negotiate business for the supply of gas-processing plants, which is what interests him most. He'll be visiting us again, with technical data for the buildings and other works which will house the American equipment. And it will also be necessary for our engineers to review the designs produced by the Americans." Kirov halted and then commented offhandedly, "We could find an opportunity for you to see George again."

"Why should I do that? Isn't my work for you finished?"

"Did you know," Kirov changed the subject, "that Pokrebsky has been released?" He stopped there, seeing her face charged with an expression of mixed horror and disbelief.

"How can that happen—after everything that he's done?"

"Political considerations." Evidently she didn't understand. "The Minister ordered it. The Sokolskoye incident is to be laid at the door of Bor'yan, the plant director."

"But that isn't true! Pokrebsky—"

"If Pokrebsky is admitted to be a crook," Kirov pressed on, "then the KGB would have to be called in to clean out the whole mess at the Inspectorate. The Army would lose control over part of the nuclear program. The Minister of Defense would not want that. A compromise was reached." He could see only her back as she played with the glasses of tea before handing him one. "That's the way things are," he said.

"What about the Englishman?"

"George Twist remains the key. He had been told that the lake at Sokolskoye has been contaminated with cadmium, but it's only a matter of time before he realizes what's going on."

"You have a better opinion of him now."

"He has his weaknesses, but he isn't a fool," Kirov conceded. "Once he knows that we have a massive nuclear-contamination problem, which only he can solve for us, he will see that he has a lever against us. That would be dangerous."

"For you?"

She imagined that he could not survive a disaster at Sokolskoye. He turned her concern against her.

"For George," he said and left her to work out the implications. He picked up the photograph of her son and asked some questions about him. "Bogdanov—you remember Bogdanov?—he has no children of his own. I think he's got a soft spot for Arkasha. He has an envelope in his desk in which he's been collecting foreign stamps. Does Arkasha collect stamps? I'll call round with them or mail them to you."

Irina asked, "How can I help? What do you want from George?"

"We need his commitment," Kirov said. What was that in her eyes? Disgust for him? "We need him to understand the scale of the human tragedy that we face." He softened his voice to her and urged, "Please, Irina Nikolaevna!" using her first two names. He had not done this before. "This matter is above politics and personal considerations. George is open to such an appeal."

"Yes," she agreed. "He's a sentimental man."

Students went by, clutching piles of books, bumping up against each other and laughing. One of them sang something that couldn't be heard through the glazing. He waved his arms, his mouth was open and his neck showed the workings of his larynx. In scarves and sweaters they seemed impervious to cold.

Kirov turned from the window.

"Can you identify this man for me?" he asked. He laid in front of her the photograph taken by Mivernadze. He expected her to pick it up and look not at the man but at her own picture, out of the instinctive vanity that makes us a care care about our passport photographs. She left the print alone.

"Are you having me spied on?"

"No." He invited her confidence. "Let me be frank with you. This photograph is an accident. There are people whose job it is to look out for trouble even where none exists. One of them took this." He gathered the picture up and handed it to her. She regarded it briefly. He continued, "This is just routine. The photograph exists as a record. It has to be explained so that we can put a stop to the nonsense and get on with serious things."

"But it makes me a suspect, doesn't it?" she challenged him.

"Of what? There is nothing to be suspected of. This is just an administrative inconvenience."

"No." Irina picked up the photograph again and scanned it apparently casually. "It doesn't require any context or explanation," she said. "It only has to be there on a police file for an accusation to exist."

"Believe me," said Kirov. "This matter is hardly worth my time.

Whatever you say, I promise to believe you."

"I don't know the man. He's just someone who stopped me to ask for directions. He had difficulty in understanding, so the explanation took time."

Kirov didn't believe her.

She passed the photograph back and checked her watch. "I have another appointment, Major. Can I go?"

Kirov nodded. But inside he was angry. He wanted her to confide in him. Whatever her secret was, he thought that she should trust him.

"Tell me," he said, "about your first husband."

She halted in the doorway, turned and examined him. She was curious but calm.

"Davidov? How can he be relevant? No, don't answer: he's relevant because you've decided that he's relevant. Well"—she hesitated but only to collect her thoughts—"what can I say? He was a violent drunk, a madman. And I divorced him."

"Was he a Zionist? Did he want to leave the Soviet Union and go to Israel? Did he have Jewish political contacts?"

She saw some humor in the questions, because she laughed mildly as she shook her head. "Osip wasn't a nationalist. He believed in the rights of humanity."

In this respect at least, Kirov thought that she was telling the truth.

He returned to Dzerzhinsky Square. Bogdanov was in the office, engaged in a wrangle over the telephone with Narodny Bank over the mechanics of transferring ten million dollars to the account in Berne that would finance George Twist. When he had finished he stretched back in his chair and only then noticed the other man.

"OK, boss, so what's new? Did you see Terekhova? What's her explanation for the guy in the photograph?"

"A stranger—a man in the street, asking for directions."

Bogdanov swiveled his chair to face his chief.

"Then she's a liar, isn't she?" he said bluntly.

"Perhaps."

"Perhaps? All right, whatever you say, boss."

Bogdanov turned back to his work. He picked up his papers but continued to talk, suggesting that they should go for a drink some place where the beer was better. He started listing bars, their good points, bad points, girls he'd met there, men he'd arrested here — he liked making arrests in pubs because he had a policeman's lust for a good brawl.

Kirov meanwhile could think only of Irina Terekhova. He suspected her secret without knowing what it was; wondering perhaps that it was not in any sense a single thing, but something that permeated her at every level at which she could be exposed, a deep, uterine secret. And then, because he wasn't a fool, he considered the opposite: that the apparent depth was an illusion, a mirror thrust in his face. There was no way to decide between interpretations.

"We need something to secure her loyalty," he said.

Bogdanov, still reminiscing, let his words trail away. He put down his pen, "Now you're talking. Any ideas?"

"The child. The person we can be sure she cares for. One way or another we can use the boy."

16

Do you know the way to San José?

George Twist seemed to remember that those were the words to a song, part of the American romance with place names that the English didn't share. Do you know the way to Rickmansworth? sounded like a request for traffic directions. But change the name to San José and suddenly the words became magical even if the place wasn't. And the place wasn't. San José was one of those sprawling conurbations like Los Angeles that you could pass right through while still looking for the center, a place where the buildings hung around like smog and you passed through them looking for whatever it was that gave the city its identity. And in the end maybe there was nothing more tangible than the song.

He hired a car in San Francisco, one with spongy suspension and no performance, the kind he had grown unused to since returning home, and drove down Highway 101 through the Santa Clara Valley, which they called Silicon Valley because the high-tech industries paid for their wives' cosmetic surgery. He felt tired and jet-lagged after the flight from Moscow via London, but this had become so normal that he had stopped thinking about it. It was enough to take it easy and let the Greyhound bus pass him on its way to Monterey, and in the same easy fashion check into the Le Baron Hotel on First Street North, unpack, shower and go to bed until he caught up with the rest of the world.

He drove out to Sep Tech's office. It was a clear, sunny morning, the way he remembered them; the traffic was light, and in the downtown area you could see maybe just a little of that magic of

American cities among the run-down clothes and record stores. For instance, the "I am" temple that he couldn't recall from the hundreds of times he had made the same journey, but there it was. He supposed it said something about California. And so, too, did the bright yellow weatherboard house that belonged to the Society of Saint Vincent de Paul, but which the board outside called "Vinh-Son" on account of the Vietnamese, he guessed, though he couldn't think why.

Little Orchard Street started out as a row of cheap housing, not much more than shacks with verandas and flaking paintwork; then it took a dogleg turn and became an industrial zone mostly flanked by plants owned by General Electric. At the further end, where the road ran into Curtner Avenue, lay Oak Hill cemetery. Sep Tech's offices and the factory where they made the membranes stared across the highway at the graveyard. George parked his car and went to see Lou Ruttger.

Lou was as he had always been but somehow larger; George's departure from running Sep Tech had given him more scope. The fact expressed itself in apparently contradictory ways. So, as Lou seemed more expansive and more confident, he also seemed in some fashion younger, with the clear-sightedness of youth or, perhaps, the capacity of youth to reduce everything to simple principles that would be seen as clear-sighted or plain naïve as events turned out.

"Hi, George, how are you doing? Coffee, Coke, something stronger? How's Lillian and the kid? Charlene!" he shouted, sticking his head out of the office door. "George's here. Bring in some coffee. Hey, George, but it's great to see you!"

"And you." George held out a hand, and Lou Ruttger clasped it warmly and steered his visitor toward a seat, all the while pumping out the usual inquiries about the flight, the jet-lag and the weather in England, to which George gave the stock answers while he tried to take in what Lou had done to his old office. The bar had been moved out and there was a computer VDT on the desk, and on the wall a photograph of Lou and his National Guard buddies grinned down at them. Ruttger had faith in honesty, decency and the American way of life that George had gone beyond mocking, and which now he found strangely touching; and Lou had made his faith concrete with talismans like the VDT or like the radiophone in his car. He was talking now about the refurbished swimming pool he had installed in his home.

". . . bigger than the old one; you should see it. Maybe you'll have a bite of dinner with us? Nancy would like to see you: she worries about Lillian. Say you'll come."

"I'll come."

"Great. Tonight?"

"Sure."

They talked around a little more until George got twitchy. Too much coffee. If the alcohol didn't get him, the caffeine would.

Lou was saying, "I hear you've been in the USSR. I thought that was a no-no ever since the Omsk Job."

"Business is business. You know the mess we're in over in England. If the Russians have money to spend, then we're prepared to talk to them. They're looking for LNG plants."

"Whatever you say. Me, I wouldn't touch them: they'll screw you to the ground. If you want a personal opinion, I wouldn't sell them any technology: communism has dug a goddamn great hole for them, and I don't see why the West should help them out of their economic problems. But I guess I'm just an old-fashioned Republican."

George nodded. He tried to remember how old the other man was—thirty, thirty-two. It seemed young to be an old-fashioned anything. But, then, George was a 1960s liberal: and, despite what he'd earlier thought, people like Lou, who had been raised in the seventies, seemed in this respect older.

For now he said, "I'll bear it in mind. If the Russians don't pay, we'll send in the Marines."

"However you want to play it, George. Just don't ask me for help. If I so much as smile at a Russian, I have the Department of Commerce and COCOM chasing me. Where this company's technology is concerned, they can get very excited about selling to the Soviet Union."

"Perish the thought," said George.

They talked away the rest of the morning on the question of Sep Tech's research and development expenditure and business prospects. George explained the cash crisis affecting the English parent company and the problems of funding the ambitious program that Lou Ruttger had mapped out.

"For Christ's sake!" Lou said in exasperation. "Alasdair Cranbourne should sell this company and be done with it! If he wants cash, there are people who would pay plenty for this operation."

"Like who?" George asked.

"Like Chaseman Industries—or maybe Abe Korman."

"Korman is still nosing about?"

"Here and there. His story about defense procurement is all bullshit: there has to be something else behind his interest. Korman is a businessman as well as a Senator, so maybe he's putting together a deal to buy Sep Tech. I hear he's tied in to a bunch in Atlantic City."

"Atlantic City—are you serious? You want to be owned by the Mafia?"

"There's no such thing as the Mafia. Edgar Hoover said so."

"And there's no such thing as the Soviet Union. I just came back and can prove it."

They both laughed together.

He took Lou to lunch at Sebastian's Restaurant and fed him a couple of stiff martinis and some broiled swordfish which they washed down with Chablis. The younger man mellowed. He began to talk about his plans in a golden voice with eyes half-closed and full of dreams. George pitied and admired him. His own dreams had long since shriveled and died somewhere on a plane or in a bar or in a hotel bedroom filled with the sour smell of tobacco and booze and sweat. He had no plans now except to reach the age of forty-four and then maybe he'd think about becoming forty-five and forty-six and so on, fighting for each day as it came. He picked at his food and drank a couple of bottles of Perrier water and, after the meal, instead of a cigar, chewed on a piece of nicotine gum.

"OK, George," said Lou when they were finished, "thanks for the meal, but why are we celebrating?"

"Because I've got some business for you, good business."

"In Russia?"

"Who mentioned Russia? I'm talking about something kosher—a client in Finland."

Lou Ruttger sat up, suddenly alive with interest. I've pulled his string, George thought bitterly; and it occurred to him that Peter Kirov would be proud of him.

Lou said, "Well? Don't leave me with my mouth hanging open. What is this business? What does the client want?"

George wiped his lips on a napkin and replaced it slowly on the table. Timing—all a matter of timing—just like any piece of salesmanship.

"He needs to remove heavy metals from water."

"Then, he's come to the right place. What scale are we talking about?"

"Three hundred and forty million gallons of water, more or less; the whole lot to be processed inside one month."

"Three . . ." Lou's answer started out as a repetition to make sure he'd got it right and trailed off in a realization of what was being said. "Jesus," he muttered, "that's a hell of a job, George."

"But you can do it?"

The younger man looked past him. A waiter came over and hung about the table expectantly. Ruttger waved him away.

"Well?" George pressed.

"I guess so," Lou ventured. He thought for a moment and then gave one of his little-boy smiles. "Shit," he murmured quietly, "why the hell not?"

They drove back to the office, Lou Ruttger behind the wheel, with his eyes glued to the route. George imagined the thoughts tumbling through his brain and waited for the questions, but Lou was in no hurry. They retired to his office, called for coffee, and Ruttger proceeded to write down a punch list on the desk pad. Then he started.

"OK, George, what's the client's program?"

"He wants the whole mess cleaned up by the beginning of next April. Working back and allowing a month to process the contaminated water, a month to erect and commission and a month in shipping times, that means we have to be ready to ship on New Year's."

Lou Ruttger put his pen down. "Come on, George, that isn't a serious proposition. It gives us two months at the outside, starting today. You couldn't find a vessel fabricator who would—"

"You don't have to," George interrupted.

"Why not?"

"Because the client will fix a lot of the project for himself. What he wants from us is the process, the detailed mechanical design, basic civils data, and delivery of Sep Tech membranes and resin. Once he has the designs, he'll put the equipment fabrication out to his own suppliers and do the building work. All we do is manufacture the membranes and buy in the resin—and that we can do inside two months: I've seen the shop-floor and they're sitting on their bums."

"I still don't see how the client can manage his end."

"That's his problem. Look, he has a lot of pull with his suppliers and can make them bust a gut to meet his deadline."

"Maybe. But with that sort of rush people make mistakes. How are we supposed to guarantee and commission the plant?"

"We don't." George said it and wished he hadn't. Lou glanced at him sharply. *It's slipping away—slipping away. Relax, take it slowly, as if this were the most normal job in the world.* "Lou," he said in that expansive older-and-wiser way, "the client knows that he's asking for a lot in a short time, but he doesn't expect the moon. He's relying on our expertise based on the West Valley project; and frankly he doesn't have much choice. I mean, how many alternative processes are there? He doesn't look for guarantees. Once we've delivered the designs, the membranes and the resin, we're off the hook: he'll erect and commission the plant himself. If it works, it works; and if it doesn't—I guess that's his tough luck."

"What kind of client is this?" Lou asked, still skeptically.

"He has a trusting nature."

"This is the client's specification: water analysis, site conditions, topography, climate, available electric power, labor, the works."

They were around the big table in Ruttger's office with the papers spread out and tacked and a scattering of coffee-cups. Outside the light was starting to fail. Lou turned a page.

"Have you studied the temperature data, George? This place sounds like the middle of Alaska."

"We're talking about Finland, not Fiji. This is a place close to the Arctic Circle and it's wintertime: what do you expect?"

"George had answered sharply—too sharply, he suspected.

"I don't know. Don't rush me. You never used to. You were always a laid-back guy. What's gotten into you, George?"

"I'm sorry," George apologized. "Maybe I'm traveling too much."

Ruttger looked up from the papers.

He thinks it's because of Lillian. Now *he's* sorry.

"That's OK. Just ease off a little." Ruttger returned to the specifications. "We're talking about a lake?" he said.

"Yes."

"Frozen. I get it: he wants to clean the place up before the spring melt—that's why the April deadline."

"Uh-huh."

"OK." Lou stopped. He was finished for the moment with the papers and was thoughtful. "Maybe I should apologize to you, George. I thought you weren't being serious. But if the spring melt is critical for the client't problem, then he just *has* to go ahead with us. He doesn't have any choice."

"That's right," George answered. He studied the other man's face. It was time to pull another level. "And that means he has to pay our price—any price."

"Damn right he does!" Ruttger cried, and his serious, youthful face had a moment of triumph.

It was evening. Light was almost gone and Little Orchard Street and Curtner Avenue were filling with cars. George was waking up. He felt like eating breakfast.

Lou Ruttger in his meticulous manner had worked through the specifications and made his notes and was now sitting back with his collar unfastened and a dream of contentment on his face. The table was strewn with cups of cold decaffeinated coffee and diet Coke.

"It's doable, George," he said. "I had my doubts, but it can be done, provided we start work now. How secure is our position? How guaranteed is the contract?"

"There's no competition. The contract will be signed within the month. Start work on my say-so—I'll take the responsibility."

"In writing?"

"You can have it in blood if that's the way you want it."

"That's OK, I trust you, George."

The remark gave George no comfort.

"There's one more question." Ruttger sounded a little cautious. "I get the feeling that there's something you're trying to avoid."

"What's that?"

"Who's the client? I've read all this stuff and nowhere does it tell me who he is or what he does. *Kosher* — that was your expression. To me, this client doesn't sound kosher."

"Put your coat on. We'll drive back to the hotel and I'll tell you on the way."

"They drove back through the downtown area. San José was putting on its night-time glamor of lights. George felt the twinge again: the romance of America, the way he had once seen it years before, through the windows of a Greyhound bus, in silence except for the bubbling breath of the sleeping passengers and sometimes a snatch of country music. In America, where they made magic out of motels.

Lou Ruttger was saying, ". . . the name. You were going to tell me the name."

"That's just what I can't do. I'm sorry."

They stopped at a traffic signal and waited. George drummed the wheel of the car.

"Why's that?" Lou asked.

"You've got to be patient with me," George answered. "Give me a couple of weeks and I'll tell you all you need to know." He touched the accelerator and they glided forward in the flow of traffic.

"What's the problem?"

"The Finnish authorities. The client runs a mining and refining operation; and you know what a business that can be for regulations. Now suddenly he finds that he's dumped a mess of toxic metals into a lake, and if the facts get out, then he's frightened they're going to close him down. You know what these Scandinavian places are like: so clean you could eat off the pavement. The environmental lobby is very powerful."

"OK — so?"

"So he's cautious. At the moment everything is on a need-to-know basis. Me, he trusts; but until we have a contract he wants confidentiality."

"I'll need the name to get an export license—COCOM—you know it comes back to that."

"Don't worry." In the darkness George gave his don't-worry smile. "Finland—who can object to Finland?"

"You going back there?"

"Just as soon as I can. I'm meeting the client in Helsinki in a couple of days."

"So soon?"

"You sound as if you care."

"What about Lillian? Moscow, San José, Helsinki—how do you know which end up you are? You should ease up on traveling, George; you look terrible."

"I feel fine," George answered; and he did. Some breakfast and he would feel even better. "You're worrying about nothing," he added. "I'm going to Finland. Snow, cleanliness and respectability. It's like selling to Santa Claus."

"I don't believe in Santa Claus," said Lou Ruttger.

17

November 7–15

Helsinki. George had a memory of trees and lakes and sea. He had been there once when he was a young, green engineer to commission a plant, and many times since; but he remembered that first time best because Ronnie Pugh had shown him the ropes; Ronnie, who was believed to know the ropes everywhere, which made all the more incredible the story that he had got himself shot in Lagos because he tried to defend a woman against being robbed. "Any tale in which Ronnie Pugh was a hero is nothing but a malicious fabrication," said Alasdair Cranbourne on the subject at a manager's Christmas lunch, when you could get away with that sort of thing. Jim Evans, the lawyer, reminded him of the story as they drove along the airport road out of Vantaa. Evans, who was less used to travel, was in a jumpy, talkative mood, which was a way it also took people. He had a string of anecdotes, more or less funny, more or less repetitive, and George let him get on with it. He did the driving, and stared out of the driver's window the while, looking for the cold, calm Baltic and the trees and the rest of it that made Helsinki unique, but saw only an airport road, which, like all other airport roads, seemed to have the topography of its kind, devoid of place.

"Helsinki?" Alasdair Cranbourne asked as he signed the travel authorization form. "On our wanderings again, are we? I should have thought you'd want to ease up on the old mileage, with all the trips you've taken lately. Can't be good for the health. Still, don't want to dampen enthusiasm, eh? Want you to be a success as sales director, eh? But Helsinki—why there? We don't have any business, do we, George?"

"I got a telephone enquiry for one of Sep Tech's units. It could be a fast mover; that's why I want to take Jim Evans with me to handle the contracts. The client is keeping the business under wraps because he has a pollution problem."

"So it's all a bit hush-hush, is it? Ah, you're too deep for me!" said Cranbourne pleasantly.

They found their hotel, the Vaakuna, close by the railway station, and the restaurant and the bar; and in no time the place had an old familiar air as they eased themselves with a few beers.

"George," said his companion, mellowed to a certain degree, "doesn"t any of this *worry* you?"

"It scares me stiff—every time. Will you have another beer, or something stronger? I've got a bottle of *koskenkorva* in my room."

They had a late breakfast, sitting in their business suits in a dining room full of men in their business suits. They had no morning appointments.

"The agenda seems all a bit loose," said Evans. "I mean, I have a list of all the things we need to investigate to get this Finnish operation on the road, but I'm not sure exactly how to proceed. A local lawyer, a property-dealer and an accountant—I've got some names and I've arranged to meet them; but what do I tell them? If I put the story baldly, setting up dummy corporations with dubious accounts: it all looks a bit, you know, *funny.*"

"Forget about it for the time being," George told him. "Cancel the appointments. Instead you can check out a few equipment suppliers, see what they can do for us in the way of machine tools for quick delivery. Then take yourself off sightseeing for a couple of hours."

"And what are you going to do?"

"I've got to see a man," said George, "about a dog."

Evans looked down at his breakfast and picked at the cold meat on his open sandwich. "You know, George," he said seriously, "the more I think about it, the more I don't fancy this business one little bit."

"I know. You've got a headache."

He called home. Bloody Brenda answered the telephone. She had left the vacuum cleaner on, and its siren sound wailed in the background as she shouted at him over the line. Lillian was asleep, couldn't be disturbed, but she, the nurse, could answer any questions. "How are you—I mean—is she?" The transposition of persons was affecting his grammar. Fine, the darling was fine. In the end Brenda would take over Lillian's power of speech.

He put on his overcoat and left the hotel. The broad street in front of the station rattled with trams. There was a drunk sitting on the station steps and a couple of kids arguing about something. The air was sharply cold.

A riverwalk fronted the university botanical gardens, except that there wasn't a river, just a narrow sea inlet from the fjord leading into a small lagoon. Beyond the line of lime trees that had lost their leaves some boats were laid up on a stretch of bank and a few squatted, moored in the water, hazy with a scum of frost. George stood for a while studying the boats, smiling at a gull that tugged at something buried in the dirt, watching two men drag a sheet over a dinghy to protect it against the coming snow. He found the *lap-lap* of the water soothing.

He walked the full length of the path and halted where it turned away by a boathouse and a restaurant that was closed for the season. He tapped his watch and whistled to himself and then turned to look along the line of parked cars, wondering whether he was supposed to check them out. What had Peter said? He had been lectured by the Russian like a child, instilled with the details of the procedures for making a contact—the safety signs, the fallbacks. "Come on, Peter, you don't really do it like that, do you?" "Please, George, this is very serious business"

"Excuse me, do you have a light?"

A stranger in a herringbone topcoat, holding out a cigarette so that it spun in his fingers. George reached into his pocket.

"I'll have to use a match; my lighter doesn't work."

"They are often unreliable." The stranger took the matches and broke two trying to light his cigarette. He inhaled and stared frankly at the Englishman.

"I must get another one soon," said George.

He put the matches in his pocket and walked on a few paces. The stranger kept step in a stilted fashion, tapping the end of his cigarette after each draw. "You were supposed to say, 'I must buy one tomorrow.'"

"I forgot. I'm sorry."

"Not good."

"I said I'm sorry," George snapped. "What do you want me to do, kill myself?"

The other man reacted blankly. "It doesn't matter, maybe. I recognized you. Shall we go this way?" He crossed the road toward the gate leading into the gardens, leaving George to follow.

"What do I call you?"

"Anton."

"You're not Finnish?"

"No."

"Or Russian?" George guessed. Perhaps it was the black hair that gave him the idea.

"Perhaps, or not." Anton paused by the railings and scraped the dirt from his shoes. They were snakeskin, and he wore them like the family jewels, not to be broken, which accounted for the stiff deliberation of his walk. He did this so meticulously that George detected an air of expectancy and wondered if he'd missed some element of etiquette. He had the bizarre notion he was supposed to give the other man a tip.

"OK, so we walk," Anton said at length. George was close to him now. They were of equal height, which made the younger man tall, too. It was in fact the other man's age that struck him: like policemen, spies were getting younger. But, then, how old were they supposed to be? Suddenly he saw Lou Ruttger in him. It was there and gone in a second. The physical resemblance was small, but there was something of youth and eagerness and tension all hidden behind the slabness of his features, the grayness of shape rather than of color. It was a face so unremarkable in its physical detail that only a couple of small razor nicks stuck in the memory. An indifferent face, but it held the menace of anonymity.

They stuck to the path; on their left stood a brick building with a lead roof, partially sheeted for renovation. Their way inclined to the right, past glasshouses and a small kiosk that sold ices in summer, and an old-fashioned hothouse, all domed and wrought, flashing panes of autumn sunlight. Anton drove the pace in a straight-legged gait. George stopped him by a small pond.

"Aren't we supposed to be talking about something? I'm sorry, mate, if I don't quite follow the form, but this is a new game for me." He caught a glimpse of his reflection in the water, overweight and breathless, and wanted to laugh.

"Please, Mr. Twist?"

"Oh, call me George; everyone else seems to." He looked back from his reflection. "Sorry, I was thinking: I've watched this scene before — in films, you understand — two men in our business, walking by the water in some park, feeding the ducks and selling secrets — yes?"

"There are no ducks," Anton responded cautiously.

"No — no, I can see that. Speaking literally, there *are* no ducks. Oh, sod it, maybe you have a different cliché in your films."

They moved off again, threading a path between bands of plant beds towards a fence where the gardens ended and some tennis courts began; and, beyond the courts, an avenue of birches.

"How reliable is your Mr. Evans?" Anton asked.

"He's all right, I suppose. I didn't have much choice. This sort of operation requires a lawyer to put it together; and Jim's the only one I've got." He brightened up and said, "That's lawyers for you: they find an opening into everything," but the comment was lost on Anton, who came from a place where they probably didn't. George retrieved the flow and went on, "He knows enough to get by, but not the whole story. You got any problems?"

"Not for the moment."

They turned left along a path leading towards an exit into Siltasaarenkatu. A gardener swept leaves from a group of tall trees. *Acer saccharinum,* according to the plaque on the ground; George must have read the word aloud, suggesting a question, for his companion looked up into the branches and said simply, "It's a tree." He said it so solemnly that George felt again that

220

there was some code between them to which he was supposed to be a party. He was missing the point of the meeting. Was Anton testing him? Or perhaps like many other meetings it was in fact pointless, just a matter of habit.

"My lawyer," he said to break the silence. "He thinks it may be hard to find the necessary local help. Our story is a little bit . . . delicate."

"Not to worry. I shall meet your lawyer and give him names of helpful people."

"In that case, why don't you arrange all this business yourself, if you know so many helpful people?"

"No," Anton answered, "sometimes it is not so easy for us. You understand that here in Helsinki there are so many American secret policemen." He let the words drift off into the cold air and put his hands in his pockets. He took out a scrap of paper and checked his watch. "I have things to do," he said. "Tonight we meet again; also your lawyer. Here are two telephone numbers." He handed the note over. "The first one you call at six o'clock."

"I'm surprised you trust me. Is there a code?

"For you we keep it simple. It is a public telephone. The second number is only for emergencies. You will remember it and destroy the paper."

"Eat it?"

"Please?"

"Never mind." George slipped the paper into his pocket.

"And now I go," Anton said and with some formality extended a hand to be shaken. Then he was gone, disappearing along the path, weaving with small steps among the piles of leaves so as to preserve his snakeskin shoes.

He met up with Evans for a snack at a pizzeria in the slag-gray shopping mausoleum on the corner of the station square and Keskuskatu. It was five o'clock, dark, and raining, and from the upper window where they sat they could watch people streaming with the rain in and out of the station. In the street lights the pink granite shone a dim brown.

Over a bowl of spaghetti George asked how Evans had spent his day.

"Oh, I got by. I found out the names of the couple of dozen manufacturers who could deliver engineering equipment off the shelf if we're not too particular in our requirements. Once we have a building, I think we could fill it with two or three million dollars' worth of stock within a week." He smiled as he cut a slice out of his pizza. "Mind you, it'll look an odd sort of factory; but it should pass muster to anyone who doesn't know what he's looking for." He wiped his mouth on a napkin and straightened his tie, a colorful spotted affair. "And you? How was your man with a dog? Some big gorilla with no neck and hairy ears?"

"No, just a kid; he couldn't have been over twenty-five."

"Doesn't sound like a kid to me."

"I suppose not," George said thoughtfully and decided he didn't want to talk any more.

Evans continued chatting over the background hubbub; now about this, now about that; changing the subject every few minutes; describing people in the street, sometimes humorously; speculating on what they were doing. "What do you think, George?" George was asking for the bill.

While they waited, Evans remarked, "I spent the afternoon dancing."

"Not in that bow tie, I hope."

"I had an hour to spare and nothing to do, and found this place, the Vanha Maestro, that did afternoon dances—well, you know how I like to dance; so I seized the chance."

"Jesus."

"Pardon, George?"

George returned a blank look so that Evans glanced away over the other's shoulder.

"Good God, what do you suppose that's doing here?"

George shuffled round. In the middle of the restaurant there was an old-fashioned red English telephone kiosk.

"That reminds me," he said. "I've got a call to make. We've got to meet our contact later this evening."

"All right," Evans agreed distractedly, still examining the kiosk. "It's a damn funny world," he commented. "An English telephone in an Italian restaurant in Finland."

"We're all living in the same country, hadn't you noticed?"

"Yes," Evans murmured and turned back to face his companion. "Sorry, George, wasn't paying attention."

"I said we're all living in the same country."

"Oh, certainly!" Evans answered brightly. "But whose country, eh?"

He crossed the square to the station; stopped to put out a cigarette on the steps; watched it fizzle out in the rain. On either side of the doors loomed pairs of monumental figures holding globes of light, where people waited and were then drawn off into the darkness. The afternoon train from Leningrad had just arrived. In the main hall a group of Russian officials, holding briefcases and shopping bags, stood fingering their papers. Unconsciously George searched for Peter Kirov among them; but, naturally, he wasn't there; just some nameless bureaucrats, one of whom stared back aridly.

"Anton?" He stood in the booth, holding a pile of silver marks in his open palm. Behind him a patient queue had formed, waiting for the telephone.

"You're late."

"Oh, come on, what's two minutes?"

"Not good," Anton replied flatly, then condescended, "but let's get down to business. I have reported our meeting, and my colleagues are happy to proceed. We shall meet tonight at eight o'clock and discuss what to do next."

George went back to the restaurant to collect Jim Evans. The lawyer was curious, excited even.

"Where are we meeting?"

"A walk by the water. Trees and birds."

"Just like the films. I love it."

"I made the same point to Anton."

"Oh?"

"He didn't understand."

Evans with his taste for the bizarre couldn't leave the subject alone. As they strolled along Kaisaniemenranta, their topcoats buttoned against the cold, he raised it again.

"Odd, don't you think, George, this fixation on holding hands in the park? It seems to happen in every thriller I've ever seen."

"It's probably in the owner's manual. Look, there he is."

223

Anton was coming toward them out of the shadow of the trees.

"Is there a password?"

"Christ, I hope not. I only know one and I got that wrong." George stepped forward, and the newcomer shook his hand gloomily.

"Tony, let me introduce you to Jim Evans, our lawyer."

"Hello, Tony."

"Anton," the other man replied tersely.

"Tony here represents our business partners," said George, and, being uncertain what custom demanded he say next, he looked away and noted other knots of men at intervals along the path. He groaned inwardly. "This isn't some queer's pick-up spot, is it? That would take the cake."

Anton returned a blank stare, then followed George's gaze. "They are other businessmen," he said laconically. "And other people to give—assistance."

"Oh, good. Yes, well, we could always use some assistance." Jim Evans grinned good-humoredly until George wished he would stop and so missed Anton's next remark.

". . . not so simple as you may think."

"Give me that again, I didn't catch you."

The younger man raised his voice.

"Our business in Finland is not so simple as you may think."

"This is simple?" George asked but, guessing Anton would not understand, he continued, "So what's our problem?" He looked at the other man cautiously. Bulgarian? There was something southern European in Anton's dark features.

"Finland is not so easy a country to work from. There are controls on imports from the United States: the importer must satisfy the authorities that the goods will only be used in Finland. Also export—very strictly controlled to the socialist countries. You must understand: Finland is a neutral country—very careful, very cautious; also very honest. It is better to use Sweden. Normally we use Sweden."

"Moscow was happy to use Finland."

"Moscow—ha! The people you deal with do not always know these things."

"You want me to tell them?"

Anton didn't reply. He gave a gesture like a sigh and reached

224

into his pockets to produce a small handful of receipts which he began to add up mentally.

George tried conciliation and without thinking suggested that afterward they all go for a drink. Anton shrugged and answered, "Thank you, but it is not possible," and it occurred to George that Anton, too, was scared. Scared because George was a beginner, prone to make slips and unpredictable, scared of what would happen to him in Moscow or Sofia or wherever these things happened when a slip was made. I'll be feeling sorry for him next, George thought; then, without resentment: I'm becoming soft as a girl. Come on, be a hero; it's what's expected. He watched the younger man worrying about his safety and his expenses without any sense of priorities; and sulking because that was all that was provided by his restricted palette of emotions. Anton sulked very close to anger and George remembered that he was a dangerous man. Damn it, we both scare the shit out of each other!

Anton replaced the money and the receipts. He looked uncomfortably at his shoes and the damp ground.

"Now I write you an address," he proposed. "It is a lawyer who is reliable. He will solve Mr. Evans's problems." He took out a pencil and wrote a few words on a scrap of paper.

" 'Matti Vuorinen,' " George read out.

"You know the street, Bulevardi?"

"I can find it."

"Good. Understand, you must speak only to Matti Vuorinen, no one else."

"I've got the message." George put the paper in his pocket. He could feel the effect of an earlier drink coming on, a prickling of his face, a sensation of heat. He had been trying to cut down on alcohol.

Evans, who had momentarily stepped away to stare into the water as if dissociating himself, inquired, "You all right? How about you, Tony?" Everything tickety-boo? What now?"

"God knows," said George.

"Oh, well, never mind." To their companion Evans said in a friendly tone, "Don't worry. This is all new for us, but we'll get the hang of it." The remark carried a suggestion that they were precocious children. George, however, was more forcefully reminded of Sandy Murchieson, fellow director and miserable bastard, who distrusted anything new because it never worked the first time. That had been Sandy's analysis of the infamous Omsk Job of company mythology. "The first, George old lad, and the biggest we ever did." Murchieson affected an ancestral solemnity to go with his Scots accent. "When you break new ground," he intoned like the law and the prophets, "never make it a big one. It just increases the cost of your mistakes." And what was this, George thought, if not a first? He looked down at his hands and wondered if the prickling might be fear.

For his part Anton was finished. He was looking at George thoughtfully and offering his hand with the same politeness that the Englishmen found odd. Then he was gone with a few murmured words of farewell and George was left with Evans, who was as cheerfully restless as a puppy waiting for a ball to be thrown.

"Let's go," George said morosely. "The spies' convention is over." The look of expectancy fell away from Evans's face. "OK," George asked, "what's getting at you?"

"Nothing," was the answer; then: "Is that what we're really doing—spying?"

George hadn't really considered that one.

"No," he said hesitantly. "I don't think so."

"What is it, then?"

George had no ready reply. He looked around for the answer, but there was only Helsinki in the nighttime, a view along a tree-lined path, water, lights, the distant railway lines bringing trains from the Soviet Union.

"It's just a different way of doing things," he said at last. "Let"s call it Alternative Business."

18

George Twist had once prided himself on his sense of place: not on knowing his way about, though a street map inside his head was a useful enough possession, but on having a feeling for the concreteness of a city, the fine distinctions that made this one different from that one. Now he had lost it.

"Reminds me of Bond Street," said Evans, meaning that there were art galleries slotted between the milliners and café-pâtisseries along Bulevardi. "London in autumn always did appeal to me." He squinted at the bright morning sunlight across the cobbled roadway at the office of Suomi Filmii. "Plane trees—are those plane trees, George? This place would suit Betjeman: 'The many bobbled planes.' "

"Sycamores." The opposite pavement was planted with saplings.

"Near enough. Mind if we sit down for a second? I've got something in my shoe."

The small garden had been a cemetery, but was now grassed and open on to the street. The headstones were still there as conversation pieces; there was a stone archway and also a monument to the Germans who had died for Finnish independence, which, as Evans observed, seemed strangely out of character for the Germans, who were normally engaged in the other thing. The lawyer sprawled on one of the green benches and flexed the toes of his right foot as he continued blithely, "Lovely weather, *crisp*," as if this were the season for buying dummy corporations and the sport wouldn't be rained off.

"Hey, George, look over there!"

George trailed his eyes around. He had been thinking that

Helskinki was still special. There had been a girl, once, before Lillian; but that had been a long time ago. She was an opera fan; they had strolled along Bulevardi to the Opera House, arm in arm, she with a white cardigan slung over her shoulders and a light cotton skirt. Otherwise her appearance was forgotten: he could remember only her seriousness about music, a certain curiosity in her eyes, a smile when he hummed a tune by Rodgers and Hammerstein.

"It's an embassy—Danish, I think. So what?"

Evans was pointing to a house standing near the corner of a side street. Helsinki was a small town, and the embassy buildings were unusually prominent. There was a cluster of the more civilized ones in the secretive, leafy avenues near Kaivopuisto, and a leper colony for the likes of the Iraqis and Chinese in the brasher suburb of Kulosaari, where, on their off days, the Chinese could be seen swarming over their building like coolies, doing a paint job.

"Next to it," Evans insisted. A travel agent with advertisements for Ibiza, Rhodes and Torremolinos stuck in the window. "The name, George, the name!"

The travel agent was called *Spies*.

"Very amusing," George assented flatly. A green streetcar went past in clanking spasms. It carried posters for Hoover and Costa Rica (where spies take their holidays George wondered, and why not?). "For fuck's sake."

A heavy wooden door with scrolled iron grilles over glass panes; on one side a gallery with a depressing line in pictures; on the other a furrier; successful high-class businesses that seemed to thrive without customers. They were across the street from the garden and a branch of the Osuuspanki and a café with large windows where women with more bags and coats than they could use gazed wanly on the parked cars. A row of shingles advertised the kind of firm that operated out of upstairs premises in nice streets, which included two or three law-offices; and a plaque said: *Matti Vuorinen, Lakiasiantoimisto*.

They found the right floor and a pale female receptionist with half-moon spectacles on a gold rope, who sang at them in English when they gave their names, and deposited them on a bench under some hunting prints, where they could look at a case of legal textbooks and be impressed. There was a background noise of typing and someone barking down a phone, and a smell of wax and fresh coffee.

"Mr. Twist and Mr. Evans!"

Vuorinen came with a tweed jacket and a meerschaum pipe, and a firm handshake that George had once been warned never to trust. He was thirty or so, playing at being fifty, and combed his hair sideways from a parting down by his left ear. His hand sported an American college ring and his wrist held a chunky gold bracelet.

"I was told to expect you," he said expansively, which was the nearest he came to mentioning Anton. "What can I do for you?"

But first there was tea, orange pekoe in dainty china cups, and madeleine biscuits, and some brittle conversation about the weather and how-do-you-like-Helsinki? Vuorinen smiled a great deal, talked a great deal, and fiddled around filling his pipe from a sealskin pouch. Acting on the principle that you set a thief to catch a thief, George let Evans take the other lawyer's measure.

"We want to acquire twelve off-the-shelf Finnish corporations," Evans began.

When Evans had first described this part of the scheme, George had asked, How long? How long to set up a dozen shell companies? "A quarter of an hour—more or less—depending on whether it's raining." George had no option but to believe him. "Believe me," said Evans with his most trustworthy smile.

To Vuorinen, Evans continued: "We're not looking for anything special—general trading companies will do. We'll take them as they stand, except that we may need to change their registered offices into separate accommodation addresses—assuming that they're all registered here. Corporations registered more than three years ago are preferred, but we don't insist."

Evans delivered the words calmly. It occurred to George that it was like laying down a card and waiting for the other player to take one out of his own hand. When that happened, they had a game. Vuorinen was counting the pits in his hand.

"I think I can help you," he said carefully and, having said it, brightened. "I have such ready-made companies available. They are capitalized at the minimum fifteen thousand marks required by law; and, of course, there will be the set-up costs and my own charges. As foreign owners, you understand that consent of the Bank of Finland will be necessary to import the funds and for the transfer of the shares."

George looked to Evans. Play another card.

"We prefer to stay in the background," Evans said. "We should be happy for the shares to stay registered in the present owners' names — as our nominees, if you like."

"I see. And you would like a trust agreement between your-selves and the present owners?"

George intervened to ask, "What's the trust agreement for?" and Evans answered: "If the shares aren't in our name, then we can't control what the registered owners do with them, unless we have a trust agreement that records our interests."

"No trust agreement," Evans said to the Finn.

"I see." Vuorinen gave George a curious look.

"We have friends who take care of our interests," George explained. "They are very serious people."

The late Ronnie Pugh had a theory about complicity.

"Keep it abstract, George. Don't go to the heart of the matter; don't tell them what it's really about; amuse them with all the detail so they don't have time for ethical speculation." At the time they were in Dubai, putting together some mildly nefarious deal in one of the emirates: Ronnie was a hot-country man. They were having one of the long, maudlin, what-the-hell-are-we-do-ing-this-for sessions that affect contractors during the wearisome waiting days while the client thinks up his next trick. "Of course," Ronnie added, "the reality is that they *do* know, bless them; but they don't want to hear the words. The words can break the spell. It's a bit like magic." And, like magic, they got the deal, and congratulated themselves on never getting caught. After-ward, of course, Ronnie got himself shot quite innocently in Lagos on the way from the airport into town.

Meanwhile they talked of mining. Vuorinen warmed to their

230

business. He sat back in his chair and smoked a sweet-smelling cavendish tobacco, nodding his way through their list of requirements.

"I want to acquire a mining company," George said without giving reasons, implying that the necessity would be immediately understood.

"Of course," Vuorinen agreed. "Mining," he repeated thoughtfully. "In Finland there are few mining companies and they are State-owned. Would any other line of business be suitable?"

George was accommodating. "Metal-plating or -finishing, or possibly, paint manufacture" — Vuorinen was taking notes — "they would all do."

"I understand. And do you have any special requirements?"

"We're looking for a long-established, dormant company," Evans answered. "It should have been set up at least twenty years ago but be no longer trading. All we want to buy is the shell — though, if there are any assets, we'd be prepared to take a look at them."

"I follow. You want a company which has closed its business during the recession." Cautiously: "In that case there may be debts to pay off."

"Within reason," said Evans. He continued somewhat airily: "Companies in this situation are often careless about formalities."

"That's so."

"About holding directors' meetings, filing accounts and so forth."

"It happens."

"Our company," Evans proposed, "should not have filed accounts for three years."

During that afternoon, Evans found a jobbing printer. He gave him the names and addresses of the twelve dummy companies provided by Vuorinen. In the case of six of them he had the printer run off blank pads of invoices bearing the company details. For the remaining six he had standard purchase orders prepared, also in blank. He then spent an hour at a clerical agency, during which he hired a translator, a secretary and a bookkeeper, all of whom were prepared to work from home.

George had lunch with Vuorinen at the Mikado restaurant in Mannerheimintie. The lawyer brought along a friend.

"George Twist. Pekka Lahtinen."

"George."

"Pekka."

They took seats at one of the clean tables, ordered drinks and food; George asked for one of the freshwater fish that don't have names in English. Vuorinen was the type who made a fuss over his eating, asked the waiter his opinion, debated the point, and then had what everyone else had ordered. Lahtinen was brisk and vigorous. He was a big, fat man with small eyes in a doughy face, and a range of expressions punctuated by warts.

"I was explaining to George," said the lawyer, breaking the ice with a deftly polite way of speaking, "that you handle industrial real estate: surveys, valuations, buying and selling and so on."

"Correct," said Lahtinen firmly.

"And George," the other man continued, "has an urgent requirement for such property. Isn't that so, George?"

"Yes."

Lahtinen prodded the Englishman with his eyes. "How much? What kind?"

George said he wanted a factory property, close to Helsinki, with about 2,500 square meters of shop-floor space. Everything else was up for discussion.

"And price?"

George looked sharply at Vuorinen. The lawyer nodded.

"I have a budget to meet," George answered slowly. "But my company wishes to purchase an asset that can appear in its books at a considerable value. Do you follow my problem?"

"Interesting," said Lahtinen without elaboration.

They drove out to Lauttasaari in Lahtinen's car, a yellow Mercedes with a floor covered in candy wrappers and with a strong smell of dog. The Finn had a line of talk that ran to which buildings along the route he had bought, sold or valued, and a general discourse on the state of the market, which like farming was always terrible. He had no curiosity. Vuorinen sat in the back, twitchy as a child, and now and again bounced up at the window to look out and ask a question. It had started to rain, blowing in sheets across the fjord from the open sea, where even the nearest islands, Melki and Pihlajasaaret, had dropped somewhere into the mist. For a few brief seconds, where the highway bridged the channel between Lauttasaari and the city, George had a feeling that the world had vanished; the sky and the open water on each side had merged in grayness, and there was nothing left but the beat of wipers clearing the windscreen, the splutter of the wet roadway and the distant horn of a freighter making its way through the fog towards Sompasaari.

Then they were in a street of apartment houses and commercial offices. Most of them were newly built, but underneath the façade lay a hint of something older and residential. On the seaward side they glimpsed warehouses and a clutch of industry, also mostly new.

"This is out of my price-bracket," George commented. "I just want a place with a roof to keep the rain off." The rain was streaming down and clearing the streets. Banks of dark cloud rolled in off the Baltic.

"This is a difficult area," Lahtinen said without answering the point. He halted at a junction and peered through the condensation forming on the windshield. "New constructions. Near to city and harbor. Increased land values. Opportunities for speculation." He turned his head in George's direction and bared his teeth in an attempt at a smile. "We go this way." He took the corner down toward the sea.

"To value older properties in such an area"—Vuorinen took up the theme with a suggestion that he was making an artistic judgment—"is hard. So much a matter of *impression*. Very difficult to put a price on the *potential* of a property." He invited sympathy.

"Sure," George agreed. "There could be two opinions on how much a property was worth."

They took another corner into a narrow lane with a badly patched roadway that would be tricky to negotiate with a large truck. It ended at a wire fence with a gate and a keeper's cabin, and, behind it, a concrete yard and a single-story brick building. The yard was full of broken crates and pallets, an oil tank and a collection of junk machinery sitting in rust and oil spills. The building was glossy with water from the broken downspouts and streaked with green slime.

"A building with potential," George said, and the others seemed to agree.

They got out of the car and ran across the streaming yard. The big double-doors needed a paint job, and the small door let into them had a brass kick-plate and a string of chains and padlocks. Lahtinen had access with a key. The interior was an open shop-floor under a roof with skylights.

"A flexible area," Lahtinen proposed as a description.

Junk lay about the floor in pools of rainwater. A pile of cardboard boxes stood against one wall. A large kettle and a blender that had not been worth moving were bolted to a concrete plinth next to a hopper with a broken shell. In the far corner a couple of offices had been assembled, with partition walls and trade calendars and a pile of furniture smashed up and dumped.

"Sound structure—tidy up—refurbish." Lahtinen went into a murmured property dealer's spiel, not especially addressing George. The rain continued to drum on the roof and gurgle down the sluices.

"What happened to the owner?"

"One of my clients," Vuorinen answered. He took his pipe from his pocket, fiddled with it, lit it and took a few violent sucks. "No longer trading—an investment property. Mr. Lahtinen was asked to revalue it for—ah—financial reasons."

"Difficult," Lahtinen affirmed.

George kicked his way through some sawdust packing and newspapers. He paced the length of the walls, running a finger along the brickwork. The walls looked sound enough even if the roof needed patching. He found a junction box and some wiring that was tolerably new.

"How much did you revalue it over the amount shown in the books?" He turned around and saw Lahtinen seventy feet away talking to the lawyer. He repeated the question and heard his words echo around the empty spaces.

"One hundred per cent!" Lahtinen shouted back.

"Jesus." George glanced into one of the offices and then rejoined the others.

Lahtinen was saying, "In Lauttasaari the land alone has value. A problem with older buildings—" He didn't get any further.

George snapped: "It's a lousy back-street location, the yard is too small for the building, the fabric is a mess, the access for trucks stinks—and your clients are a bunch of crooks." He left them with the words spread over their faces and walked towards the door.

"Everything," said Vuorinen cautiously, after a time, "is, of course, negotiable."

George stopped.

They took a seat on an upturned crate. Like three wise monkeys, George thought. He offered cigarettes: Lahtinen didn't smoke; Vuorinen messed around some more with his pipe, then delicately accepted. The smoke hung in the still air. For some reason the image stuck with George afterward: the dusty, echoing space, the smoke in coils caught by a band of daylight through the roof, the rain beating down. Maybe he smelled success and it gave him a sense of peace.

"Tell you what I'll do," he said reasonably. "If the price looks OK, you can inform your clients that I'll buy this place for ten percent over the old book value. Provided—" he stubbed the cigarette on the floor—"they give me a bill of sale, or whatever you call it, for the amount shown in the revaluation." He didn't give them time to answer. They had to be made to understand that it was all agreed. To the lawyer he said, "I want the transfer executed within the next week. Use one of the dummy companies as the buyer." Vuorinen was nodding. "One last thing," he added. "I want papers for a second transfer. The date and the sale price can be left blank."

Night fell and he returned to the hotel, taking a circuitous route through the wet streets to remind himself what had happened to Helsinki. Darkness and spangles of reflected lights. Early drunks acting out the nighttime fantasy of cities. On the quayside a Viking Line ferry made ready for the regular evening sailing to Sweden.

He made his scheduled call to Anton, fished Jim Evans from the bar and proposed that they drive out to Kulosaari and have a meal at the Casino.

Evans was excitable. He went into a long and technical explanation of what he was doing, so that he didn't have to focus on its meaning. "Do you follow me, George?" He had reduced everything to a tabulation so that he could fool himself that the whole scheme looked like a regular piece of business. He laid out his game plan in bread rolls and broken grissini. "What do you think?"

"Relax, Jim, just relax." George sipped at his wine and from time to time checked his watch. Evans took him at his word and started a recital of funny-things-that-happened-to-me-when-I-was-a-barrister, which George had heard before but didn't have the heart to stop. He sat back, smoked a little and drank a little and felt the slow passage of time ticking through his body. The slow passage of time, that was how it went: his body keyed up on adrenaline and dampened down by an effort of will; the burning tension of waiting, while Evans laughed at his own stories and waiters floated by and asked whether there was anything he wanted. Something to put out the fire inside. Something to make time and action flow together instead of tearing at his guts.

"I've got to take a walk," he said at last.

"To see a man about a dog?"

"Settle the bill and wait for me here."

"I may take some fresh air," Then, "Watch your step, George, eh?"

"Sure."

He put on his overcoat and stepped outside into the night. The rain had stopped, the sky was hung with stars, and the restaurant trailed more stars into the water of the fjord and played snatches of serenade to the moon. He crossed the open parking lot. It led down to the water's edge where a few small boats road at their moorings.

A car, showing lights, sat in the shadow of Scotch pines. As George emerged, the lamps flashed and were extinguished. A large limousine drove on to the lot and came to a halt with its headlights shining over the boats and the radio blaring. Doors slammed. A beautiful woman in jewels and a fur handed a purse to her companion and stroked his face. A man jangled the keys in his pocket and bumped past George on his way inside. There

236

was laughter all the way; nighttime and laughter.

"Tony?"

The car was a dull-green Lada with a Finnish distributor's name glued to the rear window: *Konela*.

"Get inside, George, please." The passenger door opened.

"So?" George said, once he had settled into the seat. "How's tricks?" In the darkness he had difficulty seeing the Bulgarian, but he had an idea Anton was wearing a sheepskin coat. It smelt of camphor.

"George"—a sigh—"you cause me so much trouble."

"Sorry about that, old man. Doing my best."

"But not professional—not professional."

"Look on the bright side. Maybe I'll have beginner's luck. How do you want to start? A run-down of the story so far?"

Anton nodded, so George gave him an explanation of the day's events. He had acquired twelve dummy corporations, he said. Once Vuorinen had provided him with the company that would act as the vehicle for importing the embargoed goods, the dummies would be used to launder the purchase of assets and create the company's trading past. The company would only have dealings through the dummies and all the paperwork could be backdated. Inside a week the company would have a history and accounts that would stand up to superficial inspection: and the dummies would act as reference customers for any credit checks.

Anton took all this in silence and only at the end asked: "Why so complicated? Why do you not buy an existing business? Then no need to make up all this history."

"Have you ever tried to take over a going concern?"

"No."

"Believe me, this is easier. You take over a going concern and people want to know who you are: the shareholders, the existing managers, the labor force. And then, again, they want to know what you are doing: for instance, why do you want to buy equipment from America for which the company has no use? Everything is visible; everyone wants explanations. Then there's the business itself: if it's up and running, it has to be managed. Say it's a mining company—you want to spend your time running a mining company, Tony? For sure you can't ignore it: it has decisions to take, bills to pay. And the cost: my way, you get assets for your money that you can break up and sell off when we've finished our little affair. The other way, you lay out money to purchase goodwill and reputation: you take your chances whether it's worth what you paid; and—one thing's certain—this company isn't going to have much of a reputation by the time we're through with it."

"OK, George."

"Satisfied?"

"I said OK," Anton answered testily.

They sat in silence for a minute or so. George rooted in his pockets for an antacid tablet and sucked on it gloomily. Anton had reverted to his habit under stress of counting through his small change and receipts. The Englishman found himself asking the standard site-man's question: What were Anton's foreign allowances and expenses like? Could he buy a bottle of Scotch and some scent for his missus and slip the cost to the KGB?

He broke the silence with: "I need some money. Vuorinen doesn't come cheap. I've bought twelve companies from him and I'm going to close on a property deal in the next couple of days. He only deals in cash, no credit."

Anton reached into the rear seat and brought out a folder with various bank forms in it. George made it easier for him.

"Tell Moscow I'm looking after their interests getting the job done cheaply. The property is a bargain. I've bought it at market price, but I can bring it into the books at a revaluation. It means we can inflate our asset base without having to pay for it. It makes our company look more substantial."

"Moscow will be pleased," Anton answered without believing it; and for the next couple of minutes, with the aid of a penlight, George struggled to sign the various drafts and fill in the numbers. Then it was over.

He found Evans waiting on the parking lot, breathing the night air deeply and looking at the stars.

"Brought you a nightcap," the lawyer said. He produced a brandy glass from under his coat and offered it. George took it and poured the contents on the ground. Evans was upset. "No need to throw a tantrum."

"I . . . Forget it; you're right. I'm too strung out with this business."

"Relax — isn't that what you were telling me?" Evans looked away dreamily towards the sea. "What's that light over there, George?"

His companion followed his gaze. A couple of miles away across the melancholy waters of the fjord a stationary beacon shone in the darkness. A light for mariners, vaguely comforting.

"I think it's the church on Suomenlinna." He could dimly make out the cluster of small islands.

"Suomenlinna — what's that?" Evans said.

"It's an old harbor fortress. Nowadays it's a museum, and I think the Finns have a naval academy there."

"Nice." Evans seemed to mean it. He played tunes on the word, "Suomenlinna!" George had a sense of mood and events getting out of phase with each other. Everything went up and down and there was nothing to do but throw alcohol and nicotine and anything else that worked at the problem in an attempt to smooth it out.

"Nice? Maybe," he said. "It used to belong to the Russians."

Early the following morning George Twist went to Stockmann's bookshop in Mannerheimintie and bought a route map of southern Finland and a number of topographical maps of the same area. Furnished with these, he took a spin in the countryside in his hired car. The fields and the trees had been scoured by autumn; the soil was damp and pungent with smells from the previous day's rain. By their small red cottages with tarred roofs, the farmers were bringing in wood for the winter.

He drove west beyond Espoo, then cut off along secondary roads from Route 51 north-west towards Lohja, and then on to dirt tracks in the pinewoods in an inundated landscape of spits and corridors between flat expanses of water rimmed by gray horizons of trees and mists.

He found the buildings. The map gave them a name in Finnish, but George didn't know what it meant. He guessed a lumber operation, but he couldn't be sure; the machinery had been stripped out except for some shapeless scrap and the usual collection of empty drums. Some narrow-gauge lines led out of the trees to a shed and a small turntable, and on the upper floor of

239

the wooden frame structure there was a winch; a chute on a cast-iron legs ran down to the water.

He walked around, inside and out. The roof of the main building was broken and letting in light, and there were birds nesting on the beams, and feathers, droppings and dead chicks on the floor, but the main walls were sound and there was glass in most of the windows because there was no one around to break them. He stepped outside into the sun. A boardwalk flanked the lake and a jetty with most of the planks intact jutted out into the shallows.

It could have been the lake at Sokolskoye. He hadn't seen it, but he had a feeling for its dimensions from the data provided by the Russians, and no one knew any better. He returned to the car and took a camera and some binoculars from the passenger seat and then tramped through the trees and undergrowth to the far side of the water where he could get a distance view. In the light and the mist it didn't look too bad. He shot a roll of film, went back to his car and drove back to Helsinki, where he unloaded the film and left it for fast processing before returning to the hotel.

There was a message from Matti Vuorinen waiting in reception.

"The name of the company is Siivosen Maalitehdas Oy," Vuorinen explained. "It used to manufacture paint"—which was by way of an apology underlined by much sucking on his meerschaum pipe.

"Paint—you couldn't get anything in the metal-finishing industry?"

"Please, Mr. Twist, companies with your special requirements do not grow on flowers. It was very hard to find this one in such a short time. I personally had nothing available. I have had to speak to a lot of colleagues and ask them to examine their clients to look for something suitable."

"Don't worry, you'll be paid."

"Of course," Vuorinen answered dismissively, meaning that, left to himself, he would do it for love.

"OK, OK, it'll do. Give me the details."

Siivosen, said Vuorinen, was established in 1947 in a small way of business in Porvoo. It specialized in primers and marine paints for the shipbuilding industry and got into difficulties in the mid-seventies when shipbuilding went into a decline. Most of the business closed in 1976 and the rest four years ago, since when no accounts had been filed. The assets had been stripped and sold, but there were various disputed creditors amounting to 500,000 Finnmarks. The owners hadn't liquidated the business because they had other interests and didn't want the smell of an insolvency; the creditors hadn't forced a liquidation because there were no assets and so no point; and the authorities hadn't taken action because they hadn't got round to it. The owners would give the company away to anyone who would take on the liabilities.

"I'll have it," George said. "Find me some nominees and arrange the share transfers. Pay off the creditors in full so that I get the company clean."

"Certainly," Vuorinen said and went on to discuss his own bill.

On the way back to his hotel George collected the film, which he took to his room and sorted through for the best shots. He called the office to check on other business and rang home to find out how Lillian was because he was worried about her after his last call. Then he went looking for Evans.

The lawyer had spent the day fixing up an office with a receptionist to act as a base of operations, and had arranged to have mail and calls rerouted from the various accommodation addresses of the dummy corporations to his new headquarters. He spent a couple of hours on the phone to Chemconstruct, with a pile of vendor catalogues in front of him, and, with the help of one of his fans in the procurement department who was mystified by the request, he sifted through the possibilities and produced a list of quick-delivery, resaleable items of equipment. Using the list, he called the suppliers and placed telephone orders for various items in the names of the dummy corporations for delivery inside the week to the warehouse in Lauttasaari—"which I hope, for the sake of all of us, we shall own by then." The suppliers were leery of an Englishman and of companies they had never heard of and wanted cash with the order. Evans made out the checks and had them ready for George to sign.

"I've got the name of our new company," George told him.

"Wonderful. Where do we eat tonight?" Evans replied dully. And, looking at the signatures on the checks, he added. "So *that's* how they spell 'George Twist' these days."

George stayed in his room the next morning and got down to some creative writing. Evans was out all day. The lawyer called on the printer and collected the purchase order forms and invoices that carried the dummy letterheads, and spent the morning writing up purchase orders and then arranging for them to be translated, typed and mailed together with the checks to the equipment vendors. Using some of the old Siivosen literature, which had been roughly translated overnight by Vuorinen's secretary and delivered at breakfast, George wrote a new brochure for the company and included in it a photograph of its modern lakeside factory, an artistic shot from across the water with a view of the lake and birds and trees, and, somewhere, a building in the mist. He took the result for translation and asked the girl to carry it to the printer with a request for proofs on a high-gloss paper appropriate to a good-quality company. He visited Vuorinen's office, where he had some papers to sign, while Evans watched, and afterward he had another meeting with Anton. They met in Kaisaniemenranta, the small road by the botanical gardens where they had had their first encounter; and on an upturned scull by the boathouse they sat in the fading afternoon light and signed more drafts on the Swiss bank to provide funds.

Another day.

George saw the dawn in, lying on his bed, half-reading a paperback thriller. He was having trouble sleeping, which he tried to solve with slugs of *koskenkorva* until he could barely stand. Then he crouched in the shower and doused himself in cold water while singing sea shanties he had learned at school; and afterward he lay on the bed with the book and its funny print and wondered why his life wasn't as exciting as fiction. He thought of Lillian, of the girl he had once taken to the Opera House in Bulevardi, of Ronnie Pugh who got himself shot in

Lagos or Freetown—he couldn't remember anymore—and he knew in his heart that this whole Finnish scheme couldn't work; it was being done too quickly to be perfect; it leaked at the joints—damn it, it *could* work! He hoped that Natasha hadn't suffered after their meeting in Moscow.

Evans had paid his printer to run off new letter paper, purchase stationery and invoices for Siivosen. The printer was only too glad: like everyone else he was getting premium money for breaking his back to produce results. George joined his lawyer at the new office and helped him with the paperwork. They covered the purchases of equipment by the dummies with back-to-back orders from Siivosen—the only difference being that the Siivosen orders were all dated more than three years ago. Afterward he left the other man to work on a series of phony purchase orders and invoices between Siivosen and the dummies, which would establish the trading basis for the last three years' unfiled accounts. George himself went to see Vuorinen to complete the transfer of the Lauttasaari property from the old owners into the dummy, and the second transfer from the dummy into Siivosen, which was also appropriately backdated after it had been checked by Evans.

"This Siivosen starts to sound like a substantial company," said Vuorinen with some splinters of laughter and a flash of pipe-worn teeth. "I should invest my money there, maybe?"

On the morning of 14 November the first deliveries of equipment started to roll into Lauttasaari. George had hired a man to check them against the orders and sign the delivery notes, and he had some cranes on hand and a crew to help the unloading and strip the manufacturer's packing, but he attended in person to make sure the stuff was placed around the open floor in some plausible order and not all dumped by the door.

Evans was at the airport waiting for the arrival of Dickson, one of Chemconstruct's in-house accountants. Dickson had taken a week's holiday, been paid a thousand pounds to keep his mouth shut, and told that Alasdair Cranbourne knew and approved of what was going on. He was given the outline of Siivosen's sales and purchase ledger, a sketch of its supposed history for the last three years, and told to get on with preparing the accounts for the missing years, with bonus marks for creativity. He brought some news on the Russian gas-plant business; the Soviets had placed letters of intent for the purchase of an initial two plants with more to follow; the company was like a dog with two tails, and George was the favorite son.

"Not, of course, that one can exactly *rely* on a letter of intent," Alasdair Cranbourne said when he called George at his hotel; and he added, so that George suspected that Harold Barnes had been dropping poison in his ear, "Not absolutely as *bankable* as a *regular* contract, George; so I think you'll agree that we have to get off our little bottoms and leave these diversions in Finland — whatever they are, though you know best, George — and take ourselves to Moscow to get everything properly signed in blood. Still" — he relented — "a jolly good show, and such a surprise!"

And for now that was it: George had done his best and could only hope that it was good enough. Evans agreed to stay behind with Dickson, tidy up and establish a system to handle inquiries and route them back to England. They took a half-day off, bought a few souvenirs, had a meeting with Anton to say good-bye and drove to Lauttasaari just to get some final impressions. Evans was still concerned with some technical points.

"I don't know how much difficulty we'll have filing the accounts. Auditors can be a tricky bunch."

"Ask Anton: maybe he's got some friends."

"And then there are the unpaid taxes." Evans was looking around the factory floor where the new machinery gleamed in its well-ordered ranks. "According to our accounts, Siivosen has been so damned profitable these last three years that it owes taxes."

"Make a provision in the accounts. That should satisfy the auditors; and by the time the Revenue gets round to collecting we'll have cleared off over the horizon. Remember, this business only has to stand up for a couple of months. If we can fight people off for that length of time, we're home and dry."

"Perhaps." Evans was doubtful.

"What do you want? Perfection?" George asked. "Look, the

244

only person who is seriously interested in the accounts is Lou Ruttger. So what if they are crawling with qualifications and reservations from the auditors? Lou is going to refuse to sell the Sep Tech Process? Not a chance. The worst position is that he'll ask for a letter of credit to guarantee that he gets paid, and we have the funds to fix that."

"And the U.S. Department of Commerce and the Finnish authorities? They have to issue the licenses to get around the COCOM embargo."

"They won't be looking too closely at the accounts. They'll just want to satisfy themselves that Siivosen isn't just a shell company fronting for the Russians. And they'll see what we show them: a respectable manufacturing company that's been in business for thirty years, some nice brochures, a list of happy customers. And if the CIA sends a spook from the embassy to look the company over, he'll find a factory at Lauttasaari with the best equipment money can buy. Which reminds me: we need a sign on the gate with the Siivosen name on it. Also, we should put up a notice that the place is closed for a renovation—which explains where all the staff have gone. Hire some painters, and some men to fix the roof; it'll make the story believable."

That night he called Lou Ruttger and gave him the name of the Finnish client who wanted to purchase the Sep Tech Process.

"Siivosen Maalitehdas Oy," Lou repeated carefully. "So this is the kosher outfit you promised me?"

"That's right," George told him. "These guys are so clean it isn't true."

19

Moscow: November 20

The buses were three in number, in red and cream livery, standing in the snow-covered schoolyard, their engines running with a low thrum, the air sour with their exhausts. In the white Volga saloon men sat, jammed into heavy overcoats. The windows were down and leaked warm breath and tobacco smoke into the cold day.

"Comrade Kuznetsova, are the children ready?"

She said yes, they were, with an eagerness and self-satisfaction that he knew and disliked. It went with her position—not the school's headmistress, but the possessor of another sort of power, which came from being a Party member, responsible for the staff's ideological rectitude. She was a small, plain person with a hand-knitted, passed-down look. The corridor where she met her visitor smelt of damp clothes and young bodies. The building played silent, like a children's game.

He followed her down the silent passage, followed her small legs planting solid footsteps. In his working life he was used to spaces: apartment blocks with empty staircases where neighbors never made noises in his presence; offices where he could talk to busy people for hours and yet never be interrupted. A poster of Lenin had been tacked to the wall among the notices; the Great Leader dandling boys and girls on his knee while others stood around, the children of the world in national dress. Vladimir

Lenin, meek and mild. *Suffer the little children* . . .

"You can rely on the Young Pioneers," the teacher was saying, "to keep the other children in line. You may get a few tears, but nothing that can't be handled. They're good children, by and large. And—after all—this is something like a holiday for them, isn't it?"

He agreed: it was something like a holiday.

He peered into classrooms as they passed. The pupils stood in line, their coats on, each holding a cardboard lunchbox, each child tagged with an identity.

She said: "This is Terekhov's class. A bright boy. But moody," she added, in case there were something terrible that had to be explained. "Not ill-behaved, you understand, in fact not even mischievous—quite the contrary—a lonely boy, without the collective attitude we pride ourselves on instilling here. It might be better if he were good at sports." She had her hand on the doorhandle and turned it now to admit the visitor. "Say hello, children!" she chimed. They said "Hello" in flat unison.

Having none of his own, he had forgotten how children were, the way that movement and emotion can shiver through a crowd of them like the shimmering of a shoal of fish. Fear, suspicion, excitement passing from face to face, up and down the line. And smell, the uncontrived accidental smell of children: hair, soap, dirt, dinner. Kuznetsova was saying, "Now, children, I want you to go forward in a line and collect your belongings and then go back to your place. And we are all to be quiet—yes—like mice." To him she said, "Arkady Terekhov has no belongings with him."

In careful non-explanation he answered, "I know. Don't worry, we'll provide them. Just get the kids outside and onto the buses."

"All right, she said uncertainly, and with a clap of her hands she began to bustle through the children and organize them.

The man stood and watched from his personal cone of silence.

She came back to him. "Now the children are ready," she said.

"Lead them out."

He watched them go. They held hands and walked two by two like animals into the Ark, fleeing the wrath that was to come. Arkady Terekhov saw the man for the first time and said shyly but affectionately, "Hello, Uncle Bog."

Bogdanov smiled and tousled the boy's hair.

"Hi there, kid!"

Arkady returned the smile and followed the other children out of the room. The teacher followed in turn but stopped to speak.

"I hadn't realized," she said with relief, "that you knew the boy."

"Oh, I know him," said Bogdanov. "Arkasha and I are the best of pals."

The school was in darkness except for a reading lamp burning at a window on one of the upper floors and the occasional classroom flashing on and off like a code as the cleaners made their progress from room to room. There had been more snow, and the expanse in front of the building was inert and featureless except for a patch of washed-out yellow where a transient light stained the ground. Irina Terekhova parked her blue Zhiguli and went inside.

The headmistress was in her office. Irina, tapping her way blindly through the dark recesses of the corridors, found the open door by the dim glow of the reading lamp which had filtered into the hallway where it faintly illuminated a poster advertising some moral precept of the Party. The poster cautioned work, love and duty, and now, flyblown and barely visible, it seemed subversive.

The headmistress was an elderly woman with a round, pleasant face and hair done up in tight pincurls. She wore a dress in a printed material that was too loud and too youthful; Irina, unable to bear her real thoughts, remembered the material from a period when, for a season, the shops had been full of it, their shelves lined with dusty bolts of cloth; even now it emerged from time to time when they tried to clear their old stocks. Cast the image aside. Watch as the other woman turned her neat, sad face away from the desk to look towards her, features turning into shadow, her thin gray hair charged with a penumbra of light.

"Can I help you, Dr. Terekhova? It is Dr. Terekhova, isn't it?" She was short-sighted. Her hands fumbled among her papers to find a different pair of spectacles. Fluttering fingers. Widow's fingers, thought Irina, having no reason to suppose this to be so, but seeing a fiancé lost in the war and a void blown into life, out of which came a care for other people's children.

"Where is my son?"

She sat down on a hard wooden chair by the door. She stared at her own shaking hands, clasped for firmness in her lap. Her thoughts jumped away again like a finger touching flame: she can't see me—why doesn't she turn on the light? Neither woman was fully visible to the other, but each seemed to draw a certain comfort from the fact. In the corridor a cleaner clattered her pail and whistled.

The headmistress spoke first. She spoke lightly. "Why, he's at the winter school with all the other children."

"The winter school?"

"The winter school in Gorky. All the children went there today. I don't understand. You were told, all the parents were told; Mrs. Kuznetsova sent a letter to all parents, a most detailed letter with the fullest instructions as to what had to be provided for the children. I have a copy here."

"I didn't receive it. Where is Mrs. Kuznetsova?"

"With the children, naturally. This was arranged, oh, ages ago. I really can't understand . . . " The words floated lightly across the room like transparencies in which Irina was supposed to see something else.

She's telling lies. Then it occurred to Irina that the other woman was trying to convey a truth where words were forbidden.

"Here is the letter." The headmistress stood up and crossed the room, holding out the paper, passing out of the light so that each of them was shaded from the other. "This was a decision from the Ministry," she went on. "It was considered a wonderful opportunity. Away from their homes for a few months—it is only three months—the children will learn to work as a team; they will develop a collective spirit, an appreciation of civic virtues." Tenderly she said, "This must have come as a shock to you. Please, sit there, wait as long as you wish to." Changing her tone back to detachment, she continued, "In time you will see the advantages. Other parents have. Some are delighted; they have even written to thank me—though, of course, it is not I who should be thanked. I'm sure your husband will understand. Men do."

"My husband is away."

"I'm sorry; that must make things more difficult for you. Where is he?"

"He's a soldier. He's in Afghanistan, helping to fight the bandits."

The other woman suggested that was a noble thing. Yes, it probably was. Irina must write a letter to him; explain to Terekhov what had happened. The headmistress repeated that a man would probably understand. Yes, he probably would. She should talk to a friend. "I have a friend in Leningrad." She would visit her friend, Sonya Stoletova.

And so it went on, lies and irrelevancies deadening her emotions. She wanted to cry, but the deception lying between them gave her no excuse to cry. For a son away on a scheduled school-posting to Gorky. It was an absurdity. The cruelty itself seemed merely absurd.

Kirov had no business being there. In fact he had every reason not to be there.

"Where are we going?" Lara asked. "This isn't the way to Gertsena Street." They had tickets for the Mayakovsky Theater, courtesy of Grishin, as a reward for effort. He had suddenly diverted the car.

"I have some business to take care of," he told her. Where his work was concerned, explanations were unnecessary, unavailable. And now, thinking of Irina Terekhova, he gave no thought to Lara at all.

When he saw her, she was walking the silent street outside her apartment. His car, cruising out of the night, slowed to her pace and he followed at a distance listening to the low purr of the engine, the clack of the windshield wipers.

She became aware of the car and stopped, turning to face it, but not seeing him because he was invisible behind the dazzle of lights. Her face was no longer composed; it was the face of a woman on the brink of middle age, made ugly with grief.

"Who is she?" Lara asked; and without deliberate cruelty added, "She doesn't look particularly attractive."

The object of their observation was now faced away from them. Irina Terekhova had resumed her walking. Kirov sensed an expectancy in her as if she looked for her son suddenly to spring out of the darkness with his arms open and his mouth full of excuses for being late, so that she could cry and scold him and they would both walk home in bliss.

"Wait here," he told Lara.

"Petya . . . "

He was already out of the car. The snow responded with a sharp crunch. There was music. Lara had switched on the radio and it sang a love song.

"Dr. Terekhova." He touched her gently on the shoulder. His fingers glanced against the thin nap of her coat and caught a stray hair escaping from under her nylon-fur hat. His own coat was of thick wool with an astrakhan collar; his hat was made of fox. "She has no business dressing like that," Bogdanov had once said. "Terekhova's rank gives her access to better shops. What's she doing, wearing all that Soviet-made crap?"

She halted at his touch. He felt her body stiffen and knew that she was mending the shattered fragments of her emotions to confront him again with her resistance. He heard the deep intake of breath and then the words, "Good evening, Major," in her clear, unstressed voice.

"May I walk with you?"

"If you want to."

"Where are you going?"

"Nowhere in particular. I need to walk, that's all."

"Then I'll come along."

So for a while they walked along side by side in the darkened street, she with her face away from him, watching the sky or the snow-plows moving abreast in slow tandem as they cleared the roadway while she paused only to consider and choose a route as they reached a junction. Once she slipped; he extended an arm and she took it without thinking, so that he admired her assurance; and in this fashion they went on, arm in arm as if their familiarity were such that they no longer needed to speak to each other.

After a while she began, slowly, "My son is away from home."

"Is he?"

"He's been sent to a winter school in Gorky. Do you know anything about it?"

"No."

"Ah." She considered the reply while they crossed the road, and a militia prowl car slowed to observe them and then drove

251

off in a hiss of spray. She went on: "It was a sudden matter—sudden from my point of view—the other parents were notified some time ago. But the letter to me was somehow or other lost. Don't you find that curious?"

"Things happen that way—accidents, inefficiency."

"Yes," she answered. "I tell myself that. But Gorky?" She had stopped, and he could see her face, where even her massive self-control could not hide completely the depths of her anguish. And it came to Kirov as a shock because he had considered the situation only in terms of the nexus of power between them. She was still speaking. "Gorky is further down-river than Sokolskoye. If the Chiraka dam doesn't hold back the lake . . . " Her voice was rising, not hysterically but because everything behind it was unbearable. "Do you follow me, Major?" It fell away as she repeated: "Do you follow me, Major? The coincidence?"

"Coincidences happen," he said. But in his world they didn't, and in this respect he stood apart from others.

They halted again. She said, "I think we should go back." Then, "Am I under suspicion?"

"What for?" Her question had arrested him with one foot out like a dancer catching his timing. "Yes, let's go back." He offered his arm, and she took it again. He said, "You should trust me," which might have referred to the physical support of his arm or might not. "Do you feel under suspicion?"

He waited for an answer, conscious that he had no rational ground for suspecting her. A photograph taken by a nobody. A nothing in itself; no more than a speck on which he could focus aspects of himself. He was reminded of the interrogations he had conducted: of those where he had faced some deep and tenacious deceit—not, it sometimes seemed to him, the masking of some fact or the keeping of some secret, but a deceit that had no content, that existed in itself, unwilling to share itself. A deceit that could only be broken by patient wearing away at the core of resistance. Then there would come a moment—the senses distracted and detached by the place of interrogation, which was no place, and the lights which emphasized the darkness, and the tiredness that came of being alert—when interrogator and accused alone recognized a truth emergent from the subtle interplay of lies. Then, between himself and that other, there would be established that recognition of his sympathetic power which invited confession even at the cost of life. So it went, like an exchange of intimacies between strangers on a train, freed by the knowledge that beyond the confines of the compartment where they talked there was no future and no commitment; and, because it was transitory, the experience was more poignant and more intense than anything else that life could offer. And, at the end, what? He had gained a truth, but he, too, had made a confession: because interrogation was indeed an exchange, a barter of his sympathy against the other's knowledge. But, of all the truths evoked in the trade between them, Kirov did not know what he himself had revealed.

Irina Terekhova said at last, "I don't know whether I'm under suspicion or not." She looked at him frankly but without hatred. "I don't know whether or not you are responsible for taking away my son."

A car horn sounded. Lara, he supposed. A bottle breaking. There was a drunk on the pavement across the street.

"I'll make inquiries about the boy," he said, recognizing the feebleness of his response. "I can help you," he ventured, "if only you will trust me."

"With what?" she asked, her voice rising again; the pain so palpable that he had almost the physical sensation of being touched, and inwardly recoiled. "Haven't I cooperated with you? What is it you are looking for that you think I have?"

"You misunderstand me," he said; and in that failure to press her — press until the pieces flew apart and needed his help to make them whole — he knew he had lost the moment. Her breathing, which had quickened, halted in its rhythm, picked up, halted and then slowly resumed its normal, inaudible pace. He found that he had stopped walking, but Irina Terekhova had not. She was already a few yards ahead, not looking back, pressing on away from him with a stride that seemed long for her small frame. He watched her but did not follow. They were near to his car, both of them made muzzy by its lights; Lara still had the radio switched on, and above his thoughts he could hear two comedians exchanging repartee. She crossed the road ahead of a heavy wagon which came between them and halted at the junction, the tailgate flapping loosely with a metallic clatter. When it moved off, she was gone. There were only the swimming after-images of the vehicle's headlights, the expanses of the dark street, and the taste of salt droplets on his tongue from the wagon's spray.

20

December 4-12

George visited the house where he and Lillian had lived in America. In his own mind he manufactured a reason to go there: check the roof, make sure the place wasn't flooded, walk around the garden to see that the grass was cut and everything tidied up, which was part of the deal with the realtor. The house wasn't selling. "It's a matter of atmosphere," said the realtor, which was as near as he could get to saying that the place was haunted by Lillian's presence. There were concrete ramps to all the outside doors and breaks in the porch fence where the nicely turned spindles had been removed to allow access. Big chrome handles on the doorjambs could be reached from a sitting position, as could rails along all the walls, and there was a contraption for winching Lillian's wheelchair to the bedroom level. George had spent a small fortune stripping out and refurbishing the bathrooms and the kitchen so that Lillian could use them. She was delighted. Together they had sat on the lawn amidst the bougainvillea and stared at the house, and she had clapped her hands at the result and kissed him on the cheek as if they were newlyweds.

"We've tried a few ideas," said the realtor. The railed pathways in the garden had been taken up and some children's toys posed about the lawn. When they had a prospective purchaser, an apple pie was popped into the oven to flood the kitchen with its smell. Still the house didn't sell.

He called on Lou Ruttger at Sep Tech's offices to collect the drawings for the vessels that were to be fabricated by the Russians; he already had another trip to Moscow lined up to deliver them. "A first-rate job," he told Ruttger. "You guys really pulled out the stops to produce them." He had a walk around the shop-floor where he could see that the progress in manufacturing the membrane units was well in hand, and he heard the expeditor's report on the production of the zeolite ion-exchange resin. "Fine." Everything was fine.

"Aren't you giving Siivosen the Rolls-Royce treatment?" Lou asked. "Why come yourself to collect the drawings when we could send them by courier?"

"The personal touch," George answered. "These people are not engineers. They have a big problem on their plate. They need reassurance. It's just a matter of style."

"You can say that."

George caught the note of concern. "You have a problem?"

"Problem? No, I guess it's not a problem. But it's strange. We can't talk to these guys. We raise engineering queries and we don't get an answer. We propose a site visit—I mean this is *normal,* George—and they tell us we can't come. So they're inexperienced—but unless they have some hot-shot engineers we don't know about, they're taking a hell of a risk. Believe me, I've read Jim Evans's contract, and there are no comebacks. It's weird."

"I thought you were getting answers to your engineering queries."

"OK—we get answers. Always it's the same girl who picks up the phone. 'Speak to Mr. Twist,' she says. 'Mr. Twist knows our position.' It's like you were running the project for them. Then, a bit later, back comes a telex or a letter. So we get answers, but it's not the way these things are managed. It's like there's nobody there, George!"

"They're in a difficult position. And who cares as long as they pay? They're good for the money, aren't they?"

"Sure," Lou answered without enthusiasm. "We ran a few checks on them and they came out clean. Their customers gave them references that were absolutely the best—you could hand Siivosen your billfold and expect to get it back. And they have so much cash in the bank it's an embarrassment. Every payment is prompt."

"That's Finnish morality for you."

256

"Maybe. I had some queries on the accounts: they were sloppy; there were unfiled returns and unpaid taxes, and the auditors made a few noises—but nothing to worry about since they could raise a letter of credit for the money they owed us. There was some story about a reorganization—kicking out the old management and putting in some new who were trying to clean up Siivosen's act—and maybe that explains everything."

"Sure it does," said George.

He had dinner with the Ruttgers. Lou's wife, Nancy, was a small, energetic creature with too much suntan and legs that were firmly muscled by tennis. She was studying *haute cuisine* and produced a succession of French dishes which they washed down with French wine. Later Lou showed George a mound in the garden that he had in mind to dig out to establish a cellar.

"But I ask myself: how long am I going to be here?" He was in a confiding mood. "This is the place of opportunities. I've got to seize my chances while I'm young—am I right, George?"

"Of course."

"You bet I am! And this Finnish project—my first and right on top of taking over the running of Sep Tech—it does me no harm at all, none at all." He patted his visitor's shoulder. "I owe you one."

"Good of you to say so," George replied.

They decided to adjourn to the garden. Lou disappeared to see to some music and generally fix things up. George joined Nancy in the kitchen and helped around a bit despite her weak protests. He was tired of Lou's company and had always found his wife to be a sensible enough woman. She asked how he had enjoyed the meal and told him that she personally didn't care overly for French food: the classes were Lou's idea—that or a course on philosophy. He had a passion for self-improvement. "Self-realization," he called it, with a suggestion that the human character was an object to be manipulated.

"He's out of his depth," she said suddenly and acutely, so that George didn't know what to say.

"Lou?"

She dried her hands and occupied herself with some glasses

and other practical activities. "He hasn't been around as long as you. He doesn't know people and places the way you do." She turned and flicked some hair out of her eyes. "You won't let him get hurt, will you, George?"

George laughed, one of the little laughs like a couple of pennies in an empty pocket. "Where did you get that idea from?" he said.

They sat in the evening air under some colored lights, while a fat moth fluttered lazily and a night bird called. The house was in darkness except for a block of light in the doorway and a flicker from an upstairs room where the kids watched television. The colored baubles threw reflections on the still surface of the pool.

Lou had a book of recipes for mixing cocktails and a mess of gadgets to do it. George accepted a nominal daiquiri and a glass of mineral water to go with it, and together they sat in the evening quiet, lulled faintly by the music, and breathed the heavy fragrance of night-scented flowers.

"Alasdair has been over here again," said Lou in a leisurely way. "Sorry; you didn't know?"

"I've been away. Finland—Russia—you know how it is."

"Is this man-talk?" Nancy asked.

"What's that?" said George, and added to Lou: "Go on."

"He came on his own. Left Harold Barnes locked up in his cage, I guess. John Chaseman didn't like Harold—too negative. You know Chaseman: he looks for people who can see the high frontier of achievement. He can probably take Alasdair only as some quaint British ruin."

"So he came to see Chaseman?"

"That's what I'm telling you."

"What for?"

Lou fiddled with the debris in his glass. George thought: He doesn't know what to tell me; and—remembering what Nancy had said—he's out of his depth. Peter Kirov would eat him alive. What had they offered him? A plum job in their new scheme?

"Alasdair spent a couple of days here. The accounts, the order book—he wanted to know the lot, a complete picture of the company. He went into the Siivosen deal. He didn't seem to know much about it, called it 'the product of George's dark

258

confabulations.' I think those were the words."

"And what was the point? He had the whole of Sep Tech laid open. So . . . ?

"He wanted to know everything, George, *everything*. He was looking in the cupboards and under the carpets: he said he didn't want to be taken by surprise. 'Have we got any little social diseases that we haven't mentioned?' You know the way he talks." Lou glanced at his wife, who simply shrugged her shoulders. "This is takeover talk, George. With that level of information he's got beyond talking generalities with Chaseman: near as damn they have a deal for Chaseman to buy Sep Tech. I heard—I've got my sources, too—that Alasdair and Chaseman were close to shaking hands a month ago, but then your Russian business, the gas-plant contracts, made Alasdair think that maybe Chemconstruct wasn't going to be short of cash for long and he could afford to hang on for a few dollars more."

"That must have sickened Chaseman."

"It did—or that's what I'm told. Not that Alasdair told him that it was because of business in Russia. You've heard my views about the Soviets, but they're nothing compared with Chaseman's: he'd go crazy."

He'd go even crazier if he bought Sep Tech and found that it was involved in some highly illegal transactions with the Soviet Union. George would have to think this one through. But not tonight; it was too late and he was too tired. He turned to Nancy and exchanged a few words about the children, and, when she suggested she bring out the family photographs, he said he would like to see them. She disappeared into the house and left the two men with a jumpy, palpable silence between them. Lou broke it.

"You should lose some weight; anyone ever told you that?"

George patted the soft flesh around his abdomen and nodded. Lou fired off another couple of random shots at conversation, and then the older man stopped him.

"There's some purpose to this story about Chaseman? Something you want me to do?"

"Do? No, I guess there's nothing to do. I just want reassurance, that's all."

"About what?"

"About Siivosen. It's the biggest job going through the shop. If

Chaseman is serious, he's going to know more about what he's buying into: his lawyers will want to know more."

"You have the facts: tell them."

"It's not that—it's how I *feel* about them. When Alasdair asked me the question—'George's dark confabulations,' I mean what the hell kind of name is that for a regular deal?—when Alasdair asked me the question, and I gave him the answer, I felt like a crook." Lou stood up, smoothed down his trousers and fixed himself another drink. George sensed the nervousness and, more, the pain. "It's as simple as that. I feel like a crook, and I don't know why. Can you tell me?"

"No."

"You want another drink?"

"No."

"You sure?" He added something about how good the recipe was and his own special way of mixing; then, suddenly: "You'd tell me, George, if there was something else about Siivosen that I should know? For old times' sake, huh?"

The question caught George when he wasn't listening; when he was thinking of Alasdair Cranbourne and what that shrewd, effete bastard might have guessed. And now there was Lou Ruttger to handle. Lou, who was easier to like when he wasn't there with a few drinks inside him and his ambitions and emotions hanging out. Yet George was concerned for him; he wanted to help, give him some reassurance that everything would come out all right.

"Forget about Finland," he said. "Siivosen is OK. The deal is perfectly clean." He looked up and caught the other man looking at him.

"I believe you," Lou Ruttger answered with relief.

The following morning George took Joe Czarnecki, Sep Tech's shipping manager, aside and told him that he, George, was to be informed as soon as the membrane units and the ion-exchange resin were ready for shipment. There were to be no hiccups in getting the stuff onto the boat.

In the days that followed the transfer of her son to the winter school in Gorky, Irina Terekhova came slowly to a decision. It was not a matter of narrow logic, something that flowed inevitably from what had happened. It was implicit in the corruption and incompetence that had caused the Sokolskoye Incident, in their machinations to acquire American technology to solve their problem, and in the action of the KGB in taking her son to secure her loyalty—if that was what they had done. Somewhere in their paranoia and desperate need to save face they had lost control, and were shoring up the fragile structure of their world with faulty reasoning and appeals to necessity. They had taken Arkasha because it was necessary. They would do anything if they thought it were necessary. They would even sacrifice the millions living in the Volga basin in the name of necessity because the necessity above all others was to maintain their illusions about their own power and the nature of things. They could not be trusted to avoid disaster.

Since the taking of Arkasha she had lived in a torpor of unresolved misery, like a woman whose husband is reported missing in action, who can feel no grief (why grieve? he may be alive) but only shock and fear and a bitter confusion as the channel between joy and sorrow is dammed and the muddied waters of emotion mingle. The realization that this was all caused by no more than the fear and folly of others made everything suddenly clear.

At the first opportunity, Irina went into the city and scoured GUM and the shops in the Arbat for a typewriter, eventually finding a secondhand Colibri. Among her husband's possessions she found his camera and a flash attachment. She bought three rolls of film.

The following day she worked as normal. In the evening she laid out a copy of *Pravda* on her working table and, using a chair placed on the table to give a fixed height from which to take a shot, she used a roll of film in photographing the newspaper. The next morning she took the film to be processed and afterward took the Metro to Komosomolskaya Square to queue for hours to buy a ticket at the Leningrad Station.

The prints, when they came back, were a failure. She was unused to cameras but thought that the problem was of both focus and lighting. She laid out the newspaper again and, after varying the height of her shot and the lighting, she used her second roll of film.

During the next two days she spent her evenings writing a summary of the events surrounding the Sokolskoye Incident, including the lake water analysis and a description of the technology that was necessary if the disaster were to be avoided. She concluded the summary with a plea to help the Soviet Union out of its difficulties. The third roll of film was used to photograph the results, after which she destroyed the original document and the prints and the negatives from her earlier experiments.

She went to her doctor and complained of abdominal pains. The doctor was sympathetic; she suggested that Irina take a week off work and made an appointment for a hospital visit. Irina advised her superiors of her ill health and asked for leave of absence. She spent that first day of sickness filing the identification marks off the typewriter and also defaced the individual letters on the typing heads. Next she took the Metro to Izmailovski Park and found an unobserved spot among the trees to dump the machine.

The next day Irina Terekhova took the train to Leningrad.

21

The Chiraka lake froze on October 21 and brought a change to Sokolskoye. Instead of water, gray stretches of ice, swept clean by the wind, piled up behind the dam to the dark horizon. There were fewer trees. During November a swathe of forest had been cut back and a construction camp, in ranks of gray hutments, established on the slope leading down to the lakeside. At all hours of the night fierce lights illuminated the winter-dead expanses and the air vibrated with the rumble of heavy plant moving in the shadow of the trees. In the hospital, men continued to die.

For Klyuev, the KGB resident, the days were a continuous inquest. After the first hectic spell when the thing happened and Kirov and the other Moscow chekists descended on him to investigate the causes of the disaster, there had been a lull until the construction crew arrived in their hundreds. Then the deaths, which had tailed off, started again; and with each one there was an investigation. Had the man been near the lake? Had he drunk the water? The answer was always no; and maybe it was true, technically. But the lake was a permanent, unavoidable presence: all their actions were focused on the lake, on trying to change its state. And sometimes it seemed as if the lake fought back.

So Klyuev attended the inquests as the KGB representative. They were held in what had once been a dining room for the plant managers. The concrete walls had a thin paneling of pine that had come loose from its battens and was scarred from being knocked by the backs of chairs. There were a couple of portraits, a couple of slogans, and a pennant belonging to the works ice hockey team. The investigating committee sat at a long table formed by several smaller ones, and called witnesses, and came to no convincing conclusions.

"Pointless," said Rudin, a project manager for the construction work. It was during a pause in the proceedings, when the room was cleared of witnesses and sandwiches had been brought in. Rudin resented the time he had to spend on the inquests, but Klyuev wasn't sure he was referring to that. All along there had been doubts expressed about the so-called "civil engineering solution," which meant raising the height of the dam and stopping any further inflow of water. They discussed another solution, cleaning up the lake as it was—and some of the building work was rumored to be for the equipment to carry this out—but there were no details. When Klyuev tested one of his contacts in Moscow, all he got was a bloodcurdling warning to stay out of it.

From the administration building you could see the large face of the dam, the side away from the lake, a great concrete mass wedged between the rock outcrops of the valley, and, at its foot, the dried-up bed of the stream that led to the Gorkovskoye reservoir and the Volga. Men were dotted like pygmies among the machinery. And further off there were other signs of the massive effort to undo the disastrous effects of the Sokolskoye Incident. Day and night, at irregular intervals, from the forest miles away, there would be a plume of smoke and a dull explosion as men attacked the sources that fed the lake, and tried to divert them.

"Pointless," Rudin repeated, holding a glass of tea in one hand, staring out of the window. Klyuev watched with him, and it was in this accidental fashion that he happened to see the collapse of the dam.

Kirov got the news on the telephone from the plant site. There was bedlam in the background and other lines and calls switching in and out of his as the Army, the construction team and the plant management yammered after their superiors. Klyuev had completely lost his head at something outside his control and

264

understanding, and in his broken account kept jabbering "Disaster!" until Kirov told him to shut up.

"Now, tell me what's happened," he commanded.

Klyuev breathed in. "OK, OK." There were sirens going crazy somewhere and feet stampeding. "The dam's collapsed—crumbled—fucking broke!" Klyuev had seen it: twenty to thirty feet of masonry, cracking and folding like icing from the top of the dam wall, careering down the sheer side of concrete into the valley; heavy machinery heaving and tumbling like toys; men in their dozens, falling and screaming, except that you couldn't hear the screams, just see the puppets with their limbs waving and dropping headlong, swallowed up in the great slide of rubble. Dust—the air was orange with the great cloud that had billowed out of the valley and blocked the light of the low winter sun. And noise—all hell had broken loose; every alarm in the place seemed to have sounded, every truck and wagon seemed to be on the move with its horn going; and the Army was shooting. Klyuev thought it was just shots in the air: the workers had fled, and the soldiers were trying to make some order out of the chaos. The place was a living nightmare.

"The lake!" Kirov snapped. "What about the lake?"

"I don't know."

"Don't know?"

"Jesus—you're not here! You can hardly see for the dust! It's a madhouse!"

"Ask someone, damn it! Go out and look for yourself! Find out!" Kirov could sense the other man freeze; then Klyuev was yelling at someone in the room with him, demanding information, threatening the way that only the KGB could threaten. He came back on the line.

"OK—maybe the lake's OK. They think it's only the new construction that's gone." He was trying hard to sound calm. "Yeah, maybe just the new construction. It's all going to be OK. Just the new construction—yeah. Christ!"

And that was the call. Kirov gave Klyuev an instruction to make a sweep of arrests among the management team of the construction crew, mainly to protect the KGB's position against the Army when it came to the inevitable investigation, and then he called Bogdanov and told him to make some arrests at the

Moscow end for the sake of form, and only then did he call Grishin.

Grishin was phlegmatic. "Raising the height of the dam wasn't our idea," he said. "Everyone warned that it wouldn't work." He paused to pick over the options in his head, and then said, "It looks as though it comes down to George Twist, doesn't it? His solution is the only one guaranteed to work."

"I think so."

"Does he really know what's going on?"

"He hasn't been told, but he's shrewd enough to work it out for himself."

Grishin considered the point carefully. Kirov waited, and while he waited signed a sheet of arrest warrants that Bogdanov had produced. Then Grishin came back.

"We need a lever against him. Has he been threatened?"

"Not George. We need to keep him positively motivated. Crude violence can paralyze action." Kirov didn't want to hurt the Englishman. There had to be other ways. The KGB had to find them.

"What's his vulnerability?" Grishin asked.

His vulnerability. Kirov knew. He had known from the moment Irina Terekhova had explained the Englishman's character to him.

"Terekhova," he said. "We can use Terekhova against him."

Those few words made it sound like nothing.

"Then use her," said Grishin. "Whatever it takes. The woman is expendable."

The house was one of those that have no location, like the houses we know in our childhood which are warm emotions rather than places. Sonya had invited them there once, herself and Davidov, sneaking away in the dead of winter like eloping lovers; then locked in Sonya's apartment for two whole days with all the good things they had spent weeks finding. A secret place, even then.

Konstantin had called. It was no surprise. He expected to find his sister at home. Davidov, in one of his moods of exhausting generosity, asked him to come in, "Come in! Come in!" in his voice of a lisping homosexual, which was Davidov's satire against the popular view of poets. Terekhov accepted with a grave dignity that understood the joke. He brought some food, red caviar from Astrakhan and a bottle of Armenian brandy—from a training tour he had completed down south, he said; he was on secondment from the Frunze Military Academy. And they ate the food and drank the brandy; and Davidov and the soldier struck that odd note of sympathy between them. There in that warm apartment where Davidov played his one Buddy Holly record again and again, and outside it was Leningrad and snowing.

She found the house among the trees off Morskoy Prospekt where she imagined the rich Leningrad bourgeoisie had lived before the Revolution. To own such a house—the possibility was so remote that she could think of it almost clinically. A whole house.

Irina stood before a paneled door in a corridor of broken linoleum and walls scuffed by the boots of drunks and children. She could hear an argument; someone was running water, the pipes clanked from an airlock; music played behind the door— Mozart, she thought, which she remembered would appeal to Kirov. She heard the sound of shuffling and of bolts being drawn and the door opened as much as was allowed by a short chain; and a face appeared in the gap, there and gone like a child peeping.

"Irina!"

This was the moment Irina had longed for and dreaded during that tedious train journey.

"May I come in?"

"Yes! Oh, yes—please," and again "Irina!" as if the name were a new toy, so that Irina felt as though she were making a present of herself. Then she was holding Sonya Stoletova's small, unsteady body and looking into that affectionate face with its blue eyes and shock of fair, unruly hair.

"How? Why?" Sonya launched into a string of questions, then stopped and said, "But you didn't tell me you were coming."

"No. I'm sorry." Irina put her suitcase down. Sonya had already forgotten her own questions; she was plumping cushions and turning off the music, swinging through the small apartment in a series of pivots. The caliper on her left leg gave her movements the curious appearance of agility, perhaps because it made the observer more conscious of them.

Irina took a seat on an overstuffed chair that smelled of dust. The room was crammed with furniture: a heavy mahogany table with turned legs, a bookcase carved with leaves and branches, another chair upholstered in faded plush with horsehair in bunches at the worn corners, and everywhere small ornaments. "Sonya's treasure-house," Davidov had called it, though the objects were only old photographs in tarnished silver frames and bits of broken jewelry. The bookcase was filled with music scores and a cello stood in one corner. A pot was simmering on the stove.

They sat and stared at each other for a while in the manner of friends who rarely meet and lack the small exchange of day-to-day trivia. Then Sonya ventured a few inquiries about Konstantin, who never wrote to her. That weekend, when she and Davidov had borrowed the apartment, Irina remembered that she had seen Terekhov before. She had given a lecture on the effects of radiation on plant life to an audience picked by the Army. Terekhov had been there and had spoken to her afterward. Later—when Davidov had disappeared, effectively if not literally—Terekhov confessed that he had all along known that Sonya would not be at home that weekend. He had wanted to see her again, he said; that was all.

Irina turned the conversation to the orchestra tour. Sonya had written to her about it. She was going to see the West for the first time. Wasn't that wonderful? Yes, Sonya admitted, it was wonderful. Paris! Just think! Paris, where there were such wonderful things to buy—if only she had the money, she added wryly, and she looked at her woollen skirt and the caliper peeping out of the bottom. She smoothed the material down and proceeded to make a glass of tea.

"Where is Arkasha?" she asked. "Who is taking care of him while you are here?"

"He's in Gorky. His school has been moved there for the winter to—to teach the children about . . ."

"About what?"

"About . . ." Irina's voice felt as fragile as her story. "About . . . something." Sonya turned from the stove to look at her cautiously, then smiled, assuming that the "something" was some worthy object of the Party which would naturally be a joke. Irina joined with her smile, knowing it wasn't what she wanted to say; but she could not tell her. It would be unfair, cruel. Sonya meanwhile was saying something sympathetic about how she must be missing him.

How would a man ask for help? Irina wondered what Kirov would do. Ask directly? Or not ask at all, out of self-reliance or pride? Why think of Kirov?

She stopped, realizing she was daydreaming her way out of distress. It made her conscious of her smallness and absurdity. She was trying to shake a fist at reality, at the way things were.

"Why are you crying?"

Sonya was holding out a glass of tea.

"Am I?" Irina put a hand to her face and felt a tear hang on her cheek. She laughed gently.

"There's something wrong with Arkasha?"

"Yes." Irina hesitated. "I don't know," she murmured. The tear was stinging her skin. She wished she hadn't come. Seeing Sonya's innocent eagerness to help, it struck her that she was trying to manipulate her friend just as she herself was manipulated. But she said, "The KGB have taken him — I think." The first tear had dried and was replaced by others. "I think so, but I can't be sure. I shouldn't be here. I'm sorry . . . I'm sorry." Sonya was already by her, holding her, rocking her softly, unsteadily, as she limped and righted herself.

"What happened?"

Irina didn't know how to begin, wasn't sure she wanted to begin. She had never recognized so acutely before the terrible danger that went with loving other people.

"There's been a disaster." She pulled away to put some distance between herself and Sonya, who deserved at least that.

"It has to do with your work?"

"Yes. A nuclear accident. *Please*, stop me if you don't want to hear this."

"Go on."

"*Please*," Irina repeated, feeling already that she had lost track of what she wanted to say, as though Sokolskoye were an irrelevance or at best a small example of a thing far more important that she needed to talk about. But for now only the hard facts obtruded, and in apology she went on: "If the accident is not contained, then millions of people will be threatened by the poison it has released." She tried to sound urgent. "The matter is desperate. A solution *has* to be found."

"I see." There was something touching in the solemnity with which Sonya said this. After their painful embrace she had sat quietly and attentively, her thin body folded into sharp angles, as though the mechanical contrivance of her caliper were just the visible part of the frame that held her together.

Irina said, "I'm working with the KGB—trying to find a solution."

"You're helping them? But Arkasha?"

"They don't trust me," Irina said helplessly. "They want a hostage to make sure that I am loyal. To them it's only"—she searched for words to express the impersonal nature of their actions—"logical, necessary." She didn't want an answer, only some evidence of Sonya's understanding, and that was written on her face with such compassion that Irina couldn't bear the guilt of evoking it. As a distraction she suggested some music. Sonya turned to the record player and replaced the needle at the beginning of the record. Mozart was Kirov's music. As she listened, Irina was conscious of the reason she did not hate him. Because his cruelty was blind, unintended, the result of some void in his capacity to make contact with others. Instead of hate her mind experienced only a coldness; and her body—her body still felt the unwanted taints and traces of his sexual presence. The shock of that physical realization was still there. She felt betrayed by the limited vocabulary of her body to express the complexity of her emotions.

Sonya was waiting for her to continue. Irina caught her breath and resumed with the story of the efforts being made to obtain the embargoed American technology.

"But why don't they simply ask for help?"

"I don't know. No, that's not true. Perhaps I do know, but it's difficult to explain. They see things differently from us. It has to do with . . ."

"What?"

"Their pride—their fear. They don't want to expose their own weakness. They're frightened even to admit that it exists."

"And who are 'they'?" Sonya asked.

Irina halted. She hadn't thought of "them" except as some indefinable antithesis. She supposed that it was the *apparatchiks* who worked the system, or perhaps just the KGB. But the KGB was in reality only Kirov. Had she all along meant him?

"You sound as though you're talking about men," Sonya said. She had herself been married at one time. After she was crippled her husband left her. Even so, she still observed men with an affectionate eye, and there was some humor in her voice when she spoke now.

"Perhaps," Irina admitted reluctantly. "But only because they control things." She didn't want to take that thought any further. She remembered that the purpose of her visit lay within her suitcase. She took it and placed it on the convertible couch that Sonya used as a bed. Sonya was speaking.

"I still like men." She smiled her particular smile. She had small teeth like seed pearls that added to her air of fragility. The smile closed wistfully. "But I don't understand their strangeness."

The use of "strangeness" to describe men took Irina by surprise. She paused with her thumbs frozen over the hasps of the locks. The idea of men as strange, somehow foreign to reality, was like the final twist to some obscure piece of a puzzle that at last causes it to fit and make the pattern whole. It was this strangeness that explained their pride in their capacity for reasoning and their failure to see that their reasoning was a sham ultimately reducible to power and violence. Strangeness was the explanation of their terrible inner anger; the severing of their minds and emotions that made them foreign to themselves and mute, except for the anger they denied. Her fingers worked the locks.

"What are you looking for?"

Irina opened the case and took out the roll of film she had used in Moscow.

"What is it?"

Irina held up the roll cupped in the closed palm of her hand. She had still not decided to go through with her plan. The fact that it was necessary had ceased to be sufficient justification. Sonya was eyeing her with an almost animal curiosity.

"You need my help, don't you?"

Irina gripped the film, her fist so tight that the metal of the spool seemed to burn.

"It's something dangerous." Irina found her lips struggling round the words. "I'm frightened to tell you, Sonya." She glanced at her friend. "I'm frightened! I don't know what to do, and it isn't right to ask you. That would be giving in to the way *they* do things. Do you understand?"

Sonya nodded and answered quietly, "If I agree to help, because we're friends, you think you would be using me."

Irina opened her fingers to stare at the film and then looked to her coat which lay on the couch. "I must go," she murmured. "I don't really have an explanation for being here. If I'm missing too long, it will be noticed in Moscow. I—I'm sorry."

"If we both know what we're doing"—Sonya looked up from her own hands directly into Irina's eyes—"then you can't be using me. Can you?" Her gaze drifted back to her hands, folded limply on her lap. Her weakness was visible there. They were old hands with coarsened skin, tied with a skein of veins. She rearranged them nervously. Irina had moved to get out of her chair but was stayed by Sonya's touch on her forearm. "Please—don't go!"

Irina rested her weight back on the seat. In that second it was understood between them, though neither could afterward identify the moment. Irina would remember only the feeling that in some subtle way she had manipulated and trapped the other woman. But she had not wanted that. She told herself she had not wanted that.

"What . . .?" Sonya began after a moment's silence between them.

"Arkasha is in Gorky. If they cannot cure this disaster, then Gorky will be wiped out by what follows. They"—she was trying to restrain the passion of her fear—"they can't be trusted! The risks they take in getting the American technology are too great. But I believe that the Americans would give us their help freely if they were told honestly what our problem is."

"Would they?" The question wasn't skeptical, but it touched at Irina's frail certainty.

"I don't know," she admitted. "I think so."

"I see," Sonya answered quietly. She furrowed her brow so that in the declining winter daylight the lines on her forehead were emphasized by shadow. "I think so, too."

"I think so," Irina repeated, then with an effort she made her tone businesslike. "I've written an account of what's happened and what is needed to solve the problem. It's on this film." She extended her hand with the roll held loose on her open palm. "I—I don't know how to get it to the West. I'm frightened to approach any Westerners in Moscow."

"You want me to deliver it when I'm in Paris with the orchestra."

"Yes. In the orchestra baggage it should be easy to hide. And, even though your group will be supervised, there will be opportunities to meet Westerners, or perhaps even to mail the film."

"To whom?"

"To . . ." Irina didn't know. She had thought hard for an answer many times in Moscow but her knowledge of the West was so small that she could never be sure. But she couldn't burden Sonya with her doubts. "Not to the American embassy," she said, "nor to their government. We can't trust them completely. But if in some way the facts were made public by a prominent person—a politician or—"

"I can find someone," Sonya interrupted her.

"Or—"

"Leave it to me," Sonya reassured her. Irina looked down at her hand and found Sonya clasping it. The record had stopped and the music by Mozart had finished.

22

December 17-18

Moscow was becoming as familiar as a repetitive dream. George Twist knew where to find the good bars and the good restaurants, he could use the telephone system, catch a cab and not get screwed, and he could buy cheap records, including sentimental Russian ballads Bloody Brenda seemed to like as a change from Jim Reeves. She played them as she glided round the house doused in "Moscow Nights," the perfume he bought her on his last trip. For Lillian there was a set of Russian dolls, bought at Beriozka. He sat on the corner of her bed at home and steadied her hands while her fingers took them apart for the therapy. And when she dropped the pieces he apologized for his clumsiness and scrabbled around the floor on his knees, hoping her tears were because she was happy to be with him.

Jack Melchior was there, as always. He had become concerned for George and taken to offering small services like the use of his car.

"You know me, George, I like to earn my bread. But the Russkies won't talk to me. Oh, I'm hammering on the door all right, but they'll have none of it. 'We'll see Mr. Twist about it, we'll talk to Mr. Twist directly.' You'd think the record was stuck. Bloody rum, I call it. But, as I say, you know me, George. Just say the word. Anything within reason."

"It's all right, Jack, I can handle it. I'll call you if I need you."

"You know best, George. But the way, did you bring those windshield wipers I asked for?"

Kirov was waiting, too. George found him sitting in his hotel bedroom. The Russian had brought a bottle of champagne and there was a plate of *zakuski* laid out on the table and a bottle of iced vodka in a bucket.

"A small celebration, George," he said. "So far so good. I thought we could show our appreciation. How are you, how was the trip, how is your wife?"

"I get by. The traveling is killing me, but I get by."

"And your wife? I hope it's OK to ask?" Kirov spoke softly. They had shaken hands and the Russian was reaching into the bag he had brought with him. He held out his hand tentatively. "Here—take—this is something for her." It was a brown bottle with a glass stopper.

"What is it?"

"An old folk remedy. It's an oil, to rub on the limbs. It makes supple and takes away pain. This is OK? I don't know exactly what is wrong with your wife but perhaps this helps. It's from the Ukraine, where they live to be one hundred and fifty. Try it." Kirov paused, and for once George thought the other man looked embarrassed. When he spoke again he said, "This is a gift from me, do you understand? Personal, nothing to do with business. We both know there is a lot of insincerity around, but this small present comes from the heart."

"Thanks, Peter." George looked at the bottle and its plain label minutely scrawled in Cyrillic script, and placed it on the bedside table. "I'm afraid I've got nothing for you. How about some Scotch? Duty-free? I have a bottle in my case."

"No, please, I wasn't expecting anything." Kirov's hand waved the gesture away. "But all the same, let's have that drink. Champagne? Vodka? I think champagne because we are celebrating cooperation and success. But you—whatever you want."

"Vodka."

"Good. The brand is Starka, very old, very good, but the color is perhaps not what you are expecting." He poured a measure of pale brown liquor, then pulled the cork on the champagne. They sat across the table, glasses in front of them. Kirov coughed and made a remark about the air-conditioning, then his face became serious and he spoke.

"So, George, how is business going? How are things in Helsinki?"

"Fine at our end. Sep Tech is in full production with the resin and membranes for Sokolskoye. The Finnish operation is all dressed up and looks good, but your guy in Berne is causing us trouble."

"With the bank accounts?"

"He's too slow at processing our expenses. I think he's looking for a bribe to speed things up. Can you do anything with him?"

"I'll get him transferred. Don't worry, George, we want everything to go smoothly. Is there anything else?"

"Not at the Helskini end," George answered. Kirov picked up the hesitation.

"But?"

The Englishman looked up from his drink into the other man's eyes. How much did Kirov know? He had no feeling of the extent of the Russian's power, just the creeping sensation of Moscow drifting like wind-blown snow across all the worlds he had ever known. Maybe by now it had reached Helsinki. Maybe the whole operation there was bugged and staked out and the KGB knew when the flies landed on the lampshades. There was no way of telling. *I know about the radiation leak*, he repeated to himself. *They need me*. He had to keep saying it to be sure he still had some power, some grip on the situation.

"Well, George?"

"What? Oh, sure—did I ever mention Lou Ruttger to you, the guy who took over Sep Tech in the States when I left?"

"I know the name. Yes?"

George finished his drink and looked around for the bottle. "I should stay off this stuff. With the flying it messes up my guts." He poured another.

"This is a party, George. We'll both get drunk. You're in Russia; everyone gets drunk and nobody cares. We'll both get— tiddly?"

"Tiddly? Oh, sure, tiddly!" George coughed into his glass, then waved an arm. "So, there's Lou Ruttger, a regular guy, an all-American boy, who's not in the picture because he has—what do you call it—*ethics!* You understand? He's working on this project, but he doesn't *know*."

276

"I understand you. This is a problem?" Kirov finished his champagne and deliberately poured another glass. "Try the *zakuski*, George. Go on with your story."

"I don't know that there is a story. It's just a feeling, Peter, a sense that things could go wrong."

"Oh?"

"If Lou knew what I was doing, he'd go crazy. He'd tell COCOM, tell the FBI, tell God-knows-who. And then we're finished."

"But he doesn't know—that's right, isn't it? He thinks he's selling equipment to a company in Finland."

"Sure, and he thinks that Finland is somewhere north of Canada," said George without conviction. "Forget it. Maybe I'm just over-cautious. It's just an impression I get that he's worried about something: that this Finnish business doesn't look right to him."

"I'll think about it," said Kirov. He took a snack from the tray and fingered the stem of his wineglass. "But not tonight, George. Tonight no talk of business. Tonight we're going to get tiddly and talk about philosophy and football."

They sat in their shirt-sleeves, sweating in the air-conditioned coldness. There was a cassette player and they put on alternate tapes of Mozart and jazz. George studied the crumbs accumulated in his lap and stretched out a hand for another spoonful of red caviar.

He said, "Have I told you about John Chaseman?"

"No, George, you have not told me about John Chaseman."

"Then, I shall tell you about John Chaseman."

"Please, tell me about John Chaseman."

"John"—George gulped a mouthful of air—"too much bloody smoke in here—John Chaseman is an honest-to-God hero. I've read that somewhere."

Kirov rolled over on the bed where he had been lounging with the champagne bottle and the remains of the *zakuski*. He put his chin on one hand. "How is Chaseman a hero?" he asked.

George waved his hands and stared up at the ceiling. "Hell, I don't know what makes a hero. He's honest, upright, religious,

277

industrious, brave, a good family-man. Shit, he's even likeable! Chaseman Industries would fall apart without him. Turn the music up, Peter."

Kirov leaned over and tweaked the cassette-player.

"Rum tum—bebop—dum—you like jazz, Peter?"

"It's OK. Are you trying to tell me something, something about Chaseman?"

"Oh, *that*." George stared at the glistening red globules of caviar, and they winked back. "Only that John Chaseman wants to buy Sep Tech. How's that for a story? End of our project, that's what, because John Chaseman won't supply equipment to the Soviet Union—no sirree!—no way!"

He laughed, and Kirov laughed with him, then asked, "But, seriously, is this really going to happen?"

George shrugged. "Ask Alasdair Cranbourne, he's the bloke who's flying into Salt Lake City every other week to see Chaseman and fix the price. *Bap—bap—pow*—how did you know I liked Ella Fitzgerald, Peter?"

"It was a guess, George, just a guess."

"I've got something for you."

They were drinking coffee laced with brandy. George had the cup balanced in one hand and with the other was fumbling in his suitcase.

"A present, George?"

"A cuddly toy—only kidding. Here." He passed across a file and a roll of drawings.

"What are these?"

"The reason for my being here. These are the specifications and drawings for the vessels and the other equipment that has to be manufactured in the Soviet Union. Give them to your factories for fabrication. If they have any questions, I'll be available to talk them through."

Kirov took the papers and placed them on the floor by his own case. "This will take some time," he said. "Our people will need to study these documents before they can formulate their questions. Can you stay in Moscow for a few days?"

278

"Whatever it takes. I want to fix up a meeting with the Ministry of Gas to talk about the other business—you remember the other business, Peter, the sale of gas plants? We responded to the enquiries from Techmachimport and since then we've heard fuck-all. Those contracts and more like them are part of the deal."

"Don't get excited, George, it's all some bureaucratic mix-up, I'm sure. I'll see what I can do."

"You do that, Peter. I'm not going to let myself get screwed."

They had another drink and played another tune. Kirov rang for some more coffee, which arrived promptly.

"George," he said, "I'm glad you're sticking around for a few days. I've arranged a little sight-seeing for you—a little thank-you. A trip to Suzdal."

"As long as it doesn't interfere with business."

"You'll have time on your hands while I arrange for meetings with Techmashimport and while our engineers consider your technical information. Do you remember Dr. Terekhova?"

"No."

"She was at the dinner party given by the Minister. She will act as your guide."

"I still don't remember. There was a flashy-looking woman, but I thought she was the Minister's mistress. Are you trying to set me up with some tart?"

Kirov smiled and shook his head. "Not with Dr. Terekhova. She is not even beautiful."

"George."

"Peter?"

The music had stopped. The coffee was cold. The room was quiet, still enough to hear the breathing of the night and the building, hear the pitter-patter of things that go pitter-patter and the distant closing of doors that sounds like time retreating.

Kirov was languid with tiredness, smiling with yawns, yawning as he spoke.

"Are you asking me to arrange something for Ruttger and Chaseman?" he asked.

"Arrange something?" George answered without interest. He

had placed his cup by the window and was looking out on Moscow and the night and breathing in deeply, as if the clean winter air beyond the glass could clear his lungs. He turned and focused on the other man and felt his thoughts drop into place like bricks. "Oh, Christ, Peter!" he said softly. "I didn't mean that—not that. Is killing people all that you blokes can think of?"

"Killing?" said Kirov. "Who mentioned killing? Did I mention killing? I've told you, it's not like that any more."

They walked by the river. It was past midnight. The Moskva was white and frozen under a waning moon, and the air was sharp as a knife. They walked slowly, keeping close because the ear-flaps on their hats made hearing difficult, and as they walked each supported the other when he stumbled. Kirov had thoughtfully provided them with a flask of brandy.

"Did you ever hear of a man called Oleg Ouspensky?"

"No." George had halted and was leaning on the parapet staring across the ice. The car that was following them at a snail's pace along the embankment stopped. It didn't matter; George had decided it didn't exist.

Kirov joined him. They stood together, staring into the night and snow, trying to identify objects on the further bank.

"He was a defector. He went over to the Americans. In the West it was a famous case."

"I'd never even heard of Neville Lucas—and he was one of *our* traitors. Am I supposed to remember one of yours?"

"I suppose not."

They walked on a while. George said, "What happens if you want to throw up in the street? Is that against the law here?"

"I don't know. Probably. Are you feeling all right, George?"

"I'm fine. Just curious as to what makes Moscow different from anywhere else. In England drunks are always throwing up in the street."

"Here also—but your question was whether it was against the law."

"You're right. Maybe it's secretly against the law in England, too. Maybe it's just like Moscow. So who was Oleg Ouspensky?

Has he anything to do with our business?"

"No" — Kirov had walked a few steps while George had been thinking over the last matter, and now he waited and while he waited looked at the stars and the ice-halo around the moon — "no, George, he was just someone I knew, someone I met in Washington."

Somehow they got to talking about cars. The Russian talked of the Pontiac he had once owned in America.

"You owned that car when you knew Ouspensky?"

"No, I had a Ford then, a Mustang. Good car."

George looked back at the black limousine stationary twenty yards behind them with its exhaust gases condensing in the cold. From this distance it could have been a Pontiac. In this light. Maybe Moscow had spread and was now so big that it reached Detroit, or wherever it was that they made Pontiacs.

"Was he important?"

"Ouspensky? He was a military attaché in Paris."

George whistled to show he was impressed. Then he wondered: Why? What the hell was a military attaché anyway?

Kirov was saying, "He came *back*, George! He returned to the Soviet Union. I persuaded him to."

"Good for you. That must have made you top of the class. Do you still see him? Talk over old times/"

"No, I haven't seen him since. He has a small staff job somewhere in the east. Not as good as before, but that you wouldn't expect."

"So Mother Russia forgave its erring son — is that the point, Peter?"

"Something like that."

They were sitting on the parapet, passing the flask of brandy. George suggested they offer a drink to the guys in the car. Kirov appeared not to hear him.

"George."

"Yes, Peter?"

"Oleg was my closest friend."

"Oleg? — oh fuck, I'm drunk — is that Ouspensky?"

"Yes."

"He was your friend. You mean you knew him before that

281

time in Washington?"

"No."

"No?"

Kirov screwed the cap on to the flask and slipped it into his pocket. He got back to his feet and stood for a moment batting his arms for warmth. He said, "I didn't know him before Washington. We met on business but we became friends." He added, "I know what you're thinking, George, but it was nothing like that."

"What was I thinking?"

"You have a Western attitude. Over here we don't think like that. To have close friends who are men, it's normal. Perhaps we drink ourselves into that situation. We Russians are an emotional people. See, George? I'm being more open than you are." Kirov laughed. "Think of the risks I'm running, telling you these things!"

"I'm cold," said George. Kirov helped him down from the parapet and they walked on a while.

Lillian. Kirov was still speaking, but George was losing his concentration. He was thinking of Lillian as he stared along the empty boulevard. Where the hell *was* he? Everything formless under the snow. Even the river looked like a highway. Maybe it was. Maybe it led to Detroit and all those Soviet-made Pontiacs. Would he ever get the hang of this bloody city? *Lillian!*

He had called her before they left the hotel. Kirov had sat by the cassette, listing to the Jupiter Symphony; so maybe he hadn't been overhearing. Bloody Brenda answered the phone and assured him that her "darling girl" was well but sleeping. Lillian had heard her and demanded to speak to him, but all she could say was "George! George!" in the way that small children call to their parents when they come home from work. Distant. Lillian had become far away even when he was near her. "George!" and a clasp of his hand, and her eyes far away.

Do you remember, do you remember?

Lillian didn't remember. She had become detached from her own past, separated from all those other Lillians that George had known and loved, left only with the thin present, which was so insubstantial that when George saw her now she was like an image painted on gauze. When next he heard Kirov's voice and turned to focus on him, Lillian might have been there, a part of Moscow, without form or shape in the snow.

"We are in an unusual business," Kirov was saying.

George stopped. "Sorry, Peter, I was thinking of something else. What did you say?"

"Are you all right?"

"I'm fine. Go on."

"OK, OK, it's just that I was worried for you." He took George by the arm to stop him from falling on the frozen pavement. He planted him upright and they stood facing each other.

"George."

"Peter!"

"This is a personal business, do you understand? Success and failure aren't things that happen somewhere out there—they happen to *me!*"

"It isn't like that any more—you told me so." George was looking into the other's eyes and he found himself suddenly sober.

"Please, George, be serious! You seem to have killing on your mind. OK, so nobody is going to kill me if we fail. But there are other things that can happen. And for you, too, George, eh? If we fail, then what? No gas-plant contracts? You lose your job? This is a disaster for you and for Lillian and your daughter. That is why we have to trust each other. That is why we must be friends."

Friends. Peter and George, friends for ever.

George shook the other man's hands from his arms. "I'm not Oleg Ouspensky. Stay outside of my head, Peter. This is business pure and simple—buying and selling and trying to screw the other bloke and not get screwed. *Listen!*" he silenced Kirov before the Russian could reply. "I know what's going on here. I know that somewhere in this godforsaken wilderness you've had a nuclear disaster and that I'm the only person who can help you out of the mess."

"Please, George—"

"Shut up! I'm an honest man and I've offered you an honest deal. But you—the KGB, the Party, God knows who—are so fucked up with paranoia that you can't leave it at that! You want

283

power, you want a lever against other people because you can't trust anyone to be straight!"

"*George!*"

"No!" George stopped. And suddenly he was sorry for Kirov — sorry the way these days he was sorry for everyone except himself: because to his eyes they carried their suffering on their faces, nailed and battened even on to their smiles.

Forget it. This was business.

"You need me, Peter," he said, "not the other way round. I've got the whole of bloody Russia by the balls. And I'm not going to let go!"

23

George found her waiting for him in the hotel lobby, a small, neat woman with auburn hair. Now he remembered her from the dinner at Zhukovka; not her appearance particularly, which in his eyes was plain and undistinguished, but that momentary flash of sympathy she had shown. On the other hand, she had been sent by Peter. George didn't trust her.

"Mr. Twist?" Her manner was nervous or perhaps embarrassed. "You have your overnight bag? Please, we must be quick; I have left my car outside the hotel, which is not very permitted." She offered to take the bag, but George held on to it and followed her out.

"This place we're visiting—"

"Suzdal."

"Suzdal—we have to stay the night there?" he asked.

"Yes. Please place your bag in the trunk." She indicated a space in the back of her blue Zhiguli next to a fiber suitcase and a plastic shopping bag. "It is necessary. Suzdal is at three hundred forty kilometers from Moscow, which is far. Also we have sights to see in Suzdal and perhaps we are stopping at Vladimir and other noteworthy places on the road. Rooms in a hotel are arranged." She closed the trunk, forcing down the catch to lock it.

"You didn't want to go on this trip?" George asked. They were in the car and driving. She sat bolt upright with her eyes fixed along the embankment. "Me neither. But they need time to consider my business so they suggested that for once I act like a tourist and see the sights. What is Suzdal, anyway?"

"It is an old town, very folkish. There is a castle and many churches. It is very antique. I have never been there myself, so I am having my first chance."

"But you didn't really want to go—that was my question and you didn't answer."

She still didn't answer.

"Did Peter give you orders?"

"Peter?"

"Kirov."

"You call him 'Peter'?"

She bit her lip and continued staring through the windshield. "Do you," she began, "do you wish me to call you 'George' or 'Mr. Twist'? My name is Irina. Perhaps you consider 'George' too friendly between us. I do not know your customs exactly."

He smiled because her frankness appealed to him. "Whichever makes you feel comfortable. There's nothing in the name."

"I shall call you 'Mr. Twist'."

"That's fine. Lots of my enemies call me 'George'."

At that she turned round with a question in her eyes, but seeing George's smile recognized the joke, so that her face was suddenly transformed and George saw for a second the girl she once was as well as the woman she had become. She had been beautiful and in a way still was; not that it mattered now. He put it out of his mind.

They drove east through the industrial suburbs aiming for Route 8. There were snowplows on the highway. For a while they traveled in silence. Whoever she was, she made no effort to win him over.

"Any music?" George asked. He looked for a radio and found none.

"In the back seat."

He leaned over and found a cassette player with a loaded tape. He started it. Ella Fitzgerald began to sing.

"Thanks, Peter," he murmured.

"Please?"

"Forget it." He turned the machine off. Screw you, Peter, he thought. The tune continued to play inside his head.

An hour gone. The road was straight and gray, the verges covered in frozen slush. There were white fields and dark trees and villages standing off in the middle distance, inaccessible. Irina Terekhova had not spoken once, but George didn't care. He was starting to relax. Whatever Kirov had in mind when he fixed this trip, it wasn't to arrange some compromising sexual adventure. Maybe for once the Russian even had an innocent motive—to provide George with some harmless recreation, for instance.

There were two cars. George woke up to them after dozing. A white one in front and a gray one behind, matching their speed.

"How long have they been with us?"

"You were sleeping?" she said.

"Travel—I get what sleep I can. The cars?"

"Half an hour."

"Who are they?"

"KGB probably. I don't know; I wasn't told." She glanced at him. "I should not worry. You are an important foreign guest and they wish to protect you and are suspicious of you at the same time. It is normal. So long as we do not deviate from our route, they will not trouble us." Her voice was reassuring. "Do you wish to eat?" There was a paper bag on the back seat. It held bread and some apples. George took an apple; its red color was turning to bronze, and the taste was floury. He wondered whether he could sell the Soviets a cold store.

Snow began to fall in large, lazy flakes. The car dropped speed, and the world started to close in. In the reduced visibility the two escorts fell out of sight. The temperature in the vehicle had risen, and with it George could smell his aftershave and the clean smell of the woman's soap. He took off his topcoat and felt easier without it. Before he had noticed, she had begun to talk, small talk about points on the route, then a few hesitant comments about life in Moscow. He found himself answering questions about London before he was conscious of being asked. And without thinking he inquired casually, "Are you in the KGB?"

Christ, George, what made you ask that?

"No," she answered coldly, and for a while there was nothing more between them.

They were stopped. She was tapping her watch and checking a map.

"I must have dozed off again," he said.

"I was just finding out where we are. The snow has delayed." She put the map away, slipped the clutch and the car was moving again.

"I am not in the KGB," she said.

"I shouldn't have asked. Really, I'm sorry."

"It was a reasonable question. I didn't expect . . . it's not a Russian question." She gave him the flutter of a smile.

"I'm sorry. I don't want to cause you any trouble."

"It causes no trouble," she assured him, then appeared to think that some word of explanation was necessary. "The KGB . . ."

"Yes?"

"It is not as you think. It is not just a police force. It has many, many interests. Some of them are bad—this you would think as a Westerner—but some of them are good, things that anyone would approve of."

"I understand."

"Do you, Mr. Twist?"

"I think so."

She considered that answer quietly, then went on: "The good things must be done by somebody—even by the KGB. And people who are not KGB must work with them to see that these things are done. I must work with them because there are very important security problems which must be solved—very important problems. I am a scientist."

"I see."

"Perhaps," she agreed. Then: "I think that we are going to be hungry. It was intended that we shall stop and eat, but I do not know where we are, so we shall be late. This will make some people very discomfortable, but it cannot be helped. Are you hungry, Mr. Twist?"

"Don't worry about me. I'm used to it; I travel a lot. And you?"

"An apple will suffice." She took one and ate it as she drove. "These are very good, yes?"

"Delicious. Tell me," he said, "the involvement of the KGB in this business is one of the good things?"

"Yes," she said simply.

"Why?"

"It is complicated."

"Tell me."

She finished the apple and looked for somewhere to place the core. George extended a hand to take it and for a second accidentally held her fingers in his. She spoke with the undertone of certainty.

"It is a serious problem—Sokolskoye—serious also for the people involved, you understand. So there are many lies, and all of this interferes with a solution. The KGB wishes to know the truth so that a correct solution may be found. The technology of your company is part of the solution. This is why you are so important to us, Mr. Twist."

"Then why not tell me the truth!" George snapped. Immediately he said, "I'm sorry. It's not your fault."

"Please do not apologize. I understand. But for us the truth is very difficult, very dangerous. Also very unclear. You cause concern to Major Kirov because he does not know what you will do with the truth."

"Then he'll have to learn to trust me."

Irina Terekhova nodded, but George wasn't sure whether she agreed.

"I know that you have a serious plutonium contamination problem," he said abruptly.

He had broken new ground with her. Did she dare to reply?

He went on, "How big is it? What happens if you don't solve it?"

Did she have the courage? Kirov must have known that this would happen and had dumped the problem on those small, frail shoulders. George was suddenly frightened for her.

"There are five kilograms of plutonium nitrate in the cooling-water lake at Sokolskoye," she answered slowly. "The lake is frozen and we have until the spring thaw to process the water to remove the plutonium."

"What happens in the spring?"

"The lake will flood and the water will contaminate the Volga from Gorky all the way down to the sea." She turned her head for a moment and fixed George's eyes with her own. "There are more than sixty million people living in the Volga Basin who may be poisoned or suffer cancer from this disaster. That is why you must help us, Mr. Twist."

It was said with quiet sincerity, but all George could fix on were the words in his own head. *I don't want to know this! I've got the whole of Russia by the balls and I can't afford to let go!*

At that moment the engine cut out and the car rolled to a halt.

They sat for a minute, both taken by surprise. Then George shook himself into action.

"Open the hood."

She obeyed.

He put on his topcoat, got out of the car and went round to the front. He stared under the hood. OK, so there was an engine in there and the usual bits and pieces. What was he looking at them for, when he knew nothing about cars? Why did he always do that? He went around to the driver's door.

"I can't fix it," he said. "I don't know what's wrong."

"But you are an engineer, yes?"

"Only on my good days." He looked around. The road was bounded by frozen fields. Ahead and behind, the two escorting vehicles were halted with their engines running. It was still snowing lightly. "Look, I've got an idea." He turned and left her to walk toward the forward vehicle. He got to within fifty yards when it started to move slowly away. He stopped and it stopped. He shouted and ran towards it. It retreated at the same pace until he halted, when it did the same. The engine was still running. The rear window had misted up and the occupants were invisible.

"The AAA are never there when you need them."

George had returned to Irina Terekhova.

"Please?"

"English joke—forget about it. I'll try the other blokes." He left her again and walked back along the road. He heard the driver of the other car crashing the gears into reverse. They engaged, there was a jerk and the gray sedan rolled backward at an angle and landed in a wheel-spin in a drift at the edge of the field. George bolted before the driver could extricate himself, and with a sprint reached the driver's door. He bent to speak to the man.

He hadn't expected to be staring into the barrel of a gun.

24

Kirov worked out at an army sports club. He went early when the gym was empty, and found solace and relaxation in the rhythm of movement. By nine o'clock he was finished and showered, and by ten he was back at his apartment in the Sivtsev Vrazhek district.

The car was a black Volga. Kirov knew the people who lived in the apartments, and their cars. They saved for cars, envied cars, boasted about cars. They kept them clean, waxed them when they could, took off the wiper blades and laid the cars up under tarpaulins when they were out of use. They didn't drive black Volgas that showed signs of bad panel-beating and heavy road spray, the sort of car that came out of the Sluzhba motor-pool with two men inside it as a standard fitting, both wearing overcoats cut to the house style and shapeless from sitting around too long waiting for something to happen. They were waiting for him, and didn't care that he knew it.

Kirov turned off the engine and locked his vehicle. In the side-mirror he saw the two men moving, getting out of the black car, stretching their legs, buttoning their coats, watching him in a relaxed fashion. One of them leaned on the car next to theirs, and he recognized Bogdanov's, but there was no sign of the owner. Kirov turned his steps in the direction of the apartment house and heard the other footsteps matching his without closing. They joined him when he reached the lift.

"Where's Bogdanov?" He spoke to the taller one.

"Your place." This came from the smaller one. His partner

smiled without parting his lips. They looked like a ventriloquist act.

"Why is he here?"

"Search me," said the dummy. "You still going up?"

"Shouldn't I?" said Kirov. He called the lift and punched out the floor number.

The apartment door was open. Bogdanov was inside, sitting in an armchair with his coat on and his hands knotted on his lap, screwing his cap as if he were a peasant just come out of the country. Lara was in the kitchen making coffee.

"Hi, boss." Bogdanov knitted his teeth into a welcome.

Kirov dropped his sports bag and closed the door on his escort.

"What's the idea of those two characters?" he asked. He could see Lara in the next room. Her large, dark eyes, which had always seemed to float in the hollows of her face, searched out his and registered fear as her body tried to dissemble. She went through a dance routine of pouring the drinks.

Bogdanov was saying, "I tried to call first. Larissa Arkadyevna didn't know where you were or when you would be back. I had no option but to come around. What was it? Working out? Our club or one of the others?" He took a cup from Lara and nursed it like he didn't know he wasn't supposed to drink from the side with the handle. "Sorry, boss," he added.

"For you—a drink?" Lara said. She had the coffeepot in one hand extended towards Kirov. Her face was frozen in the rictus of the smile that she wore on stage. "Sugar?"

"Thanks." Kirov took a lump while Bogdanov continued murmuring, this time saying something about Grishin. Kirov said, "It's Saturday. Grishin is at his dacha for the weekend." But he was looking at Lara, and her eyes were still eloquent. *What should I have said? Should I have told them where you were?* For a moment he felt grateful toward her; but he didn't know why. He turned now to the other man. "What's the problem?" he asked calmly.

"Let's talk in the car," Bogdanov answered.

"Why?"

A shrug. Bogdanov looked as if he didn't know what the rules were any more.

"An emergency," he said. "Let's just say we've had a disaster."

They took Bogdanov's car. Bogdanov drove: he said he knew the way to Grishin's dacha; he'd done it before, a mail drop.

Kirov asked, "Why didn't Grishin come into Moscow if there's a crisis?"

"I don't know," Bogdanov answered. "Maybe he doesn't like the company he has to keep at the office—too many spies. He's always been a homebody, likes to spend weekends with his old lady and his mother."

Kirov looked at the driver's mirror. Bogdanov had tilted it so that he could watch his passenger. In the side-mirror, the two Sluzhba men in the black sedan were visible.

"Grishin told you to bring them?"

Bogdanov nodded.

"Why?"

"Atmosphere? A bit of pressure to throw you off balance? You know Grishin's style."

"Sure," said Kirov, and for a while they drove in silence. Then Bogdanov began.

"It seems a package came in from Washington—Thursday night." He had his eyes on the traffic, and the words came out in spurts. "A report from Yatsin—you know Yatsin?"

"The Washington resident. I know him."

"I guess so. Anyway, the report surfaced yesterday morning in the regular evaluation committee—item twenty-five on the agenda, after briefings on the White House and the Pentagon and ahead of Rumors, Miscellany and Dirty Stories—and they held up distribution pending further analysis."

"Meaning?"

"That the report was direct from one of the resident's illegals and the committee wanted to clean it up to make it untraceable—you know what they're like about their sources, jealous bitches. Whatever the reason, it sat around, missed the afternoon circulation, got picked up by the night-desk, and some bright spark recognized that it had to do with our business and got the report carried to Grishin at his dacha."

"Who told you all this?"

"Volodya—the queer who works permanent nights in Registry

294

because of his boyfriend. But he's not saying any more. He fancies his chances for promotion."

Kirov gazed out of the window. He didn't recognize the highway. It ran parallel with a railway line, and a heavy locomotive with a train of dry-bulk wagons was beating down the track with its siren blowing.

What was happening in America?

Beneath his air of good humor, Grishin was a private man. Kirov had never been to the dacha before; so now he took it in, the brick main building, big enough to have four rooms, a couple of wooden sheds, a smokehouse, a pile of logs under a tarpaulin, and a square of dug earth where the Colonel probably had in mind to grow vegetables. There were two or three neighbors close by, whose kids were playing in the snow, an unfinished building under construction on the next lot, and, behind the dacha, some scrub and birch saplings and the edge of a dark wood. In the windless air, the smell of wood smoke sat on the ground.

Grishin answered the door himself. He looked less than usually glossy, his apple-cheeked face being drawn and pale; but the change could have been an effect of the clothes, which were old — a woollen shirt and a pair of thick cord trousers with suspenders. His voice was cheerful enough, bright and brittle as cut glass.

"Pyotr Andreevitch! Please come in!"

He handed a bottle of vodka to Bogdanov. "Wait in the car. Share this with the other two, but take it easy. If we haven't finished by one o'clock, go around the back of the house and my wife will give you a bite to eat." To Kirov he said, "You must meet my wife and my mother. They never see anyone." He placed a hand on Kirov's shoulder.

They went into a small room furnished with old overstuffed chairs, some heavy oak objects and a litter of ornaments and framed photographs placed carefully on pieces of lace. It smelt of pine resin and the old lady, who sat in one of the chairs and looked as if she herself had been carved, upholstered and lace-trimmed. Next to her, her daughter-in-law, a sallow-skinned, neat woman, stared at Kirov with the same ignorant, fearful expression he had seen on Lara's face.

Grishin was saying with a sort of solemn complacency, "Pyotr Andreevitch Kirov, may I introduce my spouse and my parent?" He gave names, and the women bobbed, then, without speaking, gathered up their needlework and retired to another room. Grishin's eyes followed them with quiet admiration before returning to his guest. Then, remembering Kirov, he offered a seat, took one himself and stretched out so that his feet touched the iron stove. His features displayed contentment and pride in his family, but to Kirov the expressions looked fleeting, fragile. And then Grishin was speaking.

"Sokolskoye," he intoned, "how goes it?"

"Everything is fine. No more incidents that I know of—not since the collapse of the new work on the dam. The Americans are in production on the membranes and the resin. Our own factories make progress with the other equipment."

"Good, good." There was no interest behind the words. "And George Twist?"

"He's being dealt with," Kirov answered without amplification.

"That's good—fine—and no other problems?"

"Nothing unmanageable. Chaseman Industries continues to give a little concern. I've reported the rumors that they may want to take over Sep Tech; there may be some truth in them." Kirov paused for a reaction to that one, but it didn't come. The problem wasn't Chaseman.

Grishin stooped to pick up a log; he lifted the lid on the stove and dropped it in. He asked casually, "What do you know of this agent, Source David?"

"Source David? Very little. He's an Illegal, a deep-cover agent run by the Washington residency. If I had to guess, I should say he was a U.S. Defense Department bureaucrat; but I haven't given him much thought. Why?"

Grishin didn't answer. Instead, he said, "And what is our connection?"

"Negligible. When we identified Sep Tech as a source of technology, we put out a routine background enquiry and the American Desk came back with one of his reports. Its value was marginal and there was only one follow-up. Then the First Chief Directorate placed a stop-notice on all Source David material, to preserve confidentiality. We didn't object." Kirov halted there, leaving Grishin hanging for more. Why? He remembered the Source David material. He had been mildly curious about the agency's identity, but the material itself was almost useless. It didn't make sense. He said, "Source David doesn't know about Sokolskoye."

"He does now," Grishin answered. "There's been a leak."

They stepped outside the dacha. Immediately Bogdanov and the two Sluzhba men piled out of the black car, wiping the vodka from their lips and at the ready. The ventriloquist and his dummy were eager to go, but Kirov could see the doubtful look on Bogdanov's face. Grishin waved them away.

He had proposed that they take a stroll for an hour's shooting while the light was good. There was no game, but there were rooks in the trees who ravaged his vegetables. It would relax him to take potshots while they talked. He was sorry he couldn't loan Kirov a gun, but he had a spare pair of boots. Together they stepped off into the trees behind the house, Grishin with a shotgun lodged in the crook of his arm, leaving Bogdanov and the other two staring after them, wondering what was happening.

Beyond the scrub and the saplings the wood thickened. Underfoot lay a dense mat of pine needles, patchily covered by snow. The dead silence was broken only by their own muffled footfalls and Grishin's stertorous breathing as he negotiated fallen branches and forest debris. He seemed to ignore Kirov's presence, being focused on his gun and, from time to time, the tops of the trees. He fired one shot which resounded dully, and halted to reload.

"How much does David know?" Kirov asked.

Grishin snapped the gun back into a firing position.

"Everything." He raised the barrel and swung it in an arc pointing at the upper branches. "Apparently. It's difficult to be sure. It seems he's received a technical digest of the whole problem. And"—he let the barrel fall without firing and looked at Kirov—"a cry for help."

"Is this a joke?" Kirov asked, but Grishin was still musing.

". . . astonishing," he was saying quietly. "The naivety!" He fired again, and again there was only the flat report and the rattle of buckshot among the branches. "It seems our traitor wants us to come clean with them, the Americans. He believes that the Americans would volunteer their technology if they really knew the potential scale of the disaster—on humanitarian grounds, apparently. The Americans would *care*. Do you think so?"

"Possibly."

"Highly probable, I imagine." Grishin ejected a cartridge and reloaded. "But after Chernobyl"—he mused—"you understand: we can cope with a nuclear disaster; but a *political* disaster. . . . To tell the world a second time that we cannot be trusted with our nuclear technology: it would be a national confession of failure—a humiliation."

"Yes," Kirov answered. Grishin's words, if analyzed, were unexceptionable, but they left the faintly seditious aftertaste that was part of his style.

"How did Source David come by this material?"

"We don't know the details. Evidently someone had heard of his public position and thought that he was a likely recipient for this sort of revelation. Difficult to say without knowing his identity."

"And what was his reaction?" Kirov asked.

"To contact his control and ask whether it was true. Naturally he has been told that the story is a piece of lying propaganda."

"Is he secure?"

"The resident says that he is—but he would. I don't know. Whatever hold there may be over David—sex, money, commitment—a piece of information like this one is so potent it alters the chemistry of the relationship. Who knows what conclusions David will come to when he's thought the matter over? Greed, sympathy, lust—the combinations change. Now, for me, I'd be worried about David's stability, about his continuing loyalty. The resident, however, has different views."

Kirov waited as Grishin let his theme run down. He waited for the barb. Grishin had his back to him and he was scanning the treetops so that his words, with nothing to echo on, came flatly.

"Do you have any idea who the traitor may be?"

"Me? How should I know?"

"It was just a thought. You more than anyone know the people involved."

"That's true." Kirov felt a dryness in his throat. "But if I had my suspicions I would have revealed them. Even without evidence, I could have someone reposted."

"Of course. I can see the logic of that," Grishin agreed. "Do you remember—yes, you obviously would—the Ouspensky Case?" Kirov tried rapidly to recall the other man's background; Grishin's file was closed to anyone beneath his rank, but there were stories. Meanwhile, the flow of words went on: "I was involved at the Paris end, the clean-up at the embassy after he defected. This was two or three years before your encounter with him in Washington."

"I didn't know."

"No? Well, it's the case. I never met Ouspensky himself. I mean, at that time he was still being debriefed by the CIA, not that he knew anything important, as they soon found out: but, then, it isn't what they know that makes them important so much as the simple fact of defection. Later, of course, I read the account of your recapture of him. But, myself, I never . . . well, I should like to have met him. I did in fact interrogate people who had known him and worked with him."

"I'm sorry, I don't follow," said Kirov.

"No?" Grishin seemed put out. "The point is: when Ouspensky defected, no one was *surprised*. You see, they knew all along that he was unreliable. He was incomprehensible to them, they said, he was mysterious"—Grishin emphasized each adjective—"distant; his character was unintelligible. Of course"—he dismissed the idea—"it wasn't. His character and behavior made perfect sense, and they knew all along that they made sense." He paused now and watched Kirov closely so that Kirov wondered whether he, too, was unintelligible. Then Grishin went on: "What I didn't discover, what I have never understood, was *why*? Why wasn't Ouspensky betrayed by those who themselves stayed loyal? A competing loyalty to Ouspensky? Hardly; he wasn't even popular. Under the pressure of his treason, he was argumentative, a drunk, a recluse. Then, what? What did they identify in Ouspensky that struck some chord within themselves?" Grishin raised the gun so that the barrel pointed at Kirov's chest. The gesture lasted only a second, the muzzle hovering over heart and lungs; then the upward sweep continued and he fired at a target beyond Kirov, and continued to speak while something clattered through the trees.

"In the end, I thought I knew; but I can never be sure. Perhaps you know, too."

"I know what?" Kirov asked. Grishin had set off at an ungainly trot toward a spot among the trees beyond a shallow, ice-choked stream, causing him to follow until he caught the Colonel standing in stillness examining an object on the ground. Grishin touched it with his foot.

"What do I know?"

"Know?" Grishin repeated meditatively. "I thought that from talking to Ouspensky, from becoming his friend—you were his friend, weren't you?—you would understand why everyone was blind to the signs. You see, I ask myself, Pyotr Andreevitch, whether those, even the most loyal, who saw the signs doubted what they saw: whether they wondered if they were placing constructions on Ouspensky's behavior that came from their own feelings, not from reality. In short, I ask: did these loyal men and women look on Ouspensky and see instead some little core of treason in their own hearts?"

And with that Grishin was finished. He was looking at his feet. Kirov saw the shredded carcass of a rook lying bloodied on the pine needles.

Grishin seemed satisfied with his kill; he suggested they return to the dacha. They set off back, the Colonel leading the way. They crossed the frozen stream and a foresters' roadway deep in frosted ruts, and found a clearing bedded with forest litter, where the sun broke through the long shadows of the trees and striped the ground with bars of amber light In the middle of the clearing someone had built a low hearth of stones, now covered in snow, and here Grishin stopped and waited for his companion.

"Invigorating!" he said. His face had taken on a glow of color. "Don't you agree?"

"Yes." Kirov looked around. He had no idea where he was. Dark alleys ran off between the trees to a dark distance. He turned to Grishin. "What is it you want me to do?" he asked.

"Clear the business up, that's all. Go to Washington, see

David, learn what he knows, form your own view as to his loyalty; and take any appropriate action. Solve the Chaseman problem. And, above all," Grishin added, "catch the traitor."

Kirov had no chance to reply. Grishin knew what he was asking. The Colonel went on: "We have no power in this. The Washington resident doesn't take orders from this department: if he wants to, he can refuse you access to Source David. And, as to the traitor, the file has been sent to Special Investigations. Don't look for any help there. As far as they are concerned, we are also suspects—after all, Pyotr Andreevitch, you and I have both had sufficient access to the Sokolskoye material to betray it to the Americans. And, if necessary, they would sacrifice us to preserve the greater integrity of the KGB."

"What do I have to work with?" Kirov asked.

Grishin looked at him sharply. "You used to work in the field. What did you use then?"

"Anything that worked."

"*Anything.*" Grishin threw the word back like a blow in the face.

Kirov thought of Washington and the pursuit of Oleg Ouspensky. Anything that worked. Even humanity.

Grishin meanwhile was saying, "You still have Bogdanov and the Sluzhba team. They may not have much style, but something tells me our traitor isn't the fancy kind. Get them to break a few skulls." He waved a hand to paint in the rest of the picture. Then, "Yatsin—him you know from your days in Washington. Use your influence with him to get to David. But don't expect too much. Yatsin will never act against his own agent: he'll temporize, make excuses that the problem is under control. It's the residents' way: they put pressure on an agent and grind him into the dirt; but at bottom they feel sorry for the poor devil. Where their own creatures are concerned, they can be almost romantically faithful."

"I know," said Kirov.

Grishin stopped.

"Let's get back." He looked at his watch. "I'm hungry. Are you hungry?"

"No."

"We'll see. My wife is a fine cook. My mother taught her. Good cooking—peasant-style! Enough to make a statue drool."

The Colonel gave a smile which started as hearty and turned to wistful. "Cheer up, eh? It's a living!"

"It's a living," Kirov agreed.

They left the clearing and continued toward the house. Grishin began describing details of the way: what fungus grew here; what bird lived in this tree. He suggested that Kirov come for lunch one weekend in the summer, bringing Larissa Arkadyevna with him.

"I have no clearance for Washington," Kirov interrupted as if it were an irrelevant aside.

"Ah." Grishin broke his stride through the trees. "The Ouspensky Case?"

"My clearance was taken away."

"Now I remember. Well . . . I'll get you a new one."

"Thanks."

Grishin regarded him curiously. "Don't thank me," he said. "Just solve our problems. We're finished with subtlety. I want a clear path cutting through to the end of this business. And that includes George Twist."

25

The gun was bigger, blacker and more menacing than George expected. It looked big enough to blow his head off; he didn't know what he was supposed to do about it. These things weren't supposed to happen.

He said, "I was wondering if you could help fix our car." It seemed as good a question as any.

The driver's window wound slowly down. The man was still watching him over the line of the gun. He had tired eyes and yellow skin. His passenger reached casually inside his jacket for his own weapon. He had a pair of Zeiss binoculars on his lap.

"Our car is broken. Can you fix it?" George tried the words louder and more slowly. It usually worked with waiters. "Shit," he murmured. He realized that he wasn't frightened. To get shot somewhere out in the sticks on a Russian roadside because his car wouldn't work—it was too crazy to believe in.

The passenger began to speak. He addressed the driver in Russian. He looked a smoother type, in a nice suit and a quilted car coat, and the smile on his face might have been amusement. The driver let the point of the gun fall and carefully slipped it under his jacket.

"We'll see what we can do."

This came from the passenger. The driver got out of the car and went to the trunk to open it. The passenger came around from his side and offered George a cigarette.

"We are running late." The Russian looked up at the sky. "But no more snow according to my opinion." He spoke with the same slight American accent as Peter Kirov. "Do you intend to go on to Suzdal?"

"I don't know. We hadn't thought about it. What do you want to do?"

The other man was mildly surprised by the question. "It's for you to decide, Mr. Twist. I have a wife, it would be good to get home tonight, but it doesn't matter so much."

"I'll think about it. We'll see how long it takes to get the car going. OK?"

"OK."

They walked back to the blue Zhiguli. The second KGB man followed with a box of tools. George opened the driver's door and spoke to Irina Terekhova.

"Get out. Let's go for a walk. What's-his-name, Ivan, here and his mate Boris will see to the car. Is that all right with you, Ivan? A little stroll. We promise not to go far."

The Russian nodded. "Stay where we can see you, please, Mr. Twist."

"Sure. We'll not get far in the snow."

He took hold of Irina's arm and she yielded to him.

He had noticed a narrow dirt road leading off to one side of the main highway towards a horizon of trees and a curl of smoke which, he guessed, indicated a village. The road had been cleared and was tricky but manageable. They walked along it for a few hundred yards, her arm resting on his. He felt the cold snow against his boots, a pair he had bought in the States, with pointed toes and medallions stitched into the leather.

For a while they walked silently. He found her presence comfortable. Before her illness, he had been in the habit of going for walks with Lillian. Now, if he didn't think too hard about it, he could imagine himself in Norfolk, strolling through the flat winter landscape.

He asked, "Are you married, Dr. Terekhova?"

"Yes."

"And . . . ?"

"My husband is a soldier. He is away on active duty."

"So, a hero, eh?"

"I suppose so. I had not thought of that."

"I'm a bit of a hero myself."

She glanced at him abruptly.

"Sorry," he added. "That was another joke."

They paused by a tree that overhung the road. George looked back at the Russians clustered around the Zhiguli. The men from the front escort car had joined the others. He waved at Ivan, and the KGB man waved back.

"You haven't asked me whether I'm married," he said.

"I know already."

"I see. Well, at least that's an honest answer." He took her arm again and they walked a little further. There was a patch of brambles at the edge of the field, bent under a load of snow. A few withered berries clung to the dry canes.

"I don't think we'll get to Suzdal."

"No."

"Am I missing much?"

"Are you interested in folkloric antiquities?"

"Folkloric antiquities? No, I don't think I'm interested in folkloric antiquities. I don't suppose I'm interested in anything much. My work doesn't allow it."

"That's a pity."

"Yes, I guess it is." He kicked at the snow and uncovered a fungus. He stooped to examine it. "Can you eat this?" he asked. "Isn't that something you do in Russia, eat toadstools?"

"Yes, in autumn it is permitted to go into the forests and pick them. They are very good, especially the milk-caps—I think you say 'milk-caps'?"

"I don't know. You speak better English than I do."

"I think so. But, no, this one you cannot eat."

"Shame." George stood up and breathed out. "So—tell me about Suzdal."

"I have never been there." She thought for a moment. Then, "But I shall tell you a story."

"Go on."

"There was an emperor," she began. George caught her looking beyond him at the horizon where the dome of a church was just visible over the trees. "Our Tsar, Vasily the Third."

"Yes?"

"He had a wife, the Tsarina Solomoniya, who could not give him children. So after many years the Tsar abandoned his wife

305

and took another, and Solomoniya was imprisoned in the Po-
krevsky Convent—which is in Suzdal. And there she gave birth
to a son."

"What happened?"

Irina's eyes turned from the horizon to focus on his. "According to the legend, the Tsarina, fearing that the child would be
murdered by the Tsar or his new wife, arranged for the boy to
be taken from the convent and brought up by peasants. That was
the story."

"And is it true?" George asked, not knowing how else to
respond.

"I don't know. In Stalin's time the tomb of the Tsarina was
opened, and inside, with the body of Solomoniya, there was a
wooden doll. It was wrapped in silk embroidered with pearls—as
one would wrap a royal baby."

There was a gunshot. George turned from the woman. It's
started, he thought. The killing. But he couldn't feel concerned.
The sweep of his vision took in the car and Ivan waving and, in
the direction of the village, birds rising from the wood. Ivan had
fired his gun to attract George's attention; or perhaps someone
was hunting in the trees. George couldn't tell. The woman was
speaking.

"How do you understand my story?"

"How? Oh, I don't know. I suppose the legend must be true:
the boy got away and the Tsarina hid the fact by keeping the
wooden doll. The boy was lucky." He was having difficulty concentrating. There was the unexplained shot. He could see his
body lying at the foot of the bramble bush seeping blood into the
snow.

Then Irina Terekhova did something he didn't expect. She
laughed. It was a frank, open laugh, directed at him but without
any real mockery or malice; if anything, it was regretful, compassionate. It rose and fell like music. Lillian used to laugh like
that.

"What's wrong? What did I say?"

She shook her head, and George found that he was laughing
with her. Her dark eyes were bright with laughter and her voice
was limpid with it, so that for a second she was the most beautiful woman he had ever seen. Then it was gone and she was again

unremarkable.

She was saying, "You are such a Westerner, Mr. Twist, such an optimist. You think that the child escaped. But a Russian would know that there was no child. That is the point." She could see his failure to understand. "You must figure to yourself the poor, mad Tsarina nursing her little wooden savior in order to keep a sort of sanity, a hope for the future."

"And what is your wooden doll, Dr. Terekhova?" he asked, but she appeared not to hear; she was waving at the men by the car. When she next spoke, it was to suggest that they return.

They walked back and reached the tree. She slipped on the ice, and George caught her clumsily in his arms so that as she righted herself her breasts pressed against his chest. Then she was on her feet and holding his arm, and they continued.

"Do you have any children?" he asked.

"I have a son."

"He must miss his father."

"Yes." She stopped. The hem of her coat was dusted with snow 'from the fall. She brushed it off. "My son is in Gorky," she said.

My son is in Gorky.

The words at first didn't register with George. He said something to the effect that he hoped the boy was enjoying himself there, and she agreed: she hoped so, too. Then he realized: Gorky—it was on the river below Sokolskoye!

"Why is he in Gorky?"

"His school has been moved there for the winter."

"Why?" He arrested her arm and turned her to face him. Her expression was pained, but she was asking nothing of him.

"Shall we go on to Suzdal?"

"Why is he in Gorky?" George repeated.

"I think it is too late to continue."

"Damn it, why is he in Gorky! Is it Kirov? Has he done this?"

She shook her arm free and stepped away from him. "It isn't your concern, Mr. Twist. You don't understand the way things are." He was about to speak again but she forestalled him. "I don't know why my son is in Gorky. It is not possible to tell. Please, I do not wish to talk about it." George wanted to cry out—but what? Already she was ahead of him on the path, a small woman in a drab coat, picking her way through the ice and

307

snow.

They were back at the car. Ivan advanced to meet them, like a *maître d'hôtel* to a customer, with a beam on his face and his arms open.

"It is ready!"

"Yes, we know," said George. "We heard the shot."

"Shot?"

"When you fired your gun."

"I didn't fire my gun."

"Ah, sorry, my mistake. It must have been someone out shooting in the woods."

"I don't think so. It is not permitted."

George watched Irina Terekhova. She was climbing into the driving seat. Nothing different, nothing changed. He remembered the KGB man and reached into the pocket of his parka to produce a hip flask.

"OK, whatever you say; I must have been imagining things. Do you want a drink?"

"Thank you." Ivan took the flask and dipped his lips to the neck. He wiped the rim on his sleeve. "Do you go on to Suzdal?"

"I thought we'd go home."

The Russian passed the flask back. "I think that is better," he said, then hesitated. "You are satisfied? We have caused you no problems?"

"The service was terrific," George answered. "You can quote me." He returned to the car.

They drove back to Moscow in silence. The night fell and there was nothing but himself and Dr. Irina Terekhova and a patch of snow and road lit wanly yellow in the headlights. He thought of the present and of the past and of all the women he knew. He thought even of Bloody Brenda with her brogue and bottles of Bass—which she drank, she said, on account of the iron. She had a son in the Army in Northern Ireland, and at night she watched television, fixed to the news from the province in fear for his safety. And George looked on with his pointless compassion.

Peter, of course, had known how it would be. Kirov had arranged the journey with precisely that object in view, because he could not trust George—because he needed a lever. And for a similar reason he had caused the son of Irina Terekhova to be sent to Gorky — but here George couldn't be so sure because in Russia the line between the deliberate and the accidental was blurred and the improbable became actual, and Stalin lived and slaughtered, and, somewhere on the River Volga, there was a place called Sokolskoye which was going to wipe out sixty million people.

I don't want to know, I don't want to know! Peter, you bastard!

Irina Terekhova drove with her eyes on the road, not mentioning her child, only stating the time when George asked, and identifying the landmarks of Moscow when he inquired what they were, which he did because they took his mind off her. And he could only pray to himself: Don't let me care what happens to her. Don't let me think about a woman that I'll never meet again in my life.

26

Kirov arrived without incident. From Moscow he flew to Frankfurt under his Russian work name, spending twenty-four hours there, collecting a Dutch passport from a safe drop and buying some clothes suitable for a West German businessman: a plain suit and a dull green overcoat — the type with a pleat in the back running to the shoulders which identifies Germans wherever you see them. There, too, he changed his purchases for his own clothes, packed the latter into a canvas bag which he consigned to a luggage depository before mailing the chit to an address used by the local *referentura* in the hope rather than the expectation that they would some day turn up back in Moscow and he wouldn't be faced with a wrangle about his expenses.

From Frankfurt he flew to London. For the benefit of transients through Heathrow, the KGB had a number of drops in the Slough area, and from one of them he collected a West German passport and his airline tickets. It was as Herr Hans Jürgen Goetz that he sat in a 747 and listened to the woman next to him, who was returning to Virginia from a conference of psychoanalysts in Tel Aviv. He slept calmly for most of the way.

So now he was in Washington and it was snowing. Dulles Airport had problems handling snow. National had fewer problems but was liable to dump its aircraft into the Potomac if they ran out of runway; so everyone was glad that National couldn't take a 747 and comforted themselves with a few drinks and a tray of canapés until the flight was cleared to land.

From habit Kirov took the second cab that offered itself. He felt relaxed about security—there was no reason to suppose that the CIA knew he was in the country, and the airport had the right feel to it—but he went through the stock precautions. It was late and the traffic on Interstate 66 was light—a couple of trucks and a midnight-blue Washington Flyer bus. There was a gold-colored sedan that passed the bus and slipped in just behind, but that, too, had the right feel. Kirov let it stay with the cab for three miles, then directed the driver to leave the highway at Fairfax Drive and take him through Clarendon just to see what would happen. And when the sedan stuck to Interstate 66 as he knew it would, he felt more comfortable. His instincts were still sound. He told the cabbie to take him to the Marriott Hotel in Rosslyn.

They sat in the lobby of the hotel, facing the door and the gray morning. Of the three, Yatsin, who might have been expected to be most at home, seemed the most nervous. He drummed his fingers on the dark-green floral upholstery of the couch, and when he wasn't doing that, his hands drifted around as if he had too many of them. It was, he said, because after all these years he had finally given up smoking: a renunciation his American friends approved of. He also refused breakfast because he had recently adopted a macrobiotic diet. "These Yanks," he said, "they have some crazy ideas; but I'm telling you I haven't felt so well for ages. Look—no fat!" He tapped his belly with pleasure. Kirov thought he looked terrible.

"America . . ." Yatsin began some remark.

"You seem nervous," Kirov interrupted patiently. Out beyond the door he could see the heavy that the resident had brought with him. Oblensky was standing under the car porch, staring at the RCA building and then at the traffic rolling over Key Bridge into Georgetown across the frozen Potomac. "You think you weren't careful enough coming here?"

"Please, Petya, don't embarrass me."

"OK, so it isn't that"—Kirov's eyes returned to the speaker—"so what is it?"

"You." Yatsin's face held a simple pleasure that Kirov hadn't expected. A reunion—Yatsin was attending a reunion. He said,

311

"I just wasn't expecting to see you again. We've laid a lot of girls together, but after the Ouspensky Case I thought it was all over with you. It was like saying goodbye to youth." He smiled and patted Kirov's hand. It was a big smile, and the teeth had been expensively capped. Yatsin had a tan, the sort that comes from a solarium, and the white teeth contrasted with his skin.

Ouspensky. It always came back to that.

"When you left," said Yatsin, "we all held our breath. We didn't know whether Center would bury you or make you a star. I guess they didn't know, either. They blazed the case in the training manuals but posted you to a crummy job back home with no chance to travel."

"But I was right about Ouspensky," Kirov reminded him. "I got him for them."

"Sure you did." Now Yatsin sounded as though he were humoring him. "But it was the way you did it." This from Yatsin, who had never understood. "You got too close to him. Screw your mother, I read the transcripts and even I didn't know whether Ouspensky was coming over to us or you were going over to them. OK," he conceded, "so everyone admired the technique. But at bottom this is an old-fashioned business. Give them violence—screams, blood and shit—it makes them feel secure." He shrugged, a sign to change the topic, and reached into his pocket to produce a whole-grain candy-bar which he broke into and nibbled. Oblensky wandered over from the door. He was big and as old-fashioned as anybody could have wished.

"It's this Sokolskoye business that brings you here?" Yatsin asked. "I read the stuff," he added, "the package that was sent to our man. It's really that bad? I mean, total disaster?"

"It's under control," Kirov replied blandly. He stood up because travel had made him tired of sitting around, and looked at the pictures on the wall behind. A man in a wideawake hat, a woman in a crinoline, a girl in blue stooping to pick flowers, an antebellum mansion lodged among trees.

"I want to talk to Source David," he said.

"To find out who your traitor is? You're wasting your time. Source David doesn't know. He got an anonymous package in the mail, posted from Paris, and he handed it over to us. That's all there is to it. I've done some checking of my own, and there was

312

a crowd from the Leningrad Symphony Orchestra in Paris on the date of posting. So maybe your traitor got the package to some creep of a musician who mailed it to Source David as soon as he got to the West."

"And that's it? Who is David? Why were the papers sent to him? How secure is he now that he knows about Sokolskoye?" Kirov recognized the other's reluctance. "I have orders . . ."

"From Grishin? So who's Grishin? I mean: I know who Grishin is, but since when have I been taking orders from outside the First Chief Directorate? Please, Petya," he said, his voice falling, "for friendship maybe I can do something for you. But for Grishin? I wouldn't fart for Grishin."

He wants to do me a favor, Kirov realized. Why? Why so sentimental? Because he hung around for my leavings once upon a time, and now he's the Washington resident? Ouspensky—all because of Ouspensky. He feels guilty at his own success.

They let the conversation fall. The lobby was suddenly filling with people, clamoring for service at the reception desk. Kirov was struck with how innocent they looked, how innocent all Americans looked. With almost equal suddenness the flood subsided. Yatsin was speaking.

"You can meet David. This I am doing for you, Petya, for nobody else, for old times' sake. But understand: you must be easy on him; he trusts us. I'm making the point because sometimes he seems like a rough, tough character. It's all charade—understand?"

"Who is he?"

"A politician. That's why your traitor saw him as an outlet for the story. He keeps a high profile—very anti-Soviet, pro-Israel stance: beats the drum up and down Capitol Hill. This makes him a focus for anti-Soviet propaganda. We use him as a touchstone for monitoring the political right wing."

"A 'touchstone'—what sort of agent is a 'touchstone'?" Kirov suppressed his impatience. "You mean he has no hard intelligence value?"

"Yes. I mean, no!" Yatsin was confused. "You should know: it started in your time. This is a media age and we have to keep in touch with all sections of public opinion."

"And that's what David does—keeps you in touch with right-wing opinion?"

"Yes."

"And we pay him?"

"Yes."

Yatsin shrugged and gave one of his uncertain smiles, the sort he used to give when trailing Kirov and being introduced to his smart American friends. He made a remark about keeping up with the times. Kirov had ceased to listen. Washington had changed as he hadn't expected it to. It lacked the permanence and solidity of Moscow, and he had forgotten.

". . . I mean, what sort of traitor has information like this and can't think of anything better to do with it than send it to the Americans with a plea to help the Soviet Union out of a disaster? It's so naïve it's almost incredible!"

Kirov looked up from his thoughts. "It happens."

"I know," Yatsin agreed and shook his head in disbelief. "But this sort of traitor is an embarrassment. No style—no class. If it wasn't so serious, I'd cry."

"So who am I looking for?" Kirov asked. "What sort of traitor would send a package to Source David?"

"An amateur, a beginner." Yatsin thought it over. "A Jew or a Jew-lover."

They walked to the back of the lobby where a window gave on to the hotel pool. There were chairs and lounge's stacked around the poolside. They had white frames and pale-yellow slats. Even this early there were people swimming.

"I'm thinking of taking it up," Yatsin said. He tapped the glass and pointed. "This, or maybe jogging. I haven't decided. I need the exercise."

"Has anyone told you that you're starting to look and talk like an American?"

"Sure!" Yatsin laughed. "But what matters is what's in the heart. Russia is a state of mind: you can take it with you anywhere. By the way, what do you think of the weather? Remind you of home?" He laughed again and from his pocket offered one of his wholefood snacks.

"Vanya, I have another favor to ask."

314

"Try me!" Yatsin seemed pleased.

They walked back to the front of the lobby where Oblensky was lounging on one of the couches, keeping an eye on the door and pulling long black hairs from the lobes of his ears.

"I have a wet job that needs to be done urgently."

"Fuck your mother," Yatsin murmured and slipped into a chair thoughtfully.

"Well?"

"Well?"

"You can plead orders. I have them with me. What can you do for me?"

"Nothing Petya and that's a fact."

"But the orders?"

"General stuff. Nothing said about killing people. For that I need a specific authorization from Moscow. And in any case I don't have the resources."

"What sort of story is that?"

"Nor more than the truth. I'm embarrassed, but that's the way it is."

He sent Oblensky to get some coffee, then moved to the couch to seat his bulk next to Kirov. "You want to know how it is nowadays?" he said with quiet emphasis. "I'll tell you.

"Here on the ground we get the idea that a little wet job on some guy we don't like would be in order. First thing: we have to put forward an Application in Principle to Center. This gives them an outline of why we want to do it, what will happen if we do it, and a rough idea of how we go ahead. Moscow sits on this for a month—maybe two—and *then,* if someone likes the idea, we get the nod and we move to step two: the Detailed Plan. You sure you don't know about this?"

"No longer my area."

Yatsin sucked air sympathetically.

"OK—the Detailed Plan—what can I tell you? We draw up details for the hit: time, place, method—lots of color. This"—he let the word draw out—"is all bullshit, since we all know we have to make it up as we go along; but it looks good. And—this is the important point—the Plan contains an estimate of cost so that they can make an appropriation from the budget. I'm not kidding you: they want to know what it *costs!*"

Oblensky had brought cartons of coffee from the bar. They nursed them on their laps in silence.

Then: "What happened, Vanya? I thought you said that this was an old-fashioned business?"

"I don't know," Yatsin said. "I thought maybe you could tell me after the Ouspensky Case. All that technique, all that emphasis on the human factor, the sheer subtlety of it all. Part of a trend? The spirit of the times? All I know is that some people have lost the stomach for the rough stuff. There are guys back home who are only concerned about our image and the costs." He sighed. "I tell you, these days the KGB is run by advertising executives and fucking accountants!"

They sat for a while longer. As far as they could, they talked about mutual friends. Whatever happened to them? Kirov thought about George Twist. What did George want? What did he expect when he brought up his problems with Chaseman and Ruttger? *Oh, Christ, Peter! I didn't mean that—not that.*

"What do you do in an emergency?" he asked Yatsin. The other man looked up from his coffee.

"Is this decaffeinated?" he asked Oblensky.

"I don't know, boss."

Kirov let the little scene play itself out, then reminded Yatsin: "Emergencies?"

"I heard you. We don't have emergencies. That's official."

"Everyone has emergencies."

"Only in the real world, not in Moscow." Yatsin was checking his watch. "I've got to go," he said. "I've got an appointment with my chiropractor. If you want to chat, talk to Oblensky." He seemed unsure how to say goodbye, and in the end settled for squeezing Kirov's hand in both of his. "If I don't see you again, think of all the girls we've had together." When the hands withdrew, Kirov was left with a piece of paper and on it the time and place to meet Source David. To Oblensky, Yatsin said, "Take your time and catch me at the car." Then he was gone.

Kirov slipped the paper into his pocket. Oblensky stayed, hopping around on his big feet like a kid with a secret. A bellhop came past paging a Mr. Daniels.

"Well?" Kirov let his gaze drift back from the door to Oblensky. "So what do you do in an emergency?"

"We call this number," Oblensky said and he gave the number slowly as if he were in the habit of counting on his fingers.

"Who is it?"

"The name is Maurice, but the number is only the cut-out. The real Maurice is a crazy but a know-nothing who can't touch us. The price for a wet job is five thousand dollars."

"Thanks."

"It's OK." Oblensky, too, seemed short on farewells. He shuffled a few grins about, stuck his hands in his pockets and muttered in English: "Have a nice day."

He took a Diamond cab to Bethesda. During the Ouspensky Case, he and Yatsin had taken a house there—this was at a time when there was a truce with the CIA, an understanding that neither side was to leave bodies around the other side's patch, which in itself was a sign of the times. Langley had allowed Ouspensky to live more or less openly in a neat white frame house complete with little woman and apple pie, and travel in daily by car with a minimal escort.

Oleg had loved it; he had joined chess clubs, become a Rotarian, and was looking forward to the day when he could vote Republican—not because of his politics, but because it would mark him as assimilated. He was swamped by America, drowning in American ideals, not sure how far he was supposed to drink them in; unaware that even the Americans couldn't take in all American values at the same time.

So he had checked in at Langley every day like a lawyer going to the office, and filled his diary with social appointments. And in his quiet moments he had painted landscapes, expansive Russian landscapes that he couldn't see when he looked out of the window across his well trimmed, well-watered lawn. And he had begun to forget the way things were.

Kirov went back to the house. It was still as neat as he remembered, maybe neater because the new owners had given it a fresh paint job. They had children; there was a swing on the lawn with its seat covered in snow, and a ball lying in the long grass under the hedge. They were liberals, with an old station-wagon parked in the drive with ecology stickers glued to its windows.

On the other side of the street the CIA had rented another place for Oleg's minder, a man called Harry, who was married and ready for his pension. Ouspensky had become part of the family, gone on holiday with Harry and Charlotte and learned to play poker in the evenings over a few beers. George would have liked him.

He leaned forward, tapped the driver on the shouder, and told him to move on. There was no going back. He was acting like George and people like George who made journeys into the sentimental past. George couldn't have handled the Ouspensky Case. *"Oh, Christ, Peter—not that!"* What did he want? Why had he mentioned Chaseman if he didn't want something arranged? Kirov didn't underestimate George. He was tired and under stress, but the Englishman had a core of strength and intelligence. Yet in the end, he couldn't face up to the logic of his own actions. *"Not that!"* He preferred to forget, to ignore, to leave Kirov with the consequences of his own unadmitted thoughts. And Kirov accepted the burden. He was prepared to occupy the middle ground between people like George and animals like Oblensky. And at times like now he hated them both.

He told the cab to drop him along Wisconsin Avenue, walked a stretch to check for tails, then found a bar and a pay phone and made his call. He fixed the arrangements for Maurice and arranged for the bill for five thousand dollars to be sent to the resident: Yatsin would have to explain it to the accountants. Next he hired a car locally, using his West German driver's license, and drove it by a circuitous route back into town and then out over the Potomac by the Key Bridge.

Opposite Georgetown the bank and the heights had been redeveloped, the old riverside industries had closed and offices, hotels and shopping malls spread up the slopes. They were still building. Between the high-rise blocks the jibs of tall cranes were stenciled against a cold sky.

He took Wilson Boulevard, cut off Fairfax near Virginia Square station and then drove up and down Ballston by small streets until he felt comfortable and then moved direct, following the instructions in Yatsin's note.

He found the spot—a building lot. It was a half-finished condominium fenced off by hoarding and chicken wire, with an open gate and a burned-out site cabin next to it because the developer had gone broke. On the snow-covered ground lay patches of icy water and piles of frozen rubble; and a single set of tire marks where a car had driven on to the site and not yet left.

Kirov parked the hired car. There was a spot in the shelter of the site cabin. He remained in the driver's seat and scanned the open ground. A bird flapped around hunting for thin pickings among the rubble. A rusty cement mixer lay on its side in a scattering of bricks. Some sheeting hanging from the building billowed loosely, and dust blew off the empty floors. There was no sign of the other car, just tracks trailing off to a vanishing point in a fold of ground.

He got out of the car and fastened his coat against the cold. The earth was slippery underfoot, and he had to walk with his eyes down to avoid the ice, so that he saw nothing but a few yards of dirt and snow and he could have been anywhere.

During that winter—the winter of the Ouspensky Case—he used to go walking with the traitor. Parks, gardens, public places—just the two of them strolling, watching their feet to avoid slipping, and behind them, a couple of CIA men jogging along in track suits, and a third one, a fat man in a tartan mackinaw they called Fred because he turned up all the time like an old friend, though they didn't know his real name.

"*Persuade* me, Oleg! Tell me why I should stay in America."

Ouspensky hadn't expected that. The traitor thought that Kirov would take the opposite line, feeding him reasons why he should return to the Soviet Union.

"Read the poems," said Ouspensky, the inadequacy of the answer audible in his thin voice. It was then that he had pressed Kirov with the volume of Walt Whitman's verse. "Let this tell you."

"*You* tell me," was Kirov's answer. "Help me."

An invitation to return, veiled in threats or deceit, could have been reacted to defensively: all the forces that had driven Ouspensky to defect were marshaled to respond to it. But to Kirov's plea there was no ready answer: it left the other man naked to his own feelings and recollections so that in the end—as Kirov always knew would be the case—Ouspensky persuaded himself to go home. That was how it was done and why the Ouspensky Case was different. That and the winter, which, while the snow lasted, made Washington look like Moscow; but a Moscow stripped of memories, so that when Ouspensky looked around him he saw a world filled with emptiness, and knew that he would float in that void forever.

Kirov walked on. The tracks led erratically over the site. The driver was a careful man and had spared his vehicle's suspension by negotiating a route around the ruts and half-buried bricks. Kirov was coldly amused: Source David had translated his fears of discovery into care for his car, like a scared rabbit washing its ears. What was he doing now? Emptying the ashtrays and cleaning the side-mirrors? More likely he was going over his story, dredging up details, anything that would identify the traitor who had sent him the package of papers on the Sokolskoye Incident. Could he implicate anybody, or was it as Yatsin said, that Source David knew nothing? And if he could lead Kirov to the traitor—what then? Was Grishin right? Did Kirov know the answer already, if he could face the question?

He found the car parked behind the brick and steelwork of the unfinished construction, the engine running and the exhaust gases collecting in a gray puddle around the wheels. The driver was in the seat with the window closed. He wore a hat with the brim tipped forward and a scarf up to his nose. A nervous man.

Kirov approached him.

"Hello, David?" he said. The window wound down.

"Who the shit are you?" snapped Senator Abe Korman.

"I'm one of your friends."

320

27

Salt Lake City: January 2

Place. If anyone had a more acute sense of place than George Twist, it was an American known simply as "Maurice"—because, for Maurice, place meant in every real sense the difference between life and death. So, for Maurice, the shopping mall in central Salt Lake City known as the Crossroads Plaza was something more than a system of chain stores and covered pedestrian walkways. It was a theater in which a drama was to be enacted.

For John Chaseman the day was, in all respects but one, a good day. In the matter of business, after a long conference-call to Alasdair Cranbourne in England, he had resolved some outstanding commercial queries and settled on a price for the purchase of Sep Tech Inc.; he would conclude the deal within two weeks, provided that his lawyers were satisfied with Sep Tech's Finnish contract, which seemed to be the company's major piece of current business. In the matter of religion, too, which he took sincerely, seriously and humbly, he had sorted out a number of problems that affected him as a senior churchman within the Church of Jesus Christ of Latter-Day Saints, and felt particularly at peace with his God. As for leisure, he was looking forward to a dinner-party arranged for that evening, and he had also arranged a skiing weekend with his wife and two eldest boys. It was because of the dinner engagement that he left his office promptly at five-thirty and took one of the six lifts that serviced the Commercial Security Bank Tower where Chaseman Industries had its headquarters. The lifts led to the Crossroads Plaza.

The exit from the lifts was into a blind passage, open on one side into the shopping mall. Anyone leaving by this route walks out with Weinstock's clothes shop and the bank on the left before the walkway out on to Main Street, and, on the right, a battery of three public telephones and a shoe shop called The Wild Pair. Maurice stood at the telephones with a pile of nickels and a problem on the line that explained why Maurice was there so long.

So John Chaseman took the lift. He entered the blind passage, walked out past the telephones and turned right by the shoe shop, pausing only momentarily because a glance at the Deseret Federal Savings Bank acted as a cue to his memory to check that he was carrying enough cash for the following day, which he was. So he continued.

He walked erectly and smartly. His faith commanded him to take good care of his body, and he did so. He was mulling over some problem in his mind and so took minimal notice of his surroundings. This, too, was normal, and when Maurice passed him as he paused to check his money it signified nothing and he paid no attention to the figure walking briskly away through the other shoppers toward the central concourse and the escalators.

He went on, walking past a line of shops. On his left, a place that sold ices, a men's clothes shop and another that sold boots and Western gear; on his right, Waldenbooks, with its racks of bestsellers stacked up to the entrance, then a fast-food outlet called Mrs. Fields. Chaseman passed them every working day but, if asked, couldn't have named them, nor the shops in the concourse; not Orange Julius, another fast-food joint; but, perhaps, Bohm Allen, the jeweler, because he had once bought his wife a gold clip there.

Opposite Orange Julius was a bench next to the down escalator. By the bench stood a brown trash can. Looking down the escalator into the concourse below, one could see a red automobile and a demonstrator in a two-piece suit, there as part of a promotion. Maurice was sitting on the bench, sharing it with a black adolescent in Levis and sneakers and an elderly man in sunglasses and a wide-brimmed hat, who read his paper and scratched his nose, and read his paper and scratched his cheek.

Crossroads Plaza was in every sense a very concrete place, a very particular location in which things happened. And yet, to John Chaseman, who would claim to know it, it was a place without shape or detail. He had in mind to cross the concourse and take the exit directly opposite, which led to the carpark, and to do this, as Maurice had noted on two previous occasions (though Chaseman was unware of his own habit), he took the right-hand route, past Orange Julius and the exit to the South Temple, walking close by the benches and the down escalator. He was there — just there — when Maurice stuck a knife into the thigh of the black adolescent.

"Jesus Christ!"

The boy was on his feet, his arms flailing and his eyes looking wildly around.

"Holy shit!"

The old man had rocketed from his seat as if he had suddenly caught fire, and his forward propulsion caused him to career into John Chaseman, who recoiled, froze, caught the old man in his arms and stared as the shoppers halted and stared at the commotion.

Maurice rose, too, and stepped forward as if to help. A plastic bag was clutched to Maurice's front, and from it a muted shot was fired that caught John Chaseman in the chest and blew away two vertebrae in his upper spine and sundry pieces of flesh.

Maurice shouted, "The nigger's got a gun!" and at the same time slipped the bag and the weapon into the brown trash can, while the boy gave a yell, hesitated for a second and then broke into a limping run toward the South Temple exit.

Blood. The crowd was mesmerized by it. John Chaseman was lying on the ground with a neat hole in his chest but blood leaking from the wound in his back and his lips mouthing blood as he murmured a prayer. The boy's leg streamed with blood from the cut in his thigh as he ran in a circuit like an animal at bay because already his exit was blocked and he was dizzy with pain. Blood.

Maurice turned away from the scene.

No one noticed the young woman in the smart business outfit who descended by the escalator to the lower concourse.

28

DAVIDOV—OSIP ABRAMOVITCH

Date of Birth:	MARCH 4, 1946
Place of Birth:	MOSCOW RSFSR
Parents — Father:	DAVIDOV—ABRAM ABRAMOVITCH (DECEASED)
Mother:	CHAKOVSKA—ANNA ALEKSANDROVNA (DECEASED)
Education:	WORK-POLYTECHNICAL MIDDLE SCHOOL NO. 27
	MOSCOW UNIVERSITY (RUSSIAN LANGUAGE AND LITERATURE)
Military Service:	EXEMPT ON HEALTH GROUNDS
Marital State:	DAVIDOVA—IRINA NIKOLAEVNA
	SEE TEREKHOVA IRINA NIKOLAEVNA
	FILE REF 2/555372
	Married MARCH 14, 1971
	Divorced JANUARY 4, 1977
Children:	NONE

The hospital was outside Tula, an old country house with acres of ill-tended grounds, some woods and an orchard full of apple trees that no one cared about any more. It was a place built in the indolent style of the old Russian nobility to no particular plan. The roofline went up and down where the past owners had made additions; there was a classical doorway and some steps tacked on the front; around the back, among the old laundry, ovens and brewhouse, a row of shacks for the house serfs had been converted into garages; a ruined summerhouse stood in the small English garden.

Kirov presented the pass given him by Fifth Chief Directorate. An orderly in a dirty white coat and trodden-down slippers showed him into a waiting room before sloping off to find the chief. The room contained some tubular chairs with canvas backs and a table with cabriole legs and ormolu mounts. There were names gouged into the rosewood veneer of the tabletop.

The chief medical officer was called Grigoriev. He looked misplaced for the job: too young, too eager, stuck with a profession mainly reserved for women; somewhere he had screwed up. Even so he seemed cheerful. He had a shock of curly brown hair and a glossy bright face that looked as if he didn't need to shave. Under his medic's coat he sported a KGB uniform jacket, unbuttoned at the collar, a pair of gray slacks and sneakers. He spoke with a stammer, and when he moved it was with a series of jerks. In any other line, his mental health might have been in doubt.

He didn't appear to know what to do with his visitor, tried a salute, missed it, shrugged and said: "Hail, Major, and welcome to the rubbish dump."

"Good morning, Comrade Doctor."

"You, too." Grigoriev slid into one of the chairs and sat with his legs stretched out. He waved to the newcomer to do the same. "I'd invite you to my office," he explained, "but the place looks as if it's been burgled. Long trip? Want a drink? Tea? Vodka? There's even some coffee around someplace." He smiled, thought twice about it and said, "Excuse the informality, but we don't get many visitors."

"No?"

"No. This place is the sump of the system. We get the people that nobody wants; and we keep them because somebody loses the files. Understand that and you get a picture of what we can do for you. OK? So, f-fire away."

"I've found Davidov for you," said Bogdanov.

Kirov asked, "Where?"

"Number Four Special Hospital, Tula. I got the papers from Fifth. My guy says there's an even chance that Davidov is dead but the paperwork hasn't caught up."

"Where is this Number Four Special Hospital?"

"Nowhere. Are you sure you want to go there?"

"Davidov," said Kirov. He took the papers from his briefcase and laid them out on the scarred table. Beyond the open door an old man in worn overalls slopped water around the corridor with a mop. Grigoriev spotted him and yelled, "Hey, you! Fuck off to the dispensary and take your medicine!" To his visitor he said, "We're understaffed. The patients do most of the cleaning." He got up to close the door.

"Why did she marry him?"

"Why does anybody marry?" asked Bogdanov without interest. "She probably thought she was marrying somebody else. How is she to know she's marrying a nutcase? Ask my wife. Women think about these things. Men don't."

"If I knew why, then I'd know something about her."

"Not this way, boss, believe me. We only want to know whether she's loyal. A couple of black eyes would answer that."

"Davidov," he repeated. "Osip Abramovitch." Grigoriev had resumed his seat.

"Sure—the Jew—I know him."

"What can you tell me?"

Grigoriev scratched his nose. "I didn't know you were coming," he began cautiously.

"I have orders."

"Yeah, yeah. My copy is probably floating around in the post. It'll arrive in a week or two. But for now I've got to take you on trust."

"Here they are." Kirov offered them, but Grigoriev waved his hand away.

"Like I said: I believe you."

"So?"

"We don't hold the political files here. Maybe Moscow was going to send them with my orders. We just have the medical records—an edited version, if you take my meaning."

"But your patients are politicos?"

"Oh, sure, but by the time they reach here they've already been through the sausage machine and are no longer of any interest. They're knocked about and out of their skulls on drugs. We clean them up and detoxify them; then put them on a maintenance dose and tranquilizers so they don't cause trouble. It's a quiet life. Sometimes they get released. Mostly they don't. They stay here till they die and then we get rid of the corpses. Did you notice the crematorium? We show it to visitors. It's the newest building in the place. The point is"—he said, leaning forward—"I don't know why they're here."

"I see."

Kirov saw what was wrong with the other man. Grigoriev saw things too clearly and didn't know how to keep his mouth shut. He would finish up talking to strangers in bars and end his days . . .

"Cigarette?"

Grigoriev took one, lit it and sat back.

"Of course I get the odd clue," he went on casually. "They talk about it themselves. Mostly they're 'loyal communists,' do you get me? It's the Politburo and that crowd who've got the wrong idea about c-communism—that's their story, not mine. And even then you can't believe them. There's a guy in here who claims he murdered Stalin. So did he knock off the old man, or is it just wish fulfillment? And is that why he's here—just because of his dreams?"

"Davidov was a poet," said Kirov, bringing the conversation around to the point.

"Yes, I know," said Grigoriev.

He stubbed his cigarette in the line of burns on the table.

"His file says that he's not to be allowed paper. Have you read any of his poems?"

Kirov nodded.

"Terrible, aren't they?"

"Yes."

Grigoriev reconsidered his remark; his face became thoughtful. Kirov had already detected an up-and-down of mood and put it down to stress, as to which the KGB knew as much as any doctor. Grigoriev said, "But occasionally he hits the mark."

"Oh?" Kirov thought of the poem he had read, the one that mirrored Davidov's own arrest. The doctor was thinking of another.

Have you read a verse that goes: *Will they give me a shot of their truth drug?*"

"*That profoundest miracle of Soviet chemistry. . . .* Yes, I've read it."

"Ah." Grigoriev paused for a second. "Clever, that—don't you think? And only too accurate in his case. It doesn't make you fall off your chair laughing, but it's witty all the same."

"Yes."

Abruptly Grigoriev said, "His problem is drink."

"Davidov's?"

"Every so often he gets roaring drunk and runs amok. Don't ask me where he gets the booze from—probably steals it: in this place they'd steal the teeth out of your mouth."

"So what is he, a politico or an alcoholic?"

Grigoriev suddenly laughed, as though he thought the idea of any diagnosis funny. His face went red and he was caught by a fit of coughing. Equally suddenly he apologized. "Forget I did that."

"It doesn't matter."

"It's just that I'm not usually asked for a medical opinion."

"I said it didn't matter," Kirov repeated. He got out of his chair and went over to the window. He was tired with traveling and needed to stretch his legs. He remembered George briefly and that the Englishman was kept deliberately burdened with travel to enervate him. He stared out through the bars and saw nothing but the level snow stretched out to a pale sky. I should leave, he thought. He was conscious of the dirt and smell of the place, the feel of people ground down to blood, fat and bone; reduced to the grit and grease on the floor. Grigoriev was right: this was the sump of the system, the opaque and inert place where the massive forces of entropy found their mute expression. This was the way things were.

". . . a sociopath with pathologically individualistic tendencies manifested in p-paranoid delusions, complexed by alcohol abuse."

"Forgive me, I wasn't listening." Kirov turned from the window. He had been watching one of the inmates, a shambling figure in a greatcoat, who was following the regular path trodden by the guards, picking up their cigarette butts from the snow.

"I just told you the official diagnosis of Davidov," said Grigoriev.

"Please?"

"He's a violent drunk—civilized, pleasant even—but a piss-artist who bangs people off walls when he's had a few. That's why his wife d-divorced him."

"Is it?"

"That's what the records say."

Grigoriev meant that the records couldn't be questioned.

"Drunkenness doesn't necessarily mean insanity," Kirov suggested. He offered his cigarettes again. His own addiction, which he had almost given up in Washington because Oleg Ouspensky didn't smoke and had warned him of the health hazards.

"Thanks. You're thinking of the political angle? I wouldn't know about that." Grigoriev paused and frowned as if he wasn't used to thinking about patients as individuals and it came to him only with difficulty. He said: "But Davidov's crazy, that's for sure. Even in here, why not? The law of averages says that some of our madmen have actually got to be insane."

"Because they dissent from the system?"

"I've heard that one before. Only a madman would dare to disagree—yes?"

"Well?"

"The irony is that it's true!" Grigoriev answered with a bark of laughter. He went on: "Oh, sure, plenty of sane people don't like the way things are; but they keep their opinions up here." He tapped his head. "It takes detachment from reality and a special sort of anger to do something about it. I . . ."

"Yes?"

Grigoriev had stopped but seemed on the point of wanting to say more; and Kirov guessed what it was. The doctor wanted to say something that would make him insane by his own definition. One day he probably would.

"Davidov is in love with humanity."

Kirov detected the subtle change of subject.

"That's a pathological condition?"

"Sure it is. Sane people love warm, living, breathing individuals. Only crazies fall in love with abstractions."

"I understand."

Grigoriev looked up. "Do you?"

"Yes."

Kirov remembered a maxim of this sort of conversation. *If in ignorance, say you understand; bring out that self-destructive impulse to tell the truth.* Then, he remembered this wasn't supposed to be an interrogation. It was just happening that way, as if the tension of power in an interrogation was the only form of human relationship he could know.

"Marx was the same," said Grigoriev, then laughed to imply that this was a joke.

"Marx was insane?"

"An absolute lunatic. I'm talking about the man, not the doctrine," Grigoriev added hurriedly. "Marxism is a scientific proposition, like two plus two equals four—you can't quarrel with that."

"No," Kirov agreed.

"No. But you can look at the underlying mentality. Take Newton. He discovered the laws of gravity because he was interested in demonstrating numerology and magic. You follow?"

"And Marx?" Kirov asked good-humoredly.

"Communism, freedom from want, human brotherhood, they're all fine—but they're for the future, for our children. The thing for here and now is the *Revolution,* the chance to slaughter the people we actually know!"

"I hadn't thought of that."

"No, I suppose not." Grigoriev continued to speak lightly, gliding over the fragile joke like ice.

Kirov asked, because a thought had briefly occurred to him: "This analysis would apply to Jesus, too?" He waited for an answer.

"I thought we were talking about Davidov."

"Jesus you wouldn't know about?"

"No."

"I see."

"I deal in human psychology, not divinity." Grigoriev paused, then went on more clinically: "In Davidov's case, his love of humanity is simply a manifestation of his failures at the level of real human relationships. Where it counts, he is motivated by hatred." He looked about him as if he had left something in the room, but there were only the pale green daylit walls and the steel chairs posed against the rosewood table like a setting for a still life. He proposed coolly: "Would you like to see the patient?"

Kirov nodded. The moment of confiding had gone as he knew it would, because he was trained to search out such moments, to pick at them until they were exposed and then pick at them again until they fell apart.

He thanked the other man for his diagnosis of Davidov and agreed it was time to see him.

Grigoriev nodded in return. His final remark was: "You should be cautious of the love of humanity, Major. It's a very sadistic impulse."

They walked along a corridor. Patients lounged against the walls like derelicts under a railway bridge. Grigoriev doled out sugar cubes to them as he passed. At the end of the corridor was a steel door with a judas hole. It stood ajar, and the doctor went in.

The room had originally been a *grand salon*. The fireplace was of marble, the mantel held by up a pair of *putti,* and, over the hearth, a carved armorial hatchment. On the wall over the fireplace a mirror in a gilt gesso frame reflected the beds in two lines, with footlockers and patients sitting on them folded like the bedlinen.

"Davidov!"

A figure by one of the windows turned. Kirov had the impression of a small man, compact and neatly made; put together like a mechanical toy and wound up until the spring would almost snap. There was no movement after that first negligent turn. A pair of feral eyes examined Grigoriev and the stranger and dismissed them. A sly smile hung from full lips. Kirov knew that smile. It said: "I'm fooling you by playing at being crazy." Lots of crazy people had it.

Kirov had seen Davidov before. His picture appeared on the dust jacket of one of his books: wild and soulful. It was a kitsch portrait taken by the publishing house. Then there was his work pass. Here he stared out, wide-eyed and boyish as if caught at some petty crime. Finally there were the shots taken at the time of his arrest: this time of a man tired and embittered; a thin face, unshaven and heavily shaded by bruises, looking through the camera at something else. Which one had Irina Terekhova married?

"Davidov!"

The man got up and shook himself loosely in his slack blue cotton clothes. The impression of smallness was confirmed.

He looked nothing like his photographs.

"This is Major Kirov," said Grigoriev. "He wishes to speak to you."

"OK, whatever you say." Davidov's voice was hoarse. Kirov had noticed that, like children at school, many of the patients had colds. They also showed signs of vitamin deficiency: their sallow skin had a flaky quality. Davidov's mass of dark curls, which had been consistent throughout his changes, was gone, replaced by stubble over a gray scalp.

"Where can we talk?"

"We don't have any interview rooms," answered Grigoriev. "Here, or my office, or the place we've just come from. Suit yourself."

"Where do you do your treatment?"

"What treatment? We have a dispensary, that's all. And there's a sickbay; but at the moment it's full of food poisoning cases. We get two or three outbreaks a year; it's what carries off the older ones. We can't get the antibiotics."

Kirov looked around. The other men in the ward were all turned away. A group of them had assembled at the other end of the room surrounding an elderly man with a shaven head and a full Mosaic beard. He was speaking, an unintelligible drone resonating on the drum-taut air.

"Screens?" Kirov snatched himself back.

"We could probably manage those," said Grigoriev. He glanced at two of the patients and snapped out an order. The insistent droning ceased.

Kirov handed a cigarette to Davidov and held out a light. Davidov had a poor man's way of smoking; his hands cupped the lighter as if it were a match, and after the first deep lungful of smoke he held the cigarette secretively, hiding it in the palm of his hand. He inhaled again and repeated the action of covering the cigarette. And so the two men stood studying each other while Grigoriev went away on his rounds and the screens were brought.

Kirov spoke first.

"Who's the old man?" He nodded toward the group. Davidov's empty eyes followed the gesture round.

"A Polack—name of Kosciusko." He pinched out his cigarette and pocketed the butt. He spat out some loose strands of tobacco like cherry pits, then wiped his nose. "He used to run an illegal Baptist congregation. One of the faithful shopped him to your lot. That's why he's in here."

"And he still preaches?"

Davidov shrugged. "Why not? Here he's got immunity from arrest. He says it's the best flock he ever had. But that's not why you're here. I don't suppose you've got a drink on you?"

"No."

"Pity." Davidov moved away slightly while the screens rattled into place, then took a seat on the bed. He made room for Kirov, who sat down beside him, so that they looked out together on the scene like strangers seated in a train; and Kirov was reminded—as interrogation always reminded him—of the intimacy of strangers meeting.

"So . . ."

Kirov heard the long exhalation of Davidov's breath blowing out the air in a remembrance of cigarette smoke.

"Yes?"

"So . . . what have I done, what do you want me for? This is an honor—you—here—it shows I'm still officially alive."

"I want to talk to you about the past."

"The past?" Davidov wasn't interested. "They want to charge me with some other crimes? What's the point?"

"That's not it."

"No?" Davidov thought for a moment. Then: "Don't tell me I'm going to be rehabilitated?" He laughed one loud, explosive "Ha!" that silenced the room. Through a rent in the screen Kirov glimpsed the old man. He had paused briefly but now he resumed, intoning those words that Kirov could not hear. Grigoriev had wandered back into the room and was standing some distance from the congregation, observing them expressionlessly.

Kirov asked, "How are they treating you here?"

"What's this, you want to play the nice guy?" Davidov reconsidered the smart reply and his lips fluttered uncertainly. He said: "Grigoriev's OK. I was a mess after the other place. Here they leave my head alone and I go crazy my own way. I have a violent temper and I drink too much—did they tell you that?"

"Yes. Is that why your wife divorced you?"

Davidov appeared thrown by the slight change of subject. He looked up, down, away—anywhere but at Kirov. Then with equal suddenness he was back.

"Have you been talking to the bitch?"

Kirov avoided a direct reply.

"It's in your papers, and Grigoriev confirmed it."

"Well, then, it must be true!"

"Maybe."

"Sure. Most days I'd get drunk and then I'd knock the bitch about a bit."

"Hard? You hit her hard?"

Davidov looked around without answering; his head rolled slightly as he fingered for the cigarette stub in his pocket. Kirov held out the pack again and he accepted greedily.

"We Russians smoke too much," he said, exhaling between words. "Haven't you noticed the difference from the West? You've been to the West, haven't you? Me, I've only read about it. Where were you?"

"Washington," said Kirov, remembering parties where people talked about jogging and wholefood with the intensity of the Party Faithful, until it got finally to the men in the Soviet embassy, so that even his old friend Yatsin, now the KGB resident, started to worry about blood cholesterol. "Did you hit your wife hard?"

"Yes!" Davidov blurted out sharply. "I beat the shit out of her as hard and as often as I could! I knocked her across the room! I jammed her head against the wall and screamed at her! I burned her with cigarettes! What the hell do you want?"

Before Kirov could answer, Grigoriev put his head round the corner of the screen and inquired: "Is everything all right?"

"Fuck off!" said Davidov.

Kirov waved a hand at the door and told him calmly, "Go away, please. Everything is OK." He turned back to Davidov. The other man had quieted down.

"I've studied your wife's file."

"So?"

"Her medical reports show no history of physical violence."

"She never went to a doctor. If you've met the bitch, you'd know that she's—what's the word?" Davidov's voice was rising again; his eyes were glistening. "Tight—compact—like a diamond—oh, Jesus!"—he put a sleeve to his face to catch the tears—"I've lost the words—the words—they took out my brain and they took out the words!" He fell forward, folded up so that his face was invisible.

They sat for a while in silence until Davidov slowly recovered. He retrieved his sly, mad smile and said, "OK, go on."

"I'm only trying to understand."

"You should be a poet."

"Should I?"

"What do you want?"

"There are other reports on file," Kirov resumed. "Not medical—you know what I mean—neighbors, colleagues. They don't mention violence; no talk of hearing arguments, of seeing bruises."

"Men and women fighting—who's interested? It's not political."

"And there's your own record."

"Mine? How?"

"Police files—I'm talking of the regular criminal police. You have criminal convictions."

"I was in the drunk tank a few times. And once or twice there were some fights."

"I know. But the point is that your troubles with the police started in 1976—after you left your wife."

"After the bitch threw me out!" Davidov shouted.

"If you like," Kirov assented. "But you see what I mean? According to the record—the public record—until 1976, until you separated from your wife, there was no violence, no drunkenness; you were a respected member of the Writers' Union, an established poet whose works were officially approved of; a Good Communist. And yet behind the front visible to your neighbors and colleagues and the police—what? A secret life? A conspiracy of violence between yourself and Irina Nikolaevna?"

"Yes, yes, *yes,* yes!" Davidov said volubly. "Whatever you like—whatever you like!" The tears were there again. He rocked back and forth but continued, now speaking fast, stringing words like animals fleeing a trap: "I was a toad, an official creep. I had the truth inside me, I knew the truth and couldn't say it, and it beat at me to come out—beat at me—beat at me. And the truth and the anger came out as blows against Irina because blows are mute like the dumb truth that was inside me and beating at my head!" He rolled forward, then back, and to Kirov, although the movements in themselves were slow, Davidov seemed to blur as his emotions swept in fluid, plastic succession across his face. And even to Kirov the other man had become unbearable so that he wanted to say something that would stop him.

"Shall we talk about poetry?"

Davidov stared so that his features fixed and his shape seemed to cohere. Then he laughed. "My favorite poets—it sounds like the title of a kid's essay!" He recited a list: Mandelshtam, Okudzhava, the younger Voznesensky, Akmadulina—they were conventionally unconventional, not an adventurous choice, and yet all better poets than Davidov himself. "What do you think?"

Kirov was embarrassed at the ordinariness of the other man's taste. He had expected something more, wanted Davidov to be something more. "I've read some of your poems," he said.

"Mine! Ha!" Davidov spat. The action brought on a fit of coughing. For a while he was doubled up, mucus trailing his lip. Finally he said, "Me, I'm a lousy poet. I never could find the words." He hesitated with an air of vagueness, as if the words were a missing limb that left him with a phantom feeling; so when he stretched himself and splayed the open fingers of his hand he seemed to count them in case one were gone. "And now . . . They've cut them out . . . here, up here, with their sharp knives." He focused on his interrogator. "You know I'm a lousy poet."

"Do I?"

"Yes. The good poets are in internal exile because world opinion doesn't allow them to be imprisoned. Only the lousy poets—the poor, mute, stinking, lousy poets that the world has never heard of—are locked up here. The KGB are the world's most discerning literary critics."

Davidov rubbed his hand over the stubble on his scalp, then drew the fingers slowly down his face and peeped between them like gray prison bars, pale and veined.

"Until 1976—until you left your wife," Kirov resumed, "you were an orthodox writer, thoroughly respectable."

"That was the effect of the bitch. She was respectable—bloody respectable! Why do you think she married that arsehole, Terekhov? For the excitement? She was a good, proper, prim little communist. What do you think we argued about?"

"But you didn't argue," Kirov answered. "At least, not according to the record."

"So you say. It just shows that even the KGB doesn't know it all." Davidov stood up, reverting to his earlier sly carelessness. "I've had enough of this," he said. "What else do you want?"

"You've answered my questions."

"Liar."

Kirov picked up his file and folded back the screen. As an after-thought he held out the pack of cigarettes.

"Thanks." Davidov took them with an exhausted gratitude.

"Can I do anything else for you?"

"Like what?"

"Take a message to your wife."

"The bitch? Why should I want to speak to the bitch?"

"Perhaps I can arrange for you to have some paper—I understand that at present this is not allowed."

Davidov laughed again—his coarse, degraded, destroyed laughter.

"Sure," he agreed. "I need something to wipe my arse with."

Grigoriev escorted his visitor out of the ward. The doctor had become more cautious, but Kirov had expected nothing more.

Grigoriev asked, "Did you discover what you wanted? Do you have any instructions for dealing with Davidov?"

"Let him have writing materials if he wants them. Just make sure that he accounts for every piece of paper."

The doctor showed surprise. "That wasn't what I meant—but

thanks: it should help in controlling his aggressions if he can work them out in poetry."

"Don't thank me: I'm not a barbarian."

"I didn't mean to suggest . . ."

"No? No, of course not." Kirov halted outside the waiting room. He examined the other man: tense with a desire to get his visitor off the premises. Grigoriev was hiding something—he had sensed it all along. Probably it was something irrelevant, a part of another story; but there it was between them. He said, "I need to make a phone call. May I use your office?"

"Yes, of course."

"Where is it?"

They doubled back and found a small room off the main corridor. It was as expected: standard office furniture, a chaos of misplaced papers, some remnants of uneaten food.

"I'd like to be left alone."

"Oh—yes—if you like." Grigoriev began tidying the table. He picked up the phone and tapped it vigorously to raise a line. "Here, please," he said, and left the room.

Kirov replaced the receiver and lit a cigarette. The action made him think of Washington. He had had a mistress there, an actress he shared with a Congressman. She was a diet freak who made a point of lecturing him on smoking. For the rest he could remember nothing of her; even her name had only the familiar-unfamiliar ring of a film credit. He inhaled the smoke and moved to the far side of the desk. There were two pedestals holding the writing top, each with four drawers. The top left had scratch marks around the cheap lock indicating frequent use. He took a clasp knife from his pocket and with easy technique forced it.

It was there as he knew it would be—that or something like it—because his instincts were sound. He picked the object up and let it run through his fingers: a plain wooden cross on a leather thong strung with beads.

As a secret it was pitiful and immaterial.

29

January 5

She's dead," said Bogdanov, meaning you couldn't expect anything else, and what could you do about it anyway?

"Who?" Kirov thought for a second of Irina Terekhova, who could be beaten by the poet, Davidov, and not show any injuries. But he had spoken to her that morning. He had no reason other than to hear her voice.

Bogdanov said, "You should read your mail. There's a report from Special Investigations. They're mad as hell." This gave him some satisfaction.

Kirov reached listlessly for his papers and scanned them.

"Sonya Stoletova. Who is she?"

"A musician, a cellist with the Leningrad Symphony Orchestra. She was on the Paris tour. A suspect — she could have mailed the package to Source David. See?"

"I see." There was a photocopy of the death certificate with the papers. It was gray and illegible. He asked, "What did she die of?" Bogdanov shrugged his shoulders.

"Heart failure — what does anybody die of? Or enthusiasm," he offered as an alternative, "but you can't write 'enthusiasm' on a death certificate. The boys in Leningrad pulled her in. They wanted to get a jump ahead of Special Investigations — find the traitor before Special Investigations did. Leningrad figured that, if the culprit was on the orchestra tour, then they'd be held responsible because they did all the vetting and were responsible for security on the trip. So, if they could find a candidate for the crime and sweat the truth out of her, then they'd look good and

339

everybody would forgive and forget." He paused. "They were a bit too energetic."

"Too energetic?"

"She was a cripple. Motor accident or something. Poor health. Come on, boss," he added as if he were being accused, "it's happened before. You let bumpkins handle interrogations and all you get is sausage meat."

"Sure."

There was a photograph with the papers. No one that Kirov knew. A thin, frail, blonde face, with eyes full of uncertainty. He turned the pages to find the confession, but there was nothing. She had denied the offense and died for it.

"What a waste," he said.

"You win a few, you lose a few. That's how it goes." But even Bogdanov seemed saddened.

"What was the case against her?"

"Something or nothing—who can say?" The older man fished up another sheet from the mess on his desk. He moved his sandwiches aside and brushed away the crumbs. "They did a check of all the orchestra bags and instrument cases, looking for any way the package might have been smuggled out of the country. Inside Stoletova's cello they found traces of gum, nothing much, but maybe the residue from some adhesive tape. You see the way they think? Something had been taped to the inside and wasn't there any more."

"Something?"

"But they don't know what." Bogdanov dropped the sheet back on the desk. "And now they never will."

Kirov picked the photograph up again. Now she reminded him of Davidov in one of his many guises—not in the surface of her appearance, but in the fragility, the vulnerability of her. People— the threads of their characters could be taken apart.

"You should tidy this place up," he changed the subject sharply.

Bogdanov leaned back in his chair with his brute, ignorant grin. "The hospital get to you, eh, boss? I've been to those places. You didn't like the mess. So—what?—you saw the Jew-boy. Did he help you get to the bottom of our little Terekhova?" With sudden emotion he lowered his voice and urged. "Pull her

340

in! Let someone give her the business. Nothing violent—don't get me wrong. Christ, I don't want the bitch hurt—but you're getting too close. Leave the personal side out of it. Listen to your Uncle Bog and get someone else to handle her." Just as abruptly he shut up. He was waiting for an answer.

"No." Kirov couldn't bring himself to make any other reply. But Bogdanov was right. He was too close. He examined the other man's bony face for a response and saw what he hadn't expected: pain.

Then Bogdanov collected himself and assembled his usual loose, easy expression. He said ironically, "The Ouspensky Case: one day you said you were going to tell me about it. That was a case of the human touch, wasn't it? That was why it was so special—why it made you a star."

"Forget about Ouspensky."

"Whatever you say. But where did it get you? Where did it get Ouspensky after all that great technique to get him off the street and into our embassy? Was it two crates they shipped him home in, or three? Remind me."

"He left the embassy alive," said Kirov, quietly.

He had attended the funeral.

It was held in winter in some godforsaken hole near Novossibirsk, where they heated the ground with torches and broke it with pickaxes, and the body of Oleg Ouspensky, having stood outside all night, was covered in white frost. Watching from the heated limousine, Kirov remembered the training film shown to all intelligence personnel. There was a special fate for traitors: to be thrown alive into the flames of a furnace, to burn and pop like moths, while the roar of the fire drowned the screams. But Ouspensky had a bullet hole in the back of the neck. "You're a true friend," he said without rancor or irony at their last interrogation. And now his body wore the bullet hole as a badge of mercy.

And then he could hear Bogdanov apologizing and suggesting that maybe they should go for a drink somewhere. Maybe. Maybe. Bogdanov gave his papers a halfhearted shuffle. He began to talk about George Twist: the American equipment should be near to shipment. Was everything OK on that front? He had made administrative arrangements for Kirov to be in

Finland when the stuff arrived. The last hurdle.

He came back to the investigation slowly.

"The dead woman was Terekhov's sister—that's right, our fine hero of Afghanistan, Colonel Terekhov."

Kirov understood. It was the connection.

"You got it," Bogdanov nodded. "Irina Terekhov meets a stranger—witness that clown Mivernadze and his camera. She visits her sister-in-law, taking the package with her. Sister-in-law smuggles the package to the West and mails it to Source David, who is an American politician supposedly hostile to the Soviet Union. QED. It's logical."

"It's speculation," Kirov answered. Speculation—looking into mirrors and seeing one's own reflection—he had speculated about Irina Terekhova, and her character seemed only to recede behind the image of his own. "Where's the evidence? We have a photograph of her meeting a stranger, but nothing to connect the meeting with this business or with anything else: she says it was a man who wanted street directions, and maybe it was. What else? The package was mailed from Paris. Was it someone from the orchestra tour who mailed it? Maybe there's a traitor in the embassy. Maybe in the trade mission. We don't know. And, if it was a member of the orchestra, what proof is there that it was Stoletova? A trace of gum inside a cello? That's it? A trace of gum?"

"Evidence?" Bogdanov's voice was loud and incredulous. "You want to be a lawyer? Listen!" he hissed, and Kirov recognized the fear behind the anger, the fear that Kirov would involve him in his own destruction. "Who cares? I've handled these cases before. Amateur traitors"—Bogdanov snorted contemptuously—"no craft, no style, no system. They do it once, because something gets to them, and then they revert to being Loyal Soviet Citizens. And, unless you're lucky, you never catch them because there's no method to crack, no tie-in to anyone under surveillance—nothing. Amateurs can kill you!"

His thin, skeletal face was tired. "Shit," he groaned, "I don't care whether it's Terekhova or anybody else. The main thing is to close the investigation. Throw them a victim. Get a result." He let it fall there.

Kirov allowed the silence to lie for a few moments, then said,

"Did you know that Pokrebsky has a cousin in Paris?"

"You're joking," Bogdanov answered. He put down the pencil that his fingers had been tensely playing with. He eyed Kirov suspiciously.

"He works for Aeroflot out of their French office."

"How do you know?"

"Grishin told me. He did a tour of Paris cleaning up the mess after Ouspensky defected. He worked his way through the embassy, then tackled the outstations: Tass, Aeroflot and all the rest. Pokrebsky's cousin isn't one of ours, but after Grishin and his team had turned the residency inside out, they started on the civilians in case Ouspensky had been recruiting on the outside."

"Find anything?"

"No. Ouspensky was a loner." Kirov paused. "I could have told him that."

"Well, what do you know?"

"I checked Leonid Pokrebsky out. He still holds his French posting, but he paid a visit home last month to see his old mother. He was back in Paris in time to mail a package to Source David. Do I have to spell it out?"

"No, I love it." Bogdanov's face broke into one of his friendly leers and dissipated the tension. He mused on the idea. "So Grishin is still determined to have Pokrebsky's hide. It makes you wonder whether the bastard did it himself just to set Pokrebsky up, know what I mean?"

"Make a start with the cousin," said Kirov. "Have him recalled from Paris. Pokrebsky is prepared for any maneuver by Grishin, but the cousin won't know what's hit him. Offer him a deal in exchange for a confession, and explain some of the alternatives."

"Will do," Bogdanov answered enthusiastically. He was already reaching for the telephone, leaving Kirov with his thoughts. Was Pokrebsky the traitor? It was an alternative as credible as Irina Terekhova, who had always cooperated with the KGB and whose son was a hostage in Gorky. Two possibilities with nothing to choose between them. Except that according to Grishin the truth about treachery was always known—if only the truth could be faced.

It was time to see Colonel Konstantin Terekhov.

* * *

The call from Joe Czarnecki, Sep Tech's shipping manager, reached George Twist at home. George was home because Lillian's condition had taken a turn for the worse; a chest infection threatened her weakened state. The doctor, an imposing Sikh with an Oxbridge accent, was with her now. Bloody Brenda was busying herself in the kitchen. The nurse had recently taken to attending early-morning mass, and her devotional bric-a-brac—plaster statuettes of the Virgin and papal medallions—had started to invade the house. George had to clear some of the junk off the hall table to take the call.

"George! George! Are you there?" Czarnecki sounded overwrought, which wasn't his style; he was ordinarily a slow, even-tempered character who pushed pieces of paper and never complained.

"OK, Joe, take it easy." George calmed him down. "What's the problem that you have to call me at home?"

"The shipment for Finland," said Czarnecki. "Lou has put a block on it. He won't make the delivery!"

He won't make the delivery. George tried to take it in, but there was a cry from Lillian and then Brenda rushing out of the kitchen with her face in anguish and shouting upstairs, and then the doctor's measured tones saying: "Not to worry. Just a tender spot. Bedsores." *He won't make delivery.*

"What do you mean? What's got into Lou? For Christ's sake, what's going on up there, Brenda? No, not you, Joe." *Not to worry.* "Where are the goods now?"

"How should I know what's going on in Lou's head? The equipment is all ready and packed in containers on the quayside. The vessel is fixed to leave this evening and the shipping agent is going crazy because Lou countermanded the shipping instructions. If I don't get back to him in the next hour, you can forget about getting this stuff to Finland—it just ain't going to happen. George? You still listening, George?"

"I'm still listening." He was listening to Brenda trying to soothe his wife with lullabies. "Get back to the agent. Tell him to load the goods and ship them."

"But Lou—"

"Stuff Lou!"

"He'll have my job if I do this."

"I'll make sure he doesn't. But listen to me," George said coldly, "if those goods don't get shipped, then *I'll* have your hide. Got me?"

"I get you," Czarnecki answered; and then, plaintively, "This isn't like you, George."

It was another hour and a half before Lou Ruttger called. George could hear his rage boiling down the telephone. Not like this, George wished it didn't have to be like this, over the phone, which made everything sound like an ultimatum and there was no chance to see the other man's face, to guess at his real reactions and pitch and play with the words. Keep it calm. Please God, I don't want to hurt you, Lou!

"George, what the hell are you doing to me?"

"What are you doing to me?"

"You went behind my back and told Joe Czarnecki to ship this Finnish stuff."

"You tried to put a stop to it—the biggest deal that Sep Tech ever had."

"Damn right I did! I don't *believe* in your Finnish contract. You hear me, George? I think the whole business is a scam, a pack of lies to cover a deal that's too dirty to live with!"

"Bullshit! Where did you get that idea from?"

"From the facts."

"Facts—what facts?" George waited, and wondered all the while: what could have gone wrong?

"John Chaseman is dead," said Lou Ruttger. "Murdered."

The line went silent.

"Lou? Lou?" No answer. They were cut off. George swore and looked around for his directory of private numbers. The doctor had come downstairs and was in the hallway, putting on his overcoat and giving bland reassurances about Lillian and instructions to the nurse. Brenda was at his shoulder with her grief-stricken face, asking George whether he would like a cup of tea and which sort of biscuit he would prefer, and talking about looking on the bright side and that Lillian was in Father Rafferty's prayers.

"George?"

Lou Ruttger was back on the line before George could find his number. Suddenly Lou was apologizing, but only because they had been cut off. The doctor was gripping George's free hand in a firm two-handed grasp that was intended to impart some comfort. "Thanks, Doctor. No, Lou, I wasn't talking to you. Look, can you hang on?" He knew that there were formalities he was supposed to go through; he was supposed to open the front door and see the doctor down the path to his car parked amongst the snow and suburban laburnums; there was a question he was supposed to ask. What was it? What was it?

"Lillian, how is she?"

She was poorly, but this time the infection had been caught: this time it would be all right.

"Thank you, Doctor. Lou, are you still there?" He was still there. "Thank you, Doctor."

"John Chaseman is dead."

George remembered that Lou had already said that.

"He was gunned down two days ago."

"So what's new?" George said as lightly as he could, and if it was Lillian's soft whimper that was drifting downstairs he forced himself not to hear it. "That's America. Doesn't everyone expect to be shot? What else do you have? A signed confession?"

"Abe Korman is dead, too," Lou persisted. "His body was found on a building lot in Washington. Someone had damn near taken his head off with a piece of piano wire. I've seen the photographs, George; they're all over the paper."

"Maybe it was his friends in Atlantic City. Didn't you tell me about them?"

"George, listen to me! This is not a joke!"

"Who's joking?" George answered quietly. The names were hammering into his head — Chaseman, Korman. Had it started? Was this Peter's arrangement? He tried again. "It's just a coincidence. It happens. America is a place where people get killed."

"Come on, you've been reading too many papers. You know it isn't really like that."

Peter Kirov was always saying the same thing. Nowhere was really like that; and yet the two men who had shown an interest in Sep Tech that might have interfered with the Russian business were now dead. And there was Lou.

Lou was saying, "If anyone was determined that Sep Tech stayed how it was until the Finnish deal was completed, they couldn't have fixed it better. Chaseman Industries is at a standstill while the chiefs fight over the succession, and I guess the same applies to Korman and his associates. There—"

"Drop it," George said suddenly.

There was a silence. Then: "That sounds like a threat."

George caught his breath. Was that what he was doing?

Ruttger asked, "Whatever happened to friendship, huh? To old times' sake?"

"I'm trying to be a friend to you. This is serious business, Lou, not a game, not a morality play. The bad guys sometimes win."

"I don't believe what I'm hearing."

"Drop it," George repeated.

"Or else? Come on, George, give me the 'or else'! A threat, huh? Concrete shoes and a trip down the river? An offer I can't refuse—isn't that what the mobsters call it? You a mobster, George? Been fooling me all these years, is that it? Is *that* it?"

"For Christ's sake!"

"Fuck you, George! Give me the threat—give me the 'or else.' " Lou's voice was rising, breaking with the breaking of his illusions.

George said with deadly calm, "Don't cross me, Lou, or I'll have your arse out of the door so quick you won't know what's happening. I can do it; you know I can do it."

"I don't believe this," Lou was repeating, this time quietly, over and over again. George didn't want to say it. *Don't force me, Lou! Don't force me! There are worse things that can happen.*

He began again. This time he was quiet, too. "It's not just you. My job's on the line as well. I need this sale."

"How come? You've brought in the Russian business, the gas-plant contracts."

"They haven't been signed yet. Jim Evans is in Moscow, still negotiating the words. There are no guarantees that we'll get the jobs." He couldn't say that there was no chance of getting them if the Sep Tech deal fell through. "I need this sale," he repeated. Then: "I have Lillian to think of."

There was silence again, but he knew that Lou was still there. Thinking of Nancy, maybe? And George remembered that there were others, sixty million people living in the Volga basin, whose lives could be destroyed by the disaster at Sokolskoye; and he wanted to tell Lou, but Lou didn't believe in him anymore. And there was Irina Terekhova, who touched him so that he didn't dare to think about her.

"So we're hiding behind our women?" Lou asked scornfully. "It's nothing to do with your ambition; it's all Lillian's fault. Is that the story, George?"

"Believe me."

"I don't believe you. You got me into this, and there's nothing I can do now to stop the shipment to Finland. But I don't trust you, George; I don't give any promises. One way or another I'm going to find out what's really going on. If it takes a trip to Finland, I'll get the truth out of this business."

George wanted to say: *Don't do it! It could kill you!*

But Lou had already put the phone down.

30

His memory would be of mountains, of the rearing masses of the Hindu Kush barren under the winter snow, and then the descent into the alluvial plains and the cold glitter of the Kabul river. He would remember the passengers, greedy and fearful like the young civil engineer who was going to work on the road-building program, and who talked in the same breath of the exotic goods that were there for the having and of his fear of the natives, as if he were a burglar about to break into a rich house possessed by a resolute and well-defended householder.

He shared a car into the city with a KGB captain returning from a break in his tour of duty and asked him for local color and some details of the system. The KGB were thick as flies, the captain said: in the government offices, from ministerial advisers down to chauffeurs, pale Russian faces opened doors or peered over desks, Russian voices answered telephones; Russian vehicles and their drivers caused traffic jams in the narrow streets. In the markets, their womenfolk, swathed in heavy Soviet clothing and often escorted, maintained their own special purdah as they pawed over the goods for the bargains unobtainable back home.

"This is our show," said the resident. He operated from an air-conditioned office in the embassy, where he was collecting brassware and flintlock firearms with chased barrels and inlaid stocks, so that the place looked like a bazaar. He outranked Kirov but he knew from his visitor's papers that the distinction didn't count, so he went through the form of being relaxed and greeted the younger man as an equal. From somewhere or other he had acquired a bar with a curved mahogany top stacked with a couple of cases of spirits. It stood in a corner and held an icebox that rumbled over the sound of the air-conditioning.

"Drink? Smoke?" He threw an unopened pack of cigarettes to Kirov and broke into a fresh pack for himself. The wrapping and the foil went into a fancy brass pot that stood on the floor.

"You have it all your own way. Doesn't the Army make for problems?" Kirov asked.

Vorontsev laughed. "They couldn't keep themselves in dope and women without our help." He had big teeth and tanned skin and the manners of an impresario. Kirov recognized the signs of a long posting away from the center of things. When Vorontsev left Kabul there would be a string of mistresses and small children crying in the street, and back in Moscow he would take to drink and reminiscences and trying to fix black-market deals.

"Most of our men are just country lads fresh off the farm," Vorontsev was saying indulgently. "Green, goggle-eyed, stupid and bloody useless. They huddle inside their tanks like girls in a shower, and if they step outside they get their bollocks shot off by the locals, who're very good at that sort of thing. It takes six months before they're fit for anything, and after twelve we send them home before they're totally incapacitated by clap, drugs and bad nerves."

There was more of the same stuff. The older man told it with experienced cynicism and occasional dry laughter. Kirov assumed that Vorontsev had friends in Moscow Center and had read Kirov's record and knew about Washington and the Ouspensky Case, and that the visiting KGB major was no more immune than anybody else. And then he would know, too, that Kirov was a professional with more sense than to step outside his mission to report on someone at no advantage to himself, so that it was safe for Vorontsev to play games and take chances with the truth. Kirov let him.

"So what about Terekhov?" he asked at last. "What do you have on him?"

"The files, you've read the files; it's all in there."

"I've read the files," Kirov agreed, as if they were irrelevant. He looked away from the other man, suggesting that his opinions, too, were of no real interest. Beyond the window smoke blew in a dark haze over the mountains, white jet-streams in the sky, helicopters hesitating in their flight like strangers meeting, and silence through the glazing, just the rumble of the icebox and the air-conditioning. "What do *you* have?" he asked.

"I don't follow you."

"Yes, you do," Kirov stated flatly. "What information do you carry in your head? What do you know that you haven't put on his file?"

Vorontsev said uncomfortably, "I don't carry on like that. It's not my style."

Kirov didn't answer. He looked around at the cases of spirits on the bar and at the fowling-piece with silver mounts and ivory inlay that hung on the wall.

Vorontsev was saying: "Terekhov is cleaner than clean, the Great Hero, the soldier on a white horse. He likes action, isn't scared to take risks with the enemy. When his men go in, he goes in with them; the troops love him. He shits rose petals."

"Then how do you control him?"

Kirov's voice remained mild. He lowered it to force Vorontsev to concentrate.

"Don't tell me you don't try to, that isn't your style; it isn't the business we're in. So what is it? Some little thing that only you know: because if it were on file it would be common property and there'd be no lever. Well? Boys? Our good clean Colonel is partial to sodomy, is he? Or is it drugs? Or is he trading on the black market—though I don't suppose that counts for anything out here, does it? Well?"

Vorontsev hesitated only a moment and then said, "Why shouldn't you know? OK—it's a woman."

"Ah."

Kirov took a seat. He helped himself to another cigarette. Vorontsev got up and went over to the bar. He poured himself a shot of vodka, tipped the neck of the bottle in the other man's direction, waited for a sign, then poured a second drink. He returned with the glasses.

"So," Kirov said, "a woman. Where's the novelty? Who cares?"

"It's not so much the woman," Vorontsev said. He threw back the drink and went on: "Somewhere he picked up a dose"—a shrug meaning men-will-be-men — "not usual — something exotic. So far the medics haven't been able to shift it; you know how it is with antibiotics. I've promised him help, American drugs, that sort of thing: I told him that my brother-in-law is a pox doctor to the Kremlin."

"You have the drugs?"

"How is he to know?" Vorontsev smiled his big-toothed smile. "He must be worried for his wife, our Colonel. You married?"

"I was once."

"I'm on my third. I married tne first when I was a student so that hardly counts. The second was a bitch; I never understood her. The third one is OK: I've left her back home and that makes for a happy married life. Another drink?"

"No." The first was untouched in front of him. Vorontsev moved to get another one, thought better of it, sat down and fiddled with the glass. Kirov asked, "How long has Terekhov been infected?"

"Twelve months, more or less."

"He had home-leave six months ago."

"Ho! Did he, now? Slip the missus a present, did he?"

"No."

"Ah — must have told her a tale: got shot in the waterworks; shriveled up in the infernal Afghan heat; or maybe it was stolen by the fucking bandits when he was asleep. You want to know what I told my wife?"

"I want to know what he told his."

"Don't ask him," Vorontsev answered, and now he was giving a warning. "Our Colonel can be very touchy where his wife is concerned."

Terekhov was pointed out to him, a figure among other figures standing by the helicopter gunships. The blades of the machines were rotating, the tarmac swept by eddies of dust, the men crouched and shouted over the roar of the engines.

"Colonel."

Terekhov turned round. He asked, "Who are you?" — and, without waiting for an answer, snapped an order at one of the other men. He looked around again as if Kirov should have disappeared and repeated the question. Kirov showed his badge, the sword and shield of the KGB.

"Wait here." Terekhov walked away to one of the other machines. Kirov stood and watched him while the dust blew around and settled on his fur hat and civilian overcoat. The Colonel harangued someone. He was a big man with large gestures. His arms swung and appointed like semaphore against a sharp blue sky and the mountain line. He walked back through the flickering shadows of the rotating blades and the hard bright winter light across the sandy tarmac.

"So you're the spook from Moscow?" he said.

"You were told to expect me?"

Terekhov nodded. "Get aboard." He waved to the pilot and climbed into the machine. He shouted to Kirov, "You want to talk—you get on board."

The other man followed him.

They sat opposite each other in the body of the machine, in dark contrast to the day except where sharp patches of light were cast through the gunports. Terekhov sat with his head in his hands as the helicopter lifted. White hair in thick waves. Tanned skin, deeply lined over a handsome, hard-boned face with a great nose and a heavy brow. He looked up as the first heave of the machine flattened out and the flight steadied.

"I hate flying," he said. "Air sickness." He spat a gobbet of bile into a handkerchief and stuffed it in the pocket of his combat-jacket. He shouted something to the pilot, then to Kirov he said, "Still, it's got to be done." He bent over, picked up an automatic rifle from the floor and checked it over. Kirov noticed the other man's jacket carried no insignia of rank. He didn't carry a pistol.

"So?" Terekhov licked the sourness from his lips. "What do you want?"

"Not here."

Terekhov looked around at the other men in the helicopter. "These men are Azerbaijanis. They don't understand Russian, other than orders and talking dirty." Kirov didn't answer.

The flight of helicopters swung out over the city. Terekhov crept forward and looked down on the Babur gardens. He looked at the other machines, each glued to its patch of sky. He returned to his seat.

"We're the air cavalry," he remarked to Kirov and carried on as if some explanation had been requested: "This is an old-fashioned war. The enemy isn't like us—no humanity, no civilized values—he'd pluck out your eyes and spill your guts given the chance. It makes our men afraid. Understand? Primitive fear. They feel like victims in a blood sacrifice." He moved to one of the gunports and beckoned his passenger. "Come here." Kirov looked out. In a cleft in the hills, in their dark ocher shadow, a road ran in a series of curves. There was a convoy on it, a couple of tanks, a self-propelled gun and some personnel carriers, driving in a cloud of dust. "They're going to clear a village of bandits," said Terekhov.

They sat down again and whiled away a few minutes in silence. Terekhov took out his handkerchief once more and spat into it. One of the soldiers, a dark Azerbaijani with black hair and gleaming teeth, looked up, smiled and nudged the man next to him.

Terekhov said, "You saw them down there. They're scared shitless, locked in those tin cans. The bandits have a few rockets. One hit and you roast alive. They don't even hear it coming. Just a bang and a hell of flames." He picked up the AK47 again and fiddled with the parts as he spoke. "But don't think that they want to get out of those things."

"No"

"No." He snapped the magazine in place. "At least they offer a sort of security. Open the door and let in the light, and you have a world out there of bandits that you never see. Step outside and get a bullet in the head from a man who's a better shot than you'll ever be. Stay here twelve months, watch your friends get killed, and still you'll never see a bandit, just rocks—and once in a while you'll hear a bang."

"So?"

Terekhov replaced the rifle carefully on the floor. He wiped oil from his hands. "So they need heroes to make them into heroes. They need a man on a white horse."

Kirov remembered that Vorontsev had said something similar.

Minutes elapsing, spent studying that gaunt, massive face and seeing it against Irina Terekhova and the Jew, Osip Abramovitch

354

Davidov, and speculating on the relationship between the three. Was there something in it that spelled the betrayal of the Sokolskoye Incident? Terekhov checked his watch. "Nearly time," he said and stood up to go forward and speak to the pilot. Kirov followed him as far as one of the gunports. He felt the helicopter swing and saw the mountainside rising like a wall. The craft swayed in the air currents.

Flash. The first explosion came as a packet of flame unfolding slowly without any sound of its own above the noise of the aircraft. The second followed, then a third, all in a straight line and the patterns of the expanding flame so regular that they seemed like presents being unwrapped. There was a chatter now of gunfire dissociated from what was going on on the ground, and then cheering. Kirov looked behind him and saw the soldiers laughing and stamping their feet. He looked out again. The picture had changed, with smoke drifting over the arid hillside, and the explosions as they came seemed random. *Rat-tat*. The cacophony of firing had its own rise and fall. A rocket came past, flinging out a long trail until it hit the bare rocks and exploded. A fall of stones tumbled silently down the slope. A plume of smoke drifted up and hid everything for a second. A flash. A gap in the smoke and a momentary glimpse of some dun-colored houses clustered either side of a gully amongst a few sparse bushes. The machine swinging through the smoke so that the mountain seemed to spin, and then nothing but sky so clear and blue and so hard to look at that it might have been touched.

Kirov returned to his seat. He could still feel the machine swinging away, and the gunfire had become remote. The soldiers were still in their places, grinning. Terekhov came back. He picked up a steel helmet and wordlessly vomited into it, and only afterwards said, "My guts," without concern.

The helicopter completed its circuit and returned. The gunfire rose again to a crescendo *rat-tat*, above the roar of the engines, and the soldiers grinned or giggled, *rat-tat*. Terekhov sat with his head between his knees.

And then it was suddenly over. The sound of engines seemed like silence, and the *chop-chop* of the blades lulled the senses. Terekhov went forward and came back. He slapped the nearest men on the back and turned to Kirov. "We're going down," he said, and one of the others heard and a cheer went up. Terekhov smiled thinly and murmured: "See? We're the cavalry."

The note of the engines changed. They were descending. Kirov's hearing was fixed on the changing music of the machine.

Terekhov was saying: "There's no need to worry. They don't stick around for a fight."

"I wasn't worrying," Kirov answered. He looked up into Terekhov's hard, lined face.

"Good." He had picked up the Kalishnikov in a pair of knotted hands, and around him the men had stopped grinning and sat as still as icons with their rifles on their knees.

"Now!"

Kirov hadn't felt the landing, but suddenly the place was alive and the men were pushing and eager and pouring out of the helicopter, and he was picked up and carried along in their wake. And then there was sunlight so bright as to hurt, and the cold mountain air that made him pull at his civilian overcoat.

They were on a level space of beaten earth. On the north side was scrub. On the south the mountain fell away in rock-strewn gullies and withered grass. In the valley the tanks were still pumping out shells on to the further slope, but on this side men were strung out in a loose line between the rocks, advancing in a crackle of small-arms fire.

"Come on," said Terekhov. Kirov looked round and saw the village under its veil of smoke and dust.

They walked towards the houses. Terekhov offered some chewing gum. Kirov offered a cigarette. Soldiers flickered among the ruins. A helicopter passed over them, shedding fierce anti-missile flares; they could feel the down-draft of its blades. The whirring faded down the valley towards the dull thump of shell fire.

In the first street a building had collapsed and poured rubble across the narrow space. Another had flames coming from its roof. The rest appeared undamaged but derelict. Terekhov sat on a pile of stones to smoke his cigarette, and gave directions to the passing men; but all the while his cool eyes studied his companion.

Kirov asked, "Why did you drag me out here?"

"You angry?"

"No, just curious."

Terekhov grunted and flung the butt of his cigarette into the dust. He took up his rifle and carried on down the street. At the corner the corpse of a tethered goat was gathering flies. He stopped and examined the buildings in both streets where his men were crouched in the shadows. He looked back and saw Kirov in his mohair coat and fur hat and seemed to recognize him for the first time.

"So why here?" Kirov asked. Terekhov poked his rifle at the ribs of the goat before answering.

"It's a question of morale." He waved a hand. "All of this is a question of morale. They"—he indicated a couple of soldiers who were advancing back to back down the street with their guns pointed at doorways—"need a hero. They want to see Tukhachevsky charging across the steppe with his horseman."

Tukhachevsky was shot by Stalin."

"So what? He was still a hero."

They reached the small *maidan* at the center of the village. The mosque had received a direct hit, the minaret had collapsed and was lying in a line of stone across the square. One of the troop carriers had been brought up and was parked with its engine running and the soldiers in a tight ring around it.

"Look at them," Terekhov urged. He sounded like a father. Kirov could imagine him as a father to Irina Terekhova's child. "Kids, bloody kids; I could cry for them." He took a few steps in their direction, kicking pebbles. His shoulders were thrown back, almost jaunty. His white hair caught the sun. The soldiers snapped to attention and then relaxed as Terekhov handed around pieces of gum before returning to Kirov, who was sitting now on the rubble of the minaret. The soldiers stared at the civilian in his dusty overcoat.

"They see you."

Kirov nodded.

"I want them to," said Terekhov and he gave leisurely wave of the hand in the direction of his troops, who returned it. "If I'd skipped this mission just to see some hood from Moscow, they'd think that the KGB was trying to saw my legs off. I can't allow them to think that. Get me?"

He sat down heavily. Kirov remembered the other man's age—fifty. The General stretched his legs and rubbed the right one. He suffered from arthritis in that knee.

Kirov began slowly: "I want to talk about your wife."

"Oh? Now, why is that? You've come all this way to talk about her?"

"I've got other business in Kabul."

"That so?"

They sat side by side and looked in the sky where the helicopters were still making passes like magicians. Terekhov asked: "Is Irina in trouble?"

"No. But her work involves many confidential matters."

"I imagine so."

"She is currently involved in a highly secret project."

"I wouldn't know. She doesn't write about her work."

"And she has applied to attend a conference of nuclear scientists in Geneva in the summer."

"She deserves it."

Kirov paused. Then, "Before you married her, she was married to a Jew."

Terekhov seemed genuinely curious. "Davidov? Sure. So what? I've got nothing against Jews."

"She has Jewish sympathies?"

"Not that I noticed. Davidov wasn't that kind of Jew."

"What kind?"

"A Zionist. He never applied for a visa for Israel that I heard of. He was interested in humanity, or whatever it is that poets write about. Does that answer your question?" Terekhov stood up and took a few steps forward to stare into the cold sunlit sky. He made a remark about rain: in a couple of months it would be the brief rainy season; the roads would become impassable.

"Do you love your wife, Colonel?"

Kirov watched the other man's back stiffen.

"Have you met Irina?"

"Yes."

"What do you think?"

"That you're in love with her."

In love with her, Kirov thought, but the Colonel doesn't make

358

love to her; he screws soldiers' whores from the Kabul bazaars and contracts diseases that need American antibiotics.

"Well, there you have it. You need a hostage for my good behavior?"

"And does she love you?"

Terekhov stooped to pick up a pebble and roll it through his fingers.

"That's a lot to ask of anyone."

"Is it?"

"Try it," said Terekhov and he walked away towards the troop carrier in the middle of the *maidan*, where the soldiers were roughing up a couple of Afghans who had been pulled out of the ruins.

"Who are they?" His men came to attention at the question. One of the soldiers began to yell at the two prisoners in their own language. They were boys, barely fifteen, with scared eyes and down on their lips.

"Did they have weapons?" Kirov asked the soldier, who put the question to the boys.

"If they had guns, they'd have buried them," Terekhov said. He grabbed one of the boys by the chin and jerked his head from side to side.

"Or it could be they have no guns."

"They're religious fanatics," the older man answered. He let the boy's head fall. "Take a look." He pointed out the *ghatt* on the prisoner's forehead. "They get that bruise from praying. Search them," he said to his men, and turned his back on the scene.

They crossed the *maidan*. Kirov asked, "How did you meet your wife?"

"Before I got this operational command, I had a staff job at the Frunze Military Academy: nuclear defense planning. There was a conference given to a mixed bag of engineers, physicists and military. Irina was reading one of the papers. It didn't interest me: I couldn't understand it; wasn't really trying to; but —" Terekhov halted and his eyes fixed themselves on a party of soldiers scurrying through the buildings in a street leading off the *maidan*. He's going to tell me, thought Kirov, because I'm a stranger. The rest of Terekhov's words seemed distant, like an aside. "There was something about Irina, the way she looked, stood, her voice. Nothing obvious," he explained. "Her clothes were—well, she made her own, still does. You could say she was plain—yes, plain. But to me there was something beautiful about her. I don't know. Maybe we create women in our imagination."

They resumed walking.

"When was this?"

"Seventy-four—seventy-five?"

"She was still living with Davidov?"

"Yes."

"But you met her again—while she was still living with Davidov."

"Sometimes."

"You were having an affair."

"No!" Terekhov answered sharply.

They sat down again amid the ruins of the mosque. The wind had started and was blowing dust around them.

"You have a sister," said Kirov, changing the subject.

"Yes?" Terekhov reacted cautiously.

He doesn't know that she's dead.

"I'm afraid I have some bad news for you."

He told it.

"How did it happen?" Terekhov asked slowly.

"I don't know the details. An accident, heart failure. Her health was poor, wasn't it?"

"Yes." Terekhov didn't want to speak about her—had to speak about her. "She had an accident a few years ago. It left her crippled."

"She was married? Her surname . . ."

"The bastard deserted her after she was injured!" Terekhov said angrily. Then he apologized: it wasn't Kirov's fault. He made a few more inquiries about how she had died, and Kirov fed him the stock lies; but he took care to make them sound like the truth, because he had decided that he liked this Colonel.

Had she helped Irina Terekhova to betray the secret of the Sokolskoye Incident? Behind his questions this one remained. Did she have the courage? How had Irina persuaded her? What were Irina's own motives? But that was to fall into the trap of assuming Irina Terekhova's guilt, as to which there was no evidence.

"To overcome her handicap and become a successful musician, your sister must have been a brave woman," Kirov said.

Terekhov, who had been staring at his hands as if his grief were written on them, raised his head and answered obliquely, "Women are braver than we are, or hadn't you noticed? They can cope with everyday life. They don't need"—he gestured contemptuously at his surroundings—"all this fantasy." In the valley the self-propelled gun had taken position and they could hear the sound of its shells dropping on the opposite hillside.

Their few moments of personal silence following this last exchange were interrupted by a soldier, who came at a run across the *maidan* and stood at attention in front of the Colonel. He held out a closed fist and dropped something into Terekhov's palm. Terekhov glanced at the contents and passed them to Kirov. Three buttons.

"Well?"

Kirov turned the buttons over. "From a uniform."

"One of ours. The boys had them?"

"Stitched into their turbans," answered the soldier.

Terekhov let them fall to the ground. "Souvenirs," he said. "Stripped from a corpse."

"Or a prisoner," said Kirov.

"They don't take prisoners," said Terekhov, without emphasis. He exchanged glances with the soldier. "OK, shoot them." The man smiled, turned and set off back at a trot.

"Drink?" Terekhov held out a water bottle. Kirov took a mouthful and passed the bottle back.

"There's something I don't understand," he began.

"What?"

"Your wife; she was unhappy with Davidov. He was violent, he was a drunkard, he hated him—I suppose, towards the end, she hated him."

"She never talked about him. Not at that time, before I married her."

"It's on the record. He was a madman who drank all the time and beat her."

"So I heard when she divorced him."

Kirov paused—because his training told him when to pause—until the older man was stressed by the silence. Then he asked quietly: "Then, why didn't she have an affair with you? For Davidov's sake? She didn't love him; she divorced him. For the sake of the children? But there are no children, only your son."

Terekhov shook his head. "I don't know," he said. In the distance there were shots as the prisoners were killed; but neither man was paying attention.

On his return to the embassy there was a message waiting for him. It was encoded except for the transmittal details and the "eyes only" classification, but that hadn't stopped Vorontsev picking it up. It lay on the resident's desk. Kirov guessed that Vorontsev had tried to have it decoded and then discovered that his own cipher clerks didn't have the key. He was impressed and annoyed, and disguised both by offering Kirov a drink.

"You'd better have this, too," said Vorontsev, handing over a copy of the transmittal. Kirov read quickly the uncoded sections: the message had been sent directly from the KGB in Helsinki, avoiding Moscow and any delay in clearance and retransmission. Someone wanted his attention, wanted it badly.

"I need a room," he said.

"Of course—somewhere to do your homework," Vorontsev responded sarcastically. He put down his glass and made a call to his secretary to arrange something for his visitor, then lit a cigarette which he smoked with long, leisurely style. His eyes drifted around his trophies and lit upon a small brass figure. "You looking for—souvenirs?" he inquired speculatively.

"No." Kirov was impatient to decode the rest of the message. The other man seemed to have taken his refusal as a ploy, and, while they waited for the secretary to return, he skated around the same subject like an Arab street trader.

"I'm not interested," Kirov reemphasized.

"OK, OK." Vorontsev put down the small piece he was handling. He gave a shrug and a laugh and said, "Who needs this sort of junk when the West is open to you? Finland—Helsinki—a great place to have business."

"I don't talk about my business."

362

"Sure you don't." Vorontsev smiled narrowly and, holding out a hand, tapped the edge of the paper that the other man held. "Who needs to?" he asked. "Top-secret messages in your own custom-built code. Urgency stamped all over it. What's more to tell?" He tipped his glass as a toast to Kirov. "It looks like your business in Finland is getting into deep trouble."

31

The engine was Finnish, the rolling stock Russian, gray-green and dull as the northern sky, seven sleeper cars, a restaurant and another sleeper, gray and gritty from the journey, from standing in stations during the long mysterious Soviet delays, from waiting in the falling snow at Vainikkala where the railway crosses the frontier, from the long halts on the empty line between trees and frozen lakes when no one knows why the delay has happened and the carriages clank and bump against each other like nuzzling calves. It was twelve-thirty, and the daily train from Moscow had arrived.

Kirov and his companion descended from their carriage and walked the length of the empty platform. There was no one to meet them. On the other platforms passengers queued for trains for the Finnish provincial cities.

They took a cab to Vantas where they were booked into a cheap hotel as German businessmen. They shared a room with bare pine walls and sparse furniture and a view to the back of the building where snow lay on the fire escape and the trash cans, and cats played among the moldering pile of cardboard boxes. It smelled of fish, which perhaps explained the cats. The soap in the bathroom was roughly cut from a larger block and the towels bore the name of a different hotel altogether.

"The Englishman is here," said their host, who had not bothered to take off his overcoat. He stood with his backside steaming against the radiator. Valchev—Anton Valchev—a Bulgarian who did the local legwork. He had been George's babysitter, and this time had fixed the hotel and other arrangements. Kirov remembered his reports, blandly factual like children's compositions on "What I did during the holidays," and not a trace in there of George Twist.

"He turned up, and so I contacted you," said Valchev. "Kabul, wasn't it? What were you doing there?"

"I got your message," said Kirov. He looked around for a wardrobe, opened his case and took out a couple of suits.

"He hasn't been in touch. That's what worried me. It's obvious he doesn't want us to know he's here."

"Have you tried to contact him?"

"No. I had no instructions."

"I understand."

While Kirov and his companion unpacked, Valchev sat on one of the beds, crossing and uncrossing his legs and trying to make conversation. He made a few enquiries about the journey and then asked their opinion of the hotel, its location, its comfort; it was owned by a Mrs. Murdoch, who had been married to a Scot.

"I'm right, aren't I?" he said at last. "Twist isn't supposed to be here . . . I understood his business ended when the stuff was shipped out of America, and that our side would take delivery in Finland and arrange transport out of the country."

"That's right."

"So what's he up to? Has he betrayed us?"

"How has he been behaving?" Kirov asked, ignoring the other man's question.

"Very quiet. He's booked into the Vaakuna and stays there. He takes his meals there, keeps away from the bars and doesn't chase after women. He came out once to buy an English newspaper and a bottle of *koskenkorva;* so he must be drinking in his room. Otherwise nothing."

"Then he must be doing his business by telephone. Have you intercepted his calls?"

"Too risky," Valchev answered. His attention was distracted by Kirov's silent companion. The man was unpacking his suitcase, hanging up an odd-looking overcoat, placing by his bedside a carton of cigarettes, an unfamiliar brand. "We couldn't break into his room, not with him there. We tried directional microphones, but without any luck. Our people are still working on the problem."

"Naturally," said Kirov and left the matter there.

He changed the subject.

"Where is the American equipment?"

"It's arrived," said Valchev, happier with the topic. "The containers are on the quayside at Sornäinen."

"Get them out," Kirov ordered, and then softened the command: "It's a precaution. As long as the containers are in the dock area they can be impounded by the authorities if they become suspicious. Move them to the factory at Lauttasaari and be prepared to move them again . . ."

"Yes?"

Kirov had paused. Travel—he smiled ironically—he was suffering along with George. "Fine, fine," he sighed wearily. Then, remembering Valchev, he said, "There is a contingency plan for emergencies. Do you have it?"

"There's a sealed package. Even the resident can't open it without instructions."

"Open it. You have my authority. Read the plan and put it into operation."

"Yes, Major."

Kirov turned from the Bulgarian to his colleague. "I need to sleep for a few hours and then think. I need time to think." To Valchev he said, "You can go."

The Bulgarian left and the two men were alone. Kirov's partner was going through a mess of socks and shorts at the bottom of his case, picking out each item and sniffing it lightly.

"Packed in a rush," he said without embarrassment, in heavily accented Russian. And, feeling an explanation was needed, added, "I normally do my washing on Thursdays. Plenty of hot water. It can be a bugger on other days."

Kirov asked, "What is George doing here? Can you tell me, Neville?"

Lucas put a finger through a hole in the toe of one sock, and turned with it dangling like a puppet.

"I should have thought that was clear," he said. "He's stuck in his hotel because he's waiting for someone else to arrive before he can do whatever it is he has planned. It can't be us that he's waiting for, or he would have contacted Valchev. So it has to be someone else—someone he doesn't want to tell us about."

Kirov nodded. The only question in his mind was—who?

George, of course, knew. Lou Ruttger was in Helsinki, invisible but as tangible as the prickling of his skin. One day he was in San José, and the next he had disappeared. Joe Czarnecki called when Lou failed to turn up at the office: Joe had become George's spy—not that he would have considered himself such—because he knew that in a fight George was stronger and more cunning. "I called Lou's home and said it was urgent business. Nancy said that Lou was sick; he wouldn't talk to anybody, even if the factory was burning down." George phoned Nancy on his own account and got the same story. She was a poor liar: her lies faltered, and long bitter silences lay between the words.

The same day, George took a flight to Finland. Allowing for time differences and the added length of the flight from the States, he calculated that Lou couldn't be more than twenty-four hours ahead of him and probably less. As a test he had put his call to Nancy through the operator to see how she would react to receiving an international call. She hadn't been surprised that it was him. If Lou had already reached Helsinki, she would have expected the call to have been from him and her voice would have betrayed the fact.

So now he was in the Vaakuna, placing calls to all the other hotels he could name in the Finnish capital and not finding Lou at any of them. And if he did find the American he didn't know what he was going to do.

George had guessed rightly that Lou Ruttger was avoiding the hotels. He had found a bed at a cheap hostel, the Matkakoti Tarmo, a shabby place on the sixth floor of a red-brick block at the grimy end of Siltasaarenkatu near the subway station. It was managed by a fat woman with greasy hair and a big smile, who spoke no English, and had queues for the bathroom and mysterious handwritten notes pinned to the doors that probably told him to wash his hands after urinating and pointed out the fire exits. Outside, the northern winter night closed early; in Silta-saarenkatu the traffic ground the snow to mush; and it was time for him to sleep after the flight. Maybe sleep would make sense of it all.

"George has got a problem." That was how he put it to himself and what he told Nancy. In his restless sleep he couldn't remember what the problem was. *George has got a problem.* It could be personal freshness or excessive drinking; the words didn't indicate. Good and evil had dropped out of the vocabulary and people simply had "problems," like sin and tooth decay. "If only he'd come clean, maybe I could help him," Lou said.

"George Twist is a bastard," Nancy answered and she looked at him with a simple pity. "Can't you see it? Can't you see?"

No! He told himself it wasn't as easy as that. George wouldn't really let him down. He told himself the same thing over and over again, and was still saying it when he woke in a cold sweat and the gray daylight was washing out his room.

Over breakfast he tried to work out a plan. So far he hadn't got one, perhaps because he couldn't bring himself to look at the situation coldly. He had come to Finland simply because he knew that the Sep Tech equipment was arriving and what happened next would tell him all he needed to know. He decided to make checks at the docks that the consignment was actually there, and then to call Siivosen, who were supposed to be taking delivery. He toyed with the idea of visiting the American embassy.

The checking of the cargo took him longer than he had expected: what Joe Czarnecki could have done in a couple of calls took him all morning. The only telephone to which he had access was the pay phone in the hostel, and there was competition from the other residents.

After lunch he called Siivosen's number and got a recorded message in Finnish. There was a student in the next room to his who spoke English. He caught her coming down the corridor in a bathrobe after a shower and asked her to listen and translate.

"It says the business is closed."

"The business, or the office? How do I leave a message?"

The girl smiled and shrugged her shoulders, so that her bathrobe slipped and she had to grab it. She looked beyond him at the great fat woman, who was leering her happy leer, and then vanished into her room.

He took a cab to an address in Frederikinkatu where Siivosen had its office. At street level it was a camera shop with a window full of Japanese stuff and a display of framed photographs of high-school graduates in their white graduation caps. There was an open side door with some nameplates on it and a cage lift that took him to the second floor and a dark landing with a green exit sign at the far end and a little light behind the sign.

He found a couple of doors; the first was a toilet, the second a broom closet. He lit a match and searched out an office door. It had a name stenciled on the glass, but nothing he could make out. He struck another match and found a second office. A sheet of lined paper was taped over the frosted pane, and someone had written a legend in crayon. Most of the words meant nothing to him, but he recognized "Siivosen Maalitehdas Oy." He had the right place. The door was locked.

For a moment he stood, bereft of ideas. At the back of his mind he had thought in terms of finding the right people and asking a few questions; then everything would naturally clear itself up. He put his preconceptions aside, took off a shoe and used the heel to smash the glass. There was plenty of noise, but no alarms and no one was listening. He slipped a hand through the hole and opened the door from the inside. The room stood empty and silent under the onset of darkness, though it was only mid-afternoon.

The light switch worked. A low-powered bulb picked out the cheap office furnishings: a desk, a couple of chairs, a filing cabinet; a window gave on to the street. The office had been cleaned out but not cleaned. He trod on paper clips and cigarette butts, and there were bread crumbs on the desk and sandwich wrappers in the basket. On the blotter someone had scrawled telephone numbers and odd words of Finnish — names, he guessed — and had pinned a sheet of paper to the wall. It had a cartoon drawn on it: a man with his trousers down and a speech bubble coming out of his arse. Office jokes were the same the whole world over. There were paper handkerchiefs and old typewriter ribbons in the desk drawers and an empty bottle of nail polish; and from the collection of rubbish that had slipped into the gap behind the filing cabinet he hooked out a brochure using a wire coat hanger. The brochure was one of Siivosen's own, and it reminded him of what he already knew: that the company had a factory in Helsinki, at a place called Lauttasaari.

He found another cab with a driver who would only acknowledge him in Finnish, but who seemed to understand well enough, and gave him the factory address. The dark streets were full of people in dark clothing, struggling in the cold and snow to go home. The roads were packed with the evening traffic. He had noticed that in Helsinki the sea turned up in unexpected places, now on the left, now on the right, flat expanses of Baltic ice, glimmering in the moon like a misted mirror; black channels cut by the ice-breakers; a ferry or freighter in the distance, Silja Line or Viking Line, or a Finnjet vessel sailing to Travemünde; sea mist on the horizon and the melancholy wailing of ships' horns.

The cab dropped him at the top of a broken lane that led between depots and warehouses. He paid the driver but told him to wait, with the promise of a tip, and then set off on foot between the buildings. He was sweating; he could feel the cold sting on his forehead. It was the effect of the overheated car, he told himself; and, if he tried hard, he could believe that it was true.

The lane ended at a wire fence and a gate that was open. Beyond the wire lay a concrete yard and a building and a blue Saab sedan parked with side lights. He wondered whether it was George Twist's. He thought he could hear someone kicking about the yard, but there was no one visible, just a streak of the light from a small door and a suggestion of light from a window.

He crossed the yard cautiously. The door stood ajar, let into a pair of double doors that could take a truck. The source of the light was a single lamp just inside the entrance, and further down the length of the interior two or three others were lit at intervals. At the farthest end there was an office, and from the office came distant voices.

Hi, George! How are you doing? He had the crazy idea that he only had to speak and the lights would go on, George Twist would appear, and everything would explain itself. But was the idea so crazy when all possibilities seemed insane? George wouldn't play tricks. Damn it, he knew George!

Then, why am I so scared?

He stepped through the door. The inside of the building started to come alive with shapes, the shadowed masses of machinery ranked against the walls. The voices again, the rise and fall of their echo. A door to the far office opening, a figure emerging, being called back, returning. The door closing. Water dripping.

He followed the wall to the shelter of one of the machines. There were wooden battens piled in a heap against the brickwork. He extended a hand to touch the metal. It was slick with grease. His fingers followed the machine's contours, then he withdrew them and sniffed the grease. On the floor a cable ran from the machine and ended in a coil going nowhere.

He moved to the next machine in line. The dim light caught the clean paintwork and the manufacturer's nameplate. At the base traces of loose packing hadn't been swept up. He let a handful trickle through his fingers, polystyrene chips, white as snowflakes. He was still examining them when the office door opened and three men emerged.

They were talking tensely, walking the length of the shop-floor and pausing to point out details and discuss them. Lou had a glimpse of them from his position crouched in the shadows. A tall man, stooping slightly, with an amiable sleepy face and hands shoved into the pockets of a gray coat. A younger man with a sharp look of intelligence about him. The third man was a ship's officer; a weatherbeaten cap was pulled down to shade his features, and he took broad strides in a pair of worn sea-boots. They paced out the floor measuring it for something and returned to the office. All the while they talked, and Lou listened while, carefully, he scooped up some of the white chips and slipped them into his pocket.

He didn't understand the language, but he recognized well enough that it was Russian.

He had always known it would be.

32

He was sitting in darkness in his hotel room when the call came through. He hadn't moved from his room all day; hadn't called Anton; hadn't called anybody except Lillian, who was well, cross-her-heart-and-hope-to-die as Brenda put it. He had a few drinks, but not many, smoked a pack of cigarettes, whiled away an hour filling in the letter 'o' in the first chapter of Genesis in the hotel's Gideon Bible. This way he could tell himself he didn't have any problems at all.

"George."

In his present frame of mind he was beyond surprises.

"Hi, Lou. Nice to hear from you. Where are you?"

"In the lobby. You were expecting me? Can I come up?"

"No." George hesitated long enough to let some reality wash over him. "I'd like to see you, but not here."

"Being careful, huh?"

George heard the cynicism. It wasn't like Lou, but what the hell: everybody was changing.

"Let's keep it friendly," he proposed, and Lou grunted something that sounded like a "maybe." He went on: "Listen hard. Go across the square to the main railway station and follow the building around to the right. There's a street runs off parallel to the tracks; you can't miss it: the railway is on one side and there's a basketball court on the other. Got me?"

"OK."

"OK—yeah, OK." George wiped his forehead; the room was suddenly warm. "Follow the street until it takes a bend to the right.

There's a restaurant on the bend, but it only opens for the summer, so you'll find it closed. I'll meet you there in fifteen minutes."

He waited for an answer.

"Sure," Lou agreed. And out of the past added, "Good luck, George."

"What? Oh — good luck to you, too, kid."

He put the telephone down and sat for a moment on the bed. He told himself it was time to go: he had an appointment to keep. He still didn't know what he was going to do. Nothing in his past had prepared him for this, and all his resources of bullshit and improvisation were useless. This was Peter Kirov's game.

No! If he let himself believe that, he was lost. It wasn't just Peter's game, it was — what had he called it? — Alternative Business. And that was something he knew about. He checked the room in case there was anything he had forgotten, put on his overcoat and closed the door.

In the square all the snow had been cleared except for the frozen dregs in the gutters. The trams clattered past with their windows lit but veiled in the hot breath of the passengers. It occurred to him that he might be followed. He hadn't been in contact with Anton, but this close to success there was a good chance that the KGB were watching movements into Helsinki, in which case they would have picked up his trail, and maybe Lou's, though there was less chance that they would expect the American. How was he supposed to spot a tail? In any case, what could he do about it?

Improvise, make it up as you go along. As a salesman it was what he was supposed to be good at.

He crossed the square along the station façade, passing the grim statues with their globes of light and the crowds jostling up and down the steps. He broke his pace with unexplained halts and short dashes, and checks over his shoulder.

He told himself he must look like a damned idiot.

He had read somewhere — probably in a thriller picked up at an airport bookstore — of fancy systems for tailing people, with unmarked cars, relays of watchers, frequent switches. What would Anton use? Did he have the manpower resources here in Helsinki?

Maybe he wouldn't think all that effort worthwhile—after all, he and George were both on the same side.

That's right: he was working for the KGB. If it weren't for Lou—if it weren't for Lou!

A figure singled himself out from the crowd. George recognized his man, a gray type in a heavy woollen coat with a tartan scarf and a fur hat with the flaps down, who looked uncomfortable with all his hopping about. He was ten yards behind, dragging his heels in the slush at the base of the station steps. George turned left. There were more steps, leading up to some doors and the entrance to the railway restaurant, a long flight of pink granite, and people in crowds as black and thick as beetles under a stone pressing up and down them. He continued walking, sticking to the contours while the pavement took a right into a street called Vilhonkatu and a dark lane cut off to the left to run in line with the tracks. He turned down the lane and almost collided with a drunk.

Now! In two minutes he would be with Lou. He had to ditch his follower now!

Damn it, what do I do?

The drunk was swaying and muttering obscenities. There was an empty bottle at his feet. George picked it up and flattened himself against the wall in the uncertain shadow of the drunk.

Now! The watcher had no sense of caution. Someone had told him that the Englishman was an ally, and in any case not a professional. He came round the corner with nothing on his face except mild curiosity. George smacked him in the face with the bottle.

He felt a second of paralysis. The bottle broke on impact and cut the other man's forehead so that the blood flowed and he couldn't see. The drunk opened his mouth to yell murder and immediately shut it again.

What do I do? George felt himself frozen by the question. *This isn't me!*

The stranger staggered against the wall. George grabbed his neck with one hand and with the other seized the back of his overcoat. He drove the man forward, heard his head crack against the wall, heard feet scrabbling for a hold on the ice. He drove him forward again. The man groaned; he uttered two words in English, quite quietly as if apologizing. "Please, no."

George loosed his grip on the coat, took the other man's head in both hands and smashed it as hard as he could against the granite. The stranger collapsed, and his unconscious form slid down the wall as George watched. And as he watched he shook, and sweat rolled down his face and froze. The drunk meanwhile was laughing.

George ran. His feet slid on the ice and he half-skated. He looked back but no one had been attracted by the disturbance. The drunk was stooped over the body, rifling the pockets of the overcoat. George ran on, to the pounding of his feet and the pounding of blood in his temples. And then he stopped. He caught his breath and walked slowly toward the dark shadow of the deserted restaurant.

"Hello, George."

Lou came out from behind the wooden pavilion. He took a hand from his pocket and extended it to be shaken. George accepted it as if he had been suddenly passed a smoking revolver. Ruttger sensed his reluctance and gave one of his half-cocked smiles.

"Looks like we've got ourselves in a mess, huh?" he said philosophically.

"Could be," George agreed. He looked about for somewhere out of view. They were in the empty beer garden, standing in the uncleared snow. On their right a boathouse faced on a narrow frozen sea inlet. In front of them was the railway and view across more water to the distant gardens behind the Finlandia Hall and the glow from the lights along Mannerheimintie. He took a few steps to the rear of the building and stood with his back to the shuttered windows. He gazed at the railway sidings, where cars from the Moscow train were laid up for the night. Lou joined him.

"How did you find me?" George asked. He was reaching into his pockets. "Smoke? I didn't leave any address with head office."

"I called your home. The nurse told me."

"Brenda? Did she, now? I hadn't thought of that. Where are you staying?"

"You don't expect me to tell you, do you?"

375

"Maybe not," George answered. "Your choice."

They looked at the clouds and said something about the snow.

"I know what's going on," Lou said mildly. He drew his eyes back from the sky to his companion. "Hey, you want a drink? I brought a bottle with me. Christ, but this place is cold after California!"

"What *is* going on?" George asked. "Surprise me."

"Please, let's skip the bullshit, huh?"

"Whatever you say."

They passed the bottle between them and took a mouthful apiece. Lou corked the bottle and placed it on the ground where they could both reach.

"So this is Eastern Europe," he said. "Can't say I like it."

"It isn't Eastern Europe."

"It isn't?"

"No."

Lou kicked at a lump of ice. It broke, and a scrap of wrapper was folded in it. He picked it up lazily and stared blankly at the unintelligible words.

"I've been to the factory," he said.

"Siivosen?"

"It's a fraud, George."

"How so?"

Lou put his hand into his pocket and produced some white beads.

"Recognize these?"

"Polystyrene?"

"Packing. I found them on the factory floor. There was wood there, too — from the cases the machinery was delivered in, I guess. The manufacturer's grease was still on them, and the ones I saw hadn't been connected to power. You see where I'm going? The stuff in that place has never been used. And it doesn't fit with the business. I'm no expert, but when someone says 'paint factory' I look for hoppers and blenders and can-filling lines. The equipment at Siivosen is machine tools, like they were turning out automobile engines. Do I have to spell it out?"

"Why should we care?"

"Because"—Lou's voice rose sharply and he struggled to pull it back—"because we're selling high technology, George, embargoed technology. And I want to know who I'm selling it to!"

Before George could reply the other man had already calmed down.

"I'm sorry. I thought I was past losing my temper with you. But there's nothing personal in this, is there, George? It's just business, like you taught me; like you learned from—Ronnie Pugh, was it?"

"Ronnie Pugh," George agreed.

Lou scratched his nose. "I know you're dealing with the Russians. Don't bother to lie—I told you: I was there, at Siivosen; and I saw them."

"You want me to put my hand up and confess?"

Lou ignored the wisecrack.

"What I don't understand is why. Even business doesn't explain it, or we'd all be selling heroin plants to the Mafia—or does it, George? Tell me." He looked away, at his feet, at the lights across the water, at the sky. "Well?"

"I don't know."

"Isn't it time you found out?"

"It isn't that simple." George stooped and picked up the bottle. He caught sight of the knuckles of his right hand. The skin was scraped and there was dried blood between the fingers; but no pain.

He thought: I've stopped feeling.

What he said was, "Has it never occurred to you that sometimes the Russians may be in the right? You know, just once in a while? I mean, why should they be wrong all the time?"

"I don't have an opinion," Lou answered. "Governments make those decisions. The other way is how traitors are made. They think they know better."

"Maybe sometimes they do. Following government orders—isn't that how they make mass murderers? Which do you want to be, Lou?"

"It's a moral issue, is that what you're telling me? George Twist doesn't do it for money anymore?"

"For Christ's sake!"

"C'mon, George, tell me how it really is."

"You've become cynical, Lou."

"We all learn and change. You're different, too."

They fell silent. The sound of a police siren blew in on the wind, and they froze in the shadows of the darkened pavilion, waiting. It came and went, not even close. A train rattled slowly down the tracks, its cars a string of lights. George broke the tension.

"They have a pollution problem. Don't stop me," he said. "They've fouled up the operation of one of their plants and dropped five kilograms of plutonium nitrate into a lake. It's locked up there until April when the spring thaw will wash it into one of the river systems." He halted there because reciting the facts as Irina Terekhova had told them reminded him of her. He could see her now: her tenderness masked by a fragile shell of reserve. It was crazy to think of her because he would never see her again. "There are sixty million people at risk," he went on. "If they don't solve the problem, then it's farewell to Russia, I guess. They need our help," he ended quietly.

What now? Did Lou believe him.

"Who told you?" Lou asked, and he gave his own reply: "The Russians, who else?" He laughed bitterly. "And you believed them, George, *you* believed them!"

"I suppose I did—I do." He thought for a moment of telling Lou about Irina. But what was there to tell that would make any sense? He had met a womanly briefly and—fallen in love?—except that wasn't it: people fell in and out of love every day. Instead he had been caught in a more subtle trap, though not one of her deliberate making. He simply cared what happened.

Lou meanwhile was saying, "You've been listening to lies. They've been telling you stories. If they really had such a problem, do you suppose that Uncle Sam wouldn't volunteer to help them out? All they'd need to do is ask."

George shook his head. "It isn't their way. Not a second time. Not after Chernobyl."

There was nothing else to say. Lou would trust him or he wouldn't. And trust was all used up.

378

Lou was looking at his watch.

"I've got to go. You won't follow me, will you, George?"

"No."

The younger man smiled. He held out his hand again and George took it distractedly. He asked, "How's Nancy?" and Lou said she was OK: he was calling home, morning and evening. George said he was doing the same.

"You know I'm going to try to stop you, don't you?" Lou said.

"I guessed," George answered, and added: "Don't try too hard, though, eh? Think of the risks."

"Hey, fella, don't get excited. I'm not taking any chances. The government pays people to do that. I only have to tell them."

Geoge nodded. "I suppose so."

"Sure they do."

"They must," George agreed and felt relieved until he realized the absurdity of the wish. He looked up and saw that Lou shared the realization, and he grinned because there was nothing else to do, and said, "Anyone would think we were on the same side." He paused. "So which of us is the good guy?"

Lou laughed. "Damned if I know any more!" He laughed again and carried on until it snapped like a broken spring. "Well," he said at last, "I got to go."

"I've got to leave, too."

"See you, George."

"Yes . . . of course."

And that was it, and even then the parting seemed too brief as though there was something altogether different they should have talked about. But now it was over, the snow had started to fall and Lou was disappearing into the white haze along the water's edge. George turned away, because he didn't want to see Lou any more.

He stayed there for a while, kicking around in the snow, pulling the flakes of paint from the peeling shutters, thinking the whole business over and telling himself he was right with the certainty of a man who wasn't sure. He found the bottle that Lou had left behind, uncorked it, sniffed the contents and poured the liquor onto the snow. He became slowly aware of the biting cold and the pain in his

379

hand; it was time to return to his hotel.

It was then that he saw the car.

It came out of the darkness and snow along the waterside, its headlights sweeping over the ice, over the small craft beached on the bank, over the boathouse, trapping him as he stepped out into the roadway. He heard the purring of the engine, the slamming of doors, the slosh of feet in the churned-up mess.

Four men in hats and coats and muffled to the eyes came at him just as they were supposed to come, stringing out to cover any direction in case he ran, though they weren't to know that he was too tired to run. A fifth man came up slowly behind them.

Anton, looking thin and cruel and young, splashed the snow in his snakeskin moccasins, which he had guarded with rubber overshoes.

"Hello, Tony." George tried to smile, in case charm might work.

"Hello, George," the other man replied dully. He fixed the Englishman with a pair of eyes that were moist and glittering with cold. He flexed his fingers with each lungful of misty breath. "Let's go," he said.

Then he drove his fist into George's guts so hard that the world went dark.

33

He decided he wasn't unconscious. He could feel the vomit bubbling up in his mouth and see the tips of his shoes dragging along the roadway as they picked him up by the armpits. They jerked his head back and shone a flashlight in his eyes, then stood him upright and steadied him while he spewed bright colors into the snow. They then bundled him into the back seat of the car and held him down with his head staring at the damp newspapers on the floor and his nose filled with the smell of their shabby suits and the wet wool of their overcoats.

They drove, he couldn't tell how far or how long. When he tried to raise his head, someone chopped him on the back of the neck—but carefully, always carefully. They spoke seldom and in Russian, except for one who had a loud cheerful voice and told what seemed to be jokes, to judge from their reception. As far as he could tell, they were having a good time.

The car stopped. The doors flew open, and he was dragged out again and given another punch in the guts to keep him docile, then half-carried across a dark, bare yard towards a building that seemed vaguely familiar. He heard a reassuring English voice saying, "Easy does it. Don't break the goods," and his own murmuring, "Get them off me, Neville, I want to be sick again."

"Not to worry, George." Lucas's face was visible only hazily. Before George could focus there were more orders barked in Russian and he was being dragged through a door, and into an empty space where voices ricocheted off the walls. Someone was turning an engine over, and in the vastness it still seemed like silence. But there was no time to take it in.

"Have a seat."

He felt himself slammed into a chair, and his hands were whipped behind him and bound, and someone was rolling up his sleeve and swabbing his arm.

"No! Not that! Not that!"

Maybe he didn't shout it. Maybe they just weren't listening.

"Clean him up, someone," Lucas said plaintively, and George felt the other man's breath on his face and a grubby handkerchief wiping the bile from his chin; and his abdomen ached as though something had burst.

"Oh, Christ, Neville, it hurts."

"Yes . . . well, it would. No more rough stuff, though, promise."

"You never said it was going to be like this."

"You should learn to stick by your deals, George."

"Maybe it was in the small print." He tried a smile, but someone was sticking a needle into his arm. And then it was all different.

The world was full of lights, so full he couldn't see for them. And someone was speaking.

"George . . . George." Slowly. "Geor-ge."

He knew the voice, but now it was cold. It used to belong to a friend.

"Peter?" He screwed up his eyes and a face appeared, suspended in the light, bodiless.

"George Twist, sometimes you can make me"—the younger man was looking for words, as he often did—"cross."

"Cross?" George wanted to laugh. Something told him he wasn't supposed to. "What happens when you're bloody angry?"

"Please," Kirov snapped. "No jokes."

The face disappeared and was replaced by the scraping of a chair. When Kirov spoke again it was from behind him. He spoke slowly and evenly, and George had to strain to catch the low tones.

"What have I done, George? What did I do that you have to keep secrets from me?" He sounded hurt, and George tried to remember. What had Peter done?

"You killed John Chaseman and . . . and . . . some other guy, I forget." The words were so dry in his mouth that he could spit them out like crumbs.

"Water," Kirov ordered. He waited patiently while it came and then held the cup to the Englishman's lips. "Better? I think so." He moved to the front again so that his face filled George's vision.

"I didn't do it," he said earnestly. "I promise you, George: I've had nobody killed. Trust me. Believe me."

Kirov vanished again.

Now Neville Lucas's voice drifted in, posing a casual question as if it were the time of day.

"You were with . . . oh, what's-his-name, thingummy . . . name on the tip of my tongue . . ."

"Lou Ruttger."

"Lou. Of course. How's he getting on?"

"He's fine." George was inexplicably pleased that they seemed to know about Lou. "He's a good guy."

"Absolutely," Lucas affirmed, "a great chap!"

"Why is he here?" Kirov resumed.

George tried to remember the answer to that one.

"He knows. I didn't tell him. He just guessed."

There was a halt from the other side, a rapid fire of Russian that ignored him.

He went on: "I wanted to stop Lou, persuade him to back off before he got hurt."

"Of course," said Kirov. "But you failed, didn't you? Ruttger still wants to prevent our plans, he wants to be a hero, doesn't he?"

"Yes!" George agreed painfully, and the light broke up into a spray of gold flowers and he could feel the tears running down his cheeks.

He felt the needle entering his arm again, and suddenly the

383

questions were coming at him like punches.

Where was Ruttger now?

He didn't know.

Had Ruttger spoken to the Finnish authorities?

He didn't know.

To the American embassy?

He didn't know.

Had they arranged to meet again?

No—no—no!

They came so fast he couldn't think about the answers, couldn't lie even if he had wanted to. His voice was babbling, saying anything, anything they wanted to know.

"Stop it, Peter! Stop it!" He could hear the words screaming inside his head, but had no idea if he was speaking or not.

Then there was silence punctuated only by the dripping of water. And the light was gone, and the darkness swam with phantom shapes.

Afterward he thought that he had gone to sleep and emerged gradually into a world that was right-side up. The light was soft. He could see. He was in the warehouse at Lauttasaari, his hands were unbound and someone was offering him a drink that he thought was tea.

"How are you feeling?" Kirov was asking, and his voice sounded concerned.

"I'm OK. Fine. How did I do?"

"You did all right."

"You did all right," Neville Lucas concurred.

"Good. I just wanted to help."

"Of course you did, George."

Shapes cohered into real things. There were four goods-containers parked on their trailers in the middle of the shop-floor. In his muddied thoughts they suggested something.

"I thought there were supposed to be only two," he said, and pointed.

"No, four. Your memory must be playing tricks," said Kirov.

"I suppose so," George agreed, and realized he didn't care.

Something had been blown out of him; he had lost something like all the other things he had lost in aircraft and hotels. Reflexively he asked, "Did it all arrive? The Sep Tech equipment—it's all here?"

"Every last bit," said Kirov. "And soon, if we make no mistakes, it will be in my country, and millions of lives will be saved. That will be your achievement, George."

"Will it?" He found he didn't care about that, either. There was something else he wanted to ask, if only he could dredge it out of his memory.

"What happens to me now—and afterward?"

Kirov smiled. "You can go." He saw George's surprise. "Neville will take you back to your hotel. There are still things you can do to help," he explained.

"And afterward?" George repeated.

"Don't worry," Kirov said with a hint of sympathy. "We understand. Tonight—Lou Ruttger—all that. It was a lapse by you, not a betrayal. We know that you are still on our side."

"I don't know whether to believe—"

"Don't say it," Kirov interrupted. He picked up the cup of tea, and offered it again. "If the heart is in the right place, we know how to forgive human weakness."

"After all," said Neville Lucas, "we're human, too."

His memory of the next few hours was hazy. They got him into the car and somehow back to the hotel and his room. He was bundled on to the bed like a drunk and somewhere around then he finally passed out from the drugs, the beating he had taken, and exhaustion. From time to time afterward he surfaced in the stillness of the night, and by a dim table lamp he saw Neville Lucas sitting peaceably in one corner, smoking and reading a magazine.

When he finally awoke it was five in the morning by the bedside clock, and Lucas was dozing in his chair with the magazine open on his lap. As George got out of bed, the other man stirred and gave one of his diffident, good-humored smiles.

"You all right?" he inquired.

"My head aches," George answered, which was an understated summary of how he felt.

"Ah, yes. That's probably an effect of the . . . the you-know-what."

George went to the bathroom and stripped out of his filthy suit. He examined his face. It was yellow and flaccid, and his eyes looked like those of a dead man. He shaved and took a shower.

"Are you my guard?" he called out to Lucas.

"Guard? No, not exactly," Lucas answered. "I'm not into all this rough stuff. Anton has people who do that sort of thing. They're hanging around the hotel, I expect: well, you can understand that Peter is a little bit nervous of you, George. No, when he heard that you were in Helsinki, he asked me to come along and give moral support. Another English face, that was the idea. I said it mightn't appeal to you, what with my being a traitor and all that. I thought it was rubbing salt into the wounds—not that you're a traitor yourself, old chap, don't get me wrong."

George stopped him. "I'm glad you're here."

"Peter was right, then," Lucas said with some surprise, and brightened up. "Well, thanks for saying so. I mean it."

George came back into the bedroom and got dressed. He switched on the radio but nothing much was playing, so he turned it off again. He glanced at Lucas, who was sitting expectantly.

George remembered what was troubling him. He asked: "Tell me, Neville, what's really going to happen to me?"

"Peter still wants your help. He's going to move the equipment tonight, try to get it out of Helsinki. It could be difficult if the authorities here know what's going on. Dangerous, even, if the Americans get to know; they can be very hot-headed."

"That wasn't my question."

"No?" Lucas paused, and his innocent face was ruffled with

thought. He started again, slowly. "I don't think you've ever understood properly about the Russians. Your suspicions have got the better of you"—he hesitated—"which is only natural, I suppose. But the truth is that, in their own funny way, they're very honest. I mean, you've got to admit that Peter has kept to his side of the bargain, hasn't he? Everything has been paid for promptly and in full, and your fellow Evans is negotiating the gas-plant contracts, isn't he? Can't say fairer than that."

"I suppose not."

"Just so. And that's what Peter will keep right on doing. The Russians take great pride in sticking by their deals. It's just . . ."

"Just what?"

"It's just that the deals can be a bit tougher than you first expected."

They had an early breakfast brought to their room, and afterwards George announced that he wanted to clear his head by going for a walk. To his surprise, Neville Lucas agreed.

They strolled, side by side in the pre-dawn darkness, two of Anton's men ahead of them, one on each flank and two at the rear, and perhaps it was their presence, or his tiredness, or the cold air acting on the remnant of some drug within his system, but for a second George felt himself overwhelmed by a wave of panic. *He didn't know where he was!*

He halted and felt Lucas's big friendly arm stretch out to steady him, and gradually solid things emerged in his vision, but only grayly: lines of darkened shops, their details etched out in snow, unfamiliar cars parked with snow on their roofs, a veil of snow hanging lightly in the air and the cold feel of the flakes falling on his face. He told himself that he was in Helsinki but he couldn't be sure. He was tired that all places were the same grey place and all values the same grey values because they stemmed from one's sense of place. He wanted to go back to a time when places seemed real so that people could become real from being rooted in them. Values were not abstract: they existed concretely only from a sense of place and of belonging to it with all the other real people. To people from nowhere, nothing was owed. They became travelers preyed on by bandits.

He was in this frame of mind when he heard the shot and the squeal of car wheels. He looked at Neville Lucas and then at the men forming his escort. They seemed unaffected.

"Here's a rum do, George," said Lucas with a flicker of amusement. Then: "Are you all right, old chap? You look a bit green around the gills."

"I think it's the stuff Peter used," George answered uncertainly. "I thought I heard a shot."

"Oh!" Lucas snorted. "You heard that right enough!"

George stared in the direction Lucas was pointing and saw that out of the darkness a scene had been cut in lights. In the cold pre-dawn, a film crew was working in the Kaupatorri, the marketplace on the quayside. On the opposite side of the road a group of actors was clustered around a car and a thick Scottish voice could be heard growling; "Right, darling, now this take let's try to show a bit of real terror in our pretty face." Then a burly figure in a sheepskin coat and calf-length boots broke away from the group and recrossed the road to the camera.

"Let's go back," said George. He watched as the car screeched to a halt again and two men wrestled with a woman before flinging her into the vehicle.

"Whatever you say," said Lucas.

George screwed up his eyes as though, if he tried hard enough, he could recognize the woman.

"Cut!" yelled the Scot, and the woman looked up, but her face was unrecognizable under the light and makeup. "OK, boys, let's get breakfast."

One by one the lights went out, and George heard Neville Lucas saying, "I gather that they filmed *Gorky Park* here."

He kept his eyes on the fading scene but asked, "Why Helsinki?"

Lucas kicked his toes idly at the cobbles and signaled to the others that they would be returning to the hotel.

"I should have thought it was obvious," he said. "It's the nearest they can get to Moscow."

* * *

Lou Ruttger woke at 8 a.m. It was still dark, and he was covered in the cold sweat that had affected his sleeping ever since his arrival in Helsinki. He told himself it was due to the change of diet, or the water. So he queued for the shower, and bought a bite of breakfast from the fat woman, and, as he ate it in his room, made up his mind what to do next.

The Sep Tech equipment was still in Helsinki, he was sure of it. Otherwise there was no reason for George Twist to be there. But for how long? Stacked in its containers, it wouldn't take much to move it. They could do it today. In fact, now that George knew he was here, they had to move it today.

He decided to go to the American embassy and confess the whole story. It was something he should have done before: he should have confronted George when he first had his suspicions. But when was that? There was a point when he ought to have faced up to where the facts were leading, but the truth had taken him so subtly that there was no telling when he knew, and now . . . there was no point thinking about it. He would tell the embassy and stand the consequences. Like he said it to George: the government had people to take care of these things. It was simple, really.

He walked. The exercise and the cold air cleared his thoughts. The pale sun came up and lay in the southeast over the frozen sea. He took the route along the embankment and the quays.

The ship, when he first saw it, looked like the others moored around the South Harbor. It had a white hull with a blue stripe, and a band of reed around the smokestack; and the name painted on the bow said it was *Georg Ots* out of Talinn, which didn't meant a lot unless you knew where Talinn was. It sat peaceably against the quayside with a few lamps showing faintly in the morning light and a few sailors on deck lounging over the rail; and Ruttger wouldn't have given it any attention, except that when he glanced at the smokestack he caught the emblem painted in yellow on the red band. It was the hammer and sickle.

And he remembered that one of the Russians he had seen was a ship's officer.

The American embassy was in Itäinen Puistotie, a narrow suburban street with its share of trees and expensive apartment houses. It looked like something from colonial times, a two-story hollow square of light-brown brick with a mansard roof, eagles on the gateposts, and a pair of Finnish embassy guards to make sure it couldn't have been quieter. Lou Ruttger found the public entrance and presented himself at the reception desk, and it was only there that he realized he had a small problem. How was he supposed to ask to see someone from the CIA?

"I'd like to see someone from the CIA," he said, And, if it sounded stupid, it was the only way he knew how.

"Ruttger is at the American embassy," said Valchev, putting down the telephone.

Kirov nodded and continued with his breakfast.

Valchev was impatient. "We know where he is staying. He walked from his lodgings. We could have taken him at any time. He's on his own and he takes no precautions. He's an amateur."

"There's no need for haste," Kirov answered. He balanced the other man's anxiety with his own patience. "Look, we don't know what previous contact he has had with his authorities. Perhaps he saw them also yesterday. Perhaps he telephoned them this morning before making his visit. We can't say. Ruttger is an amateur and therefore unpredictable. But"—Kirov wiped his mouth and turned to examine his companion coldly—"if he has told his story, then any action against him will only add to his credibility." He saw Valchev nod, but he guessed that the Bulgarian was already writing a report to protect himself. The responsibility for tactics in these last critical hours would be Kirov's. He asked, "Have the containers been moved from Lauttasaari?"

Valchev grunted his assent and added, "They're safe until tonight."

"Then, there's no way they can stop us, is there?" said Kirov quietly, and he waited until the waiting forced Valchev's grudging agreement.

But the truth was that there was always something that could go wrong.

"Mr. Ruttger," said the embassy official, who looked smiling and wholesome and called himself Jacob Renbacker, but-you-can-call-me-Jake.

"What can I do for you?"

"Excuse me, but first things first. Am I talking to the CIA?"

"You're talking to the U.S. government," Renbacker said expansively, "and if any action is needed, I personally guarantee that anything you tell me will go to the right quarters."

"Then I guess that will have to do," Lou Ruttger answered, and he breathed in, ready for the big one. "What I have to tell you is that my company is trading illegally with the Soviet Union."

Having said that, there was no stopping. He told the whole story as best he understood it, from the initial inquiry to the arrival of the goods in Finland. He explained about Siivosen and described his visit to the factory at Lauttasaari, his sight of the Russians and his subsequent meeting with George Twist. He told Renbacker of his belief that the Russians intended to ship the equipment on the *Georg Ots,* which was waiting in the south harbor. He had few preconceptions about the response he would get: anything from righteous anger to outright panic. What he didn't expect was to be received as if he were selling encyclopedias in a polite neighborhood.

"Well, Lou, that's quite a story," said Renbacker with his overtrained friendliness that was starting to sound like insincerity.

"Except that it's not a story. I am who I say I am. You can check my credentials."

"I guess we could, too," Renbacker agreed, but his Ivy League manner indicated that it would be bad form to do any such thing. Instead he smiled and waited a few seconds in case there was any more, and, having realized that there wasn't, he suggested coffee. While they waited for it he made a call.

The newcomer was bigger and more spare than Renbacker. He had the sort of large shoulders that look out of place in a suit, and a long face with features hanging off it like clothes in a wardrobe. His manner was easy enough. He took a seat on Renbacker's desk with one leg draped over the end and one resting on the floor. Renbacker started the ball rolling.

"Henry Krewinkle, this is Lou Ruttger. Lou and I are having coffee—Hank, you want coffee? Lou, tell Hank what you just told me. Hank, you should listen to this. Lou, is that with or without cream and sugar?"

So, while Renbacker wrestled with the coffeepot and the china cups and the low-fat cream-substitute, Lou Ruttger went over the same ground, and this time got no reaction except the occasional nod to tell him that the point was noted and he should move on to the next one. And, as he did so, he became aware of time passing, of the morning going before he had accomplished anything. He wanted to shout out and tell them to stop wasting the day, because this was the last day and tomorrow would be too late.

"So, what do you think?" asked Renbacker.

Krewinkle shrugged. "When Sep Tech applied for an export license, we looked Siivosen over. Reputable company—long-established—they looked OK. To be frank, Lou," he said directly to Ruttger, "we've seen some of these Soviet front-companies before, and Siivosen doesn't fit the bill."

"Meaning?"

"Did it ever occur to you that you might be wrong?"

They watched Lou Ruttger leaving by the street exit. Renbacker let the slats on the blinds fall and turned to his companion. The friendliness was gone.

"You didn't believe him."

"On the contrary, I think he's telling essentially the truth."

"Then why did you let him go like that? He thinks we just turned him down."

"I want to see what happens if we leave him running around. In the meantime I'll warn the British in case he pays them a call, and I'll ask the Finns to take a look at that place at Lauttasaari and maybe the *Georg Ots* too. The ship's been lying in harbor overdue for two days with what the captain says is engine trouble. It would fit if she were waiting for an illegal cargo."

"You had a feeling something like this was in the cards?"

"Maybe," said Krewinkle, and he began on his telephone calls and only afterward explained.

"We think there's a Moscow Center hood in town. We caught sight of him at the main station yesterday, posing as a German, name of Bauer, just off the Moscow train. The identification was confirmed by Langley only this morning. They're not sure, but they think he could be a guy called Borisov, who used to work out of the Washington *rezidentura,* also known as Kirov. If it is Kirov, then the Company would be very interested."

"Why?"

"A few years ago the KGB decided to clean up their act. They thought that they'd get more flexibility and better results if they stopped running their operations like the Five-Year Plan; also the strong-arm tactics were giving them a bad name. So they trained a new breed of agent, just a small batch of them, to see how they would look. These characters were to be re-laxed, civilized, independent—Moscow was going to let them freewheel a little.

"The Company was just as curious as the Center to see how it all panned out. They targeted one of the new men working out of Washington and played a burned-out defector against him as bait, with the aim of bringing him over to our side. I'm talking now about Kirov.

"At first it went like a dream. Kirov gave the right response. He was going to defect as soon as he could put together the price of admission, his wedding trousseau. He made all the arrangements with Ouspensky—that was the name of our man—and we had everything ready for the jump. Then—whoosh!—Ouspensky turns on us and vanishes into the Soviet embassy, the Soviets score a big publicity coup, and a few of our guys have their careers wrecked."

"And Kirov?"

"I don't know," said Krewinkle. "For some reason Moscow decided that the experiment was a failure. Kirov and all the others we identified were recalled. Until now, not one of them has ever shown his face again outside the Soviet Union. Maybe Kirov's success frightened his masters. Maybe they don't really want to leave the old Russia they know and love. Who can tell how they think? But then, suddenly, this. Kirov has been put into Helsinki to run an operation with a bunch of amateurs like the British guy, Twist. It's tailor-made for someone with fluidity and style."

"You sound as though you have some respect for him."

"I've never met him. But I've met guys who have. Kirov is a high-profile, high-risk operator. He'll let you see both his hands, while all the time he's stealing your watch."

Renbacker understood. "This has something to do with Lou Ruttger."

Krewinkle nodded.

"After Ruttger met Twist, the Russians must know that Ruttger is in town and liable to tell his story to anyone who'll listen, and yet Kirov is letting him run loose."

"Put that way, it does sound odd."

"Damned right," said Krewinkle thoughtfully. "All the time Ruttger was telling us his story I kept asking myself one question."

"Which was?"

"Why isn't he dead?"

* * *

At 11 a.m., while Lou Ruttger was still at the embassy, Kirov arrived in Espoo, one of Helsinki's satellite towns, where the KGB had rented a warehouse in a quiet area away from the center. The containers with the Sep Tech equipment were already there, standing under cover on the open floor, being resprayed. From his position in the office Kirov could watch the activity. He smoked and thought through his tactics in the light of each new report brought to him by Valchev.

At noon, Ruttger was seen leaving the American embassy. He was on foot, walking slowly and uncertainly, orienting himself by a street map. He took a route down Ullankatu, where he paused briefly, and then, suddenly realizing that the dark gray classical block behind the railings and garden on his left was the Soviet embassy, hurried off and at the next corner took a left into Vuorimiehenkatu. It was there that the American team appeared.

"They have him in a box," said Valchev. "Four men on foot and a car somewhere around. It makes life difficult for us. If we try to maintain close surveillance, we'll be tripping over the Yanks." He explained that Ruttger had stopped walking for the time being. Vuormiehenkatu was a quiet street of apartment houses and small shops. On the south side it was divided from the next street by open ground, which rose at its eastern end into one of the granite outcrops that underlay the thin soil all about the city. Ruttger had climbed to the top of this low knoll, and was watching children in the small play area that occupied the open ground. "Doing nothing," Valchev emphasized, meaning why? what? how? as if Kirov could read minds.

And Kirov thought he could read the American's well enough. Ruttger had children of his own. George had told him about the terrible threat to life posed by the incident at Sokolskoye; what if George had been telling the truth? Ah, yes: Ruttger was motivated by conscience and patriotism, and patterned by movie images of heroism, just as George could be moved by compassion and sentiment. It was not too difficult to conclude what

Lou Ruttger was thinking, and the courses of action that flowed from that.

"What do we do about surveillance?" Valchev was asking.

"Pull your men back and avoid the Americans. If necessary, they can lose Ruttger."

"Whatever you say."

The next report had Ruttger turning right into Laivurinkatu, where one of the CIA team held back to check his own rear. Valchev's men followed orders and broke off contact. For five minutes Kirov was blind as to his target's movements, but after a circuit of the streets the watchers identified the American again in Frederikinkatu. Valchev was glad to have reestablished contact but puzzled.

"He's completely off-route to return to his hostel. He's up to something. But what? Now that he's given his story to the embassy, what's left for him to do?"

"He thinks that the embassy didn't believe him," Kirov answered briefly. "Or that they won't take action." He wasn't looking at the Bulgarian, but out of the office window onto the shop-floor, where he could see a new set of identification marks being stenciled onto the containers. Ruttger had a spurious clear-sightedness: to him the problem and its solution must have been self-evident. He wouldn't understand the embassy's guarded response. Or so Kirov supposed, though he had never met Ruttger, only divined his character at second-hand from George Twist—which, naturally, only added to the risk. "He'll do whatever he thinks is necessary."

"I don't like it," Valchev complained. "It's all too loose. I don't know why you let him get as far as the embassy."

"No?" Kirov inquired. Valchev wasn't listening. He was taking the next report. Ruttger was in Uudenmaankatu, walking slowly and checking addresses.

"What could he be looking for?"

"The British embassy," suggested Kirov. "It's logical. George Twist works for a British company. If the Americans won't help him, maybe the British will."

"The British embassy! It gets worse!" Valchev gave a short laugh. Kirov began to lose patience with his obtuseness and brutality.

"At no stage have we known what the British or the Americans suspected. Perhaps their export licensing authorities never believed in the Siivosen contract and want to know what was behind it. Perhaps Ruttger voiced his suspicions or informed his government before he came to Finland. Perhaps your contacts with George Twist were observed, or I was identified when I arrived here."

Perhaps Senator Abe Korman had told the CIA about the package he had received which described the Sokolskoye Incident. Kirov didn't mention that possibility. The interrogation of Korman, in the back of a car parked on an empty building lot, exposed the limitations of violence. Korman had died before he could answer that critical question. Not that Yatsin, the Washington resident, could complain, since Kirov had never officially seen Korman. In that connection he had merely turned another friend into an enemy. He returned to Valchev's point.

"Whatever the truth, it has never been safe to assume that British and American intelligence have been entirely ignorant of our operation."

"And what does letting Ruttger run around achieve?" Valchev asked.

Kirov was impatient of explanations, but he recognized that the other man was also feeling the strain of waiting for the final move.

"It gives the CIA something to do. They will follow Ruttger; and, if they lose Ruttger, they'll follow George Twist. Either way, we shall have focused their attention. They're looking at those two, and believe that they are seeing us. But the truth is the reverse: we can see exactly what the Americans are doing. And it doesn't hurt us at all."

Uudenmaankatu was a broad street full of second-rate shops.

On the south side stood a modern building with a tiled face and a limp flag hanging at the fourth-floor level. Between the shops was a recessed entrance and a door with a modest sign advertising Her Britannic Majesty's Embassy to Finland as if it were a firm of dubious accountants with an office far enough from the street to allow the files to be cleared before the police could break down the door. In the lobby a lift gave access to the fourth floor and a shabby reception area which suggested that the owners assumed any callers to be on welfare.

Lou Ruttger presented himself at the desk.

"I want to talk to your commercial counselor."

"Would you mind speaking up, sir?" The man behind the desk was a comfortable type with a myopic gaze and an air of forced politeness.

"I'd like to see the commercial counselor," Ruttger repeated.

"Ah—and may I ask what about?"

"The subject is confidential."

"Is it? Oh dear. Could you give me—a hint?"

"For Christ's sake."

"Possibly."

Lou tried again. "I want to report that a British company is about to break the law."

"I see." The man had a certain unflappability that seemed only to become more pronounced as Lou Ruttger showed excitement. He asked, "Are you a British citizen, sir? Or from the Empire?"

"I didn't know you had an empire?"

"I was speaking loosely, sir. Have you reported this matter to the Finnish authorities?"

"No."

"Ah." The receptionist's mouth flickered wanly. He picked up a telephone and punched out a number. There was no answer, so he replaced the receiver and apologized. "Engaged. Mr. Fairbrother did say something about having a meeting all day."

"Interrupt him."

"I couldn't do that."

"Then get me someone else."

The man spared another of his thin smiles and reached for a well-thumbed copy of a typed list. "Let's see." He hummed as his finger went down the lines. Then he put the list down. "We're running a bit lean at the moment. The cuts . . ." he explained vaguely. "Tomorrow any good?"

"It has to be today," Ruttger answered, but less emphatically. He knew when he was wasting his time. He turned away from the desk and took a seat while he decided what he was going to do next. In the adjacent seat a man in his early twenties with a backpack and traveling gear dozed as he waited. It gave Lou an idea.

By the lift in the lobby of the building a CIA agent waited for Lou Ruttger to descend from the embassy. In Undenmaankatu, two more Americans were posted on the corners at the end of the block. The fourth man was stationed in Iso-Roobertinkatu, and the car that controlled the operation was parked in Bulevardi, which completed the four sides of the box. Because of the CIA presence, Valchev was limited to one man, who kept watch from a shop across the street from the embassy block.

At 2 p.m. the doors to the lift opened and a man with a moustache, wearing a travel-stained sheepskin coat, dashed out and bumped into the agent in the lobby. He dropped a brown attaché case which bore the initials "L.R." in brass letters, picked it up, apologized and asked whether the other man had just been passed by an American. The American, he said, had left his attaché case at the embassy. Receiving the answer "no," the man hurried out into the street and, holding the case in front of him, looked up and down the pavement, then returned to the lobby and took the lift back to the fourth floor.

The agent in the lobby waited uncertainly. He gave Ruttger five minutes to appear, then himself called the lift, went up to the fourth floor and entered the embassy reception area. Ruttger wasn't there.

He inquired after the men's room, got an answer and followed it. The toilet was empty except for the man in the sheepskin

399

coat who was at the urinal. The agent checked the stall, closed the door, returned to the lift and descended again to street level, He posted himself by the door again and gave Ruttger another fifteen minutes. At the end of that time Ruttger still hadn't appeared.

He pressed the panic button.

At 2:30 p.m. a convoy of three cars rattled down the broken lane to the Siivosen factory. The gate in the chain-link fence was chained and padlocked. The yard behind was snow-covered and empty.

From the first car four men got out. One went to the hood, opened it and took out a pair of heavy cutters, which were applied to the chain until it snapped. The man opened the gate and admitted the cars.

A quarter of an hour later the vehicles left, having established that the building was empty of anything other than some machine tools.

Aboard the *Georg Ots* the master was interrupted in his reading of a newspaper by the entry of the chief engineer. He asked what the problem was and checked his watch. It was 2:30. The chief engineer said that Finnish customs officers were waiting on the quayside with a request to inspect the vessel for contraband goods. The men were allowed on board and shown to the master's cabin. He offered them a drink and explained good-naturedly that he would lodge a protest at the search, to which the Customs officers replied that a search was necessary and that an apology would be forthcoming if nothing was found.

Nothing was found.

Between 2:30 p.m. and 3:00 p.m., according to distance and communication, extra personnel were stationed by the Finnish authorities at crossing points to the Soviet Union: at Raja-Jooseppi, where a road led to Murmansk; at Vartius, where road and rail crossed to Kostamuksa; at Imatra, where there was a short railway link; at Vainikkala, which was the checkpoint for the Moscow and Leningrad trains; and at Vaalimaa, where the main highway handled traffic to Vyborg.

Simultaneously, further watch was placed on airports and harbors throughout Finland.

34

For a few minutes Kirov let himself doze. It was a trick he had developed to handle stress: let sleep wash ideas through his mind. Cold recognition of stress was halfway to its resolution. Kirov picked over the spare bones of his own character with the same thoroughness that he dissected others. In his case no more than any other did he assume that his motives were wholly rational; but he could convert that irrationality into an engine to drive at his goal.

So he considered again his tactics. By them he had brought the Americans down on his head, unless they had already known before Ruttger told them. He had assumed that they had, because it was prudent to make that assumption; or because he had allowed himself to fall victim to the fear and paranoia that dogs illegal operations; or because he needed to heighten the tension and risk the better to demonstrate his own brilliance.

He even considered the possibility that he had designed the operation to fail so that he could be punished for some obscure and unrelated guilt. This view he eventually discounted, though it haunted him. He watched others and himself, and sometimes it seemed that he was a visitor, a spy from some dark country of the mind where only the guilty could live; a country to which no farewells could be made.

As Valchev shook his shoulder he stirred and glanced at his watch. It was three o'clock; night was already around them.

"We've lost track of Ruttger. So have the Americans. Somewhere in the British Embassy building he managed to give everybody the slip. He's on his own now."

Kirov nodded. He asked for coffee, stood up, stretched his legs and looked through the window. The repainting of the containers was complete. It was cold, and he wrapped his coat around him.

"The Finns have raided Siivosen. They've also done a search of the *Georg Ots*," said Valchev. "I told you that we shouldn't have run this operation through Finland. They're very careful about their neutrality. Sweden would have been better. The authorities will probably tighten up the frontiers, try to box us in."

"Probably. How is George Twist?"

"Twist? I think he's OK. Sleeping, according to Lucas."

"Sleeping, yes, he would."

Kirov looked down at the containers. They were connected to their tractor units.

"I want those dispersed," he said. "Until tonight. Get them out of here."

"Why?"

"They were moved out of Lauttasaari in their original colors. We must assume that their route will be traced and that this place will also be raided. See to it."

He returned to the window and examined the shop-floor again. One of the drivers was lounging by his cab, reading. The other three were kicking a ball around, banging it off the echoing walls like gunshots. They had also adjusted to tension, to the long waits before action.

Lou Ruttger waited. He stood at the urinal, where the light had failed, and counted the minutes until he was safe, except that safety could only exist in his head. He took off the sheepskin coat that had covered him in the dimness and walked back to the reception area where he gave it to the owner and got possession of his case again.

"You took your time," said the stranger.

"Here are your twenty dollars."

"Nice doing business with you." The stranger was gap-toothed and pallid. He probably paid his way on his travels by selling blood.

Ruttger returned to the urinal and locked himself in the stall. He checked his watch and sat down. He would wait the Russians out, assuming that they were watching him, as to which he had no idea.

How did you tell? How long would they wait?

In the gathering darkness he alleviated his boredom by remembering birthdays: his own, Nancy's, the children's; George's wedding anniversary, when he had forgotten to send a card. He wondered what sort of car to buy next and where to take a holiday when this was all over. He even thought of the Russians. George had mentioned millions of people who were threatened by whatever disaster the Soviets had engineered. He tried to picture them, but he couldn't get them to seem real, probably because they weren't.

An hour later he descended to the street and stepped out into the shops and the streetlights of Uudenmaankatu. No one was following him.

George, too, awoke to darkness — in his hotel room, he guessed, though his memory was uncertain.

"How long have I been asleep? What time is it?"

"Four o'clock," said Neville Lucas from somewhere in the shadows.

"Morning? Afternoon?"

"Afternoon."

"I don't remember anything since breakfast. I've been asleep all that time?"

"You've been knocked about a bit. You should take it easy," said Lucas kindly.

"Have I slept through it all? Have the goods been shipped?"

"Not yet."

Lucas turned on the light and sat blinking.

"A few hours still to go," he commented, and yawned, then smacked his lips and stretched himself. "Feeling a bit tired myself. What do you want to do, George? Fancy a game of cards?"

"I'm hungry."

"There are some sandwiches on the table. Cards? Three-card brag?"

George shook himself into an upright position and let the room swim around for a bit since that was what it seemed inclined to do.

He remembered Lucas and answered, "Cards? Why not?"

While George doused his head in cold water, Lucas laid out the sandwiches and dealt a hand. He heard Lucas calling, "I hope you don't mind playing for rubles. I'm a bit short of the other stuff."

"Whatever you like." George dried himself, returned to the bedroom and briefly scanned his cards.

"Two rubles," said Lucas. "By the way, I've got to leave in an hour or so. A few things to do."

"I'll see your hand. Finnmarks or sterling OK? So you're going to see a man about a dog. What do I do?"

"Sterling is all right. A pair of kings." Lucas laid his cards down and went on wistfully: " 'Going to see a man about a dog'—I haven't heard that expression in years. Looks like I win." He scooped up the cards, and redealt. "You just stay here and wait for a call. And, George, don't do anything silly, will you? Some of Anton's boys are hanging around this place, and they can be very bad-tempered."

They played another few hands, ate the sandwiches, had a couple of drinks. Lucas asked conversationally, "What will Lou Ruttger do now? The embassy people didn't believe him. He's roaming about out there on his own."

George stopped with his hand frozen on the down-turned cards. Lucas's expression was inconsequential, as if he didn't care about the answer. He pushed a handful of small Russian coins into the pot and clucked over the cards he held. He took his winnings in sterling and paid his losses in rubles.

"I suppose he'll try to stop the containers from being moved. I don't know. He's turned into a hero. He's a man of principle."

"Is he? Pity. Ace high." Lucas snapped the cards. "I'm not a man of principle myself; well, I wouldn't be, would I? Used to be, though." He paused. "Pity about Lou."

He took a car. He had never thought before how easy it was. There was a parking lot in the jumble of side streets west of Mannerheimintie somewhere near the bus station. It was an old Renault, but when he started the engine it sounded sweet enough.

There was just one more thing to do.

From his case he took two empty bottles and a length of plastic tube. He went to the back of the car and unscrewed the gas cap, and using the tube he siphoned off gasoline into the bottles. He unfastened his coat, pausing for a second as the cold air struck his chest; then he pulled out the tail of his shirt and tore off two strips, which he fitted into the necks of the bottles. He placed the bottles carefully on the floor of the car by the front passenger seat and wedged them with his case. He placed his cigarette lighter on the dashboard.

As Neville Lucas was putting on his coat to leave, George said, "I keep thinking that somewhere in all of this we forgot about Sokolskoye. I have to keep telling myself that we're trying to save human lives."

"That's the ticket; just bear the human side in mind." Lucas stood in the dim light, looking absurd in his duffel coat, his fingers fumbling over the wooden toggles.

George asked, "Is it true? About Sokolskoye?" He had believed it once. He had worked it out rationally from the data, and then Irina Terekhova had told him. That ought to have been enough, but it wasn't. Certainty was like love; it faded without renewal, and as time went on he longed for both with ever greater intensity.

Lucas hesitated and sighed.

"Search me, George. We never know, do we? Only what they tell us. But you have to believe in something. I think it's true. We'll look bloody daft if it isn't."

Kirov closed the door on the empty warehouse at Espoo and pocketed the key. The Finnish police hadn't raided the place; obviously they hadn't tracked the movement of the trucks. Not that it mattered now. He had assessed the risk, and it hadn't happened. Not all his assumptions had proved true. Nor had all his plans worked.

In the dark interior of the car Valchev said, "The latest reports say that the Finnish authorities have stepped up border checks everywhere. They have the *Georg Ots* buttoned up tight. We have only one shot to get the goods out of the country in time. For all our sakes, I hope it works."

Kirov didn't answer. He checked the dashboard clock and saw that it was midnight. The streets were silent under the mute snow.

"I left my heart in San Francisco," Lou Ruttger sang to himself in the quiet of the car, and a few other songs as well, but he could never remember a complete verse. From time to time he glanced at his watch. George had still not emerged from the Hotel Vaakuna, and maybe he never would; maybe they had taken him out by some other route; maybe he couldn't lead Lou to the spot where the containers were stashed until they were to be moved. He couldn't be sure of the facts and he was lonely.

George slept, woke, slept, ate when he could. His actions were unrelated to time; it no longer seemed to have anything to do with him. He read a few pages of a novel and did the crossword from an out-of-date newspaper. He stalked about his room, examining the bric-a-brac as if there were some mystery in the way hotels were put together. Like why was the leading edge of the toilet paper folded every day into a triangular point? Who told hotels that anybody cared?

He tried to telephone Lillian, but the lines were engaged.

He was awake when the call came, sitting in the darkness by a pile of cigarette butts and the discarded newspaper. He scrabbled after the receiver, dropped it, swore and finally got the it to his ear. It was Anton.

"We're ready, George."

Ready for what?

"I want you to leave the hotel, find a callbox and telephone the emergency number."

George called out, "Anton! Anton!" and found that the line was dead and there was nothing to do but obey.

He put on his coat, and locked the door behind him. In the empty corridor of the silent hotel he realized how alone he was and wondered how he had ever got there. At what point had he really made his decision?

The square was a white expanse of fresh snow, leper-pale under night clouds. A police wagon cruised by on a mission of mercy, hunting out drunks who would freeze in the bitter cold. The air creaked to his footfalls, and somewhere a siren issued laments.

He found a telephone and made his call. The tone rang only once before the call was picked up and Anton's breathless voice was sounding his name.

"I'm here, Tony."

"Good — good." A voice so stressed that you could break the words into pieces.

"What do you want me to do?"

"It's time for you to join us, George."

"Yes, OK, I suppose. Where do I have to go?"

"Suomenlinna."

Snap. George had a picture of himself and Jim Evans by the waterside at Kulosaari, staring across the fjord at the distant lights of the islands.

"George?"

"Suomenlinna!" George didn't believe it. "It's two o'clock in the morning and the place is in the middle of the bloody sea!"

Anton laughed with brutal abruptness.

"Be brave, George! Remember the Winter Way!"

35

Suomenlinna. George had been there once before, more years
ago than he cared to think about. It had been summer, the
ferryboat from the terminal by Kaupatorri had been packed
with tourists wanting to see the islands and maybe bathe from
the rocks and the narrow sand; but there was no bathing for
George: he had a few hours free during some negotiation or
other, and he trod the gravel paths in the wake of the guide, his
parka pulled close about him against the wind and his hand
gripping a case full of business papers. He remembered some
weatherboard cottages, a decrepit barrack block built of brick,
and a ruined dry dock inside a meandering circuit of old stone
fortifications which had been reinforced with mounds of earth.
That and the church with its green dome and lantern, and its
fence of heavy cable slung between cannon barrels, which the
Russians had built. And someone had pointed out the Winter
Way. It had seemed a crazy route for anyone to use.

But that was in the past: now he was driving slowly through
the night along Eteläranta, where a Soviet vessel, the *Georg Ots,*
was moored and the quayside was dotted with lights and police
cars and a Soviet embassy limousine with a bunch of excited
officials standing by it waving their arms. By the Olympia
terminal he took the left-hand fork to follow the sea along
Ehrenströmintie, and the city lights dropped away. On his right,
the ground rose to the quiet streets of the embassy quarter. On
his left, the sea was a faint sheen of ice broken by a scatter of
rocks and islets, and somewhere the black slash of the shipping

lane.

The Winter Way. He was supposed to drive on it.

The road became an embankment bordered by a low sea-wall. He could see the dark mass of Suomenlinna now, a mile offshore across the frozen fjord, maybe less if you wanted to believe that. The embankment ended and there was another of the beer gardens in which the Finns like to while their fleeting summer, the Café Ursula, shut and battened for the season against the elements. He stopped the car and got out to investigate.

The pavilion was silent, the beer garden lay under a thin cover of snow. Across the road was a place to leave cars and the entrance to a public park. Further along on the seaward side a short stretch of turf had been swept clear of snow by the wind. Beyond the turf stood a few trees, and beyond the trees a small jetty jutted out into the ice.

He walked over to the jetty; it was a low line of stone with a wooden handrail, ending in a square landing stage. He paced its length, now looking across the fjord to the islands, then at the ice just a few feet below him. You could drive a tank on to that ice, Anton assured him. And Anton's mother wouldn't let him tell lies.

He turned back. He scanned the shoreline and saw that beyond the jetty the sea wall ran out, and, instead, the ground sloped away from the road across a flat granite shelf and a narrow strand of gravel easy enough to drive a car over if you cared to take the chance. If you cared to take a chance — which wasn't his style where physical risk was concerned. But he had found the beginning of the Winter Way and the only thing now was to take it. He returned to the car.

Lou Ruttger had no difficulty following George. The Englishman took no precautions, or perhaps there was none worth taking in the drive from his hotel through the empty nighttime streets. The blind led the blind, just as it had been from the

410

very beginning. It suited Lou's cruel mood.

At first he thought George was going to a rendezvous with the Soviet ship that still lay at anchor in the South Harbor. He didn't know the names of the streets, but the direction was clear enough: toward the quayside. But then, with the *Georg Ots* in view, the other car carried on along the waterside boulevard, heading south. He couldn't help a flicker of excitement. George had to be leading him to the containers and the embargoed equipment.

They cruised slowly. He guessed the other man was looking for something, but he didn't know what. He tried to recall what he had seen on the maps and had an idea that the road curved around a stumpy promontory and then bent backward and north through a dockyard area towards the bridges, taking the highway across the neck of the Seurasaarenselkä fjord to the island of Lauttasaari. So maybe George was heading for the Siivosen warehouse, or maybe there was another Russian freighter in one of the southwestern docks.

But why so slow? Why now, when the docks had to be a couple of miles away and Lauttasaari even further? There was nothing along this stretch except a small suburb of old-fashioned houses up the hill on one side of the highway and the sea on the other. It made no sense!

And then George stopped.

Lou didn't have time to do anything about it without the risk of attracting attention. He let the car glide past and then, in a couple of hundred yards where the road made a shallow bend, he pulled up near an emergency telephone and switched off the lights. For a few moments he sat in the darkness listening to the wind play tunes over the car and then got out.

The wind came in sharp and bitter gusts across the sea, blowing fine particles of snow. Looking back along the road, he took his bearings. Close by on his right was a small island. Beyond it an open plain of ice dotted with low flat rocks. Then a larger island mass, with buildings and a bright pinpoint. In the direction he had come from the stub of a pier with a chain of lamps on it obtruded into the ice, and behind the pier and a line of small trees a low building formed a dim shape veiled by the lamps.

And that was all. There was no car, no George.

With nowhere to go, George had vanished from the road.

The car swayed and heaved over the rock. In the headlights George could see that the strip of gravel was scored with deep wheel marks from some heavy vehicle that had been there before him. He thought maybe Anton was right: it was going to be OK. He let the clutch out, and the car crept forward on to the ice and out across the fjord.

Slow—he couldn't believe how slow it was, his nerves racing but his body responding with small, deliberate movements. Steadily forward to the creaks and crepitations of the ice and the buffets of wind that forced him to grip the steering wheel till his fingers felt numb.

He dimmed the lights to reduce the glare from the powdered snow that was scoured off the sea by the wind. It stopped the glare, but without lights he saw only by the febrile moon in a sky of scudding cloud. On his right an island was stamped black on black against the horizon. Directly ahead, too small and too close to be Suomenlinna, was another low island with its western shore broken by a line of jetties. He bore left, steering by the beacon on the church. In the windblown snow it flickered like starlight.

Now he was closer, isolated without shelter on the open ice sheet. On the nearer islands of the Suomenlinna group, details were picked out by the moonlight. He could identify at the water's edge the long block of the naval school and, to its right, the inlet that marked the narrow channel between Pikku Mutasaari and its neighbor. Flanking the channel entrance was a headland in the form of a whale-shaped hump. George steered slowly toward it.

The headland came nearer, lying squat on his right as he

412

reached the mouth of the channel. He could see now that the mound was artificial; the designers of the fortress had piled earth to cover a magazine or armory; the side looking on to the channel was faced with concrete arches, now bricked up, and a disused chimney stuck out of the ground like an obelisk. Ahead of him a flimsy-looking bridge linked the two islands, and on his left loomed more darkened buildings of the naval school. He looked for a place to land.

The lamps on the bridge reflected faintly from the ice and threw some light on the shore. On the left, just this side of the bridge, it seemed to George that the ground sloped easily away from the water and there was something lying on the snow and gravel that might have been a ramp. He edged in that direction and by degrees felt the wheels of the car bite on to solid earth. He was ashore.

He got out of the car. He found himself on a small patch of rough ground by the brick gable of a two-story building. To his left was a square bordered on three sides by more old buildings and a few birch trees streaked white by moonlight. To his right a narrow unmade road ran away from the bridge and out of sight around a corner. There was no sound except the wind and the blood pounding in his ears.

Where now? What time was it? He looked at his watch but it was too dark to see. He took a few steps towards the bridge and saw a figure standing by the nearest lamp. It was Neville Lucas, muffled in a scarf and with the hood of his ancient coat pulled up.

"Hello, George. Glad you could make it."

"Never again. That drive just scared the shit out of me." George heard his own nervous bad temper and moderated it. He thought of lighting a cigarette, but in this wind it would be impossible. Instead he asked, "What are we doing here, Neville?"

"All in good time," said Lucas. "By the way, were you followed?"

"Buggered if I know. That's your game, isn't it?"

413

"Of course." Lucas answered lightly as if it didn't matter. Then, "Well, we'd better get this show on the road."

He set off across the bridge, ambling in his big easy way with George in tow. The road ended shortly at another square with stuccoed buildings looking half-ruined in the darkness. Lucas turned right, following a path that ran parallel with the channel, so that George could look back and see across the narrow strip of ice his car parked on the further island. The going was easy: there were lamps along one side of the lane and a few small cottages of yellow board: the last one with the frozen remains of a garden. On their right rose the whale-backed hump by which he had steered to the channel. There were two men on top of it, black against the sky.

The lane ran out, and a few yards of steep sandy path led up to the crest of the mound. On this exposed high ground the wind blew fiercely, but from the top there was a view across the mile of ice that separated Suomenlinna from the city over the only approach, the Winter Way. On the leeward side a stunted tree clung to the slope, and the two men that George had seen were waiting there.

Kirov glanced in the Englishman's direction as the group crouched in the shelter of the tree. George was inexplicably glad he was there.

"We have a problem," Kirov said neutrally as if discussing some point of theory. "The American CIA and the Finnish authorities know that we intend to ship embargoed goods out of the country. At the moment all exits are effectively closed to us, and the Americans are pressuring the Finns to search for the trucks and containers. The premises at Lauttasaari have been raided, and the latest report is that a second holding point we had arranged at Espoo has also been discovered."

"Can't you just stash the stuff in the forest somewhere until this all blows over?"

"You are forgetting about Sokolskoye. Already we are at our deadline if we are to deliver the equipment and erect it in time to clean the lake before spring." Kirov paused and looked

414

George in the eyes. "You do see, don't you, George? We simply *have* to move the equipment within the next twenty-four hours."

"Sure," George agreed, and wondered why Peter was trying to persuade him. Then it occurred to him that Kirov was enlisting his support to do something that George would be unable to live with.

Not that! He wanted to cry out, but he knew now that killing had always been implicit.

Kirov stood up. Valchev, squatting next to him, passed him a pair of night glasses. He made his way to the top of the mound. George followed him and found the Russian with his back to the lights of the city staring thoughtfully down into the dark cove formed behind the headland. George stared with him, but the blackness hid everything and the wind filled his eyes with freezing tears.

"What am I looking for?" he shouted.

Kirov held out the glasses and pointed into the shadows.

"There! There!" he yelled above the gale.

George put the glasses to his eyes and in the glaucous light tried to make out shapes on the ice. At first he could recognize nothing, then gradually he focused on some dim rectangular blocks and the outline of two cabs.

"Oh, Jesus," he murmured; then, louder: "It's here. You brought the bloody equipment here!"

"Where else in Helsinki could be safer?" Kirov asked. He took the night glasses back and began the steep clamber down to the shelter of the tree. Valchev was signaling.

They reached the tree. Valchev was pointing towards the city. "There was a flash of light out there," he said.

Kirov lifted the night glasses and scanned the apparently empty sea. He nodded and handed the glasses to George.

"It seems you were followed," he commented laconically.

George hesitated, then looked. His gaze swept across the open fjord, where all seemed still except the shifting eddies of snow. He wiped his eyes and looked again, and out of the featureless seascape an object slowly resolved itself. There was a car waiting on the ice.

"Lou?" he asked in disbelief. He let the glasses fall and turned to the others. He found a gun pointing at his head.

"For your own good, George," said Neville Lucas calmly. "Nothing personal. Just to stop any foolishness."

Lou Ruttger had lost sight of the other car. George had a lead on him and was driving without lights, and somewhere against the black backdrop of the islands he had disappeared. So Lou had stopped. He was afraid. His whole body was coursed by fear so that he had to lock his muscles rigid to avoid collapse. He would have run away if he could have thought to run away, but fear had its own logic that trapped him like an animal caught by the lights of a car. Then, too, he was trapped by the blind anger of a man who sees the world innocently.

He nudged the car forward. His fear was demanding: how far did the ice stretch? Surely it didn't run on forever; the sea had to begin somewhere! Did it have thin spots that would swallow the car without a second's warning? Was that what had happened to George?

He tried the lights for a second and saw that the ice appeared unbroken as far as the islands. He waited a few more moments and then drove on again slowly.

The lights came as a cluster spreading from a black point on the islands' shore. There was no sound to accompany them above the whistling of the wind, so that from the first they had an unreal quality like some glitter on the ice caused by a freak of the moon; but then the cluster broke into pairs and the bright points became sweeping beams of light, and what had been an illusion became three cars fanning out across his path. Then with equal suddenness the lights went out and he was alone again with the wind and his eyes swimming with afterimages. He slammed on the brakes and sat for a second with his hands frozen in a sweat over the steering wheel.

Where were they? He could see no light except the beacon on

top of the church; the moon was hidden by cloud. Could they see him? He supposed not; then, on reflection, he realized that they must have been able to see him to have prepared this reception. The drivers had to have night glasses or some other gadget. They could see him, but he was blind—damn it, he was blind!

Flash! A pair of headlights came on only yards away on his left flank. He stamped his foot on the accelerator and instinctively steered away to the right. He caught a glimpse of the other car as it skirted his rear, and then the lights went out again. He braked again, and the car slid to a halt. He felt urine leaking down his leg with fear, but in his insanity it did not affect his determination. What now?

He listened to the thrum of the engine—what now?—what now?—the howl of the wind. More lights, still on his left, suddenly blazing out of the darkness. This time he was quicker, he hammered the power, and the engine screamed as he forced the car, again right, careening blindly, this time longer and further so that when he finally stopped he had traveled perhaps half a mile.

Another lull. He tried to get his bearings from the shapes on the horizon but they meant nothing. He searched for the beacon and found a point of light to his left rear, which meant that he was running parallel with instead of towards the islands where George had vanished. Why were they waiting?

He remembered his own lights. He should have used them before. His hand reached out for the switch, touched it, pulled back. The reason for the lull had come to him.

Although he could not see them, he knew now that there was only one man in each of the cars, armed with a pair of image-intensifying binoculars, which was how Lou was being located. But the driver also had to steer on the ice as well as see, and that required both hands. . . . Lou didn't have time to complete the thought. This time two cars were coming at him front and right and he was caught in the crosspoint of their headlights.

He gave the wheels power and yanked the car into a spin to

face the vehicle that had come from his right. He gave his own lights a second of brightness to blind and confuse his opponent and veered left to pass the other car side by side. He put another hundred yards between them and slowed to a crawl, but this time he didn't stop.

So maybe he was blind, but at best they were one-eyed. When he was stationary they could take a line on him with the glasses and then home in blindly. But when he moved they couldn't rely on their visual fix and were effectively as sightless as he was. If he kept going and maneuvered a little, he could get some way toward evening out the odds. He had to give it a try.

For a minute or so he put the car into a slow wide circle. In the dark emptiness of the ice he had no close points of reference, so that as the glow of the city and the beacon on the church at Suomenlinna rotated at the edge of his vision he could half-believe that the world was moving around him and he had become the one fixed center of things. He wanted to believe that; he wanted to give in to the hypnosis of movement, because the illusion of himself as the fixed point of the universe supported his crumbling sense of moral stability. He didn't want to think of George's arguments and consider whether they were right. He preferred the good guys and the bad guys to be who they had always been without ambiguity and moral relativism, because if you lived by proof and argument instead of by rules there was always doubt.

A set of headlights flashed—a few seconds and then another. They were making random attempts to find him. The wind faded for a second and he heard an engine close by. Then the crazy carousel in the darkness continued. Crazy. How had he got there? Why? He looked for some sense in his response and began to see that the craziness had its own inner logic, that it all flowed from that moment when George had offered him a deal and he had suppressed his suspicions and accepted. This was all part of the deal, but the bits that weren't spelt out, the Mephistopheles pact. Somehow he and George had agreed to all this!

He let the car crawl another circuit. Then by degrees he sensed a change. Although he had not consciously altered his course, with each turn of the circle his position was drifting. It was an effect of the pursuit: each time he caught sight of one of the other cars — near or not — his instincts caused him to edge away, and this animal recoil was driving him towards an island that even in the darkness was marked by the rounded silhouette of a headland.

His reaction was more fear, another wave of cold panic that seemed to peel and loosen his skin so that it hung on him like a damp garment. From all the causes for fear he picked one to torture his mind: closer to the island the chance of wrecking his car on some invisible rock would increase. Stupid! He didn't need the car. It could be sacrificed to find the Sep Tech equipment; and if it was anywhere in this wilderness it had to be on one of the islands where George had been heading. If he couldn't get ashore in the car, he could ditch it and make his way on foot. Instead of avoiding the island he was now so close to, he should be aiming for it.

He let the next circuit take him closer to the headland, but at one glance he distrusted its steep sides for a climb in the dark. He considered following the line of the shore to the seaward side of Suomenlinna, guessing that without sight of him his pursuers would have no reason to follow. But his uncertainty as to the limits of the ice restrained him, and with the mass of the islands between himself and the city he would lose the one clearly visible point by which he took his bearings. The church wasn't enough; even this far from the headland he had lost sight of it. And the darkness frightened him. Without the lights of Helsinki his uncertain certainty of the reality of this madness would fail. He would be driving in some darkness of the mind.

He looked for shelter. To the right of the headland he thought he could make out a cove, and with the high ground covering his line of approach there was a chance he would be masked from the other cars and could risk his lights briefly to search out a beach or a path leading from the shore. He turned the wheel and drove slowly in that direction.

Slowly — he felt like a man putting his hand to the flame — the car crawling at barely walking pace; but the whole sequence from his first driving on to the ice had been like a slow-motion shot, and in the run for his life he had probably not driven faster than ten miles an hour in the darkness. He tucked into the headland as near as he dared, and as it cut off the distant glow of the city he held his breath and switched on the head-lights.

There were two trucks parked on the ice.

The cry that rose in his throat was tinged with disbelief. On the ice, goddammit! Then suddenly he was bathed in light. He turned and look into the dazzle of his enemy, a single car lying a hundred yards behind him at the entrance to the cove. They had found him.

There was no point in hiding now. He kept the lights on, slipped the clutch and rolled softly forward. The other driver hesitated then followed a parallel course. Lou reached into the well on the passenger side and fumbled after an object stashed there. His fingers fastened round the neck of a bottle. He picked it up, still trying to manage the steering. The other car was keeping its distance; a second had joined it, and the lights of both illuminated the cove. His heart raced as he struggled to set a flame to the ragged wick hanging from the neck of the bottle. The third car appeared.

What were they waiting for? He did a slow round of the two wagons. They were fully visible now, pale specters as the wind stirred up the snow and ice particles. He saw movement among the other cars and quickly he pushed open the door of his own vehicle and threw the gas bomb at the nearest truck. It glanced off the side of the cab and then skittered across the ice until it erupted in flame. But too far!

Too far. The flames were useless. The truck was untouched. He yanked at the wheel, threw the car into a spin, then closed again.

Now the brightness was glaring; car lights seemed to be everywhere; a large stretch of ice was blazing with gasoline; the air itself picked up and reflected the light. And there were men; he saw two or three near the other cars. They had guns and were trying to aim at him as his car careened in a wild ring around the trucks. Maybe they were firing, but he couldn't tell above the wind, the noise of the engine and the flames. He threw the other gas bomb.

Nothing.

Then an explosion and one of the trucks went up in a mass of flame that threw burning debris in parabolas across the cove. Cascades of fire poured from the mound of wreckage and subsidiary fires sprang up like demons across the ice. The heat came as an intense blast that scorched his face. His enemies had thrown themselves to the ground.

The car jerked insanely between the fires as Lou wrestled to avoid them. In the fierce light he could barely see. He knew only that there was one truck still intact and that he lacked the means to destroy it. But in a strange way that failure did not trouble him: it was swamped by his excitement, his sense of power. Without reason he knew that he would succeed because the narrow world of the cove which he had turned into a species of hell was the world of his manifest power.

Around, he drove around in crazy circles made crazier by the fires and the ice. His skin felt on fire from the heat and from the furious working of his body. He was terrified. He was elated. His thoughts and emotions were sweeping through him like the flames so that his own flesh felt about to explode. What now? Come and get me! I'm a madman! Come and get me!

In a split second of inspiration he flung the car door open and threw himself on to the ice while the vehicle, now out of control, sheered off and skidded for the shore. He felt the thump of his body hitting the cold ice, but no pain. He lay flat and for a moment glimpsed the silhouettes of men running towards his abandoned car. He got to his feet and made a dash for the remaining truck.

The cab door was unlocked. Out on the ice, in the middle of the night, nobody had taken any trouble to disable it, and the engine fired first time. The three Russians heard it, they stopped short in their tracks, hesitated and then ran duck-legged over the glassy surface in the direction of their cars. They scattered and went flying and gliding on their bellies as Lou Ruttger drove through the middle of them.

He had driven a truck before, but never anything of this size and weight. He found the steering erratic, but maybe that was the ice, and in any case he didn't care: he was riding high in the cab and his body was running on adrenaline so that his fear was swamped by excitement and he knew he was going to win. He would prove he was right; he would show them the goddamn truck!

He turned left without thinking as the truck swept out of the cover for the open fjord. His hands fumbled for the lights and couldn't find the switch, but maybe lights were a bad idea; and for now he could see a little way: there were breaks in the cloud and the ice was striped with bands of moonlight. But somewhere he had lost the city.

The cars appeared, a swarm of lights on his right. He swung leftwards, keeping an eye out for the shoreline, but the island ran out here in another headland and he could keep going in this direction and track the line of the rocks. His pursuers fell away to his rear.

The city—where the hell was the city? The moon was covered again and the sea lay blackly everywhere about except to his left where he could still make out the shore. He tried to relive his movements from his last bearings and guessed that he had taken a route to the seaward side of Suomenlinna. Not to worry. Stick close to the shore. Pray for the moon. How far did the islands stretch? How fast was he going?

The blackness now seemed total. Nothing in his vision said he was moving, but the cab vibrated and the engine roared. He could see nothing but his past reflected in the mirror, a faint glow over the furthest reach of the islands from the fire that was

422

still raging in the cove, the small group of headlights following his tail. They were gaining on him, but if they could risk the speed so could he. He gave the engine more power. Then light—faint but to him dazzling—light without form that created its own shapes instead of illuminating others. The bright, shapeless mass of Helsinki. The moon emerging from a ragged edge of cloud. The ice, now throwing back reflections and patches of darkness.

With the sight of the city he uttered a cry but heard it die on his lips. The black slash across his path was not some trick of vision but the cold waters of the sea lane. He hit the brakes and the steering, but the truck would not respond. It plowed on through the debris around the trough, breaking up the fragile floes edging the water. Something was screaming—the truck?—his own voice?—he couldn't tell. Broken shards of ice smacked into the cab. The windshield was starred and fractured by a hail of ice. Everything was turning and swaying crazily.

He reached for the door, fighting against the violent movements that were throwing him about. But in the chaos everything was clear to him. He knew that he was going to get out of the cab alive.

He knew it with the same heroic certainty when the sea swallowed up the truck.

The heat scorched his face, even now after the explosion when the initial force was spent and there was only wreckage and twisted metal blazing in the cove and a pall of smoke and steam rising from the melting ice. But the heat didn't stop him looking; the ruination of everything had its own fascination, and this destruction had action, noise and color, unlike the ignored drift of his own life toward entropy and apathy. So he watched the flickering light-show until he felt Neville Lucas's hand on his shoulder and heard his voice saying: "Come on, George. It's all finished. Time to go."

"But Lou . . ."

"Dead, old chap. Drove into the water with all the stuff. Know how you feel. Bloody shame."

"Then it's over. The equipment is all destroyed. We've failed."

"Yes. Pity about that." Lucas forced him to turn round, and in his peaceable way urged, "Got to go, George, eh? No point in hanging about." Recognizing George's distress, he added bizarrely, "All you need is a good night's sleep."

"But we failed!"

"You can't win them all. Be a good chap. We can't stick around here, really we can't; you must see that."

He could see Kirov now, that cold impassive presence, and Valchev hopping about excitedly and pointing across the ice to the mainland. There was a string of moving lights on the road by the Café Ursula. Cars turning on to the Winter Way.

"Someone must have been keeping an eye on Ruttger," said Lucas. "Americans, I should think, or possibly the Finns. Sorry to rush you." He was struggling to stuff a gun clumsily into his belt, and George remembered that it had been held at him to stop his taking any action. Now Lucas seemed embarrassed by it, as if it were a prop for an out-of-character part. George allowed himself to he led away.

They scrambled down from the mound and on to the path towards the bridge, Valchev and Lucas holding him by the arms to force the pace. People were stirring in the buildings, lights were going on, but so far no one had appeared. A matter of time. Everything had happened so quickly, quicker than George had imagined. He saw the crumbling building by the landing point and a car parked on the narrow shelf of dirt with the engine running, and there were noises, doors banging, feet on the gravel; someone pushing him in the back, and he was shoved into the car.

Valchev drove—Anton, who had once seemed like a clumsy kid but who was now assured. He drove fast and without lights, which made no difference to him. The car tore out of the channel, and Valchev spun it into a right-hand turn across the long face of Suomenlinna. And in the distance, blocking their exit along the Winter Way, the group of cars descending from the Café Ursula moved tentatively across the ice towards them.

George shook himself out of his thoughts. He asked, "How do we get out of here?" The question was directed at Kirov, who was sitting in the front passenger seat, but Kirov didn't answer. He sat riveted in silence like a machine. And George knew that that was how it was: Peter wasn't human; he was a machine for taking real human beings apart and rearranging them to the required specifics.

"How do we get out of here?" he repeated to Lucas.

"There are ways," said Lucas, but he was tight-lipped and drawn. The cars moving after them had formed a cordon across the ice. Their own car was probably invisible for the moment, but there was no route back to the mainland.

Valchev was still forcing the car blindly across the ice, responding only to curt instrucitons whispered by Kirov. George wanted to shout out: the course they were taking was insane; they were going to finish up in the sea!

Like Lou.

"Peter, you bastard! You killed Lou!" George rose out of his seat. There were tears in his eyes. Lucas forced him down again.

"Calm down," Lucas murmured. "He was a casualty, George, not a victim. It's not the same thing. Remember, we were in the right—*you* were in the right. Remember Sokolskoye."

"But we failed, Neville! The equipment is burned out or at the bottom of the sea! Their bloody disaster is going to happen because everything is fucked up!"

"True," said Lucas quietly, and George could see that Neville didn't care. And maybe he was right. Sokolskoye in all its enormity was just a drop in the inexhaustible pool of human suffering, a well of pain so vast and deep that it could be conceived only abstractly. To become engaged by that suffering was fatal. It had to be put away, reduced to the scale of the charity collection plate, demanding only the small change of our emotions. Which was where George had failed. He had responded to the humanity of a woman and shed the last tatters of his masculine detachment. And now he suffered because Irina Terekhova suffered, and for him Sokolskoye had become real.

They drove on. The Café Ursula grew more remote. Valchev switched on the headlights, and the sea lane became visible as a cruel gash in the purity of the ice. He swung the car over so that the lights swept over that black freezing expanse. He drove parallel to the sea lane like an animal desperately avoiding a trap. Searching for a way out.

Nothing.

Behind them a gathering of lights closing on them. They had been seen, and the hunters were on their trail. Nothing. Valchev jabbering away in Russian. Kirov stone-faced, calm.

"Fancy a toffee?" said Lucas, offering one of his little packets. His eyes looked soulless, empty, but his face contrived to keep his peculiar sweetness of expression. "Bit of a poser this, eh, George? I hope there isn't going to be any unpleasantness."

Nothing. Valchev turned the car in a spray of ice and made a pass back along the sea lane in the other direction. The other cars were so close that the lights could be broken down into individual vehicles.

"Now!" Kirov yelled.

George couldn't see what was happening, but the car was braking, sliding across the ice, skidding madly. The doors were thrown open and there was shouting and he was outside with the wind blowing cold knives at his face. And he was running, he didn't know why or where, but Lucas was with him, shouting, "Come on, George! Come on, man!" and he was running with his breath catching and his heart ready to burst. "Come on, man!"

Then he saw the boat. They were wading through the churned-up ice on the margin of the sea lane. It was moving under their feet. They stumbled, swore, ran. Men in the boat waved and yelled. The ice felt like it would tip them into the water. "Come on! You can do it!" Who was shouting? But he could do it! He could!

426

He felt hands grasping him. He was being dragged. His feet kicked at the last of the ice. His legs trailed in water so cold that it was as if they were amputated. Someone was hauling him aboard and he could see Lucas laughing with relief, but no sound. Just the wind. God, but it was cold, and he couldn't feel or stand.

But it was over. The speedboat was kicked to life and they were shooting down the sea lane. Behind them the line of pursuing cars was stationary on the ice.

36

January 20

He didn't know where they took him. He didn't even remember leaving the boat. Once on board, someone had pushed a bottle into his hand and he had drunk it. Then they were at a villa somewhere in a street with plenty of trees and little paths between the houses where the snow lay packed. He thought he was at Kulosaari, but that was just a name that came into his head, so maybe he wasn't. Yet the house was real enough, but sparse, and dirty inside, in a way that didn't go with the expensive neighborhood. People wrote on the walls and left cigarette burns on the arms of the stuffed chairs and stains on the carpets; and there were bunks in the bedrooms, six to a room, with bare lightbulbs and a smell from the toilet that nobody ever cleaned. George lay on one of the bunks and wondered what was supposed to happen to him next.

Neville Lucas woke him. Neville, standing in his socks and underpants, scratching his belly and beaming.

"Wakey-wakey, rise and shine! How are you feeling? Anything for the head?"

"They killed Lou," George said, coming out of his fitful dreams into a room smelling of bodies, where clothes and cigarette stubs were both dropped on to the floor and someone had covered the window with newspaper.

Lucas offered one of his solemn expressions, that of an apologetic child.

"Let's not be morose, eh?" he suggested helpfully. "It doesn't do to think about the past."

George slid out of the bunk and looked for his clothes. Lucas sat on one of the others and continued dressing.

George asked, "Where are we?"

"It's called a safe house. Well, we couldn't let you go back to your hotel, could we? At any rate, not straight away. Be a good fellow and put your clothes on. I can smell breakfast."

George looked out of the door and saw Kirov pass, but Peter didn't stop or glance in his direction. He thought: I'm all used up. Why don't they kill me? And even that thought didn't trouble him. He slipped into a shirt and pants and went downstairs where there was a group of Russians sitting in their underwear in the kitchen around a wooden table covered with an oilcloth and some cheap zinc bowls. Without being asked, they passed him some coffee and a piece of bread, and one of them offered him a cigarette.

"What happens to me next?" he asked Lucas, who had wandered into the room and taken a seat.

"Nothing to worry about. We have a final piece of business and then it's back to your hotel for you."

"And the authorities? What do I tell them when they come to arrest me?"

"Oh, I don't think they'll do that."

"No?"

"What's their evidence? Nothing links you to the ownership of Siivosen. There's no proof that the imported goods were actually destined for the Soviet Union. There isn't even any evidence of foul play where Lou Ruttger is concerned; he drowned under his own steam, so to speak. In fact the most they have is your hired car found abandoned at Suomenlinna—possibly stolen. All bloody suspicious, I grant you; but not what you would actually call beyond reasonable doubt." Lucas took a piece of bread and dunked it into his coffee. He smiled at the other men and continued amiably, "In any case, I don't think the Finns will be all that concerned to discover the truth. When all's said and done, they were only obliging the Americans. And now they have their own position to consider. The Soviet ambassador has protested about the additional border checks and the search of the *Georg Ots*. Very unfriendly. Not the act of a neutral. As for the Americans—well, you win a few and you lose a few; and as long as the embargoed goods were destroyed they'll be happy. But I'd sell that Sep Tech company, if I were you: the Americans may not be aggressively hostile, but they can be petty and spiteful. More coffee?" he proposed brightly. "So no problem. What do you say, George?"

"We still failed."

Lucas put the coffeepot carefully down. "Yes," he said thoughtfully. "Well, that's a different matter."

It wasn't Kulosaari, it was someplace else. They drove through the western parts of the city by a route that took them by the sea. Suomenlinna looked peaceful in daylight, a jewel in a setting of ice under a bright sky. In summer the tourist guides would tell you that the fortress used to be Russian. Now it was Finnish and in that peculiar Finnish way belonged to nobody.

The *Georg Ots* was gone from the south harbor. Peter Kirov said that the border checks had been lifted. The Sep Tech equipment had been destroyed and the Finns wished to avoid causing a diplomatic incident.

George thought that Kirov sounded calm, too calm, slightly distracted. Thinking about something else. What else was there in Kirov's arid existence? After everything that had happened, he really knew nothing about Kirov except that he had once been involved in something called the Ouspensky Case; and even that was probably a lie. Was he thinking of Lou Ruttger? How did he live with having killed Lou? How did George himself live with it? But here he was. He *had* lived through it, and already the pain was diminishing. Perhaps Lou had been too innocent to live. Someone had said the same about Ronnie Pugh after he was murdered in Lagos. Ronnie was all heart and innocence (Evans said it, and Evans would say anything to be witty: even tell the truth); and even Ronnie's extra wives were like a kid's prank, just something done out of exuberance. He shouldn't have stopped on the airport road to help a woman who was being robbed. Really he shouldn't. George wound down the window of the car and breathed the cold air. He didn't feel too bad.

They were sticking to the sea-road, heading in the direction of Sornäinen. The road signs indicated Sompasaari. Across the fjord George could see islands: Korkesaari, Mustikkamaa, Kulosaari—more islands than you could count or name. He knew the road, Sörnäistenranta; it picked up the highway going east to Porvoo through an industrial zone, past factories and a big modern power station of the kind that wins architectural prizes in Finland. They kept with the signs for Sompasaari and turned right by the power station along the route for the docks, with coal heaps for the power station on one side of the road and then a string of wholesalers' warehouses. The road bent again. On the corner was a bonded compound full of imported cars, then the road ended at a wire fence and a gate blocking off the quay by the highway bridge. And George understood why.

"You were entitled to know," said Kirov. He had been silent, but now he turned and appraised George with the cool stare that George had always thought held something else.

"This is a container terminal," George answered.

"Yes."

George nodded. He looked around, not seeing anything much. There was an East German freighter alongside the quay, a small black-and-white affair, the *Zussow*. There was a regular run between Sompasaari and Rostock.

"I saw four containers at the Siivosen place," he said. There was no reaction. George didn't want to remember that night. "I was out of my mind on the drugs and the beating your boys gave me. What were the containers? Two dummies and two that were the real thing?"

"Yes."

"And the real containers are here? Yes, of course, they are. So we won after all."

431

"We won after all."

"Three cheers for the good guys." George looked at the ship again, then at Kirov. "OK, can we go?"

"In a while. The *Zussow* is about to leave. I wanted you here where I could see you, simply to avoid any last-minute upsets."

"Whatever you say. I'm out of fight, Peter. You win the last trick."

"We both do."

"Sure we do. Just like friends."

George sat and watched the freighter going through the pre-sailing motions. Traffic rumbled overhead on the bridge and some seagulls were making a meal of something. Sunlight caught the red cabs of the dockside cranes. A couple of trucks went in and out by the gate. And George could only think of Lou Ruttger. In the end he had lost his life for nothing. How more innocent could you get?

"You tricked him," George said bitterly.

"Ruttger?"

"You lured him out to Suomenlinna, using me as bait. Why, for God's sake?"

"Because of loyalty and disloyalty," Kirov answered and he looked at George, willing him to understand. "So many people knew or might guess our business: Ruttger, your lawyer Evans, people in your company, other people you don't even know of— and even yourself, George. We could never be sure that we were not betrayed. So we anticipated events and focused attention on two particular containers. The chase at Suomenlinna was designed to lead Ruttger to them. Either he would destroy them or we would destroy them ourselves as long as he was there. It was *necessary*, George."

Necessary. Kirov said it with a sincerity that frightened George more than anything else he had done. Cynicism had its built-in moderation, the desire for self-preservation; but sincerity was the mark of the true extremist. Kirov was terrifying because, though he displayed at times a superficial humanity, there was ultimately nothing he would not do. He had the dark face

432

of innocence because he expected George to understand his motives. George saw it all now and in his revulsion looked for some weapon with which to fight back.

"Was Oleg Ouspensky another case of necessity? he asked. "What did you use against him? How did you get him? Come on, Peter, you can tell your old mate, George!"

He saw pain—Kirov for once in pain. His one bitter victory.

"Come on, Peter, tell me! Tell me!"

He hesitated. Kirov was staring at him with a coldness that could kill. Then he turned away and looked at the *Zussow* and the cranes with their red cabs, and the seagulls making a living from the scraps thrown out by men.

"There's no secret, George," Kirov answered without expression. "I used the same method I used on you."

"And what's that?" George asked, though he had always known.

"I made him care."

Epilogue

February–June

After the affair in Helsinki, the equipment which George Twist had smuggled out of America was transported safely to the Soviet Union by way of East Germany. During February it was erected at Sokolskoye with only the usual hiccups, and throughout March it processed the contaminated water in the Chiraka lake. There was no disaster as a result of the Sokolskoye Incident.

In the middle of February, Techmashimport, the foreign-trade organization acting for the Soviet Union, signed two contracts with Chemconstruct Plc for the supply of two liquefied natural gas plants to the Soviet Union. The down payments were made promptly and all subsequent payments arrived on time.

In May the Soviet Union signed two further contracts for similar plants, and this time the signing was made an opportunity for an official reception to mark an advance in Anglo-Soviet economic cooperation, and in particular the role of Chemconstruct Plc in that achievement. Alasdair Cranbourne, taking credit for his boldness in reopening business relations with the Soviet Union, accompanied George Twist. The British ambassador attended as did Archibald Lansdowne, the commercial counselor. The Russian delegation was large and included Peter Kirov as well as the Minister of Gas and the usual functionaries. The reception was held at the Hotel Peking.

In general the occasion was judged a success. Aside from the speeches, Alasdair Cranbourne's sly charm struck a chord with the Russians. The Minister commented on it. Peter Kirov made a sardonic remark on the same subject as he and George Twist found themselves together for the first time, nursing their drinks and staring, for want of anything better, at the several bowls of fresh fruit presented like jewels, which only the most senior among the Russians would touch.

"Your Mr. Cranbourne is a witty man, but perhaps there are places where his jokes would not be appreciated. By the way, George, how are you?"

George drew his eyes away from the fruit and politely weighed up the other man. A nice suit. Kirov looked suave. He always had. Maybe a little older. "I'm fine."

"Good. And your wife?"

"She died—two months ago."

"I'm sorry." Fumbling with his glass. "Really, George."

"Yes, of course. I thought I would never get over her death. But naturally I did. May I have another drink?"

Kirov signaled a waiter, who came over and poured two more vodkas.

"Well . . ." he began.

"Yes?" George regarded him curiously.

"I was going to ask whether you had met everyone here from Techmashimport."

"I think so."

"Of course. You will come back to Russia again?"

"How can I tear myself away?" A bleak smile. An empty glass. "Cigarette? Another vodka, I think." He held out a pack for Kirov to help himself and struck a match to light both cigarettes. "We've received two more inquiries for plants."

He said the same thing to Archibald Lansdowne, who lounged in his direction while his sharp-eyed Scottish wife ferreted among the fresh fruit.

"Two more plants—gosh!" said Lansdowne carelessly. His eyes were looking past George to Alasdair Cranbourne, who was arm in arm with the Minister of Gas, telling stories through an interpreter. "A good chap, your chairman," Lansdowne added, "to pull off all this business with the Soviet Union."

George looked around distractedly. He had a sense of someone

435

missing. Naturally Neville Lucas was not there, since it would have been in bad taste to invite him. But someone else.

"They're tough," the commercial counselor was saying with undue earnestness. "But essentially fair."

"The Russians?" It was Irina Terekhova who was absent.

"And *reliable,* which is what counts. Once you've broken the ice with them and proved your own reliability, then they come back again and again; there's really no limit. And they keep their deals."

"Yes, they keep their deals, all right."

"No question," Lansdowne answered, dusting ash from his sleeve.

"Sorry about that."

"That's all right. I hope Fiona hasn't filched the kiwi fruit. It's meant for the Minister and the ambassador. I'd better tell the bloody woman to stick to the apples." He extended a hand with delicately splayed fingers like an invitation to pick a card, and George shook it. "Well," said Lansdowne, "I'll say good-bye. But I'll see you again back in Moscow, I dare say. Now that you're in with the Russkies, there'll be no saying good-bye to this place."

"Probably not," George agreed, and his eyes followed the tall figure of the other man, but he still searched for someone else, another face: Irina Terekhova. He wanted to make his farewells to her; to ask after the child. There was nothing much else to say; after all, he had only met her twice and did not honestly expect that they would ever meet again. It wasn't that he was in love with her—his love was for Lillian and always would be. But his attachment to Lillian, which was a wholly different thing, had withered with her withering so that the final release left only the faintest of responses. There was some difference, some otherness in Irina Terekhova. He knew as he watched them how difficult it was for people to be totally real. They seemed to consist of behavior, lacking any ability to bring out from concealment their feelings in all their acuteness and pain. But sometimes there would be a fleeting exchange of sympathy and a transitory shared reality. He had experienced it for an hour with Irina Terekhova and he supposed that he would have to be satisfied with that.

Peter Kirov was also making his farewells.

"I don't expect we shall see each other again, George."

"No, I don't expect so." He thought that Kirov had difficulty looking at him. Peter was becoming sentimental.

They talked a little of Moscow. George had seen it during the thaw when the landscape appeared literally to dissolve. He still couldn't get the place to assume a definite shape or bounds. The conversation went nowhere; they both found themselves checking their watches without embarrassment.

"Then this is good-bye," said Kirov.

"Good-bye," George answered and felt a pang of regret which on any rational ground seemed insane.

Kirov's last words were, "I'm glad that you've become a success."

The investigation into the traitor who had attempted to betray the secret of the Sokolskoye Incident to the Americans continued, even though the business in Helsinki was concluded successfully. Then, on April 15, Yuri Maximovitch Pokrebsky, head of the All-Union Nuclear Inspectorate, was found dead at his apartment on the Frunze Embankment. The weapon was the dead man's own service revolver; and by the corpse, which lay in the bathroom the brains spattered over the walls, the police detectives found a suicide note explaining that Pokrebsky had killed himself because of his treacherous conduct in the matter of Sokolskoye.

The subject was quickly transferred from the regular murder squad at Petrovka to the Special Investigations branch of the KGB. While not rejecting the suicide theory, they raised several questions calculated to shed doubt. For example, why had the fatal shot not been heard by the deceased's wife, tucked up in bed in the next room and only mildly sedated, or by the other occupants of the apartment building? What could have been Pokrebsky's motive in leaking the secret to the Americans? In no sense would American involvement in solving the Sokolskoye business cure the suspicion that Pokrebsky had contributed to the causes of the problem by his corrupt dealings with Atommash in 1974; and in any case his protector, General Kostandov, allegedly backed by the Defense Minister, had officially cleared him of those suspicions. Also to the point, though less tangible, the common opinion was that, even if guilty, Pokrebsky was not the man either to shoot himself or, more particularly, to confess. He was too good a communist, as Bogdanov put it to Kirov.

However, the murder theory itself had problems. There was no direct evidence to support it — no forced entry, signs of struggle, unexplained injuries about the body. And who was the murderer? The real traitor — still unknown according to this hypothesis — was the obvious candidate; but this solution involved a contradiction. It was agreed by everyone that the hallmark of the traitor was amateurism; but the murder, if murder it was, was undeniably professional: indeed, the level of professionalism suggested an expertise only available with the KGB itself. And, as Special Investigations asked rhetorically in its report, who in the KGB would want to kill Pokrebsky?

In the end people had better things to do than pursue a bare speculation, and the investigation was closed.

In the aftermath of the successful conclusion of the Sokolskoye Incident, Kirov was promoted to colonel. He had every cause for satisfaction, but was not satisfied: satisfaction had become as elusive as truth. Perhaps it was the same thing. And in the matter of truth he could only remember what Grishin had implied: that there was something he knew, had always known, and was unwilling to face.

Death in its casual and not so casual way affected Irina Terekhova. On May 7, Arkady Konstantinovitch Terekhov was killed in a hit-and-run accident. Kirov knew because Irina's application for final approval to attend the long-standing conference in Geneva had been passed to him in the light of his particular knowledge of her loyalty. Noted on the file as a matter of concern was the absence of any children — a spouse one could always abandon. He thought of calling or writing but the words failed him. He went so far as to drive to her apartment and sit for an hour watching the windows. It was the beginning of spring, and when she emerged from the building on some errand and walked down the street he saw the breaking of new buds and the darkness of her face, and the contrast prevented him from speaking, so that he retreated into his overcoat, buttoning it to the lapel, and retired, a dark figure, to the waiting car.

Bogdanov, who had no children of his own, was visibly upset. "I liked that kid," he said quietly, and then: "God, the world's a terrible place!" Later Kirov found him emptying the contents of a drawer into a wastepaper basket. It consisted of stamps he had collected for the boy. That night Bogdanov got drunk and took a couple of days off work, but afterward he was all right.

It was after the death of her son that Irina Terekhova did something Kirov had not expected. She requested permission to visit the hospital at Tula to see Davidov. It seemed to him as if she were presenting him with a series of pieces like the elements of a puzzle. The woman, the soldier, the poet, the boy. Arrange them. Understand what you have always known. Kirov fixed for the request to be rejected. He called for sight of the autopsy on the child, and then the medical records.

"What for?" Bogdanov asked.

"I need to know about her."

"Why?" Bogdanov saw knowledge only as a tool, to be picked up or put down. It was intrinsically dangerous. He tried to convey that now. "It's all over!" he urged. "Leave the woman alone! Get her from under your skin. I'm serious, boss. She's poison!"

Kirov nodded. Bogdanov had sound instincts.

"Arkasha was circumcised," he said.

Bogdanov snorted. "So what? *I'm* circumcised. It happens."

"It's in the autopsy report." Kirov pushed the papers across the other man's desk. Bogdanov cleared a space of files and weighed down the pile with a tin of fish he was using as a paperweight. He looked at the papers then at Kirov, wearily. Like my father, Kirov thought, who otherwise never thought about his father. Why he should think that now he wasn't sure, except that Bogdanov had reached an age when he no longer expected promotion; he now studied life with detachment, taking an interest in the careers of others. Maybe that was why they called him Uncle Bog. Kirov said, "There's no reference to circumcision in the medical history."

Bogdanov gazed back stonily. He shoved the papers across the table unread. His hand remained in place, spread out across the typescript, thin fingers scrawny as chicken legs. How old was he? Forty-five? Fifty? He had clouded eyes in dark pits, as if smoke were blown into them. A face that was seamed and stitched with wrinkles.

"I want your advice."

"Stop being a fucking star—that's it, my advice." The impatience disguised an unexpressed fear. Bogdanov knew something also and was avoiding the knowledge. *Uncle Bog;* it was a mask to cover that evasion.

"The boy wasn't circumcised in the hospital," Kirov said. "We both know that."

"I don't know that," Bogdanov retorted. "I don't know anything except that Terekhov isn't Jewish."

Kirov agreed. The Colonel wasn't Jewish. He spent his nights with the soldiers' whores and contracted infections he didn't pass to his wife.

Bogdanov didn't answer directly. He stared at his own papers and said in a low voice, "If you want to see her, you'd better hurry before she leaves for Geneva."

He found her at Sheremetyevo, waiting with the other delegates in the milling crowd around the boarding gate. She saw him present his papers to the guard with that air of authority too natural to call arrogance. Her body stiffened. The guard saluted him, and he approached her across the departure area.

"Comrade Terekhova," he said without expression. "I need to speak with you. I have a room available and I should like you to come with me." His voice was low. Evidently he didn't mean the other delegates to hear. For that she was grateful, but his presence filled her with coldness.

"I must explain to Comrade Samsonov," she said.

"Of course."

He lit a cigarette while she went to find Samsonov. He saw her speaking to a fat, jolly man with a nodding head who broke off from a conversation in the thick of the crowd. Samsonov smiled, listened, frowned, looked frightened. She was coming back toward him. He recognized her physical tension but looked for something else. Grief? But Irina Terekhova would never let him see her grieve over the boy. He felt a flash of anger but suppressed it.

Kirov received her with the same studied reserve. He had finished playing with the cigarette and was ready to go. Irina thought: Why am I so cold? Why does he have this effect on me? He seemed to identify her reticence, and she thought she saw in his unruffled features the makings of sympathy, but it was a sympathy that gave no comfort, a cosmic sympathy—perhaps a sympathy for the dead. Are we all dead to him?

He led her through the byways of the airport hall to a room with a guard outside, and, inside, some tubular chairs and a table. The walls were dirty and had no decoration except a notice on electricity-saving posted by the light switch. It was a room too banal to be frightening except in its accidental dreariness. Kirov offered her a chair and took one himself. He checked his watch and made some remark about departure times. He said he had authority to delay the flight, but in any case mechanical problems or the usual difficulties of the airport would cause delay. She shouldn't be concerned. Irina thanked him.

"Am I under arrest?" she asked.

He appeared not to have expected such a direct question. His mouth flickered with a question in return, then changed, and he asked simply if she would like something to drink. He called the guard and asked for two glasses of fruit juice; then he returned to the table and faced her with his hands placed in front of him, palms down.

"You have been a mystery to me, Irina Nikolaevna," he said,

441

using her more familiar name.

"Am I under arrest?"

"You have betrayed your country." Her insistence had annoyed him at last, and the accusation when it came sounded like petulance. He was impatient with himself and added quickly and without interest, "You tried to ask the Americans for help in solving our problems at Sokolskoye. You sent a message to a certain American politician, using your sister-in-law Sonya Stoletova. The attempt failed. There"—he put his hands together in unintended prayer—"now I have explained and we can perhaps stop playing games."

She didn't answer. He tried again.

"Since I first came to know you, you have always shown the outward signs of loyalty. You came from a good communist background; you were married to a hero of the Red Army; you were well regarded by your colleagues; and you cooperated fully with the KGB in the Sokolskoye business. Even the lapse of your marriage to Davidov could be explained as evidence of loyalty: after all, at the time you married him he was still a respected member of the Writers' Union; and he had left you and you divorced him before he entered into his 'insane' period. Why, then, Irina Nikolaevna, has your loyalty always troubled me?"

Still she didn't answer. She tried to look at him calmly. So cold. She did not see herself as a brave woman, but she could mirror his impassivity, though in the effort his words seemed to lose themselves. Perhaps it was his use of the word "loyalty." In his mouth it became unclear as to what he had expected her to be loyal. He had misunderstood her dissent. If she were in truth a dissident, it was not against Russia, unless Russia were some dark place of the soul. Her resistance was against the lie on which their reasoning was founded, against their world of action as a substitute for feeling. Her dissent went to the core in ways so fundamental that when she opened her eyes she knew that she looked upon a different world. Before she could consider that further, he seemed to be talking about her child.

"Arkasha isn't Terekhov's child. The father is your first hus-

442

band, Davidov."

The words pulled her together.

"No. Davidov had left me and I was already married to Konstantin before I became pregnant," she murmured. But she felt that the explanation was pointless: it wasn't possible to hide things from him. He *invaded* the truth as if it were a sexual secret.

"You had the boy circumcised," he countered. "It wasn't a medical circumcision. Irina," he said more softly, "I *know*—do you understand? The circumcision was all you could do to mark the link between the boy and his true father, the Jew, Davidov. *Please,* don't lie to me."

Abruptly he stood up and moved to the corner. She closed her eyes to shut him out. When she opened them again, he was sitting composed across the table, a pack of cigarettes in front of him.

"You have had no sexual relations with Terekhov," he stated flatly, using the expression "sexual relations" in a way that struck her as subtly evasive of the complex reality of love. "Isn't that so?"

"I was willing," she answered, which was no more than the truth. It was Konstantin who had refused, not out of failure of desire but for reasons of honour and decency and other things that she understood as words but not as words with the same magical appeal that they had for men.

"But it isn't part of the arrangement—the deal between you, him and Davidov!" Kirov came back sharply, and for the first time she detected his anger.

"Davidov knew that ultimately he would be arrested." She addressed her words to the room. After that brief flare of anger, Kirov seemed as abstract of humanity as the walls.

"His poetry . . ." he prompted her.

"If he wrote the poems he wanted to write, he knew that he was doomed."

"So?"

"He was suffering—stifling on meaningless words," she said dully. Davidov had used the same expression. She had excised it from her memory so that the words had become thick and desensitized as a scar. She couldn't bear to think—couldn't bear to think!

443

"Now can *you* understand, Pyotr Andreevitch?" she said, using his more familiar names in an attempt to make contact with him. "He wanted to save me from his destruction! He wanted to save any child we might have!"

"So he gave you to Terekhov, and Terekhov accepted you with no—no personal end in view—simply to protect you!"

She did not answer—could not answer. She could only remember now that her child was dead. It was all to no purpose. Even Davidov's poems were dead, stillborn on his tongue; but she had loved him too much to tell him. And Davidov had loved her, too; yet he had sacrificed her to poetry and madness and had not seen the contradiction. It seemed to her sometimes that men were always searching for such sacrifices from some inner necessity that they cloaked in rationality. She allowed it but did not understand.

"You're crying, Irina," she heard Kirov saying with sudden tenderness. He stood up and crossed behind her. He passed a handkerchief over her shoulder. She felt the tears coursing down her face and the touch of his hand resting on her shoulder; his hand stayed on her shoulder. Taking me apart, she thought, and the coldness she had experienced became a sensation of emptiness, of dismemberment. Her body responded to an illusion of nakedness: the touch, the whisper of his breath across the nape of her neck. It doesn't mean anything, she thought. The prickling of her breasts. It was cruel.

"I think I'm in love with you," he said. He was sitting again with the table between them. Her eyes opened as he spoke, and he repeated the words, this time with more force. "I'm in love with you."

She thought: If only he could see the hatred in his eyes. He hates me more than anyone in the world for bringing him to this. In a flat tone he was continuing to explain his love. His hatred was terrible, she thought. Doesn't he see it?

"It's absurd, I agree," he said gently, "after everything that has—happened."

She looked for something to turn him away. "It's not possible," she said. "We're strangers."

"I want to stop being a stranger." He said this deliberately, and she wondered what meaning attached to "stranger." But of course he was the ultimate stranger—the interrogator. He could not share in the reality of life, only observe.

She realized that his declaration hadn't surprised her. She supposed she had always known.

"I didn't ask for this," she said. She was thinking of him but also of Davidov and Terekhov. If it came to a question of powers, then they could always prevail. But they would say that it wasn't a question of power: they were simply right. It was cruel to use love as a weapon.

"I could make you want me," Kirov said brutally, then immediately added, "but that's not what I want."

"What do you want?"

"What? Yes, what?" He gave a low, self-mocking laugh, and she found that he had become incomprehensible to her: his indifference to cruelty, his flashes of tenderness, his knowledge of people, his inability to understand and respond to them; and a longing and frightening destructiveness. He had what men assumed as a blessing but which cursed them, a deceptive heroism. They absorbed the mannerisms of heroes without the wisdom and were left with that hollowness of arrogance and anger. He was watching her carefully and she felt overwhelmed by his intense dangerousness. *He could kill me here—now.*

But his eyes drifted from her face across the table to his watch. "We must go," he said, and while they pushed back chairs and picked up the small litter of objects they had brought he began to speak like old acquaintances parting: "I should like to help you, Irina Nikolaevna. You may need other protection. Terekhov cannot give *political* protection. Davidov . . ." He paused. "I could make things better for Davidov: arrange letters, parcels, visits. Perhaps you don't want me to?"

He escorted her back to the departure gate where Samsonov, concerned and impatient, waited with the others. Kirov held her aside and inquired quietly, urgently, "Will you be coming back to Russia?" Her eyes opened with surprise, and he heard himself say,

"I'm sorry. I presumed. You have no ties here now. Whether you stay or leave, Davidov's position is beyond your help. I thought that—"

She stopped him. "It isn't something I've considered."

He gripped her forearm. "Please come back." And again: "Please."

She said something in reply, but the crowd was moving and talking as it moved. He saw only her lips, and to them he could put any words he wanted. Then she was drawn away by the pressure of others, and he saw her next standing by the interpreter, a tall, blonde woman with striking features and good Western clothes. She was looking in some direction that was not his.

From his vantage point he watched the aircraft take off and swing into the clear sky. A guard asked solicitously whether he could be of service to the colonel, but Kirov dismissed him. He stared at the plane once more and in his vision saw Irina Terekhova. She had not considered defecting, but he knew that logically the thought would in any case have come to her in the freedom of the plane and the atmosphere of Geneva. She would realize the danger he presented to her because he knew of her betrayal, and that that knowledge gave him total power over her. She would not return, he was certain. They had met for a short span and parted as strangers who have exchanged intimacies to while away a journey. She would not come back.

He watched the plane. It would take three hours, more or less, to fly to Geneva.

In that time, if he so decided, he could still have Irina Terekhova arrested.